VIKING
THE GREEN LAND

This book is a work of fiction.
Names, characters, places, and incidents
are either the product of the author's imagination
or are used fictitiously,
and any resemblance to actual persons, living or dead, business
establishments, events, or locales is entirely coincidental.

VIKING
THE GREEN LAND

ISBN-13: 978-0997876512
ISBN-10 0997876514

VIKING

THE GREEN LAND

by

Katie Aiken Ritter

For Mark,
my encouraging and blessedly-orderly husband,
who calmly navigates the endless chaos and craziness

For Zach, Gabe and Ben, our three sons,
with enormous gratitude and love

SEA

West coast of Íseland, spring equinox, circa 980 A.D.

Cast Off

"Leave! Little time is left! They must leave now!" The headman's voice rang out over a pounding surf as the setting sun sank into the waves and the sky began to darken. At his words, seventeen chained men and one woman were pulled along the shoreline and their hoods were removed.

They were right to chain us, Tiller muttered to himself.

He stood on the shoreline shackled with the other men and stared at the ship that waited for them. The sight of it silenced the boasts on their lips about coming home heroes to all the fame and fortune they could want. Facing the far-likelier prospect of dying at sea, they knew fear.

Even Tiller, so much at one with the waves, felt the same dread. *Too late to escape our fate now,* he thought, filled with bitterness. But as he looked over the smooth curves of the waiting vessel, Tiller also realized with a sudden shock that he knew this ship, even though he had never seen it before.

What had he said, so long ago? *"Build her like a young woman: give her the speed and power of a warship, but the carrying capacity of a merchant's knörr, to hold the things they'll need for life. Make her beautiful. Whoever takes the voyage you describe will need to feel proud. It'll give them strength and courage."*

The headman called again. This time, the crew was herded into the water and shoved up the boarding plank. One by one, the men lifted their wrists for the manacles to be unlocked and the watching crowd cheered, but as the irons rattled off, the crew began to argue loudly, shoving at one other.

The woman was pushed aboard last, her wrists chained as well. She would serve as their fishgirl – part cook, part healer, and crew's helper - for the voyage. As the torches flickered on her face, Tiller could clearly see wet tracks of tears.

"Stop fighting!" the headman shouted at the crew. "Look east…the moon has almost cleared the hills already! Get to your oars! Your ship is heavy and the surf is high, and you will have to row hard! Be ready!"

He turned to the man who counted the moons and seasons. "Kalendar, you be ready as well, to call the rope-release!"

The Kalendar nodded. He had prepared for this exact moment for months, watching carefully across the winter as the length of daylight drew equal to the night. "Only one or two more days," he had reported yesterday to the headman. "Spring is almost upon us, *Gothi*."

"And the moon?" the *gothi* had asked.

"Full tomorrow night. It will rise just after Sól sets in the sea." Kalendar had hesitated, the briefest pause, before he continued. "Such a rare thing…and to nearly coincide with the *even-day-and-night* that brings spring and starts our year? Inconceivable! It foretells a remarkable voyage."

"Ready the ship and the men!" the headman had cried. "They will sail at moonrise tomorrow!"

2

Last to be unlocked, Tiller watched the men who would be his crewmates for the next three years. All were seasoned in the ways of the sea, and like him, all were outlaws. Beyond that, they were as different from one another as any crew might be; some were tall, some short, some were disfigured by scars and others handsome. Some seemed talkative and others stayed morosely silent. Tiller saw all of humanity in their faces: strength, weakness, greed, fairness, brutality, and humor. What did they see in his own face? Did they see the uncertainty in him? The willingness to risk their lives to prove himself right?

The fishgirl-woman desperately looked from face to face of the people on the shore, but no one would meet her gaze. She did not watch the headman as he unlocked her wrist irons, but stared only at the face of the moon-god rising over the shoreline hills, and her face filled with dread.

How old? Tiller wondered. She looked to be about twenty-five. *And still no finger-ring for marriage?* For certain, not because of her looks. The entire crew was eyeing her. Any fool could see trouble coming. Was that the reason for the oath they'd been made to swear? *To protect her, at all cost, until they find land...?*

More importantly, why was she on this voyage at all? Women usually served as fishgirl for crews on short journeys, a couple of weeks or a month at most. Had anyone told this woman how long they'd be gone, and how terribly small their chances of returning were? Unlike the men, she did not carry the mark of an outlaw. What would compel her to come with them?

"Rowers, ready oars!"

Strong hands gripped the long oak poles, and the crew prepared to pull the ship through the surf.

Tiller held the steering oar. Through it, he could feel the waves frothing against the strong hull. The ship bucked against the ropes holding her, and exhilaration knifed through Tiller, reckless and hard. Those sweeping timbers longed to be free of land, and he in turn longed to feel the strength of them surging through the open sea.

"Almost ready!" the headman shouted. "Release the ropes on my command!" He cleared his throat.

Oh, gods, he was going to give a speech.

"You on this voyage are headed straight into the heart of danger. We pray that your courage will set us all free…"

"We're not brave! We're dead men!" shouted one of the rowers. "What difference does it make, at sea or on land?"

The headman frowned and continued his speech, his words of hope in stark contrast with the grim faces on board, and Tiller's thoughts drifted.

He had not murdered anyone, but no one else from the fight had survived to say so. Men he had counted as friends had tumbled to the ground and bled out, their open eyes as colorless as the sky. With them went testimony that might have saved him. *Guilty,* the Council had said at the trials at the quarterly trials at Thornes Thing. *Three years outside the law.*

Being outlawed might as well be a death sentence. Outlaws enjoyed no protections that the law had once offered to them: take an outlaw's tools, and he could complain to no headman about the theft. Take his fox-traps and the furs he had prepared to sell, take his last rind of cheese, his last crust of bread, and give them to your own sons and daughters, and no one would stop you from letting him starve. Take his cloak for your own, and let the rain drench him, and there was no one to whom he could turn for recourse…and giving an outlaw shelter and food meant risking the same fate. Convicted men who

4

could afford passage and bribes left for other lands. Those less fortunate gnawed hard barley grains and hid in hillside crevices in freezing cold, not daring to risk a fire.

At the country-wide mid-summer Althing trials, Tiller's law-speaker had pled his case again. The council had affirmed the guilty verdict, but afterwards, to Tiller's surprise, one of the *gothi*-councilman appeared at the jail-pens. Gold threads in his cloak glittered in the sun, and he lifted it carefully above the muddy ground.

"Come over here." He had beckoned with his free hand. "I have a proposition for you."

Tiller's heart had beat hard, but he kept his face quiet.

"The rumors that have spread throughout this Althing. I assume you've heard them?"

Tiller had hardly dared to believe they might be true. He nodded.

The gothi continued. "Everyone knows the situation here in Íseland. In the time of the Great Settlement, people came here in great numbers, and almost immediately, all of the good land was claimed. Then all the forests were cleared, and the poorer land was settled. For four or five generations, there has been no new land left at all. No more farms to feed the grandchildren and great-grandchildren of the families who settled here. Yet more mouths are born every day, and more slaves are bought and brought here. They, too, have children who must be fed. The terrible truth is that far more food is needed from too few fields." He rubbed his hand across a forehead lined with worry. "With the crop failures these past years, even the people with good land are struggling. You know what is happening to those whose farms are worked on thin soil."

The dreaded word *famine* had at first been whispered. Now, every meeting along the roadway brought news of places where people were starving, and the mounting deaths.

5

The councilman cleared his throat awkwardly. "It's been almost ten years since anyone went *viking* to look for Gunnbjörn's skerries." At those words, Tiller knew that the rumors were true.

———.———.———

Gunnbjörn's skerries. Maybe land, maybe not; a *something* in the sea far to the west, barely glimpsed by Gunnbjörn Ulfsson's crew nearly a hundred years ago, after a disastrous storm.

"You want us to make another attempt to find them," Tiller said flatly. "Because outlaws are desperate, and expendable."

"Not want, Thorvaldsson. Need." The councilman was almost pleading. "Every headman here at the Althing brings the same problem. Their people are dying for want of fields and food. If there's even a *chance* that an empty land is somewhere out there, can you imagine what that would mean to our people? We must try! That means an opportunity for you. A ship is being built, a specially-designed one. We need a crew who will go to search for whatever Gunnbjörn's men glimpsed."

Tiller had remembered then, too, the elderly shipbuilder who had asked *How would you design a vessel for an incomprehensibly long voyage?* The old man had been vague about the reasons, but had listened carefully to Tiller's ideas, and had disappeared into the crowd again.

How long had the council been planning this? How long had they been watching him?

The councilman eyed Tiller to gauge the condemned man's reaction. Fury built in Tiller, but he held it in check.

"I know what you are thinking," the *gothi* continued. "You have the means to buy your way to another country and try to ride out your

6

three years…and you know as well as I do that anyone who goes on this voyage will likely die on the sea. There will be storms, bitter cold, fights on board. You may starve, or perish of thirst. And to go so far out into the sea…" The councilman shuddered. "Freakish things live out there, they say. Monsters in the waves who swallow ships that sail too far from land." He forced a laugh. "But your odds may be just as bad on land. Too many traders know your name, if not your face. Show up in Dublin or Danmörk and someone will turn you over to us for the reward-silver that will be offered. Where could you not be found and hunted down? Do you want to live as a fugitive running and hiding for three years, or go searching for glory? Find a land where we can send people to live, and you'll have everything you could want: gold, silver, slaves, silks, furs, fame…and freedom."

Tiller had heard the stories of Gunnbjörn's skerries since childhood. After a disastrous voyage, Gunnbjörn Ulfsson had finally steered his battered ship back home, all but sinking and with most of the crew gone. The few *vikingers* who had survived told frightening tales. *"We were steering for the North Way, but we were blown west by a terrible storm. Hideous, a man-killer. A ship-sinker. We took down the sail. Not one of us believed we'd survive it. Waves…"* Their faces would still go ashen remembering the horror of that night. *"The sea tore at us like an enormous animal, berserk, clawing and screaming from every direction. Maybe the sea-goddess Rán wanted to punish us for being so far west. She pulled most of our crew overboard. Swallowed men whole in her great mouth."*

The ship had wandered, lost. Fog had swirled around them. *"That fog was as thick as cream, unnaturally warm, a feeling of something unhealthy. Were we even still alive? Maybe we were already dead, and Loki's daughter Hel was pulling us to Niflheim."* Niflheim, the *nothing-home* that lay at the very edge of the world, was a place hidden

7

by clouds and mist. Those not chosen at death for Valhalla went there, where giants of ice guarded Hel's gates.

The storyteller would hesitate, his haunted eyes remembering. The fog had suddenly lifted. They had seen something hulking in the water, gray and white, something enormous of stone and ice. Should they sail closer? They had barely survived so far. Why tempt Hel's ogres, or perhaps some huge sleeping sea-beast? If those were the actual gates to Niflheim, would there be sharp terrible rocks, tearing what was left of their hull? Would they become slaves for the dead?

Fearing for their lives, Gunnbjörn's crew had turned the ship in the opposite direction. They prayed with every passing wave to see the shores of home again, and vowed to carry a warning to others. *"The sea-goddess Rán spared us for a reason! We tell others, so that they do not go where the seas end. That place belongs to Hel. All must stay away."*

The warnings of Gunnbjörn's crew had fallen on deaf ears. Many ships set off, looking for those shapes in the sea. Most never returned, and the voyages had diminished over luckless years. The last attempt several years ago had ended in horror.

Going in search of Gunnbjörn's skerries was little different than being outlawed: both usually meant death.

———·———·———

"What's your decision?" The Althing councilman had interrupted Tiller's thoughts. "Everyone knows your reputation as a steersman. Will you go?"

Bitterness ate into Tiller's gut. "When my neighbor Thorgest accused me of murdering his sons, everyone knew the truth. He had stolen from me, and I only took what was mine: those high-seat pillars belonged to me. I never wanted the fight, never intended for anyone to be hurt – and I trusted in the law, certain I'd be found innocent. Now I know why all of you on the Althing Council ignored my law-arguer. You convicted me because you needed me."

"What difference does it make? However you got here, you're an outlaw now. Be practical."

"Do I really have a choice? You'll find one way or another to get me on your ship. I'll save you the trouble. Sea dangers don't cut a man as deep as deception from those he trusts."

But as he spoke, premonition swept through Tiller. Gunnbjorn's skerries were where he longed to go. He was meant to find them.

———·———·———

Now, as he waited for the local headman to finish his speech, Tiller wondered about that feeling of fate. A future-knowing? He winced. Maybe he was becoming too like his father, desperate for recognition, imagining his own importance. But by the gods…*Gunnbjorn's skerries!*

By the time he had grown enough to listen, the tales were old and tired, the patina of promise worn away. Some still clung to the possibility of rich land waiting in the west. Tiller's father Thorvald had been one of them, spinning stories about wealth to be found. As a youth, Tiller had pretended to be Gunnbjörn Ulfsson, finding the longed-for land. Later, loading crates as ship's boy, in his imagination he was carefully outfitting a merchant knörr with supplies for a new settlement.

Well, you're on that knörr now, he thought as the headman's speech droned on. *And you're not Ulfsson, you're Thorvaldsson, with all the stigma that name carries. Not exactly the dreams of your boyhood.*

Tiller shook off the feeling of destiny. He was an outlaw, and the son of an outlaw. Who was he to think he had any chance of succeeding where so many others had failed before? He was going to die out there. But the old longing skirled deep in him, like the smoke rising from the shoreline torches, and he knew he still longed to try.

Tiller kept his eyes on the stars as they came out, thinking of the course he would steer. The rowers waited for the command to pull. Firelight flickered on the long wet oars. Thin edges of moonlight tipped the waves. Beyond, all was now blackness.

The headman rushed his carefully-prepared words to match the moonrise. "You set off tonight, watched only by the moon-god, so that nothing in the sea will notice as you leave land in the darkness. The ship has been charmed with powerful spells. It is stocked with provisions for a long voyage. We have done all that we can to protect you, and we ask of you this: if there is land to find, find it. Find good land for us, green land, a place where people can live and thrive. Know that your journey offers hope for our people; a new birth. But make no mistake: there will be no warm arms to welcome you. This ship is your midwife, and your mother is the sea. Our future and yours lies in her cold embrace. We may never know what happens to you, but we will sing of your courage in sagas."

At that, the gleaming white circle lifted above the hills. Their moon of destiny -- or disaster -- floated full in the night sky.

"It is fully risen! They must get underway immediately!" The Kalendar's anxious voice rang out as the bottom curve of the moon-god Máni came clearly into view.

"Pull away the boarding plank!" the headman roared.

Fish-gutters, who had arrived for the spring spawning and were camped in hovels along the shoreline, jeered. "Plenty of land at the bottom of the sea! For certain, you'll find some there!" Their mocking words concealed hope they dared not admit, a longing that was buried in the lines of their too-thin faces.

The headman silenced them. He gestured to the rope-holders. "Release the ropes! Push off the ship! Row now, men! Pull hard! Row! Row!"

At the gothi's command a score of people waded forward to press their hands against the sleek lapped timbers of the ship. Cynical sarcasm shot through Tiller. How many who had jeered today would one day say *'I pushed them off,'* telling grandchildren of a part in the great discovery?

The rowers leaned forward, pulled back hard, and the voyage was born. Long years of experience told Tiller's limbs to shift from land-legs to sea legs.

The woman who would be their Fishgirl lurched at the motion. Hair blew wildly from her braids and tangled in the wind. She cried out once in agony as the ropes were released. Her eyes locked onto Tiller's.

"We die, either way, you and I," she croaked towards him, looking furtively back over her shoulder at the crew. "There is no coming back for us."

What was she talking about? Tiller needed to focus all of his attention on the rudder as he steered them away from the breakers. He gripped it hard and ignored her stare.

No one called good fortune as the knörr left. There was only silence, except for crash of waves and the wind blowing across the beach. It had been forbidden to make the good-luck striking of sticks, or to ring bells to bring safe journeys to the ship. No sense alerting whatever lurked in the deeps.

The pale faces of the crowd on the shore watched, stony and still. So much hung on this ship and the small band on board. Dozens of hands lifted in a wordless fare-thee-well. Their silence pulsed with a mute plea for land, for food, and the dark width between the knörr and the shoreline slowly widened.

Salt spray cut across the bow as strong arms pulled the ship steadily through the waves. The rowers watched the fires of the torches on shore grow fainter and dim to nothing. Tiller could see the men's eyes in the moonlight, fierce and focused as they rowed in unison. The reality of what lay ahead was locked away inside them for now.

We'll all be sick of one another and the sea soon enough, Tiller thought. How long until one of the crew panicked under the crushing uncertainty? It was only a matter of time until knives were drawn and blood spilled. *We're as dangerous to each other as the sea is to us.*

Screaming birds wheeled overhead, ghost-pale. In defiance of the headman's orders, two small vessels darted from a nearby cove and came alongside, calling encouragement.

"Get away, damn you! You were told not to come!" roared the man who had shouted at the headman. "Too much noise splashing through the waves! You want a sea-troll to come before we barely get started?"

Tiller knew full well who was on the boats following them. He called to the men who had risked their lives to shelter him for the last months, "Go back. I know you wish us well. I'm in your debt. When we return, I'll do whatever I can to repay you."

As the men in those small crafts turned away, the knörr slipped past the headlands and they were utterly alone on the nighttime sea.

Tiller felt strong and unafraid. Was it out there, somewhere? That lustful, longing promise of land? Wild exhilaration surged in him again. He and the crew would work all this night without rest or food. They would push themselves to go further and further away from land. For now, their only hunger was the yearning to return as heroes…or not at all.

———·———·———

Fishgirl

When she could no longer see the shoreline, the woman dropped to her haunches and huddled between two crates. She buried her face in her arms and kept it there until the first rowing change. At the gong, she kept her chin down, but her eyes slid to the men.

The full moon gave them dead faces, gray and grim, their eyes black pits. They moved in unison, eerily quiet. The only sound was the creak of oars and the slosh of water.

Gods, how had this happened? Her mind reeled in terror. Clawing for something to hold onto, her eyes landed on Tiller's face. It held hard lines that had not been there before. She noted that his hair had been cropped since the trial, and his beard was clipped close against his jaw.

Why did I say that to him? That man can't help me, the woman thought, angry at herself. *No one can. I am an utter fool. I should be at home, looking for a husband. Starting the spring planting.* She squeezed her eyes closed and looked for courage inside but found none.

Like it or not, a game that would hold her life in its balance had begun. *Them or me. Damned if they will win.* Her lips quivered. She cursed herself, but angry words were not enough to hold tears at bay, and her face collapsed. The rowers did not notice her weeping, concealed between the crates. Tiller saw, but he had no time or caring for her fears.

———·———·———

Through the long night, the moon climbed high into the sky and then sank into the western sea ahead of them. The crew rowed, changed shifts, and rowed more. The woman barely moved, crouching between the sea chests. She wept but stayed quiet, her thoughts too huge and harsh to be formed into human language.

As the sky lightened to gray before dawn, Tiller wondered again who she was and why she was on board. His ship of dreams had never carried a woman, and a weeping one, to boot. There was no logic to her being aboard. Lack of logic usually opened the door to trouble.

He snorted. Logic and sense lay back on land. Out here, the only thing that mattered was survival. Like the rest, she would have to hang on and do her best, and even that might not be enough.

———.———.———

Dawn brought the first battle, and a surprise.

The woman lurched to her feet and began to heave chests open, clanging cookware in the back of the knörr near Tiller's post. How hard was it to figure out where the oats were, to start a small cooking fire? Her fumbling seemed endless.

"Food? Soon?" An impatient question from Dagsson, the rowing leader at oars. "We have not eaten since yesterday noon."

The woman raked her fingers through what was left of her braids, and thrashed about faster with the cooking tools. Men stretched aching muscles, groaning. As the day grew brighter, they could see nothing but waves, endless in every direction, and their spirits darkened. Their fish girl still struggled with the fire. As their eyes turned towards her, she became the source of their resentment.

Finally, Dagsson roared. "Daybreak, Fishgirl! Time to eat!" He glared at Gierr, the other oar-leader. "And time for the other team to row again."

Gierr squinted into the rising sun, his face sullen and stubborn. Old patterns of pulling oars, taught for generations, were designed to let a man pull oars for long hours. Like everything aboard ship, the traditions had been honed over time, for endurance and for fairness. One did not tamper lightly with shipboard tradition.

Gierr snorted from where he leaned against the hull. "Sól is not fully up. Your team pulls until the end of this eighth-mark."

"Your team should take over now. Stop waiting on Fishgirl," Dagsson disagreed.

"Piss off. You know the rule." Gierr spat into the water.

"We've been rowing into the wind since dawn. Don't be such a jack's ass!"

Without warning, Gierr leaped across the crates that served as rowing benches and landed a fist on Dagsson's face. Blood spurted as the two men grappled together. As they roared and fought, the fish girl plunged along the center of the ship and into the melee.

"Stop that fighting! Stop it! Stop right now!" She grabbed at Gierr and her hand came away with handful of hair. "I said *stop!*" She slammed her hands flat against Dagsson's chest and glared him straight in the eyes, then at the other men in the ship. "This is my first meal to serve you, and I am nervous about getting it right! Get your bowls ready!"

They looked at her with mouths agape. One did not disagree with a Fishgirl.

"I mean it," she growled. "It's time to eat."

"*Fukker*," growled Dagsson. He cuffed Gierr once more, but the fight was over. Fishgirl wielded significant power, especially in matters of food. The rest of the crew shrugged their shoulders and shuffled to get in line for a bowl.

Before long, Dagsson's team stretched out to rest, their turn finished. "Enjoy your naps, sweethearts," Gierr mocked, and lifted his oar.

Hungry men snarled over things that mattered little when stomachs were full. The woman had been smart enough to know it. No matter how terrified she appeared, Tiller knew that Fishgirl had won the fight, not Gierr or Dagsson, and he found himself wondering about her again.

—·——·——

Fishgirl bent to her work board, pounding dried fish with a mortar and pestle. The sound combined with the creaking of oars. The men who had rowed the last shift were exhausted, and with the quiet rhythm, most of them were already beginning to snore.

She looked at the surrounding waves and panic rose in her. *They are used to being out of sight of the land. I am not. I cannot do this.* She pounded. *Cannot. Cannot.* The thought repeated again and again, and her fear grew with every thump of the oars. She wanted to run, but to where? *I must not let them see me be afraid!* A mad shriek began to bubble inside her.

Her workstation was close to where Tiller stood at the rudder. She glanced at the crew. They were not paying attention, their eyes glazed as they counted the rowing-rhythms. With the wind coming off the steering-board side from the stern, they would not hear her. She drew a deep breath and spoke quietly.

"Tiller?"

"Yes, Fishgirl?"

Her jaw lifted. Tiller saw stubbornness, but the upthrust chin trembled a little, too. It matched the look in her eyes: desperation, barely controlled.

"I *do* have a name," she quavered. "It's Tho-"

"Stop!" Tiller replied, his voice harsh. "I do as well, but everybody calls me Tiller. That's the work I do. Everybody will call you Fishgirl. It's tradition aboard ship."

On either side, endless water surrounded their small ship *Oh my gods, we are so far from home!* The shriek inside her threatened to explode. Tiller's words offered a miniscule distraction, and Fishgirl clutched at it.

"Why is that?"

"If someone uses your name, you're a person. They call you Fishgirl, you're a...position." Tiller hesitated. This was one of the most basic understandings of being a Fishgirl. How did this woman not know? Did she have any idea what she was doing here on board?

"You are aware of your duties, yes?" Tiller phrased the question carefully.

The Fishgirl swallowed hard and looked around at her workstation, as if she was trying to remember what her duties might be. Her voice seemed terribly uncertain as she replied.

"I am to care for the casks of food, and the bladders of water and small beer. I am to catch fish from the sea, and catch fresh rainwater to fill the spare barrels."

Again, her eyes swept across the deck, landing on the dim space under the half-deck. "Once each day if the weather is good, I am to bring the goats on deck to strengthen them, and clean their pens, along with the chickens and ducks." Now, Fishgirl's voice became rote as she said words the headman had made her repeat again and again. "No matter the weather or the seas, I am to feed the crew three meals each

18

day to keep their strength up, and satisfy their thirst whenever they ask. A thirsty man at sea becomes a dead man too quickly. If the food or water run short, I must portion it out, man by man. I must be free of allegiances, not beholden to or preferential to any man, so that I share the food fairly."

Her voice took on an edge of sarcasm. "I will not be bullied by any man, either. My words, not the headman's. But the gothi also said that I am to serve the crew in every way. *In every way.* He kept emphasizing it, over and over. Did he mean the sea-freedoms? Nobody ever talks openly about them. What are they, and what is expected of me? I deserve to know."

This time, Fishgirl looked with dread at the rowing men, and once more, her face seemed on the brink of tears. She gripped the pestle with both hands, white at the knuckles. Tiller was appalled. She might be able to rattle off a list of duties, but this woman in front of him seemed barely to be holding on to herself. Ill-prepared to serve on their voyage, that was for certain. Well, there was no helping it now. The sooner she knew what was what, the better.

"People often think sea-freedoms are just wanton behavior, away from the rules of land, but it's actually a far more complicated matter. I've nothing to do right now besides hold the steering-oar. Do you want the long explanation?"

She whispered, "Yes, please. I need something else to think about besides how terrified I am." As soon as the words were spoken, Fishgirl wished them back. Did he know about the frightening plan she had overheard?

Tiller seemed not to notice. "Let me start by saying that life works best in balance. Some believe that a woman aboard balances the crew, and that helps a voyage. Women often bear with patience those things which men find vexing. They can lighten a foul mood with a word, turning sullenness away with a well-timed joke. If a Fishgirl has a good voice, we like to hear her sing. The sound of a woman's voice, with words spoken wisely, is soothing. It heals us. At sea, just like on land, women often sustain men's spirits."

"These are not the sea-freedoms," Fishgirl retorted.

"I'm getting to them," Tiller replied. "But you need to understand the whole thing."

He thought of how to put it into words. Men who *vikked* through the waves thought of the sea as a woman, a kind of mother whose waves carried her sons, in ships, from land to land. They saw each of the ships that carried them as a female as well, a strong, beautiful brave partner who carried them and protected them. Their Fishgirl was the third woman in that trio, one who personally carried and cared for the crew the many ways women did in life: as provider, partner, leader, sister or mother or lover, advisor, healer, and friend.

Tiller lifted his own chin towards members of the crew who were chanting the rowing rhythms. "See the fellow there, with the gray beard? That's Sigmund. And the giant one with the dark skin is Tor. He's sitting next to that chatterbox half his size. That's Ekka. Nollar is the skinny one behind Ekka. To each of those men – to all of the men on board - you have a kind of magic in your very being. To some, you might symbolize the one who birthed them and kept them safe, and who will help keep him safe through this voyage. To another, you might be the one he turns to as a man who needs the counsel of someone he trusts. For another, you will be the one who ministers to the blisters on his hand or muscles strained from ship-work, or whose mischievous smile eases a bitter day. You will be their healer. Some of them will count on you to offer prayers and gifts for good passage to Rán, the Goddess of the Sea, and to your sisters the Valkyries who send the winds to our sail."

20

Fishgirl looked impatient and started to interrupt, but Tiller put up his hand. "I'm still getting there. You said you wanted the long explanation."

For an instant she started to rebel, but the corner of her mouth twitched. "I did."

Tiller continued. "Keep looking at those men. Look at their faces, so intent in work. Some of them will have foul tempers. Some will cheat. Fights will happen, there is no doubt of that! Because a Fishgirl is holy to Rán, it gives you some authority in settling everyday squabbles. Without ever saying as much, those men are going to count on your common sense to settle us down sometimes. If you can stand up to the bull-headed stupidity of men - just as you did with Gierr and Dagsson this morning – you can stop a fight without any of them having to give in, which keeps them from looking weak or foolish. Today, you showed them your strength right away. I know for a fact that it meant a lot to these men to see you do it. They need to trust that you are strong enough to do such things."

She protested. "I wasn't being strong. I didn't intend to do it. I didn't even realize what happened until I got back here with Gierr's hair in my hand."

"It doesn't matter how you did it, only *that* you did it. What I'm trying to say is that the three of you - the sea, the ship, and the woman who is Fishgirl – together, you carry us from place to place and back to home. Of all on board, you may have the least strength, yet in many ways, the most power. A Fishgirl is a figurehead, embodying balance and safety in her very person while on board. I can tell you this; a crew will rarely say any thanks, but they are deeply grateful to women strong enough to choose the work."

She nodded. She still gripped the pestle with one hand, but the fingertips of the other traced the bit of dried fish. "I can see why a crew wants a Fishgirl. But why would any woman want to do it? You must have known many through the years."

Her question added to the unease in Tiller's mind. She had been chained and forced aboard, but then, they all had been chained. He had thought it was for show. So she really had not come willingly? Something seemed terribly wrong about it. Tiller ignored the troublesome thought for the moment.

"Women seek work at sea for the same reasons men do. Some need to pay off a family debt. Some earn silver for a dowry their family cannot fund, or enough coins to start a business venture of their own, or to buy livestock or lands. Some women, like men, have a spirit that feels best in the wide horizons and the exciting uncertainty of the sea, and simply prefer to roam." He hesitated. "And now that I have told you all the rest of what a Fishgirl offers, this brings us to the sea-freedoms." He was not an awkward man, but to just spell it out... Tiller cleared his throat.

"Part of it is...well, just practical. For women who have been unable to conceive a child in their marriage, what are called the sea-freedoms offers a way past that. People choose to ignore that the child looks nothing like her husband."

Fishgirl nodded. "When I was a young girl, my cousin did not quicken, even after years of marriage. She served as a Fishgirl three times. A month at sea each time, and she bore three children. I heard whispers, that they were sea-freedom babies. But as I said, no one talked openly about what it meant. What's expected of me? Do I have to...?" Now, she had dropped the pestle completely and covered her mouth with fingers that shook, and her eyes were wide with horror.

Tiller realized with a shock that their Fishgirl was unaware of the oath they had had to swear about her. Again, the sense of foreboding, of something awry, flickered briefly, and again, he pushed it away.

22

"No. No Fishgirl ever is required to do *anything* such as that. Most, I can say, are strong, open, friendly types, but beyond that, they are as different as every woman is different. Some are prim while others are wanton. Some tease and torment, lifting their tunic or bending so that we cannot help but look. Some will smack a man for looking crosswise at her, and some happily hitch their skirts. I can tell you, in truth, there's far more talk of that than actually happens."

She looked dubious.

"Damn it!" Tiller found himself annoyed. He wasn't the Fishgirl, but here he was almost acting like one, consoling her. "Look, you seem like a decent sort. I'll try one more time." He struggled to find the right words. "How can I explain this? You three - the sea, the ship, and the fish girl -- we never admit it, because we want to seem strong, but we *want* you to care for us. If a Fishgirl welcomes any of the men to herself, whatever her reason, there's no shame in it. We congratulate the lucky fellow and hope we may get an offer as well. But it doesn't mean she will be disrespected. Crews may joke around with these women, but they are deeply respected. No matter how wanton or willing she may be, there is a line none of the men will cross. A Fishgirl is terribly important to safe travels and money earned, to the men who *vik* and to the families who wait for them, and to whoever owns the ship. *That's* the reason why no one ever speaks openly about the sea-freedoms. When the voyage is over and her service completed, the Fishgirl exists no more. The woman returns to whoever she was in life before. Her memories of work and freedom and shared laughs - and yes, maybe a bit of lust amid the waves - are memories that belong to her. No one ever questions her or comments on it."

Tiller looked earnestly into the striking eyes of the woman in front of him, who would be so critical to him and the crew in whatever lay ahead of them.

23

"Sometimes, just the *possibility* of excitement keeps a voyage lighthearted. It helps break tension more than those on land might realize. So much hangs on this voyage –our lives on this ship, and hungry mouths back at home – and each of us, including you, need to do everything possible to help it succeed. Maybe that's what the headman was trying to tell you."

"So a Fishgirl doesn't have to....? If she doesn't want?"

"Never. The crew will likely flirt openly with you, but it is all fun give-and-take. If a Fishgirl wanted more, it's she who would offer."

She scanned the men rowing and the ones, exhausted, sleeping under blankets. "But this crew? They're a rough lot."

Tiller looked the men over. "Some are. Some aren't. More than half the men are on board this ship because poverty made them desperate in one way or another. The council knew it. They could've shown mercy, but they needed a full crew on board, so here we all are. Outlaw or not, I doubt many of them would ever hurt a woman, on sea or on land. Of the rest, all I can tell you is that even the most hardened men are generally too superstitious to cross shipboard customs. You're Fishgirl now. You're powerful. I can't imagine any of them forcing you. Especially..." He stopped suddenly, thinking of the oath.

"What did you start to say?" In the back of his mind, Tiller noted that the woman's question came just a heartbeat too fast, her voice suddenly brittle.

Again that flicker of something askew. But if she didn't know of the oath, what harm would it be to tell her? He decided quickly.

"There's another reason for you to feel safe. Each of us was made to swear - in blood, with witnesses - not to lie with you. Not even to touch you, even if you offered. I've never heard the like. Who tells men and women what they can and cannot do?"

"All of them? And how did they react?"

The panicked note in her voice deepened Tiller's sense that something was not quite right. "I was certainly surprised. We all were. It happened very quickly just before they put us in irons to take us to the ship."

Fishgirl's face blanched. She said nothing. She knew too well the reason for the oath. Her terror had calmed while listening to Tiller, but at his last words, her heart began to pound again.

She would say nothing about it. The fact that she would be safe from unwanted attention offered some small comfort for now. For a moment, she had relaxed a tiny amount in the calm Tiller projected. Like nearly all of the crew, his face was hollowed, his body rangy from reduced food shares across the last few years. She had learned he had no real wealth, and a reputation for a too-quick temper, but also one for being fair and honest.

Fishgirl steadied herself, looking over the men who were rowing and sleeping once more. "While in part I'm relieved to hear of this oath, I expect some might be angry at me for it."

"So you definitely didn't know about it?" Tiller replied. "I thought perhaps it was a condition you made before volunteering to come."

"*Volunteering?*" Fishgirl snorted, her voice bitter. "That's one word for it."

Tiller could hear the rowing cadence coming to an end. "We should stop talking about this now. My advice, which you haven't asked for, is to just do your job as best you can. They need to respect you, especially if you have to make the hard choices of rationing to keep us alive. You're intelligent. You'll figure it out. But you see now that there are many reasons to stay Fishgirl and not whoever you were back on land. Better to be refused precious rations or water from 'Fishgirl' than from...what *is* your name, anyway?"

"It's Tho--"

He cut her off mid-word. The question had been a test. "You really don't know anything about this work, do you? Even *asking* your real name is forbidden. I don't want to know it."

"What if you knew me before the voyage?"

"Doesn't matter. Someone uses your name, and you become any woman, to be argued with, ignored, desired, and even abused. It could endanger the whole voyage. That's the reason for the rule."

"So I protect all of us by leaving my own self behind on land. On ship, I'm Fishgirl."

"Yes. For the duration of this voyage, that's all of who you are. If someone asks your real name, don't answer. It's not allowed."

This small conversation was helping Fishgirl to breathe again, even if only for a moment. "Talking helped. Thank you."

He nodded. "Put your mind on what you need to do each moment. It'll help you stop being overcome by fear. Right now, it looks as if the rowers are ready for a drink."

Sigmund, the big one with gray streaks in his beard, confirmed Tiller's words, calling from the head of the boat. "Fishgirl! The men are thirsty!"

She looked at the day-marking stick near Tiller as she reached for the water bladder. "It's that simple? Just focus on the task at hand? Maybe you're right. In the time we just talked, at least I haven't been nauseous with fear."

Another small smile flickered across her lips. It was a bitter one, but it showed Tiller a hint of the strength she might have. Her next words, brave enough to carry the smallest of jests, confirmed it.

"Three years, less one night and part of a morning still to go. I'll put my mind on serving water now. Then I'll put my mind on finishing this fish. Then I'll throw out a net to catch fresh ones." Fishgirl stood, wiped her hands, and headed aft towards Sigmund.

Tiller watched as she moved among the men, offering a drink to each in turn. Beautiful, strong, spirited. He found himself unexpectedly yearning for something impossible.

Ignore her, Tiller reminded himself. *You took the oath like all the rest. Besides, no matter what, one way or another she's just more trouble and you don't need that. Take your own advice and focus on what's at hand. Don't think about her or what could be.*

Suddenly he remembered Fishgirl speaking to him as they had pulled away from the shore. What had she said? Something about neither of them coming back, no matter what?

Probably just panic. Tiller shrugged, but the feeling that something was not as it should be had become a troublesome splinter he could not dislodge.

———·———·———

Towards evening, the setting sun glowed scarlet under low clouds. Rose and gold lit the crest and valley of each wave and outlined the elegant muscles of the ship. It was a good sign. Tomorrow would be clear.

Randaal, one of the tallest men, called the end of the rowing shift and yelled to Fishgirl for their ration of small beer. As the men wearily stood and stretched, Randaal flexed his aching fingers and hands, watching Fishgirl as she handed the small cask to each man in turn.

The sun brightened her hair and face. Her braids were tidy now, thick and straight, the color of ripening wheat. She had lips made for smiling above a chin that had jutted stubbornly during the morning's fight.

"When will you serve our supper?" Randaal asked. He thought of giving her a friendly swat on the backside, but remembered the oath and swore under his breath, irritated. "That *sup's* ready, I can smell it. Food could get here a little faster, maybe?" He looked around for support, but receiving none, glared at Fishgirl as if she had insulted him.

Without answering, Fishgirl lifted the soup pot from the fire and stood ready with it. Tiller had shown her the traditional way to serve. Food went first to the men who rowed the right side, then to those on the left. Teams switched sides each turn to keep their muscles balanced and for balance. Fairness kept men from fighting over small nothings.

As Fishgirl spooned portions to the left-side rowers, Randaal asked for more beer and tried to banter with her. She passed the cask to him without comment and returned to serving soup. "Sigmund, you're next. Hold your bowl closer, please. I don't want to spill any."

Randaal pressed the beer cask to his lips and drank slowly and deeply. His gaze slipped down Fishgirl's body. It was taboo to brazenly ogle her, but no one could accuse him of it while his head was tipped back to drink. "Keep the drinks coming, Fishgirl," he said, wiping his mouth with a tattooed forearm. "You should offer, not wait for me to ask."

She made no response. Randaal spoke louder. "And keep your cooking space decent. Way too many of your kind don't keep their kettle clean enough, if you know what I mean." He guffawed, making a crude gesture to ensure that no one could possibly miss his meaning.

"You are foul. And keep your eyes off me next time you drink." Fishgirl's voice was flat and cold, and she spoke without looking at him. She dipped her ladle into the pot for Dagsson.

Randaal leered, pleased to have baited her. "You can be sure that I *will* be keeping my eyes on you. Strictly on your work, I mean!"

Most of the men kept eating and looked away, uncomfortable. The fish girl...no, Randaal should not. One of the Knutsson twins forced a laugh, too loud and shrill.

"Stop it, Randaal," said Tiller. "We don't need trouble on our very first day."

Dagsson chimed in. "Fishgirl is sacred to Rán! Do you *want* the goddess to send bad seas?" To combat Randaal's insult, Dagsson spat over his shoulder into the waves and mumbled the traditional words of supplication: *water-from-me-to-thee-Rán-goddess-of-the-sea-deal-kindly-with-our-ship-we-all-of-us-beg-of-ye.* A couple of the other men followed his example, spitting and mumbling the words with worry in their eyes.

"Leave Fishgirl alone, Randaal," said gray-bearded Sigmund. "She's doing her job. No need to set everyone's teeth on edge."

Randaal grunted in irritation and turned aside. Later, Fishgirl saw him look furtively around, then surreptitiously spit and say the words as well.

At least Randaal's comments had served to get the men talking. Soon, jests were being made and the men boasted to one another. Up until this moment, the crew had barely spoken, too tense to say more than a grunted word or two. Longing for release, they were suddenly eager to look one another in the eye, to call one another 'brother', to clasp hands in bond.

Men like my father, thought Tiller. *They may be able to work like cart horses, but at some point, they will need to triumph over someone, to prove that they are not the fools the world sees them to be.*

Tiller watched Randaal more closely. That man, and the two he was joking with, had been outlawed because they had done true wrongs, not because of trumped-up circumstance. Randaal was not the kind who took punishment to heart and learned from it. He would do wrong again in a heartbeat if it suited him, for spite if nothing else.

Woe to him – or her – who stands in Randaal's way at that moment, Tiller thought.

———·———·———

Watching Randaal brought a memory of Tiller's father. Thorvald, demanding the names of stars from the thin boy who ran behind trying to keep up, and behind them was another job lost because of Thorvald's contentiousness, and a dry hay crib for sleeping that would instead now be a night shivering along the chilly roadway.

"Stop dawdling and looking back towards the farm, boy! You need a proper education, not anything that farmer could teach you. Look over there, at those stars low in the southern sky. When farmers gather hay on autumn evenings, the land-fools don't know what they mean. Tell me their names, why they matter."

Tiller would repeat the remembering-shapes his father had taught, that the position of those stars meant sea trout after the first rains of autumns.

"Right!" Thorvald crowed. "The fool could've had a rack of fish drying if he'd listened to me, but, no, I'm dismissed because his pigsty wants mucking. Me, Thorvald Asvaldsson, freeholder, *vikinger*, son of a son of chieftains!"

The boy Tiller followed silently, saying nothing about Thorvald having been hired to muck the pigsty, not to give fishing advice.

"Quit dragging your feet, you worthless lout! I'll wager you upset that hothead and he's taking it out on me. This is your fault again, isn't it? You should be ashamed!"

30

If only they knew, Tiller thought when men praised his remarkable seamanship. His father, the once-haughty landowner and seaman, reduced to working as a thrall. Too proud to admit failure, humiliating his son had become Thorvald's favorite game.

But his father had taught him the stars, so had given him a start. From others, Tiller had learned the sea routes to Éireland and Northumbria and Scotiland, and further south to where the Anglos lived, and to the Northern and Southern Isles. He'd been across the water to West Francia. Tiller had traded in all of the lands to which the *nórsvegr* carried ships - Westfoldia, Swealand, Götaland, Danmörk, Finnmark. He had plied the great *nórsvegr* current, the *north way,* straight to the country for which the current was named: Nor'way, the land which had outlawed his father, a place rich in fox fur and walrus ivory – and he could keep a knörr heavily loaded with them safe from storms. He knew how to outrun thief ships and bring safely to port valuable loads of silver, silks, spices, slaves, glassware, and quern-stones. Men who owned ships paid a premium to have Tiller Thorvaldsson aboard.

But only he knew the darkness within, the relentlessly gnawing self-doubt instilled by his father's mocking. "Thorvald, you taught as much bad as good," muttered Tiller. If only they knew.

———·———·———

That night, as the crew wrestled themselves into sleeping sacks, Fishgirl whispered to Tiller, bundled into his own warm húðfat a few steps from hers.

"Tiller?

"Hmmm?"

"Thank you."

31

"For what?" Their conversation of earlier had left his thoughts.

"Just…I'm so alone here. It felt better, talking to you."

"You're welcome. It was nothing."

A small awkward silence floated between the two of them; a woman lying almost rigid with fear in her sleeping sack, and a man who feared little in life but loathed much of it. He heard her breathe an unconscious little gasp of self-reassurance, and something in him felt not tenderness, but at least a kind of gentleness.

"Good night," she said.

Men on ships did not bid one another good night. People snug in longhouses did that. Again, it touched the cold place in his chest.

"Good night," he said back gruffly.

Fishgirl heard the sound and knew it for what it was; a man who had buried his feelings somewhere deep inside. She found herself smiling the least bit. Why did that make her feel happy?

"Sleep well, Tiller." This last, the quietest of whispers so that the crew would not hear.

He did not return the sweet, wry smile he heard in her voice, but his own lips showed a flicker of warmth.

Fishgirl closed her eyes in exhaustion. For now, the ship timbers against her furred sack felt almost like a sleeping bench in a warm longhouse, instead of a ship far at sea and drifting. With that small comfort, she was instantly asleep.

———·———·———

In the ship's fore, the man called Randaal was thinking of the Fishgirl as well. Unlike Tiller, Randaal was smiling broadly under the barely-waning full moon.

32

He pictured her naked. Her hair would be unbraided, he decided, and freshly combed, and the golden waves of it would froth around her shoulders and lie soft and gleaming on the curves of her breasts.

She would be tied up, of course. Randaal took his time thinking about her eyes, full of fear; that mouth, trembling with desire for him to do as she asked.

But that would not happen. Randaal chuckled to himself. No, he would not do as she asked. She would not be let go...but he *would* let her beg for it.

___.___.___

Challenge

"Fishgirl!"

It was the third dawn. They were another night farther from land, and another man was bleeding.

Was it Kurt Knutsson, or Karl? One of the thin twins held a bloody rag against his forearm. Fishgirl reached wearily for the packet that held the linen thread and needle, and made her way fore-ward. She had already stitched up two other men in as many days.

"What happened?"

Kurt looked away nervously.

"What happened?" she repeated. "I have to know to fix it properly."

"I tripped onto Gierr's knife. He was sharpening the blade and I did not see."

Fishgirl lifted the rag and blood gushed from a long straight draw across the skin.

"Tripped?"

He nodded and would not meet her eyes.

Fishgirl looked straight at Gierr. "When someone on my farm hit a blade by accident, it usually punctured straight in. This looks pulled across his skin on purpose."

"Just stitch it for me, Fishgirl," said Kurt. "Never mind."

"What's the point, Gierr? How will we get anywhere if you slice each other apart bit by bit? Brace yourself, Kurt." Sea water poured over the cut would sting, but the salty liquid would help offset any curses Gierr had put on his blade. She rinsed the wound carefully, and threading a needle, pushed it into Kurt's arm. He grimaced in pain as Gierr muttered and smirked to his oar mate.

"How are the nightmares?" Fishgirl asked quietly. Twice Kurt had woken screaming in the night. "Did the calming-broth help you sleep better?"

"Yes. More tonight, please?"

"For certain. Will your brother drink some if I make it for him too?" Kurt's twin Karl was barely eating. Working or resting, he stared constantly at the horizon, flinching.

"If I tell him to."

"I'll make it for you both at dusk." She poured salt water over the stitched wound again. "It's not deep. It'll heal quickly. I'll rub fat on it in a little bit." Fishgirl raised her voice. "No rowing for Kurt today or tomorrow. You can all thank Gierr."

As she made her way back to her work station, Sigmund tapped Fishgirl on the arm and nodded at Randaal. "That one put Gierr up to it. I saw him. Randaal's always looking for trouble."

"He is. You knew him before ship?"

Sigmund picked at his tooth with a fingernail. "Knew *of* him." He spat some tiny thing onto the deck flooring. "Always a troublemaker. Last thing we need here."

Fishgirl watched Sig as he shouldered his way forward. He said nothing as he passed Kurt, but gave the young man a fatherly pat on the shoulder.

Despite their bravado, Fishgirl could see that fear lay below the men's anger and bickering and the fights for no apparent reason. Kurt and Karl were the youngest and weakest aboard, and took more than their share of abuse. Kurt, looking furtively about and whispering, had choked out the images from his nightmares: vile creatures rising from foul waters, half-fish, half-dragon, their scabrous spine-backs covered with thick, ugly fins that silently broke the surface of unhealthy waters in a silent, menacing approach.

Fishgirl almost wished she would have bad dreams, for at least they meant sleep. At night, full of fatigue, she would fall asleep from the sheer exhaustion of work and worry, of wind and waves, but she often woke again not long afterwards. Under the sprawling sky, Mani the moon-god looked down, judging Fishgirl for the wayward foolishness that lead to being caught on this ship. Her sleeping sack kept her warm, but nothing could stave off the bitter tears.

I need to drink calming herbs at bedtime as well, she reminded herself. Quickly, Fishgirl washed Kurt's blood from under her fingernails, trying to keep her thoughts away from yet another long day stretching ahead, from the already-filthy men, from the pus in the knife wounds, the half-leering, half-hateful glances.

I cannot do this. I cannot do this. I cannot... Her heart pounded and the panic escalated rapidly into the inner shrieking, the wanting to run, to blurt out the whispered conversation she had overheard which caused her to fear finding land as much as she feared dying on the sea. *I cannot do this, I cannot...*

"Fishgirl! Water!"

She gulped. Thank goodness for the crew's constant thirst. Three years to go, less three days and nights, less a morning.

———·———·———

That night, another whisper.

"Tiller?"

"Yes, Fishgirl?"

A long pause, and again the indrawn gasp of hope. "Good night."

Damned if he didn't catch himself picturing her eyes.

"Mmmph," he grunted, and heard in reply a muffled whisper.
"Thank you." Was she laughing at him?

—·—·—

"We're alive! Hel didn't take us to Niflheim last night! Hel, I pray, spare us again today!"

The first few mornings, squinty-eyed Ekka's invocation to the goddess of the afterlife had elicited jeers. He repeated it each daybreak anyway. One by one, others had started to say the words along with him, partly in jest and partly in hope.

"Fishgirl, first water!"

Still alive, Fishgirl told herself, refilling the water-skin from the cask. *Three years less four days and a night. Still alive. That's something.* She drew in a deep breath, began to prepare the daybreak meal.

Suddenly Fishgirl paused and reached for her knife. Where to cut? The board on which she worked would do. She turned it edgewise. Four days. She made the marks swiftly, then turned back to preparing food, staring at her hands and letting herself think of nothing but the small movements of her fingers.

—·—·—

"What's our direction today, Tiller?" Randaal queried as he combed and braided his hair.

Tiller had known the challenge would come soon, and from Randaal. "Same as yesterday. We strive for due west, and we let the current push us."

Randaal's mouth twisted in disgust. "Why west? Why not south-west, or north-west?"

They were finally running under sail, tacking hard but with a decent wind. Men were busying themselves with bailing or mending clothing. All eyes went to Tiller.

"Snæbjörn Galti owned the last ship that sailed to Gunnbjörn's Skerries. What do we know of him?

Fishgirl startled. Tiller was asking about her cousin Snow-bear Galti? Her family never spoke of him or that fateful trip; it was too horrible. She kept her mouth firmly closed.

No one else answered Tiller either, so he continued.

"Twenty-six men and women were aboard, they said, led by Snow-bear Galti and his partner, Rolf of Red-sands. Rolf brought a friend, a man named Styrbjörn. Just before they left, Styrbjörn claimed that he had had a terrible dream of a doleful place of frost and cold and anguish. He claimed that in this dream he had foreseen the death of Snow-bear."

Heads nodded. The story was widely known.

"Who returned from that voyage? Not Snow-bear. Not his wife. None of the others; only Rolf and Styrbjörn came back, telling a story that matched Styrbjörn's dream: that they had found an ice-covered land where there was no food to be found, no game to hunt. They said that everybody died there. But did they really go on the voyage? Or did they just sail out of sight, find an empty island, and kill Snow-bear and the rest, and take the ship?"

"What's your point? Are you spinning a yarn, twisting the story around to confuse us?" Gierr was always impatient, with his thick eyebrows knitted in a constant frown.

"My point is this: Snow-bear said he was going to sail due west. If they actually *did* find land, as Rolf claimed, what good would it do

38

to go to an ice-covered stone in the sea again? We need actual *land*, not frozen rock. Rolf also claimed that the coastline was huge, that it went on and on without changing. If this place is that large, better to let the current push us southwest, and then go west again looking for a warmer shore. I've thought hard about it. It makes sense."

There was a pause while the crew considered Tiller's words. Trying to explain his theory troubled Tiller. What if he was wrong? Part of him deeply and instinctively understood navigation. He often felt an inner calling towards a particular course, and it usually turned out to be good, but another part of him did not trust the feelings.

He simply said to Randaal, "We discussed this before we left, and decided we would start by going west as best we could, working with the current. It's strong and could overturn us easily."

"You're so damned clever, I figured maybe you had another thought, now that we're actually out here!" Randaal shot back.

"Randaal, you're just spoiling for your daily fight. You want to tell me how to do my job? Sharpen your knife again. I'm just about the only person you haven't pointed it towards."

———·——·———

Randaal's annoyance festered across the next eighth-mark. When it was time for his team to take their turn, he rolled his gaze over Fishgirl again as he drank. Wiping his lips, Randaal asked, "Will you be making anything decent to eat today?"

"Will you be taking your eyes off me while you drink?"

"Did you not discuss your duties with the headman before you left?" Randaal jabbed. "Men need good food to row, fool-girl."

"We'll be out here a long time. I'm not anxious to use up our supplies," she snapped.

"You'll use what we want." Her returned glare made his voice rise. "You *will!*"

One of the men resting on the chests grunted. It was Hyulf, missing a tooth and with spiky red hair. "Randaal, I'm so sick of your blather."

Randaal turned with exaggerated slowness. "Shut your snout, Hyulf."

"You pick a fight with someone every eighth-mark. Leave Fishgirl alone."

Another voice chimed in. "Be quiet, both of you. I'm trying to rest."

Randaal ignored them both. "Fishgirl, your job is to serve the crew. Make sure men who work harder than those who slack"—he looked pointedly towards Hyulf— "are fed best."

"No," replied Fishgirl. Her face burned as it had when she challenged Gierr and Dagsson.

Hyulf lifted up on one elbow, watching.

Fishgirl's voice was deadly calm. "You will be fed equally. That, the gothi *did* make clear. None are to be fed better or worse than any other man. Feel free to test me again tomorrow, Randaal. You're not going to beat me down."

Hyulf raked his fingers through his cropped hair and laughed, a barely-heard sound over the creaking of the boat. He lay down again, pulling his tunic back over his eyes.

Randaal mouthed a word he dared not call Fishgirl aloud as she put away the water-skin. Victory spoke in the set of her shoulders and the grim curve of her mouth, even though she shook inside. *Three years, less a week. I may be powerless, but I will not yield to Randaal.*

—·——·——

"Fishgirl!" Again, the call of *come-fix-this*. By now she could tell if it meant to bring water or to hurry with food, to help mend a sealskin or a sock, to pull a splinter, or to straighten a wrenched thumb or a bloody nose.

Fishgirl sighed wearily, drew a clean bucket of sea water, and felt for the sewing kit in her pocket. "Who is it and where are you cut?" She made her way forward and began to clean the gash in Hyulf's head without much caring how it had happened.

Drenching

Rain came the next day, and turned the mild spring weather wet and dreary. It poured relentlessly. The mood on deck became morose as raw showers fell for a solid day with no wind or current. Fights broke out, but after halfhearted swings and curses, the men went back to work.

Three years, less a week and half. Fishgirl counted, and cut a mark in her workboard. Could it really be ten days away from home already? Tears squeezed from her eyes, and she fought to draw in air. How far west could a ship sail before it fell off the edge of the world? The fear rose and fell inside her as steadily and endlessly as the waves.

Breathe breathe breathe... She spat into the water, said the prayer to Rán, again, and again. *Breathe breathe breathe.*

———·———·———

"Do you see that? There, two waves away?" Karl was becoming thinner daily, the constant nervousness eating away at his flesh. He barely had strength to row, and shivered under his cloak.

Fearing she might actually see one of the nightmare sea-beasts, Fishgirl looked where he pointed, but there was nothing except ocean swells moving sluggish under the rainclouds. "It's your imagination, Karl."

"Make him shut up or I'll cut his tongue out," someone snarled. "He makes the hair stand up on my neck. He's calling bad luck."

"No one's cutting out anyone's tongue," Sigmund said laconically. "We need every hand willing and able to row. Keep your tempers, lads. The sun will be back soon." His calm tone soothed them briefly, and rowing resumed.

The men bent forward as one and the oars creaked, then splashed as they hit the water again. They gurgled beneath the waves as the men leaned back, pulling. Creak, bending forward. Splash. Gurgle, pulling back. Creak, splash, gurgle. Karl rowed and stared.

By nightfall, he was shaking with fatigue and chill. Fishgirl put a cloak over him. "Sit as close as you can to my cooking fire, Karl. The little bit of warmth will do you good." She had found the warming-stone and put it in the coals. "Here, the warming-stone is wrapped in this cloth. Keep it against your belly."

"Tell me something about land, Fishgirl," he asked, his voice plaintive. "Tell me about the farm on which you lived."

Fishgirl swallowed against the pain that rose in her throat. "I try not to think about it," she replied, a catch in her voice. "Tell me about yours instead." Almost immediately, she regretted her words.

"I've never really had a home, Fishgirl. I've always been a thrall. Sold from one master to the next as long as I can remember. Tell me of yours, please? What it's like?"

42

She let her thoughts turn to the hills and valleys of home. "The wet would be welcome there, I know that. It would be nourishing seeds, and coaxing the first soft green of crops from the fields. Rain would pull people inside to work at mending plows and repairing boots. You'd hear a wheel turning in one of the sheds, someone using a whetstone to sharpen field tools. The metallic smell would come across the still air, and mix with scents of leather and oil."

Fishgirl saw the ghost of a smile in the gaunt shadow of Karl's cheek. She leaned deeper into the image in her memory.

"I'd stand just inside the doorway of the longhouse and listen to the wet drops hitting the wood frame of the door and the ground. If the rain was hard, the water would run in rivulets along the furrows of the fields. The little ones would get their shoes all wet, running outside to stamp about in puddles, splashing and laughing."

As Fishgirl described comforting small details for Karl, his eyes grew heavy. Soon, he nodded off to sleep under his blanket. She let her voice soften to a whisper and finally stopped speaking. Her gaze softened and she looked at him; the thin face, full lips, a nose a little too big for his face. A foolish face, to be sure, but not a bad one. Asleep, Karl could be any of the thralls on their farm. Some had come as young boys. She'd helped to teach them, assigned them chores, and nursed them through sickness.

Suddenly Fishgirl realized she did not care if he knew of the plot against her. Who knew if they would ever reach land? For now, what mattered was keeping Karl alive. She put her hand against her heart, surprised to realize that thinking of being at home had eased the ache in her own breast. Something flexed within her, a sensation of strength and power.

Serve in every way, Gothi had instructed.

Part mother, part healer, Tiller had said.

She watched Karl's chest rising and falling peacefully, and felt again inside herself an understanding of true power. *I am his Fishgirl,* she thought. *He needs me. I am Fishgirl to all of these men, stupid or not. Help me, Goddess Rán. Help me, Mother Ship. Help me carry them.*

The images of home fields faded slowly from her eyes. Here, only dreary wet fell on slick gray swells, barely visible in the post-sunset light. They felt like an eternity in which the dead rested. Fishgirl shuddered and cursed for the thousandth time, but this time, there were no tears.

———·———·———

"Fishgirl?" Tonight Tiller had decided to beat her to it.

"Yes?"

"Well…I just thought I'd tell you good night."

From 'well' to 'good night', she heard his voice change from being kind enough to make a little joke to feeling foolish. Fishgirl bit her tongue to keep from laughing. Men were the same the world over.

"Thank you, Tiller," she said, her voice graceful and warm. "I hope you sleep well."

———·———·———

When the rain finally stopped the next day, heavy fog rolled in. Fishgirl tried to lighten the mood by singing, but even that felt irritating. Finally, she called aloud the question on every mind.

"Tiller? Sigmund? Olaf, Gierr…does this feel…off…to you? This weather? This fog?"

Sigmund Graybeard grunted and took the question head-on. "You want to ask if this is like the fog Ulfsson's crew described."

Ekka squinted, glad to have the question out in the open to discuss. "I wish I had heard one of them talk about it. Would've asked them many questions."

"Ulfsson's crew turned tail and ran home," Randaal scowled. "Creeping cowards!"

"Sig, answer Fishgirl's question to quiet these fools. We all are wondering the same thing," said Dagsson. "Do you think we're close to …Niflheim? The end of the world?"

"Maybe we are, maybe we aren't. No knowing anything until we see something, is there?"

Kurt gawked around, anxious. "What if we *are* close to Hel's home? Will she take us?"

"You're a creeping coward too, Kurt. You don't deserve to be aboard," Randaal jeered. Randaal loathed weakness in any form, and the twins annoyed him beyond all reason. Just hearing the question made him want to break Kurt in half. "I've seen plenty of fogs. This one is no worse than any other. Not like Ulfsson's."

Other voices rose and fell in annoyance and frustration as the crew debated the question. Fishgirl listened, in her mind matching the men with their names. Some had hair cropped short like Hyulf. Others, longhaired, carefully combed their locks each day before putting to oars. Some shaved their jaws close to the skin, while others had full beards with every variation of braiding and beading imaginable. They ranged in size from the massive Tor to the tiny Ekka. Some were cheats and some were bullies, while others seemed like men who would never have committed a crime. By now, Fishgirl knew who wheedled and who whined, who was always looking for a fight, who lashed out without warning and who calmed them down; who told foul

45

jokes, and who was courteous. Fishgirl paid attention to every detail, learning the men's weak points and their strengths, saving scraps for when she would need them.

Wonderful old Sigmund was respected, irascible and likeable. How had he possibly managed to get himself outlawed? Maybe because the council needed him; he knew the sea as well as Tiller. No one seemed to know the real reason.

The rowing leader Dagsson was as sulky as Sig was easygoing. Short of temper, he exploded easily at imagined slights, and he always wanted to stop work early. But more than once Dagsson had stood up with her against Randaal. Gierr, the other rowing leader, also had a temper that erupted often and grew quickly. But unlike Dagsson, Gierr would work well past exhaustion without complaining, and he resented those who did not work as hard.

Bolli was so lazy he never rubbed his teeth when Fishgirl gave out the tiny amount of cleaning-water allotted each morning. He had no ear-wax spoon, he sometimes smelled badly, and his belongings were always untidy, but Bolli's words were spotless. He would not lie. No matter the consequences, Bolli could be counted on to recount exactly what had happened in any situation – even when it had resulted in his own outlawing.

Unlike Bolli, Olaf groomed himself carefully every morning, even tweezing his brows in a prized tiny mirror from Hispania. His vanity sprang from fear of seeming a failure. His family had once held all of Olaf's Bay, and he longed too much for the old power. A stone fence would be moved one spring, or a planting line, and sheep would disappear and reappear, shorn and with Olaf's mark on them. Old neighbors tried not to offend with direct accusations, but Olaf grew bolder, and finally it was too much to ignore.

46

Ulf had gambled himself into debt, and then deeper debt, unable to resist betting, and unable to resist cheating to win. But Fishgirl had learned that Ulf never gave up. He would try, and try, and try again, and always believe in the possible.

Bergr could row all day, but he could not stand up for himself. He was weak of spirit and had been used by others, and took their punishment, too frightened to say that their crimes were not his doing. But he genuinely wanted to please, and would offer to help Fishgirl – to the point of annoyance.

Randaal was a bully, pure and simple. He sought out trouble at every turn, stirring up arguments for the fun of it, but like Olaf, Randaal could have been a strong leader. What caused him to go down the road where his choices became fewer, and less pleasant? Someone had taught Randaal to be cruel and crafty. His only leadership was a cobbled-together band of raiders who terrorized farmers and stole pigs.

Mitla was so pleasant of mood Fishgirl could not imagine that he beat his children and his wives viciously and often enough that they had brought suit against him. Mitla had tried to touch Fishgirl once, groping furtively for a breast as she passed. She had not expected the cowering look in his eyes when she'd hit him, hard. In that instant, she realized that Mitla had himself been beaten, and had become the same as whoever had brutalized him.

Scrawny little Nollar had been a slave from Éireland whose loyal service had bought his freedom and a small piece of hardscrabble land. He had run out of options with three years of crop failures. Is a man a thief when he steals food for his children? In another year, the council might have levied a fine and a work-repayment, but Nollar was a man skilled in everything that had to do with a ship, or rigging, or repairs.

Lars was handsome and charming, with a ready smile and strong shoulders, and always willing to work and lend a hand, but Fishgirl's skin crawled from him. The disappearances of girls who had been his companions could not be proven. All had been orphans or slaves with no one to worry much after them, except for one; a stubborn sister and bit of flesh and cloth had finally been enough to take him to trial.

Tor almost never spoke. His name suited one as massive as a mountain, and his skin shone as dark as the black lava-stone that had hardened down the side of the mountainous lava fields. He, too, was a slave, brought from far away as a child. Squinty-eyed Ekka, Tor's rowing mate and his opposite in every way, talked incessantly, but Ekka had good sense when one could bear to listen to him. They were another pair that Fishgirl suspected had been found guilty for convenient reasons.

Kurt and Karl, youngest and last in all things, were boy-men who had been ground to nothing by life. *If my brothers had taught them, tumbled in play with them...* With a decent family, the twins would have grown into strong and capable men.

These sixteen manned the oars and the sail. That left Tiller. Was he a cold-blooded killer of friends, or was it a lie, as some claimed at the All-Gathering? As she counted and named them, Fishgirl wondered how many of these men knew what was planned for her should they reach land. Did Tiller? *I don't think so,* Fishgirl thought. *Maybe, but not likely.* And if they knew, would they follow through with it? Giant, silent Tor seemed to be quietly kind to her. Dagsson, who had stood up to Randaal for her, might help her, and Hyulf, along with Sig. Kurt and Karl trusted her, but she could not trust them. They were too foolish to keep a secret. The rest would likely save their own skins first. It meant she would have to do the same.

48

I need to learn more, to test if they would stand with me or against me, should it come to that. She could not think how to do so without giving herself away. Frowning, she watched Karl rubbing his hand on his stomach where the hunger hurt, and an idea came. Fishgirl gasped at how dangerous the thought was. But with her life already on the line, what did it matter?

The *Tafl* Game

The next morning warm spring sunlight flowed over everything on the ship. Tiller stretched deeply with pleasure. Nothing lifted spirits like bright sun after rain. It would be good to finally make progress westward again. He reached for the hem of his *kyrtill*, eager to pull it off and feel the fresh air on his skin.

"Fine garments, these shipboard kyrtills!" he said to Fishgirl. "These, and our sealskin sleeping-sacks and our woolens kept us from suffering too much from the wet and cold, didn't they?" In the rain, they had covered their sleep-*húthfats* with sheepskin blankets. The thick wool, rich in sheep's oil, had held in warmth and shed water.

The crew talked aimlessly as they hung belongings in the sun to dry.

"Do you know why shipboard kyrtills are short?" asked Tiller. He continued without waiting for her answer. "Of course, so we can work and sleep without binding, but there's more."

Fishgirl shook her head. Tiller noticed that she looked unwell.

"You see how they are all the same length, just about the knee? It's to show that every man aboard has equal value, from veteran sailors to the greenest oarsman. Any of them might save the ship by holding the sail in a storm or seeing shoals in time. On land, one adds length to a kyrtill to boast of wealth, but at sea, all wear the same length tunic, even the owner of the ship."

Suddenly Fishgirl leaned over the side of the knörr and vomited into the water.

The men stared at her, perplexed. The sea was calm, almost glassy. She had endured rough waves for days with no signs of sickness. Along with them, Tiller found himself stupidly wondering. *A woman, ill in the morning for no reason? A fish girl must not be...*

No! His brain reeled from the idea.

Randaal exploded. "What's wrong with her?"

Lars whispered something to his oar-partner Bolli.

"What did Lars say?" Randaal demanded.

Bolli laughed. "We may have one more passenger on board. A stowaway --"

His laughter cut off as Randaal's eyes hardened to iron. Despite his own concerns over Fishgirl, Tiller could not help but wonder at Randaal's expression, as if he'd been betrayed. An odd memory came to Tiller, a moment out of time, of two brothers who had been playing a game of *tafl*, the older teaching the younger. The oldest had let his young brother advance easily, sometimes thwarting him without being ruthless, so that the boy would learn the game. The younger prepared for victory when the older one slowly slid his piece. Surveying the *tafl* board, the boy saw his certain victory crumble into sudden defeat.

That look of bitter betrayal was the same expression that was now on Randaal's face.

———·——·———

Randaal dropped his sleeping sack and strode towards Fishgirl. "Is it true? Are you with child?" He swayed on the half-deck, glowering at her as they squared off.

"What business is it of yours?" Fishgirl snapped.

"You can't be!"

"Who says I am?"

"Well, are you, or aren't you? Quit playing games and tell us!"

"I'll tell you nothing with you shouting at me!"

In a flash, Randaal's short knife pressed her throat. "Answer me! Answer *right now!*"

Remarkably, Fishgirl held her calm. "Put your knife down. You can't hurt me."

Her words whipped Randaal's anger into fury. The veins in his neck throbbed. He moved his dagger-point against her stomach. "Tell us or I'll cut you open and find out for myself!"

The men, momentarily caught off guard, had watched, frozen. At Randaal's threat, they exploded into movement, wrestling Randaal away, taking his knife, and pulling Fishgirl to safety. In a moment it was over, and all were panting from exertion.

Sigmund wiped his brow. "Randaal! What are you thinking? You swore the oath to protect her as we all did! Oath or no oath, do something like that again and you'll have the whole crew on you." His big head swung to Fishgirl. "As for you, our lives depend on you. Randaal's right in asking. We deserve to know."

"I can't be," Fishgirl admitted. "The last time I was with a man was…" she hesitated, mentally counting.

"The *last* time you were with a man? You've been with more than one?" Olaf practically shrieked the question.

"Again, I ask, what business is it of yours? There's no law against a single woman being with a man!" she snapped.

"Ignore Olaf! Are you sure? Count again!" demanded Sigmund.

"I don't -- I don't know. I'm not sure. I was sick when I first woke up, and again now."

Tiller startled. In the pale glow before dawn, burrowed in his sleeping-sack, he had seen Fishgirl stretch, wake, and sit up, peering around to see if anyone else was awake. Seeing none, she had gazed across the horizon where sunrise would soon sparkle. Her expression had been calculating, and she had not been sick at all. Why did she just lie to Sigmund?

Sigmund pleaded, "Fishgirl, women traveling with a husband, you see them on ships, and yes, they can lug around a belly. But on a voyage such as this? At sea so long?" Sig did not finish his thoughts. The implications were terrible and clear.

Her face was anxious. "We'll know soon enough, I guess."

All eyes were trained on Sigmund, wanting a more certain answer. He stared at Fishgirl, biting his lip. The silence stretched out uncomfortably. Feeling the pressure, he blurted, "We have to know! You have to be sure. What made you be ill?"

She looked at him guilelessly, and shrugged again.

She's lying, Tiller thought, *and she's good at it.* The thought made his skin crawl.

Poor Sig was caught between the crew's anxious fear and Fishgirl's innocent, worried look. He covered his eyes with his hands for a moment, then spoke loudly.

"Well, if you are, there's naught we can do now, is there? But no denying, it would be terrible bad luck. The weather the last couple of days has been a strain on all of us, and I don't know that we can bear one more burden just now. We need time to think about this. Give us the comfort of breakfast, at least."

He swung around to the crew and barked orders. "The rest of you, get your things out in the sun! More rain could be on us soon, so the faster they are dry, the better."

The crew returned with relief to shaking out kyrtills and rubbing oil into sealskins. The tasks gave their hands something to do while their minds struggled with the devastating possibility.

Randaal alone did not move. His eyes followed Fishgirl with malevolence. She struck the tinder to start her small cooking fire. As she measured the pounded oat grains into the pot, Fishgirl's gaze, intense and grim, flicked for just an instant at Tiller. He saw a bitter message there, but after the merest heartbeat, it disappeared.

———·———·———

Across that day, Tiller could barely take his eyes from Fishgirl. She caught him staring at her often, and other times at nothing, his mouth tight. It was the look of a man working through an idea.

Keep at it, Tiller, Fishgirl mocked him silently. *Keep watching. Figure out everything you can. You'll need it when the time comes.*

He had no idea that she watched herself more. She could not afford any mistakes.

———·———·———

The men avoided discussing Fishgirl as if merely talking about her would bring even worse luck upon them. They focused attention on the one other thing that worried them almost as much: the ship's heading. *Surely, Gunnbjorn's men weren't pushed south as hard as we have been?* The question came at Tiller over and over, in a variety of ways. One of the men would ask, or comment, but always with eyes on Fishgirl instead of Tiller.

Tiller fought their uneasiness, stubbornly insisting that they continue as before, that it was too dangerous to try to cross that southwestward wind. He had more reasons than the too-close set of the sail. He was confident that, barring a terrible storm, and assuming it actually had existed, sooner or later they would find the rocky landing place of Snow-bear Galti's ship. But with that, the crew would want to head back to Íseland and claim success. Rocks and ice were not what the council wanted. Tiller was under no illusions that the council would promptly turn them around and send the ship right back out. No, he believed they needed to keep moving south. It was more dangerous and took them much deeper into currents that he could tell grew more treacherous daily, but his instincts insisted it to a level he could not ignore.

The debate continued, from one rowing partner to another, from sail-tightener to bailer, from one meal-break to the next. Tensions on board mounted, with nothing to dissipate them: *Fishgirl...might they have to turn around, take her back home, drop her off along the shoreline of Íseland? Ulfsson's and Galti's shores...would they ever find them? Niflheim...did it lurk too close for safety?*

At every meal now, as well as at every change in rowing shifts, the entire crew lined up along the ship's side, spitting as one into the ocean and saying together the plea to the sea goddess. *Water-from-me-to-thee-Rán-goddess-of-the-sea-deal-kindly-with-our-ship-we-all-of-us-beg-of-ye.* Tiller joined them, only partly to support a sense of oneness in the journey. He was not a praying man, but if there was ever a time to invoke divine intervention, it was now.

Fishgirl doubled her prayers to Rán and the Valkyries, and released every third fish caught in her net as a thank-you offering. Her lips moved constantly, the invocation almost a sing-song. From first light until after dark, lookouts were posted on either side of the ship, to shout a warning if gods-knew-what arose from the deep.

The strain aboard ship grew as taut as a wire pulled tighter and tighter, ready to snap. Locked together, too afraid to speak of their fears, the tensions pulled them inexorably towards where disaster awaited, where a breaking point, inevitable and catastrophic, rolled relentlessly toward them from somewhere out on the nameless, endless waves.

___.___.___

Another Deception

"Still alive! Hel spared us through the night, and we pray, again today!" Ekka's words were met by murmurs of support as the first shift dragged from their sleep sacks.

While Ekka led the early-morning call, Fishgirl was already up working her net. Tiller saw her pause and dip her drinking cup into the bucket that held seawater. He started to alert her that she'd used the wrong one. To his surprise, Fishgirl shook her head slightly as she drank. *Say nothing.* A little later, with all the men watching, Fishgirl leaned over the ship's side and was sick again.

She splashed water on her mouth and wiped it, and continued preparing their breakfast as if nothing had happened. She ignored the stares of the crew, and spat once more in the ocean, then shot a quick look at Tiller.

Yes, I am creating confusion, she thought fiercely towards him. *You're the one known for figuring things out. Keep working at it.*

She turned to her workboard and nicked a little cut on the edge of the wood.

How many days now? Fishgirl started to run her fingernail against the little cuts to count them. *Three years minus....* Her hand dropped. What did it matter? The small count was only a drop in the bucket of the required time. *Three years minus eternity.*

———·———·———

That night, Fishgirl wriggled her sleeping sack a little closer to Tiller's.

"Tiller?"

"Good night, Fishgirl," he said gently.

"May I...can you give me your hand?" The whisper trembled.

Tiller frowned to himself in the darkness. An invisible line hung in the night air, and he sensed that crossing it would cause trouble of some kind, but he knew not what. Despite that, he pulled his hand from his sleeping sack, took the mitten from it, and reached towards her.

Fishgirl did not say a word. She still had on her mitten, but she pulled it off at the feel of his bare palm. Neither of them spoke again. Only their fingers moved. They had touched tentatively at first, but in the slow roll of the waves, their fingers laced together and held tightly long after the two had fallen asleep.

———·———·———

"Damn Sól! I never thought to curse you! But you rise earlier each day and set later. You've stolen an eighth from our sleep already." Bolli rubbed his face, yearning for sleep, but yearning more for a day without a new worry.

Bolli had told the truth, as usual. His plaintive words unexpectedly filled Fishgirl with compassion and a hardheaded practicality. She could see the strain growing daily in their appearance. The growing days of spring meant less sleep, and less sleep meant more work, more hours to worry, more fatigue. Fatigue meant irritation, which meant fights, and more work for Fishgirl. Every day since they had left, the arguments had increased, and every nightfall, the ship moved closer to the nothingness that troubled them so terribly. She'd stitched cuts, washed scrapes, and mended clothing that had been wrenched and ripped. They could have turned around, but they pushed on, afraid to show fear, stoic in demeanor, but with little hope.

Despite their distress, Fishgirl had to admit that for the most part, the crew had been decent to her. *I am their Fishgirl. Their balance.* Bolli's words gave her pause. If she pushed them too hard, her efforts to protect herself could backfire. Perhaps it would be wiser to lessen the crew's worries a little today, rather than add to them.

Fishgirl stood up and spoke briskly. "Karl! Stop staring at the water and fetch me another log of charcoal from the underdeck. Kurt, check everyone on your rowing team who has a wound, and tell me how many of them need fresh fat rubbed in. You can help me with that. Tor, I'll help you repair your sealskins afterwards. No fighting with fists or knives today, fellows, please. I'm using the linen thread far too fast."

No one answered. Her eyes roved across their faces as they sagged wearily on the storage-chest benches, waiting for their daybreak food.

Fishgirl clapped her hands to get their attention. "Listen to me, all of you! Too much rowing, rowing, sailing, bickering, worrying, fighting, and looking at nothing but waves is no good for any of us! We need something to look forward to each day. Something, even if it's small. I've decided we're going to have a contest, after every evening meal. I'll tell you more when I serve tonight's supper."

Later that morning as Fishgirl scrubbed her scaling board, Tiller thought he saw her give him a tiny wink. *Did I imagine that?*

He winked back.

A dazzling smile lit her face, for only the briefest instant, and Fishgirl saw the reaction it caused in Tiller.

Yes, she said to herself. *I will trust him. I will tell him.*

———·——·———

When she had finished cleaning up after the morning meal, Fishgirl edged closer to Tiller. Once again, the knörr was under oar, the rowers on the port side pulling hardest as they fought the wind that pushed them south. Most of those not rowing were watching Lars and Gierr arm-wrestling, shouting wagers. No one would hear.

"Be ready," she whispered. The briefest of nods meant he'd heard.

She called loudly, "Bolli, would you help me? My net is tangled."

Tiller was splicing spare rope. "Why ask the laziest man on board? Bolli won't help. You know that by now."

Fishgirl shouted louder, making her tone shrewish. "Bolli! Come help with my net!"

A refusal was what she wanted, and received. "Ask Tiller! He's right there!"

She made an exaggerated pout. "If he messes it up one of you will have to fix it!" Turning to Tiller, she snapped, "Here, look how it's tangled."

Tiller leaned over, but her net was floating freely. Before he could say anything, Fishgirl hissed at him. "Stay down here and listen."

___.___.___

She whispered rapidly. "I have something important to explain, but for now, just know this: I'm in mortal danger as soon as we find land. You are as well. Watch for a chance to talk without the crew hearing. If by some miracle we find land before I can tell you everything, I need you to promise me to leave the ship as soon as we land, and stay away as long as you can. Do you understand?"

He shook his head *no*.

She whispered furiously, "I can't explain! But it's true, and it matters! Do you trust me?"

Tiller hesitated, then shook his head no again.

"Fair enough," Fishgirl said. He'd seen her lie, and did not know her as Jorund's daughter, proud of her integrity. "Would you do it for," she hesitated, "…a mother from Jadar?"

He froze, and shocked, nodded yes.

"When you stand up, throw the net out, as if you fixed it. Know that I'm your ally. Don't be fooled by anything I say or do, not *anything*. And good luck, to both of us."

——·——·——

Tiller knew now that those quick looks had not been his imagination. And Jadar? How did she know about the place he had lived as a child? Suddenly, she was no longer *Fishgirl*. He needed to know who this woman was, and what she was about, what she knew of his past. Bending over the net, he asked the very question he had told her was forbidden.

"What's your real name? I mean it this time. Just for me."

"Thjodhild," she whispered, her eyes shining. "Called Thio."

——·——·——

…Thio…

——·——·——

60

Thio. Her name was like the sweet whisper of a breeze in spring. It rang in him, the chime of a pure clear bell, echoing. *Thio... Thio... Thio...*

Tiller was dismayed to feel his heart pounding. He worked the net a little longer, pulled it up, and tossed it overboard again. The waves moved past as they had a moment before, but everything had changed.

———·———·———

Questions churned through Tiller's mind as the sun crossed the eighth-marks. In a vessel that stretched mere arms-lengths through the water, far from anywhere and bound for nowhere, these small scraps were monumental.

How could Fishgirl possibly know of Jadar and his mother? Tiller had not seen her since his father had been outlawed from Nórsvegr. And this Fishgirl had deceived the whole crew, but now, she asked him to trust her? Against whom was she allied with him, and for what? Besides the sea and the fighting on board, what other dangers could possibly exist?

His brain seethed, frustrated by too few pieces of information. That oath. That damned, confusing oath. Why was she different than other fish girls? Who *was* this woman?

The frustration built. Tiller had striven to keep his impatience in check since they had left Íseland, but now he felt like Randaal, craving release by action, even if it meant a stupid brawl.

No! That clash at home when friends died and their blood soaked into the ground was not so long ago. Stay calm, Tiller told himself.

Ignore your father's quick temper. His desire to know more was met only with impossibility.

Games

"What will the big contest be?" The men were lined up for supper, smelling a tantalizing fragrance. Fishgirl had caught several fish and cooked them over the meal-fire on her iron skillet. The smell of fresh seared fish eased the lines on their faces. Thieves, abusers and cheats they may be, Thio thought, but at that moment, they looked like eager boys, longing for a distraction from the work and worry.

"We're going to have games. Of course, you've been playing matches to pass time when it's not your rowing shift, but for the contest, we're going to have teams as they do in the summer All-Gathering, and prizes. We'll start an hour before dark, every night after the evening meal, if the weather is clear."

She anticipated a possible objection and held up her hand. "Yes, of course we could row or sail for another hour, but one sunset hour a day really won't matter that much, will it? Instead, we'll all go to sleep for the night with a tiny bit of fun to fill our minds, instead of hunger, thirst, exhaustion, and monsters."

"We'll keep count of who wins, and have real wagering!" This was Ulf's voice.

"What will we use for bets?" asked Ekka.

"If we find land, you'll all be rich men. We'll wager your future silver. We can use fish bones to represent it."

"What kind of games?" Several voices came in unison.

"Anything you want. *Tafl,* knucklebones, whatever. Something everyone can do."

"And the prize? What will we win?"

62

Fishgirl smiled mysteriously. "I have a magic amulet. It's a curing-stone, one which gives great power to he who wears it. The winner of each evening's contest will get to wear this stone as he sleeps, and through the next day."

The men murmured to themselves, obviously pleased with the reward, and Thio continued. "The point is, even in the worst of circumstances, we can choose to laugh on purpose, even if just a little, to keep fear and worry from consuming us."

"Worry, my ass," said Randaal. "Mind your words, Fishgirl! You're talking to men. I claim the first game. Who wants to play against me?"

Fishgirl smiled, but her voice was iron. "It's my curing-stone. I'll decide who plays first. Don't worry, you'll get a turn, same as everyone else. Now, who wants to eat?" The men plunged into the food, their mood the best it had been since they left shore.

———·———·———

Sig tossed the knucklebone again, and it landed with the Mark of Thor up.

"Again you win, Sig! Amazing luck!" Fishgirl smiled wryly at scrawny Nollar as he sighed in defeat. "Maybe tomorrow, Nollar."

Sigmund, always generous, clapped his opponent on the back. "You almost had me, Nollar. I wager you'll beat me next time."

Fishgirl pulled her braids over her shoulders and began to unplait them. The evening breeze felt good as it lifted her hair.

"I want to play Fishgirl at *tafl* while I wait for my turn," Kurt said.

"Too complicated for me, Kurt. I'll learn it soon, I promise." It was a quick dodge. Fishgirl had beaten her brothers and father on the tafl board by the time she was in her teens, but she did not want to show her skill yet. "Tor, it's your turn to play against Ekka. Ulf, keep track!"

—·—·—

Sigmund made his way aft between the lined-up crates that served as rowing benches. He kept his voice low against the roars of the knucklebone game. "Time to talk again, Tiller."

Sig's forehead wrinkled. "How many days have we been out here, do you reckon?"

Tiller was evasive. "No more than a few weeks."

"I reckon your ideas are as good as anyone's on board," Sigmund said.

Tiller waited for the '...*but...*'

"...but what if we've gone too far? Gunnbjörn might have seen just a wee island. Lots of ocean far west of Éireland, and that's where the current's taking us, isn't it? I've never heard any reports of anyone going west of *there* and seeing any skerries."

"It's a valid concern. I worry, too, that Galti's partner exaggerated or lied. What if those skerries are the size of the sheep-islands between Íseland and the Nor'way? No matter which way we go, we might miss them. I'm wondering if we should perhaps let the wind push us far, far southwest, then work our way north, zig-zagging east and west."

Sigmund looked hard at Tiller. Would he sound foolish saying it? Ah, what the Hel... "Maybe it was just a freak chance Ulfsson's men saw anything at all. Maybe the skerries... moved."

"No, you don't, Sig. It's bad enough without imagining giants moving ice-islands about in the seas around Niflheim. There's land out there, I'm convinced of it. We just have to keep looking."

"It's a bit raw tonight."

64

Tiller understood Sigmund's meaning. "I'm sure everyone senses it, despite making jovial with Fishgirl up there. The air says a storm is coming, a hard blow. If we make it through, we'll have a vote, and all can have their say. Better that way."

As they talked, both men watched Fishgirl and the crew, intently engaged in gaming.

"Strong woman," said Sig. "She's just as afraid as anybody. Hides it well."

"Yes, and a smart woman," agreed Tiller. "These contests were a small but perfectly-timed distraction. Even a blind man could see the crew is close to a breaking point."

"Shame, really, isn't it?" said Sig over his shoulder as he made his way fore-ward again.

Tiller frowned after Sig. *Shame? What was a shame?*

That night Tiller took Fishgirl's hand almost as soon as she had climbed into her sleeping sack. Something was terribly wrong, just as Fishgirl had said, and this woman was right in the center of the mess, and, he suspected, through no fault of her own. That was not right.

———.———.———

The morning dawned red and quickly turned gray and cold. The winds picked up as the temperature dropped. Whitecaps appeared, and the waves quickly grew taller and rougher.

"We're still alive...Hel, thank you for sparing us through the night...mayhap you could spare us again today?" Ekka's voice quavered.

"We're going to lose the ship for sure," Ulf said. "Not a wager I like, but I feel it."

"Your wagers are crap. Quit talking. You too, Ekka," Olaf rebuked them.

Sigmund spoke. "Olaf speaks true. No sense speculating. We all can tell it's going to be a little rough. Get everything ready, mates. You all know what to do."

Nollar, so wise in seafaring, spoke quietly to Tiller. "A little rough? We're in for a massive gale."

"I know. Can't do anything about it, though, can we?"

As Tiller began to pull the sealskins from his sea-chest, an ironic thought crossed his mind. Gunnbjörn Ulfsson's crew was pushed off course by a terrible tempest. Today, a storm as monstrous as that one was bearing down upon their own ship. Fate had come to call.

———·———·———

A Moment, a Lifetime

"Awhoooooooo! *Awhooooooo!*" Kurt howled. "We need to call wind-wolves to the ship! Bear us up, boys! Ride against Ran! *Ride! Whoooooooooooo!*" He had wrapped his lanky arms around the mast, and yelled desperately. "They'll get us through the waves!"

Olaf cuffed him. "Get away from the mast, you fool. You've been howling all morning. The wolves are no doubt on the way. Have you stowed your gear?"

Kurt laughed, almost hysterical. "We're wolves, running with the wind! Fighting the wind-witches!" He grasped at the mast, shoving Olaf away, and gasped for air, choked, and tried to shout again. "Wolves! Come to us!"

Sigmund pulled Kurt and held him as he squirmed. "Go tighten the straps on your trunks, son." Sig's usually-genial face was grim.

Fishgirl shivered in fear, and Sigmund came to kneel beside her. "Look here. Take your sleeping sack, your *húthfat*. Stow it deep in your sea-chest so it'll be nice and dry when the storm is over. Get your sealskins on, to keep you dry when the rain starts. All your crates must be tied to each other, but not to the ship. See to it, now."

Fishgirl's teeth chattered. "What is everyone doing, breathing into the empty water bladders?"

"They're tying them to the chests. If we lose our ship, it'll give something to hold, to stay above the waves."

"Sig…" she faltered.

"Buck up, woman. You're scared, I know. But you're strong, too. Powerfully strong. I've seen enough of that in these last days. Stop thinking about what might happen, and do what you need to do."

Fishgirl nodded, teeth still chattering, and began to follow Sigmund's directions. He continued in a matter-of-fact voice. "Depending on the storm, we may take down the sail. We cannot afford to lose either our sail or rudder. We have spares, but they're precious." Sigmund worked as he talked, and Fishgirl followed his lead. She tied her fish line and net into her cook-pots, and lashed them to the crate nearest her.

"You still listening? That's a fine woman. Keep packing. Tiller decides what serves us best, sail or no sail, oars or no oars, to keep the ship from capsizing." She nodded and stuffed her *húthfat* deep into a crate, grateful for Sig's strong, steady voice. "If we pull in the oars, we slide the covers in place to keep some of the water out. Now see here, Fishgirl, storms at sea can seem frightening, but you're in good hands. This crew knows what they're doing. If Tiller warrants he can't hold the rudder safely, he'll call for the sail to be dropped, and Tiller will pull the rudder up and lash it tight to the ship."

"What if the storm is too strong…if the waves are too wild?"

Sigmund did not spare her the truth.

"The storm *is* going to be strong. The ship will rock terribly, and the waves will crash over it. That water is more powerful than you can imagine. You don't want to be swept overboard. Hold onto something as if your life depends on it, because it does. Pray if you want."

———·———·———

Fishgirl's heart pounded. Why must she ask the next question? The stubbornness in her demanded truth. "Have you been through a storm as bad as this one looks to be?"

Sigmund laughed. "Oh, many times. Clearly, we made it through."

68

She looked him straight on, her clear blue eyes unflinching against his lined green ones, and managed the tiniest of smiles. "Clearly, a complete and utter lie, Sig. Thank you for it."

———·———·———

They crew wrestled into their sealskins as the rain started, making frantic last preparations. Almost as the last crate was tied, they heard a roaring in the wind unlike any they had ever heard before, and their eyes turned to one another in astonishment and apprehension. On Tiller's abrupt order, the men scrambled to pull down the sail.

Shouts could barely be heard above the fearsome gale. "Hold the sail bag -- tie it -- no, there!" "Lash the oars!" "Forget the oar covers! Brace yourselves!"

The wind slammed into the ship before Tiller could pull up the steering-board. The deck slanted at an obscene angle as men scrambled to hold on to something, anything, and the timbers of the ship cried out, a gruesome shriek of terrible pain.

What came next was worse. Fishgirl screamed and pointed, and their eyes turned as one.

A monster wave rolled towards the ship, impossibly large, filling the whole horizon, until a ragged mountain of black water towered over knörr, dwarfing it. Impossibly, the wave swelled taller, rising straight up into a cliff that obliterated the gray rainclouds. As it grew, the sea growled in gruesome hunger, and the wave opened to swallow the ship, sucking them into its black wetness.

It was The Mouth of Rán.

The cavernous maws of the sea-goddess gaped. Gray waterfalls fell from the hideous teeth-edge high atop the dreadful height of the wave. They could smell her breath, the marine scents of mollusks and seaweeds and salt, and feel the chill of her cold wet jaws. Rán widened her mouth even more, until they could see into her very belly, as the Sea opened her throat, huge and ravenous, intent on swallowing the ship whole.

———·——·———

The crew stared in disbelief.

"Hold, hold…we're going over…" Sigmund's voice was oddly calm. Men scattered about the ship flung themselves flat, their hands reaching, slipping and flailing.

Later, Tiller reflected how close their small band came to being tumbled into the heaving sea, and choking and drowning as Rán sucked them and their ship into the watery depths of her bowels. The brave little bladder-floats would have been of no use, and their clothing, heavy with wet, would have pulled them under. The hopeful journey would suddenly be over, and those at home would never know what had happened.

They would have waited, he knew.

Those who loved the fools on this ship – the fathers, mothers, sisters, brothers, wives, and children - would have numbered the hours, plowing hope into the tasks of each day, counting first the weeks and then months. As they stacked stones for fences or stirred skyr or mended stockings and tools, they would have sent up silent prayers. Talking with neighbors about butchering pigs in autumn and birthing lambs in spring, no mention would be made of how a full year had passed. But sometimes, hands would have paused at work for no reason, and the pain of wondering would cut deeply. Those nearby would be silent, knowing the reason.

One waits a full year for those who do not return from the sea. Then, the rituals are held, and the funeral ale drunk, and the inheritance, if any, divided, and debts forgiven. But because of the outlaw sentence, the ones at home would have waited the full three years, with a last hopeful burst at the end that a sail would suddenly appear in the harbor, the ship home and the men free.

Three years.

One unnoticed day after that, they would have started letting go of the tattered rags of hope. Some whose life had been made hard by a man's offenses might have breathed a sigh of relief, but mothers who loved no matter what would finally weep with grief. Sorrowing fathers would ease their loss in work, burying pain in the set of their jaw. Many would have held a thin thread of hope for the rest of their lives.

Thio screamed and screamed, and Tiller wrenched the rudder hard, too hard, an inner voice asking *will this take us over or pull us out*, knowing in any case that it was too little, too late. The knörr keeled over, shuddered, and headed straight up the cliff of water. Thio's fingers clawed at the crates, desperate to hold on as the ship climbed and climbed the terrifying height, until it seemed the very tip of the mast must be upside down, scraping the bottom of the revolting trough. With a sudden, wrenching jerk, they pitched forward and down, and inexplicably, the dark Mouth of Rán closed, and the gigantic wave passed under them. The crew renewed their handholds and braced for the next wave, without realizing that today, fortune graced those at home who would never have stopped looking towards the sea.

———·———·———

"Hold, hold…"

Anguished encouragement to one another and to their ship sounded again and again, with no time to wonder *can we possibly hold again?* The ship raised and dropped, lifted, slammed, and wrenched and cried out. Oaken and pine boards screeched in agony as they twisted beyond reason, too far, too hard. It was impossible to see across the blinding sheets of rain and spray and waves that gushed over the rails.

"Dagsson here…Bergr here…" they cried out. "Tiller, are you still with us? Sig? Ekka? Fishgirl?" The sound of each other's voices was a lifeline, their solitary strand of survival, and they called desperately, fighting despair and grasping for hope wave by wave.

Gunnbjorn's crew had barely survived the storm. What if they had been right all along? What if this was no storm, but truly the gates of Hel? It was too fearful a thought in the moment, and their minds skittered away from it in horror. Karl's voice, whipped by the wind, wailing, "We're going to die. There is no land, we're going to die, there never was any land…" brought no response, only the repeated names: "Olaf here… Lars here… Hyulf here…"

Gigantic swells and troughs flung the ship as they crashed together. Bailing was pointless, but each time they tipped as much water ran out as came in, so somehow the knörr did not founder.

"Hold, hold…" Hands bloody from grasping slipped, scraped, and clung. Every bone ached from being tossed on the deck like slippery fish. "Hold, hold…" "Hold, hold…" "Hold, hold………" "For the gods' sakes, keep holding……"

———·———·———

The storm roared viciously across the entire day and through the night. With morning, the winds finally began to diminish, and much later, the terrible waves started to subside, but the rain continued to fall in drenching downpours. All hands began bailing. They worked for hours, soaked to the skin, ignorant of fatigue, ignoring hunger.

The rain lessened across the afternoon, and towards the second night, the storm finally ended. The setting sun shot bright streams below scattering storm clouds, turning them the colors of ripe peaches. Every wave glowed gold, every crest glittered.

After two full days and a night of the worst storm any of them had ever experienced, the small band was almost too tired to feel relief. They finished bailing and sat exhausted, falling asleep in their sodden clothing.

Olaf took charge. "Strip to the skin, everyone, and get your sleeping sacks out. You too, Fishgirl. We can't afford for anyone to catch sickness from wet and cold."

They looked towards her at Olaf's words, and stared, exhausted, as she began to pull off her soaked sealskins. Olaf realized his gaze was fixed on her as well.

"She's the *fukking* fish girl, for the gods' sake! Sigmund, take your sleeping bag and hold a screen up for her. Tiller, take the other side and look away. As for you, Fishgirl, you've seen men naked before. No false modesty on your part."

Wet clothing soon draped the mast's crossbeam, chests, and everywhere there was space. The last rays of Sól glowed across a silken sea, and the ship stood almost still. Their eyes already falling closed, they felt in their sea chests and pulled out the tightly-wrapped sealskin húthfats, climbed in, and comforted and warm, fell into sleep as deep as death. The only thing that would move tonight would be the stars and the sliver-thin crescent of a pale new moon.

——·——·——

"Get off me," Bolli said to Dagsson. "Your head is on my shoulder."

Dagsson grunted.

Bolli shifted, and both men instantly fell asleep again.

———·———·———

Dream Interrupted

He was flying.

I am a petrel, Tiller dreamed. His wingtips skimmed the surface of the water, and beat hard, lifting him. As he rose into the air, silver strings of seawater-beads dripped from his feet, falling from his dizzying height into the sea far below. Something about the beads pulled his thoughts. Beads, strung together...

He flew across the fjord and soared over forested hills. The land and the sea became smaller and smaller below him. He flew across the sea from Nórsvegr, the North-way that gave name to his people. *Norsemen.* Men from the north.

He flew over Íseland, and continued west, looking for land, but could not see it anywhere.

He carried a red berry in his beak.

Tiller startled. It was the same as an odd berry he had found as a child, a small fruit that had puzzled him. Long since dried and hard, he kept it in a leather pouch on a cord around his neck. The one in his beak was fresh and tart. The berry represented a long-unanswered question, one that had perplexed him for many years. It was that question which had made Tiller want to go in search of Gunnbjörn's skerries.

The strings of seawater-beads kept falling from his feet, and as they fell towards the sea far below, they turned into berries, round and fresh and red. Something about the strings of beads, about the red berry...it was important. What did it mean? He bit into the fruit in his beak and tasted it, sweet-sour and exhilarating.

With the berry taste on his tongue, Tiller suddenly knew where to look, and soon saw it: a darkness far on the horizon. His heart beat hard and he pumped his wings, flying harder and faster towards it, but clouds came, and he flew into a storm. He wanted to fly towards the dark line, excited to see if it was land or danger, but his wings were pinned back by the wind. The storm held him, and he could not break free. He tried to cry out, but the red berry filled his mouth, choking him.

Tiller fought to speak, and woke to find someone straddling his chest, pinning his arms to his sides with their knees, his lips and jaw held firmly shut.   The night was absolutely black. Tiller tensed to fight, but whoever sat atop him realized he was awake, and whispered *hold still.*

It was Thio.

He stopped moving, and she whispered again. *Let me into your sleeping bag.*

He mumbled back *is your húthfat wet?*

Everyone is asleep, she said. *I may not get another chance to talk to you.*

Something in his mind demurred, but he was too tired to follow the thought. It was common to share a húthfat if another's became wet, or you could use bone buttons along the side to fasten them together for warmth on bitterly cold nights. But share with a fish girl? No.

Thio slipped inside, quick and fluid. In a sack for one, her body pressed closely to Tiller's. He ached to fall back to sleep, but she was clad only in a thin sleeping shift. Fatigue wrestled with the forbidden. Her next whisper snapped him into focus.

"Tiller, they're going to kill me when we reach land."

———·———·———

Tiller recoiled from Thio's words. Why would she say such an appalling thing? Who would kill a fishgirl? He had heard her lie...was this another one? Fatigue confused Tiller, and he felt anger at her for waking him to say such a preposterous thing.

Thio began to weep, but he lay unmoving. Little by little she got ahold of herself, and gulped out a couple of sentences.

"*If* we find land. There's going to be a sacrifice to the land. But not an animal. A *human* sacrifice, in the way of the old ones. Me."

His words were flat and hard. "That cannot be true."

"It is." She whispered brokenly at first, and then faster. "I have so much to tell you. Some can wait, but this part, you need to know now."

Damn her. He was bone weary. "Get it over with, then."

"I came to Snæfellsjökull at Olaf's Bay late in winter, knowing that the ship was supposed to sail at the first days of spring. People took me to the headman. The *gothi* was not there, but his wife asked was I a fishgirl. I said yes, thinking it would serve my purpose."

"There were meetings the week before we sailed, to plan the voyage. Why did I not see you at any of them?"

"I was kept a prisoner in the headman's longhouse." Her breath caught in another sob. "When the family was not there, a guard watched me. One day, the headman's wife was called away. She told me the guard would be there any moment, and to not dare leave or she'd have me beaten. When she left, I was almost out the door when I saw the headman was coming up the path. I hid on the farthest sleeping bench under some blankets, hoping I could leave later."

Despite himself, Tiller could not help but listen. "Go on."

"The headman was moving about impatiently, back and forth through the longhouse. A little later, some other people came. I could tell from their voices it was important."

"What did they want?"

"One of them was talking about an important sacrifice to Odin. He kept saying *the old ways are under threat* and *that is why the crops have been failing.* That too many on the council disagreed with him about the old ways, about why the gods were angry. That this voyage was a great opportunity to restore the gods' favor, with an important offering in the oldest of old ways. A land-gift."

"There *was* an offering to the gods," Tiller replied. "The headman had a sheep prepared as a feast-offering for *Even-Day-and-Night,* to bless the voyage. Didn't you see them sprinkle the blood on the beach while we waited for the moon to rise?"

"Not that offering; it was about something bigger, a blood-ceremony for Odin himself. Why Odin, for Even-Night? It didn't make sense. I couldn't hear everything, but one of them spoke loud enough that his voice came clearly. *'What they need has already been packed on board the ship. What about the Fishgirl who was foretold? Has she arrived? Good. Make certain no one speaks to her about this.'"* Thio gulped, and continued. "He said, *'I'll show you the Blood-Blessing ceremony in the boathouse later, while everyone is preparing for the feast. The crew will have to know how to do it, when it's time.'* They talked a little more, and left."

"What did you do?"

"As soon as they were gone, I ran. I would have left the village, but people were watching the road in case any of the crew tried to escape, so I went to the boathouse. That's how I found it," she said. "How I saw them."

"Saw what?" he asked.

"The knife...and the noose."

———·———·———

In Hiding

"I got to the boathouse." Thio's voice grew breathless as she recalled being there. "The knörr still inside it, waiting for their *Kalendar* to verify the Even-Night-and Day before they pushed the ship down to the water."

"No one saw you?"

"Everyone was preparing for the Even-Night feast. The boathouse sides had not been lifted yet. Enough light came through the roof-reeds that I could see. No one was in there."

Thio could remember every detail: the dust motes drifting across the beams of midday sun that filtered softly thorough roof-reeds, the sweet smell of the ship's wooden timbers, and the rich aroma of the pitch used to seal cracks. She had walked around the ship, running her fingers along the perfect curves of the hull.

"There were crates stacked everywhere alongside the boathouse walls. Some were locked, some weren't. I had no idea what to look for, or where. I heard a sound on the path outside, so I climbed into the knörr and hid under the half-deck."

She continued after a gasped breath. "Some men came into the boatshed. I could barely hear their footsteps on the pine needles on the floor. Three, I'm certain. Maybe one more. One hit his knee against something. He cursed, but no one else said anything. I pulled my tunic over my nose and mouth, afraid they would hear me breathing."

Tiller wrestled with tide of sleep, trying to listen.

"They came to the ship and climbed up the ladder. I nearly died of fright right then. They dragged one of the sea chests from the stack, right over the half-deck where I was hiding."

She had heard the clasp being twisted open, almost too terrified to breathe. "One of them said *'It's under the cloak.'* I heard things being taken out of the chest and put on the deck. A whistle of admiration, then silence again."

Thio had listened intently, her heart hammering against her chest. "The man said, *'Place it on the neck, like so. Pull clean and straight.'* There was a tiny noise, something being slid. Then the same voice again, one of the men who had come to the gothi's longhouse. *'No, not like that! You must do it properly. It's a blót ceremony to bless a new land, not a hog slaughtering!'* And then another voice: *'Mmmh. First the noose, and then the knife? Or should her blood soak into the ground first, and afterwards the noose?'* "

Thio's throat choked, and she started to shake again. This time, Tiller put his arms around her as if comforting a child. "Shhhhh…. shhh…."

"The visitor kept describing how to use the …tools. What had to happen first, what next, what words should be said at each step. He was very specific, saying *'Odin must be properly thanked… you have a duty to make the land pure and safe…'* Things like that."

"Did you recognize the other voices?

"Something in me says one was Randaal, but they were speaking so quietly I can't be sure. One of them asked something. I couldn't make out the words, but he sounded frightened. I heard the leader say, *'You know the price of refusal. Don't think your son will be spared. He will suffer at my own hand if you fail.'* Then a long silence, until the visitor again, *'Any other questions?'* His voice was awful. Cold and cruel. I could hear them put everything back in the chest, and they shoved it back into place again, and climbed over the hull. Before they left the boathouse, the frightened one asked one last question. *'When should we tell the rest of the crew? Before we leave? Or only when the time arrives?'* And the leader said, *'Tell who you want when you want. If something happens to either of you, they must know what to do, and how, and when. But don't tell all of them. The fish girl was chosen by the gods, so if anything happens to her, someone else would have to serve. It should be someone strong, of decent character. Consider your tiller as the alternate. Don't tell the woman, of course, nor any who would fight the idea. Just enough of the crew. It is absolutely critical that this ceremony happens.'* Then they left."

———·———·———

Thio quivered in terror, remembering.

"When I was certain they were gone, I crawled from the hold. I could see the marks on the deck where they'd dragged the crate. I wrestled it out again and opened the hasp. They hadn't locked it! I pulled things out carefully, so I could put them back the same way. There was a cloak with a knife wrapped in it. Not an ordinary *sax*. It was longer, and covered with carvings."

"A *skramasax*. A ceremonial gash-knife. They used one at the Althing, to symbolize cutting me from the law, when I was sentenced."

Thio nodded, her head against Tiller's chest. "I saw it. The one in the cloak was nothing like that one. This looked ancient." She paused, remembering the design. "I felt again, and buried in another fold of the cloak was a thick braid of leather. It had a loop on one end, and a row of knots along the other end."

A noose.

Thio blurted, "I suddenly realized that *'her blood'* meant *me*. I had been so afraid that I would cough or sneeze, and be caught, and I was trying so hard to hear what they were saying that I paid little attention to what their words *meant*. But looking at those things in my hands, I

81

knew they had been talking about *me*. They were planning to hurt me. *Sacrifice me! Kill me!*"

She shook with silent sobs. Tiller held her, half-wondering if this, too, was a dream.

"*I* was the blót offering for Odin! They practiced pulling that knife against my throat. Mine, or yours, it appears! Since you're the reason I came to the village in the first place - to fulfill a promise which I'll explain later – I knew I had to warn you…but that landed me on this ship, fool that I am."

Tiller barely heard her last words. Human sacrifice in Íseland was illegal, had been outlawed generations ago.

"Who would revive such a vile old custom?" Tiller wondered aloud. Thio did not answer him, having no answer to give.

They lay together in the silence of the night. The sea was completely calm, barely rising and falling in soft swells that swayed the ship in tranquil rhythm. The water murmured against the hull, and over it floated the peaceful cadences of snoring men. Each had his own particular noise. All were deeply asleep.

Tiller did not want to believe Thio's story. How could it be possible? Were some of the men on board really prepared to do that to Thio if they found land? But improbable though her story was, it answered questions that had nagged at him, small details that had not made sense. He shivered, chilled to the bone.

———·——·———

Thio had not realized when she got into his sleeping sack that Tiller was completely naked. She felt awkward lying beside him. But she had been able to deliver an important message to him that she had been carrying; one of them, at least.

Weariness filled Thio. She wished she could simply stop breathing, and pass to an endless smoothness that drifted towards home, but that was impossible. Small breaths separated them and joined them. In that quiet space, Thio began to speak again.

___.___.___

In the boathouse, Thio had fallen to her knees on the sturdy boards of the half-deck. Nausea overtook her, and she vomited into the underdeck storage area again and again. Finally, trembling, she wiped her face and mouth on her tunic sleeve, replaced everything in the sea chest and pushed it back into place, and left the boathouse. The beach was empty. She ran helter-skelter to the where the grasses were tall and fell onto the ground, weeping with terror.

"I need to tell you everything, Tiller, in case it helps in any way," Thio continued. "Once I left the boathouse, I hid in the grasses for – well, I don't know how long. Then I covered my face with my shawl, and walked through the longhouses to the healing woman's dome-house. I didn't know what else to do. If someone stopped me, I planned to say the headman had sent me to her."

"Why didn't you just leave? Run away from Ólafsvík to somewhere safe?"

"When you arrived, did you see the men who guarded the road? Getting past them was impossible. Even if I could, to then cross miles of mountains, with winter just ending, and with no supplies and only my indoor clothing? And the lava stones, the *hraun*… I had on house shoes. They would have been torn to bits."

"Of course. I wasn't thinking," Tiller murmured drowsily.

"I knocked on the dome-house door. No one answered, but I went in. An old woman was there, huddled next to the fire, dozing.

"'Help, me, grandmother,' I said. I thought she was asleep, or deaf, but she asked impatiently what I wanted. How do you say *oh, I'm going to be killed in Odin's honor if this voyage is successful, and your headman is part of the plan?* But I blurted it all out. She said nothing for a long while. I was terrified that she going to turn me in."

"But she didn't. She shook her head, and poked at the fire with her stick, muttering *'idiots'*. That's all she said. Afterwards, she was quiet a long time. I thought maybe she had dropped off to sleep again, but then she clicked her tongue in exasperation, and began to rant about sacrifices, how foolish they are, that sacrifices never seemed to help the rains come or stay away, or the crops grow, that they were just a waste of good animals. She said that her husband had *vikked* everywhere, and that in some lands, they have gods who don't even *want* sacrifices, not of any kind! Something about one human sacrifice a long time ago, a man who volunteered to be the last one. She said they didn't need to kill animals after that. I didn't really understand. Why would he do that? We all eat the roast, at the feast afterwards..."

Tiller replied, abstractedly and disjointedly, "It's a faith that many have taken in other lands. Not all by choice; Harald, son of the man who took the country, is forcing people along the North-way to accept it. It's even spreading to parts of Íseland. But I don't like it. Their priests speak in a different language than ordinary people do, and they demand to be given tithes. For those reasons alone, I have little liking for it. But then, I care naught for our gods, either. I prefer the *druid-vitki*. Truth-seers offer much and take little." He shook himself, unable to focus.

"Maybe it's not as bad as you think. People have always fought over their gods. At least his doesn't sacrifice humans!"

Tiller grunted in response. "I'm too tired to talk about it."

Thio looked at the night sky, wondering momentarily about Harald's religion, then left that argument and continued telling Tiller what had happened at the village.

"The old woman grabbed my face, and said *'You know the rules of sacrifice! The ewe must not be carrying a lamb, and a ram must not have sired. They'll want your pure, and certainly not with child. Get yourself past that. It may be your only hope.'* So I did."

Thio felt Tiller stiffen in disbelief. "So quickly? You had precious little time."

"It was sheer luck. The headman's wife was often busy. The longhouse guards... I found opportunities." Thio spoke almost defensively. "I've had the morning-sickness."

Tiller suddenly wondered again if this was all some kind of trick. He exclaimed, "But at least twice, you caused it yourself! You drank salt water to make yourself be sick."

Thio drew in a long breath and let it out slowly. "Yes. I did do that. I didn't know how long it would be before I started getting sick, or if I even would. Some women don't. I needed the men – the ones who knew about the sacrifice, at least – to know as soon as possible that I was no perfect ewe, ready to be led to slaughter." In a very small voice, she added, "I'm sorry."

Truth or Lies?

What a bizarre story, Tiller thought. Again he wondered if he was really talking to Thio, or if this was some exhausted dream, when a memory swam up through the tiredness, one that lent credibility to her tale. He had been allowed to go into the boatshed to look over the ship just before their departure. As he inspected it, Tiller had smelled a nauseating odor coming from under the half-deck. *"It smells as if someone has been sick down there,"* he had remarked to the headman. *"Someone should clean that up before we leave."* He had immediately forgotten about it as he turned back to the critical work of checking the rudder and the ropes of the mast, but that small detail meant that everything Thio had said might be true.

Who, Then?

Weariness crushed Tiller. Sleep would not wait much longer, even though he was keenly aware of Thio's breasts rising and falling against his arm as she breathed. It would not do for them to be found like this. He shifted uncomfortably, pulling his arm from where it encircled her.

What he knew of sacrifices turned in his thoughts. Most farmsteads still offered an animal here and there across the year: at Yuletide to call Sól back in winter, and again to thank her on Longest-Day in summer as she began her voyage south. Sometimes during the Even-Nights of spring and autumn, to encourage good crops and plentiful harvests. They were simple ceremonies; a few words of thanks, the animal's blood poured onto the ground, and its meat cooked and eaten in honor of the sun, the earth, the harvest, the rain. Some people offered one for the birth of a child, or for a wedding. Many still observed the old custom of death-sacrifices, sheep, goats and chickens offered for those who had died, so that the dead would have wool, meat, milk, cheese, *skyr,* and eggs to sustain their afterlife. Along with other funeral gifts, the animals were put alongside the dead in a stone-ship or barrow to travel to Hel with the loved one's spirit.

86

But sacrifices of human beings… Had those ever really happened? Weren't the old sagas about them just fantastic fables, enlivening the long dark nights of winter with tales of old kings, of campaigns on sea and battles on land, of women captured and loved, and gold won and lost, and much embellished by saga-tellers for entertainment? No one paid the sacrifice bits of the sagas any more mind than the hordes of riches and faultless heroes. Tiller could not recall hearing of a single one that really happened.

He thought over Thio's description of the old healer as she mocked the men's words. "*The sacrifice to Odin and the new land must be absolutely pure. She must have known no man, have no children of her own, must not be carrying a child inside. All of her fertility must be for the land only, to bless it with productivity. If not a woman, then a man, strong but with no sons.' Bah! What nonsense! Even back in the old days, it was just an excuse for a chief to get rid of a woman who scorned him or a rival, I've always thought.*" The old woman's crisp words had belied her advanced years.

Tiller shivered again, despite the intimate warmth of his húthfat and the nearness of Thio's body. How could anyone on board consider hurting a fish girl? How could they stomach taking the life of this fine woman, even for something as important as new land? To defy the laws of the land and revert to an archaic ritual? Another chilling question occurred to Tiller. Who in Íseland had the power to authorize such a thing, and how many of those on the law council knew of it? Talk of it had not come up at the local and regional Things, or the summer Althing would have been buzzing with it. This reeked of the absolute power of kings and secret plots, an idea that was abhorrent to all Íselanders.

Thio's words broke in on his thoughts. "I said I'm sorry because I took the healer's advice. A child may save my life, but it endangers yours."

Understanding came slowly to Tiller through the fog of fatigue, and the memory of a conversation early in the voyage, a question asked in idle conversation that had rung false at the time. *How about the rest of you fellows?* Every man aboard had spoken of at least one child, even Kurt and Karl. The twins had played a trick on a girl who was unable to tell them apart, so neither knew who the father was. *Tiller,* someone had pressed. *Is there a brat with your name running around somewhere? Are you certain?*

Who had asked? Thio was right. He *had* been marked. If she carried a child, it was his throat that would feel the knife.

———·——·———

Tiller named the snoring men in his mind one by one, and then started over, listening and counting again. The moon-sliver had barely moved. Had they been talking such a short time? It seemed as if half the night had passed.

Those who planned this did not care if the sacrifice was a man or a woman, but only that it happened. In his mind's eye, Tiller saw his hands and feet tied, and Randaal smirking as he prepared a ceremonial knife, putting the noose over Tiller's head. *Damn them all to Hel.* Hearing Thio describe such things were appalling. *Pull it smoothly,* the leader had admonished. Tiller pictured the warm gush of his blood, spurting as if he were a pig at slaughtering time. He longed for Thio to stop talking, to take her horrid story away. Sleep sucked like quicksand, pulling him towards a place where malicious murder did not exist.

88

They lay side by side in silence. In a few moments, Thio spoke again, and her words wrenched Tiller back from the slide to unconsciousness.

"Tiller, I have a plan."

Worse

Since the conversation in the boatshed, Thio had thought constantly, turning over every option she could think of. While casting her net, gutting fish, feeding the men, and playing games, she'd thought about her plan, and refined it. It was careful and considered. It was bold and decisive. It could work. *There are other ways to do battle,* the old woman had said. *I'll show you.* It felt wrong, so very wrong, yet what alternative did she have?

"Tiller, those who are planning this. What if they die first? Before they can hurt us?"

___.___.___

Why did Thio's words chill him to the bone? "Die first? What do you mean?"

"I mean, no one on the ship can harm us if they're already dead."

"You mean, kill them first? You don't even know who they are! Who would you kill?"

Her silence answered the question in a way that only disturbed Tiller further. He struggled to find a response to her madness. "Thio! What about those of the crew who know nothing about this? Even if they know, I don't believe they'd do it!"

"Don't be a fool. Whoever selected the outlaws for this voyage chose men who could be used. What else can we do? I wish there was another way, but I cannot think of one! I have the right to protect myself! Besides, they are outlaw! They are entitled to no protection, no rights."

Those outside the law were safe nowhere, it seemed, not even from their Fishgirl, far out on the empty sea.

"You're wrong, Thio. Each man aboard is under the council's protection for the duration of this voyage" Tiller snorted, half in admiration and half in disgust. "I, an outlaw and you, a fish girl, are arguing fine legal points in the dark of night on a lost ship in the middle of gods-know-where. That's one for the storytellers."

———·———·———

Tiller's admiration was not for Thio, but for a suddenly-realized truth. Even though the law had betrayed him, this conversation still made Tiller fiercely proud of how it functioned in his country in a way he had never truly appreciated.

He said softly, "We are so different, you and I and all Íselanders, from those in every other country. Those owe allegiance to chieftains and kings. Our rights - nay, our very lives – lie not with the whims of a ruler, but in laws voted on by common folk like you and me. That thing, our laws - something we cannot see and cannot hold - is a wall of fairness against those who would do evil to others for their own gain. The sacrifice of another human is against the law. Even if some on the council want it, they cannot do it."

He felt Thio stiffen at his words. "And just who will stop them, out here? We may have no time at all, once we find land. We need to be ready to act, and not waste one heartbeat!"

"Thio, I lost my freedom because anger made me act rashly. Friends I cared about *died* from it! I will never – *never,* do you hear me? – act rashly from anger or fear again. What you are saying is not only illegal, but reckless. How could we ever get back to Íseland? We all need each other to stay alive!"

"They said no one would go again after Snæbjörn Galti's disastrous attempt, but with famines for three straight years, they've sent this ship. More ships will come, eventually. Maybe it'll take two years, maybe five. At least I'll be alive for them to find, not a throat-slit skeleton hanging on a pole."

"Think of this crew, these men. Some are violent, but most are not. Think of Sig. Could he do this? Or Dagsson? Hyulf? The twins? And if it comes to that, could *you* actually do it? I *have* killed, Thio. The taking of a life, even if justified, weighs heavily on your spirit."

"The ones in the boatshed, whoever they are, have already decided. All don't have to agree with them, only enough. I cannot afford to take the chance."

91

"Your plan is imprudent. I need time to think."

Tiller fought sleep heartbeat by heartbeat while they argued in fierce whispers, knowing this might be his only chance to change her mind. He clung to reason as if it was the only thing keeping them afloat. "Those of us aboard this ship voyage as people of Íseland. Your plan does not uphold the spirit of our country. Wherever there are humans, there will be good and evil. Some on the council may have wicked intentions, but others do not, I am certain, and sent us in good faith. You ignoring the council's protection of these men is as wrong as those who ignore other laws. The law is never perfect, but Thio…but if we leave it of our own accord, then we are truly lost."

———·———·———

In the end, exhaustion won. No matter the horror of hearing Thio say in a shaking voice say, *'I'm going to poison them, whoever I need to. I got the herbs from the old woman. It's already prepared, and it waits only for the right moment'*, no matter how desperately Tiller tried to find the right words to change her mind, nothing could keep him awake much longer.

Tiller said wearily, "I've seen friends die and I'm convicted of murder, Thio. Killing solves nothing. I want nothing more to do with killing, ever. I genuinely believe this will come to naught. The men aren't fools, and most of them like and trust you." He sighed deeply. "But if it does seem likely, I'll do everything in my power to protect you."

With that, weariness claimed him, and he could stay awake no more.

No Rest

Sleep should be blissfully empty for one so tired. Sleep should not be endless dreams of waves with eyes that stared accusingly as they cut past the ship, or dreams of blood seeping from storage chests jammed with knives and nooses. Sleep should not be images of Thio's head hanging back lifeless with two necklaces adorning her throat, one a twisted leather cord and the other a rich red line cut from collarbone to collarbone by the blade of an ancient skramasax, a thin precise gash from which her lifeblood poured down her beautiful pale throat and drenched her kyrtill, her leggings, her shoes, an impossible wave of red that flowed into the bottom of the ship, where Randaal bailed, tossing her blood onto the sea where sharks snapped. The sharks became waves, and their eyes the wave-eyes circling the ship, staring at Tiller, blaming him.

Sleep should not be dreams of Tiller standing with the rest of the crew while Thio faced them all, her eyes narrowed, sharpening a blade in her own hand.

———·———·———

The sun shone bright and warm, high the morning sky, when sounds of waking finally began. Snores changed to groans as men reluctantly stretched and sat up.

Thio's heart beat wildly. She had failed to convince Tiller to protect himself. Very well, then; she would try and do it for him. This thing she was about to do might help, but it might also make everything terribly worse. *I'll find out soon enough if this will help or hurt. If I do nothing and we find land soon, it might be too late then to do anything to save us.* She knew her strategy was risky at best. Thio's nature was intelligent but impulsive, and once she had latched onto an idea, she found it hard to shift herself.

As the men came more fully awake, Thio lay pretending to sleep, silent and scared. It was too late to change her mind now. Part of her wished with all her heart that she had taken Tiller's advice and been less rash.

——·——·——

"What, by Hel?"

Bergr's hoarse whisper and pointing finger had provoked Lars' shout. With her eyes closed, Thio could not see the astonished faces turning in her direction, but she heard men scrambling to their feet and coming close.

Hold, hold, Thio whispered to herself. *Like in the storm. Hold, hold.*

Lars strode the last few steps, striking a crate in the process. Angry at the pain, he kicked the sleeping sack hard, and Tiller came cursing awake.

"Why are you kicking me?" Tiller cried. He pushed himself up in his húthfat, struggling to come alert. "What is wrong with you?"

"What's wrong with *you?*" Lars shouted.

Tiller echoed Lars' question as he saw Thio still in the sleeping sack with him. "What in Hel?"

Thio stretched lazily as if she were just coming awake. She extended her bare arms, enjoying the warm air and sighing with contentment. At last, she blinked her eyes open and gazed innocently at the staring men.

"What?"

No one answered, their faces dark.

"It's not right! We swore!" Lars shouted.

"What's not right?" she countered.

Accusations came hard and fast at Tiller. He put his hands over his ears and grabbed his hair, ripping at it, and wanting, almost viciously, to shake Thio instead.

"He's naked! You're almost naked! What were you thinking?" Hyulf shouted at Fishgirl.

"I'm thinking that most of you are standing there naked-to-the-bone yourselves!" she retorted hotly. "My sleeping sack was soaking wet so I asked him to share!"

There was a momentary pause. The men looked confused. Sharing a húthfat was acceptable. Sleeping with a Fishgirl was acceptable. It was that damned oath they'd sworn that made her being with Tiller unacceptable.

Thio took advantage of their confusion. "Oh, I see. You think I should have woken someone else, asked them to double up instead? So I could take their sack and sleep alone?"

Grunts of acknowledgment said yes.

Good, thought Thio. They had nibbled at the bait. She made her voice indignant and exasperated.

"Don't you think I *tried?* You were like dead men! My braid-leather is somewhere in Kurt's sack. It fell off when I tried to wake him, to get him to double with Karl. You can look for yourselves. I wasn't about to reach my hand down around him, looking for it! I tried to get Sigmund to come alive, too, to no avail. Half of my hair ripped out on that enormous silver Thor pin on your húthfat, Sig. I tried waking every single one of you! No one would budge!"

Kurt ran to his own sack. "Look!" He reached in and pulled out the leather strap Thio used to fasten her braid and waved it overhead.

Thio had slipped from Tiller's sleeping sack, loosed her braid and tucked the strap beneath Kurt as he slept, then ripped strands of her blonde hair and twisted them around Sigmund's prized Thor pin, before returning to her own sleeping sack and pouring a quantity of water onto it.

Dagsson looked at her bag and nodded. "Wet as can be."

Looks of anger slowly changed to doubt and confusion, but Randaal challenged her still. "So the twins were asleep, we *all* were asleep, so *what?* Your bag's only wet along the bottom third. All you had to do was pull your feet up a bit! You're a disgrace to this ship, you whore!"

—·—·—

96

Whore? Thank you, Randaal, you angry, stupid fool, Thio breathed inwardly.

Long ago, she had learned how to catch fish without a hook or line. *Weave the green branches together, then put the fish-trap into the stream,* her uncle had said. *Put bait into it. Set rocks to force the fish to swim into it. Take your blade, and plunge it down.*

Thio had slept next to Tiller all night as bait for men who needed to be pushed where she wanted them to go. Kurt had nudged them towards the trap, and Randaal had swum right into it.

She let tears come to her eyes and pressed her hand against her mouth in shocked horror. "Whore, Randaal? Far from it! I tried so hard to wake each of you. I shared Tiller's sack as a last resort." Her chest heaved, and she wept. "I planned to wake early, to get up and dressed before any of you. I didn't want to upset anyone." She fetched up great gasping sobs.

Tiller watched along with the others, but with a different kind of astonishment. Whatever lies she was telling were just a prelude. More was coming, he could tell.

"Perhaps it is better this way," wept Fishgirl. "The truth is that I was *glad* to share Tiller's sack! Since I have betrayed myself, I have no choice but to tell you something I never wanted to. I am not a whore, Randaal, I am just a weak woman…because for once on this voyage, I wanted to lie beside the father of my child." She broke down in complete distress.

Jaws dropped, eyes bulged out, and Thio struck the final blow. "I was afraid to say anything before." She stared straight at Randaal, still weeping, but speaking clearly so that no one would miss her words. "Even Tiller did not know."

———·——·———

97

As sheep bunch together in the presence of a wolf, the men instinctively turned to each other in the face of danger. A Fishgirl knowingly pregnant by a man on board, before she came aboard ship? How could she possibly be fair to the rest of them? They deeply needed to trust in a beholden-free Fishgirl. More than one of the men put a hand to his chest, where such distressing news caused a physical ache.

Thio took the instant to mutter a guarded whisper to Tiller. "I understand what you won't do, and why," she muttered. "This seemed to be the only other way."

Tiller was too stunned to say anything. Thio added, "Please don't make me a liar."

He turned his face away.

Once again, Olaf took leadership. "Here is what is going to happen. No one has eaten for over two days. We're all starving. No good thinking ever gets done on empty stomachs. Fishgirl, whatever your situation, you've got a job to do. Make a meal, we'll eat it, and then we'll hold a shipboard Thing. Tiller, stay away from her. No one may discuss this until the Thing begins. Understand?"

No one objected. Tiller spoke up, confounded, his thoughts latching on the safety of the ship. "I need to inspect the sail, to see if we can put it up after we eat."

"I'll be quick with the food," Fishgirl promised loudly. The men started dressing, ignoring Olaf's command as they muttered comments to one another.

——·——·——

Thio's hands shook as she began to boil water. She tried to console her nerves. *At least I didn't fail by being too cowardly to take action.* She wanted to break down and weep, to throw the whole boatshed secret out into the open and challenge them with it and have it finished, one way or the other. Only the thinnest self-control kept the silence she knew was needed.

She sliced fish.

As Thio deliberately slowed her motions, her mind grew calmer. As she stirred oats in water, her will grew stronger, and her face more and more grim. She moved unhurriedly and let herself become hot and combative.

The Thin Line of Power

Thio did not look at anyone, but her irritation cut through the warm air like a cold knife.

"Fishgirl!" Sigmund called. "You're taking too long! Faster!"

She looked at him coldly. "You insult my virtue *and* my work?"

"Faster, please?"

"I'll work how I like." She glared at him, let it slide to the others. Stirred more slowly.

———·——·———

Another quarter-mark, and still no breakfast, even though they could smell it, delicious on the morning breeze. The men grumbled. In reply, she stared at them and put up her chin, daring any to speak.

A famished and frustrated crew of dangerous criminals, and Thio held them at bay with no greater weapon than the thin line of her lips.

———·———·———

The men shifted from one foot to another, pretending to do small tasks, when Hyulf did what was needed. He had come from a rough-and-tumble family, and did not know, or care, about the danger of a woman's lips pressed together.

"Come *on,* Fishgirl! We are famished! What is taking you so long?" he roared.

The rest of the men breathed a collective sigh of relief. Now the dam would now break, and what was irritating Fishgirl would spill out, and it would all be directed at Hyulf.

———·———·———

Thio slammed her ladle and stood up. "I am furious, that is what is wrong! You knew about the baby. Now you know who sired it. So what? Does it change the work I've done for you? Take back the meals I've cooked? All the times I've stitched one of you up?"

No one answered.

"I've been frightened out of my wits most of the time, but I've tried to be pleasant for you! Why do I deserve to be dragged to a Thing as if I am on trial?" She stood with a knife in her fist, challenging them.

Sigmund kept his words carefully neutral. "It's just that so much is different on this voyage, and now this. The men are jumpy. Talking at Thing will ease their nerves."

"Talking about what? How to punish me or Tiller?"

100

This time Gierr spoke. "Look, I just want food. Olaf called for a council meeting."

All eyes went to Olaf.

Thio stormed to him, her face in his, brandishing her knife. "Olaf. I want an answer. Exactly what have I done wrong?"

Randaal could not stand it any longer. "You have no respect for your position and your duty! Not for this voyage, not for anything! The other men are weak, succumbing to your nonsense! You will endanger us!"

Randaal realized that of all of them, he would have to be a man and show some strength. He stepped between Olaf and Fishgirl and shoved Olaf away. His face twisted in anger and Randaal slapped Fishgirl hard against the side of her jaw. Her head snapped sideways.

"You...deceitful...liar... You were supposed to be pure!"

A gasp of disbelief went around the ship. It was nothing to see men fight, but Randaal had hit a fish girl.

"How *dare* you!" Thio's eyes watered from the blow. She managed to stay on her feet, instinctively grabbing the neckline of Randaal's kyrtill and throwing him off balance. As he stumbled, Fishgirl drove her knee straight into his nose. The sound of the cartilage tearing from bone came clearly, and Randaal howled in pain.

The men of the crew hesitated, not sure whether to intervene or let Fishgirl fight it out for herself. Randaal decided for them. He cuffed Fishgirl again, this time with his hand in a hard fist.

Fishgirl cried out in pain. She burst out, "You don't know who I am! I'm not a liar! I'm...I'm a good woman!" She collapsed into a heap and burst into sobs.

———·———·———

Tiller did not remember how he got ahold of Randaal or for how long he pounded with his fists. Men pulled him away and held his arms, and Sig's voice came through the fury, *don't kill Randaal, Tiller, we need everyone to row…it's over, he's learned his lesson, let up.*

From Randaal's face, Tiller guessed that no one had rushed in too quickly to stop the blows. His fists were already beginning to swell. Randaal kicked away the men holding him, his eyes swelling shut, blood dripping from the broken nose.

"Have your damned Thing, then," Randaal shouted. "Act like a bunch of over-civilized gothi. There's not one real man here besides me, is there?" He spat with fury. "Her mistakes will cost you all more than you can imagine! I swear, if any one of you gets between me and Fishgirl again, I will kill her cold." He staggered away.

"There now, Fishgirl, don't cry," said Ekka roughly. "You *are* a good woman. Many a day I couldn't row without you working on my bad shoulder."

"So what if she growing a child, and so what if it's Tiller's? It's over and done. Can't be helped now, can it?" Hyulf glared after Randaal. "You're just on edge because with the storm, because we are *fukkin'* lost for sure now."

Olaf spoke in a placating tone. "You must have misunderstood my words, Fishgirl. We don't need a Thing about you. I meant because we've been blown by a storm, we need to discuss which way to sail now." At this, Randaal made a rude, guttural sound. Clearly Olaf was not a man either.

Gierr's words were friendly but his gaze cold and calculating. "Help her up, boys. She'll give us food, then we'll get to work on this sail. Heave to, get your bowls."

Later, Gierr pulled Randaal aside and spoke tersely to him. Randaal's head twisted away, angry. Gierr jerked at Randaal's muscled arm and spoke again. This time, Randaal nodded slightly, his eyes still averted.

———·———·———

Fishgirl served the breakfast to an unusually quiet group. The smallest of remarks from some of them let her know that they were sympathetic. Some said nothing, and others refused to even look at her, holding their bowls for food with a set, cold expression.

Ekka, for me, she counted. *Hyulf. Likely Dagsson. Olaf, I cannot tell. Gierr and Randaal, against me for certain.* When Fishgirl took the cooking pot back to her workstation, she took out her workboard. Turning it over, she started a second set of small cuts. Her fingers shook as she made a small nick for each man who might help her, and a nick for those who would not.

———·———·———

The crew gathered into a loose circle, doing their best to ignore the jarring events of the morning and focus on the most important decision of their lives. They would follow the tradition of a Thing, speaking oldest to youngest. Everything came down to a single question: *which way?*

———·———·———

As oldest, Sigmund spoke first. He opened by formally stating the matters to be decided. "We were going southwest. We do not know how far the storm blew us, or in what direction or where we are. We have been at sea for three weeks, I believe. The issue to be decided is this: where do we go now?"

Olaf spoke briefly, mostly to defer the matter to others, and Gierr did the same. Tiller heard, but with only half his attention. The strange feeling of a navigational-knowing had begun buzzing inside him. Tiller carefully reached towards this thing he could never explain and did not fully trust, but which almost always proved true. He listened inwardly, if one could call it that, and slowly an understanding grew in him. *Directly towards the star that does not move.*

Was it real, or something of his own imagination? The guidance always confused him.

Bergr was talking, emphasizing that the gods had a plan for everything. "Let the wind fill our sails, and follow it. If the gods are directing us, they will take us where we need to go."

Tor was next, but Kurt broke in, always impatient. "Hel's the only goddess directing us. She's leading us to the afterlife. We should forget this idea! Sail directly east, find work in the land of the Scoti, or in Éireland. Hide there rather than die out here."

Tor's eyes measured Kurt for a moment, frowning. Did the slight shake of his head mean he disagreed with Kurt, or would not take a turn speaking?

Sigmund was talking again, as was the right of one who had already spoken. "I don't care. I'll support either decision."

Ulf calculated the odds: "Maybe Kurt's right, crazy as it sounds. We could split up wherever we go, and keep moving. It would take all of the council's resources to track all of us. They'll give up. I'd prefer my chances on land."

Everyone was talking out of order now. Tiller decided to skip his turn and speak last. The time to sway an argument was not in the heat of it, he knew. Let others disagree until they were weary, then offer

104

good reasoning, and a plan with promise would likely be adopted. Waiting, he felt again for the trail of whispers in his mind, and knew the same words about the northern star again, but fading.

Was it right? Tiller considered the odds as Ulf might. They actually could sail for a very long time, catching water from storms and eating from the sea, but the storm had been a reminder of how vulnerable they were. The next one might be disastrous. But if they took his idea, it meant that the life of every man aboard was entrusted to it.

Tiller bided his time. It did not matter what others said. His words would carry the vote. He looked at his hands, swollen and still bleeding from the fight of the morning, and waited.

———·———·———

A sudden scuffle broke out. Tiller looked up and saw Bergr and Hyulf chest to chest, their jaws grim and faces full of anger.

"Calm down!" Olaf shouted. "We're in the middle of a Thing! Fighting is forbidden!"

"Don't *dare* tell me I'm wrong!" Bergr's voice, furious, ignoring Olaf, his red face almost touching Hyulf's. "This storm came for a reason! We must heed the messages of gods! We need to pray to Thor, to Odin, to Hel, to Ran, to all of them, for guidance!"

"You pray if you want, but I'll think whatever I want!" The midday sun reflected off the sharp blade. "This says you can't make me!"

Bergr shoved his chest against Hyulf. "You endanger us all with your wickedness!"

The young man with spiky red hair staggered backward, then surged towards Bergr again. He held his saxe high. "I'm sick of you fearmongering in the name of your gods!"

Bergr gripped Hyulf's forearm, and the two men wrestled. They tripped over a sea chest. Hyulf was not a killer and had only meant to threaten Bergr, but to his dismay, as they fell, his knife drove deep into the side of Bergr's neck. Blood spurted and their cries of anguish mingled, Bergr in pain and Hyulf in horror at what he had done.

Randaal, already nursing bitter pride from Hyulf's remarks earlier, broke from the Thing circle and shoved Hyulf away from Bergr. "Bergr is my oar-mate! Damn you to Hel! Our team loses a man? Then so does yours! Here, fool, take what you gave!" Randaal grabbed the saxe from Bergr's neck and ran it up through Hyulf's ribs, right below his heart.

Hyulf fell, his hands pressed to his chest. Blood spread rapidly down his tunic. His eyes were confused. "Fish," he choked. "I used to eat them. Now I will be food for them." He looked to Bergr. "Do we eat men when we eat fish?" In an instant, he was dead.

Randaal looked down at both bodies in contempt. He quickly stripped them of weapons and took the silver bands from Bergr's wrists. "Anybody want anything else?"

One moment ago the crew had been discussing which direction to sail. Now two of their company were dead, with Randaal standing over them, breathing heavily, his knife out as he glared around the ship. They were too dumbfounded to move, even to speak a word.

Randaal grunted and hoisted Bergr. "Here, fish. Supper is ready," he said. Two splashes, and the bodies of both men floated lifeless in the sea.

———·——·———

Randaal wiped the blade of his knife across his tongue, cleaning the blood from it. "Delicious." he sneered. "You dreamers. We are never going to find land. We should eat and drink and play knucklebones until we die."

The aghast crewmen stared at the bodies of Hyulf and Bergr, sinking below the surface. There should be words spoken, the rites for the dead at sea performed. Randaal's eyes defied anyone to speak, but they moved their lips in silent invocation, hoping it would be enough to placate the spirits of the two dead men.

"Who wants to offer the next opinion for our Thing?" Randaal taunted. "With two less men to vote, it'll go faster." He pointed his knife in each man in turn. "Speak! No? How about you, Ekka? Your mouth is always going."

Ekka tried to answer, but only a gurgle came from his throat.

"You wanted your damned Thing!" shouted Randaal. "Whoever's next, take your turn or I swear, you will join Hyulf and Bergr!" His eyes glinted around, choosing a next victim.

Bolli pointed, the whites of his eyes showing. "You're right. I think it was Ekka's turn.

"No, I'm after you. Your turn, Bolli."

With Randaal's knife still out and his face sneering at the group, Bolli wished he could say nothing. Suddenly he thought of a good distraction, a true thing.

"It's pointless to ask me. I know nothing of sea-steering. Which of us knows about navigating? He should decide." Bolli looked pointedly at Tiller.

"Yes," replied Ekka, glad of the deflection. "Tiller?"

Tiller cursed Randaal for forcing his hand. As he drew breath, Thio moved to stand in front of him.

"Do I get to speak?" she asked.

Randaal snorted in derision. "You? Vote on matters of *viking*?"

"My fate is just as much at stake as yours!"

"You think your fate matters to me? I could not care less, you contemptuous she-witch!" he sneered. Who did this woman think she was, to tell them how to do their job? Hatred goaded him against her. In two steps he had Thio. He grabbed her shoulders and shook her, his eyes bulging, and spittle hit her face as he spewed furious words. "You'll...do...what...we...decide!"

The men lunged toward the pair again, but Fishgirl's voice cut as sharp as a knife. "Stop! All of you!"

No one moved. Randaal's knife was wickedly sharp and lightning fast. No one wanted Fishgirl to be his next victim.

Thio pulled away and stood strong. "What's your big plan, then?" she shouted at him.

"I think we should be like Snowbear's men. We'll eat all the food, drain the drinking casks dry, and then we'll draw straws to see who eats who. You, my lovely, will go last, because you will dance naked for us, like the whore that you are, and I'll have you as often as I like."

Thio was stone. "You will never touch me. I'll kill you first."

"As if you could. Try it. Your sweet neck will snap like a branch in winter."

"Hold, there, man," said Olaf. "We need Fishgirl." His voice was low and smooth, placating Randaal. "We'll all get a piece, one day maybe, eh?" He reached to pull Thio away.

"Get back," Randaal rasped. He reached for his saxe again and held it against Thio's neck.

"I'm just suggesting," said Olaf. "Let's not waste our resources."

"Anyone touch me and I'll open her throat right now." Randaal gripped Thio's hair, his knifepoint pricking hard into her skin. One twist, and she would be gone.

"Nah, man, do as you choose. It's naught to me." Olaf's stare remained locked on Randaal. His determined look belied his light tone.

Randaal stared back at Olaf, squinting, calculating, and sweating. Suddenly he pushed Thio away towards Olaf. "Smart man, Olaf. Fishgirl, go ahead, try and get your revenge. Slay me whenever you want. Better succeed, because if you fail, I'm going to cut you and cut you. Not enough to kill you, just to control you. You hate me? Good. Don't give me reason to teach you another lesson."

The watching men breathed a sigh of relief. Randaal's terrible temper came up fast, but it would disappear just as quickly.

Thio's eyes were murderous. "I know how to slaughter a pig, and if I have to, I will. What I don't want is to hear another word out of your stupid mouth. You're not king of this ship! I *will* speak, like any of the crew. There's a reason the council forced me onto this ship!"

Her defiance pushed Randaal to the boiling point again. "Stupid bitch!" he cried. He snatched at her hair, and as his grip closed on one of her braids, he sawed viciously at it. The men shouted and pulled him away from Fishgirl again, and he let them, holding her severed braid aloft.

"You see this? It's mine now! I own it, and I'll own her! The only reason we exist is to find land for the council. We're going to do that job, and no one, Fishgirl or otherwise, will get in the way. Got it? *Got it?*" He spat the words at the entire crew, glaring, chin jutting, his shoulders hunched.

Tiller saw the danger that formed in that instant. Half the men glared at Randaal, and the other half at Fishgirl. *They have fully*

109

divided, he realized. Before, they had disagreed, but each one with all the others. Thio's attempt to speak on matters of sailing had firmly split the men into two camps.

Disagreement between two equal groups was far worse than each man having his own opinion. It would mean battles instead of squabbling scuffles.

War was coming.

———·———·———

Olaf tried to placate them all. "Randaal will settle down…give him a moment…"

Dagsson retorted, "You encourage him by allowing him to treat Fishgirl in this way! We swore an oath to protect her, all of us, Randaal included! He speaks of doing the council's bidding, but it is he who is defying it. Are you with us, Olaf, or for Randaal?"

The two men eyed one another. No one on board realized that they were holding their breath. The ship stood in the still water, the entire crew of men stood in frozen stillness, their breath drawn. The only thing that moved was their hearts ramming in their chests.

The terrible moment of balance could not hold, and finally, Olaf snapped.

"I'd rather stand with Randaal than someone who's always whining about work!" he shouted, knocking Dagsson down. With that, the long days of festering anger and fear burst like a boil, spewing a savage longing to hit something, someone, anyone, anything, and full-scale fighting broke out.

———·———·———

110

The men of the crew might have destroyed themselves were it not for Fishgirl's shriek. In the melee of fighting, Randaal had reached for her and was hitting her savagely. Once again, they surged as one to pull Fishgirl away from Randaal, other angers forgotten.

His arms held, bent over in pain, Randaal was still defiant. "Finish your damned Thing. Go whatever *fukking* direction Tiller says. I'm going to sharpen my knife for next time I need it."

———·———·———

Strained silence prevailed as each person tried to return to the critical issue at hand. Thio was crumpled against the side of the ship, her face in her hands, while Kurt stroked her butchered hair.

"Well, then, Tiller, let's hear what you have to say," said Olaf.

Tiller struggled to calm himself. Resentment surged in his veins, self-righteous wrath that wanted more fight, more fury, to prove his right and might with fists. Damn Randaal, for bringing that out in them, for dividing them. Damn his own father, for teaching wrath over reason. Tiller forced grim humor as he began.

"I enjoy a diet of fish, fish, and more fish as much as anyone," he said. "And sailing beats plowing any day, but one more storm and we might *all* be joining Hyulf and Bergr."

Slight nodding of heads. Good. They were ready to listen.

"We'll check the stars tonight. I believe the storm blew us pretty far south," Tiller reasoned. "We know we've gone southwest all along. If I'm right, we're an astonishing distance west of Éireland. To the best of our reasoning," he nodded at Sig, Olaf and some others, "We judged that Gunnbjörn's skerries were due west of Íseland. Put together with where I believe we are, it puts us far south of where we want to be."

They all listened intently, even Randaal, who pretended to be more interested in inspecting his knife from handle to blade tip.

"But if you sail north of anywhere -- Íseland, Nórsvegr -- sooner or later, you find ice. What then?" Dagsson was still nursing wounded pride.

"I cannot emphasize how far south I think we are, Dagsson. But no matter; if we go straight north, towards the guiding star, either we will see signs in the air and the water that Gunnbjörn Ulfsson's land is near, or we *will* reach ice. If we see signs, we keep going. If we run into ice, we can turn around and keep searching south, or go wherever you like. I know places where we might find a decent chieftain to serve, one who has no love of the council, and get off this ship."

No one argued, so Tiller finished.

"I vote to keep looking. We only want a harbor because we fear death. Even from other countries, news travels fast. When some trader sees us and word gets back to the council that we took their ship and sold it and hid for three years, rest assured, they *will* come looking for our blood. People will know we were defeated by fear, plain and simple. I would rather die trying to become a hero than live a life mocked in shame."

They frowned in concentration. Sigmund took the lead again.

"Well-reasoned." He twisted around, looking hard at each of the men in turn. "Do Tiller's words seem right? Does anyone have a better plan to put forward, or are we ready to vote?"

"Vote," said Gierr. "We need a decision."

One by one, each man spoke 'aye' aloud or nodded his head. When the last vote was heard, Sigmund spoke formally to conclude the Thing. "All votes are cast. The decision is unanimous. We go due north, as Tiller recommends. Straight to the guiding star."

They slapped one another's backs to show support. Tiller walked aft, took the steering-board in his hand, and the oarsmen poised for the call. With a deep breath, he pushed the rudder to turn the ship north, knowing that the fate of the voyage rested on his shoulders now.

"Row!" cried Gierr.

———·———·———

Late that night, when sounds of sleeping filled the ship, a dark figure slipped from one of the húthfats and moved soundlessly between the crates and snoring bodies. A sharp knife, some quick cuts, and the figure slipped back, through the darkness, unheard and unseen.

———·———·———

In the morning, no one told Randaal that his left braid was missing. Whispers and furtive nudges indicated the hacked-off thatch bristling below his sleeping-cap. When he finally discovered the prank, the crew howled in mirthful relief. Randaal kicked and threw things, seething with anger, but stopped short of incurring another beating for himself.

No one took responsibility, but a message had been sent: *Guard that you do not go so far again, or your neck might feel the blade.*

Northward

The wind blew against the knörr as it pressed northward with fresh promise, almost as if the voyage had started over with a fragile new grasp on hope. The quiet work of rowing after the terrors of the storm felt safe, and ushered in a relaxed mood. A few sang rowing-chants. Even Randaal seemed in a decent mood. Soon they felt settled, lulled by monotonous swells and the sound of the oars dipping and rising.

Only Thio remained guarded. Tiller could not risk talking to her. She was deciding something, he could tell. *Please let it not upset the hard-won calm on this ship,* he hoped, and wondered what it might be.

———·———·———

Thio finished serving the midday meal, and announced to no one in particular that she would inventory their supplies. "We took on so much water, I should check the food and seeds." She pulled open the nearest crate and began to unpack it.

It gave the men something to watch. As Thio worked, even her movements took on a peaceful rhythm, as she dragged out a box, unpacked it, spread things to check, repacked them, pushed the box back, and started on another. For a ship of criminals lost at sea, they were, for a brief time, oddly and deeply at peace.

———·———·———

As the afternoon pressed on, Tiller noticed men whispering to one another. They peered at him, then Fishgirl, leering. The first taunt came from Lars.

"Tiller. Why don't you tell us how you knocked up Fishgirl but didn't know her?"

"Yes, Tiller. How stupid is *that*?" Kurt was always eager to be part of any excitement.

114

"Why do you need to disrupt the first peace we've had in days?" Anger left over from fighting Randaal clashed with Tiller's irritation at Thio for making him part of a lie. "Me, Kurt? Stupid? An idiot could teach you. And Lars, she's not your daughter. Why do you give a *shite*?"

Lars' rude bantering gave way to the deeper issue. "You know the rule about fish girls! No brats in the belly! You're as responsible as she is for breaking it!"

"You kept track of every woman you laid last year? Nobody knows *who* you slept with, do they, Lars? No one left to say!" Tiller spat on the deck boards.

Lars pulled his knife and leaped for Tiller. None of them knew that massive Tor could move as fast as he did, catching Lars' kyrtill and holding him aloft and screaming curses.

"Tor, put him back in place at his oar or throw him overboard," Tiller railed. "I don't care if I ever get back to Íseland, and I damned sure don't care if Lars does!"

Lars glared, but hanging from Tor's grip, there was little else he could say.

Karl, who hated for anyone to fight, broke in with a silly song. "Tiller took his rudder, and steered it straight to shore, found himself a Fishgirl, and made a little oar…"

He laughed at himself, his twin joining in. Karl sang it twice more for good measure, and under such nonsense the tension diminished again. Eyes drifted to Thio, half-laughing as she tried to ignore Kurt's ditty. Rowing resumed, and once again they watched her at work.

———·———·———

It took Thio until supper to finish the crates in her work area. As the men took out the knucklebones and tafl games, eager to resume their nightly contest, she began working on the chests stacked aft on the half-deck. By nightfall, she had finished a few more.

Thio stood and stretched from bending over so long. Rubbing her back, she circled the ship, serving night-time broth to soothe them for sleep. "I'll be finished with the grain and seed chests early tomorrow, then I'll go through the crates of tools," she announced to no one in particular. "If anyone wants me to straighten their personal supplies, I'll be happy to do them too."

To no one's surprise, Bolli answered quickly. "My sea chest is a mess! All yours, Fishgirl."

Several other heads nodded in assent. Watching her work had been a pleasant diversion from just seeing her cook. It also gave them the opportunity to watch her body without accusation.

"Good," she said. "I'll start after *dagvbethr*. Bolli, I should get to yours by midday."

As he looked to where Bolli's crate was, Tiller was startled to realize what Thio was doing. Somewhere not far past it was the crate containing an ancient knife. When Thio opened that chest, all of them would see her take out the tools of the planned blood-offering.

He suddenly realized that none of them would ever beat their Fishgirl at tafl, no matter what Ulfr's tote stick might say.

———·———·———

116

As the sun climbed overhead, Thio reached Bolli's sea chest. She removed the contents, shook the clothing, and laid it out to air.

"Do you want me to oil your land boots?" He did, after which Thio carefully repacked his belongings, and started on Dagsson's chest. She tried not to glance at the crate with the knife and the noose where they sat innocently in line a few ells ahead.

"Tor, yours next?" she called. He nodded. "Your blacksmithing tools?"

"I'll pull it out. It's too heavy for you to move." Tor's deep voice, so rarely heard.

One more chest to go until she reached it. Thio could barely breathe. *Another reckless idea! What is wrong with me that I keep pushing so hard? Do I actually think I can escape this fate?* She had thought of exposing the dreaded plot via the tools and had immediately started without thinking further. Now, once again she regretted her impulsive actions.

Still... *Randaal intends it, for certain. Why else was he so angry at me?* As much as Thio wanted to believe that the whole mess would go away, she knew she was not safe.

Unmasked

Not long now, Thio thought as she nailed closed the heavy chest of tools. A thick layer of mutton grease and wrapping-skins of fat-rich sheep's wool had kept the iron free of rust. Thio had added a fresh coat, then Tor shoved the crate back into place and pulled out the one carrying tent spikes. She fixed her gaze on them, focused on each spike as if it was everything in the world. *Breathe breathe breathe...* The old nauseous fear threatened to overtake her, but suddenly Thio drew a breath in sharply, and a kind of angry strength returned to her. She forced herself to speak lightly, in case any of the men were watching her closely. "These don't need a fresh coat of mutton fat. They are quite good!" Thio replaced the spikes and closed the crate.

Watching her, Tiller wondered how she was remaining so calm. The tension had mounted in him at each chest she opened. Would someone stop her before she opened the chest holding the deadly knife? And if so, who?

As Thio struggled to push the spike-crate back, Olaf stepped in. Her heart skipped. *Was he being kind, or...?*

"Let me get that for you." His voice was friendly.

Thio smiled. "Thank you so much. Now that next one." Olaf was so close. Could he see her trembling?

Instead, Olaf pulled out three crates from the top stack behind it. "If I put these on top of the front ones, you won't have to bend so much. Better?"

He was right. They *would* ease the work.

"That's wonderful," Thio smiled again. "Will you put them back when I'm finished?"

"Of course. My wife is carrying. I wouldn't want her bending over so much either."

Thio worked the chests as quickly as she could, her eye still on the critical one.

"Olaf!" But he had started his rowing shift. Ulf stepped over the thwarts. "Let me do it."

118

Ulf moved crates back in place quickly. She almost missed seeing him push the one she wanted under completed ones. Was it deliberate, or accidental? Thio covered her gasp with a cough and pointed. "Ulf, that one. I'll do it next."

"Nay, it's one of the ones you finished already."

"No, I didn't. These here, yes," she pointed at each in turn, "but not that one. It might be the turnip tops for the garden. I haven't seen them yet."

Ulf's smile grew broader. "Turnip tops go in round casks. You're not a merchant, you wouldn't know that." He said loudly, "Fishgirl, you've worked hard. Rest before you serve supper, why don't you? Tomorrow I'll pull whichever crates you want. How's that smoked mutton coming?"

Thio dug in. "I want to finish this row now!"

Bolli offered unexpected aid. "Let her be, Ulf. Nobody else wants to do them."

"Stay out of it, Bolli," Gierr chimed. "We need cooking more than cleaning!"

Olaf? Ulf? Gierr? The shift change had complicated Thio's efforts. "The mutton isn't ready. Please pull that chest, Ulf. Whose is that one, anyway?"

"Ulf doesn't take orders from you!" Gierr's voice was sour, and Ulf's face no longer pleasant.

Randaal dropped his oar, tangling the other rowers. "Fishgirl, enough! Be done with those crates! You're here to work at cooking and fishing. Leave this tidying-up be. We're on a ship, not in some coddled longhouse!"

The rest of the crew watched. Why did Thio provoke Randaal so? It seemed that she wanted to make him lose his control. *The fool woman,* some thought. *She brings it on herself.* The rest worried that he might try to hurt her again.

Thio considered the men's faces. Who else besides Randaal might know of the boatshed plans? Perhaps, they just did not know where the… she shivered…*things* were.

She weighed a third possibility. What would happen if she held up the noose and the knife? Maybe they thought that, even seeing them, she would never guess their significance. At best, someone might play it off with a lie, say it as an old family treasure brought for good luck. At worse, full-scale battle might erupt on board again, and their voyage might end right there, the ship a drifting death-hull of corpses.

She decided to back down for now. "You could thank me more nicely for all that work."

Thio returned to her workboard, a dark smile playing across her lips. It had cost hours of backbreaking bending and lifting, but she'd narrowed the field. One of those - Gierr, Olaf, or Ulf - had been the other man in the boathouse.

———·———·———

Conflicted

Tiller caught himself again. *Daydreaming about a woman. The gods made us human, and therefore stupid.* Thunderstruck with the bold brilliance of her idea, Tiller's admiration for Thio had grown as he watched her work through those chests.

The exchange between Thio and Ulf ran through Tiller's memory. If Thio was telling the truth, the only time she'd looked in that crate she had vomited into the hold from fear. How had Thio managed to stay so calm today, facing her opponents? *If it was true, then she is brave,* he acknowledged. *Or cunning. Or both.* Thio could clearly manipulate the crew. Why did she not just save herself, and push them to sacrifice him? Her loyalty confused him.

Brave, cunning, confusing - and rash. Her 'survival plan' was abysmal. Still, the woman had ungodly courage. She'd faced Randaal better than most men could. She had patience and intelligence, but she'd allowed herself to be trapped into this voyage by some mistake, a reckless wildness taking her to Ólafsvík for a reason she had not yet revealed. Thio was a singular woman, unlike any he'd ever met. And they'd all seen her in that flimsy under-shift. Any man would want her, yet she'd managed to keep them distracted from that as well.

Ever since her astonishing announcement that her child was his, Thio had remained maddeningly aloof, ignoring him while they worked close together, with barely a word beyond *Tiller, can you hold this while I tie it?* An invisible wall separated them.

Love was a luxury Tiller had never allowed himself. Too busy, too much work to do. Was this love, or just fascination? Whatever it was, it had slipped in subtly, filling Tiller with longing. Desire, he realized, was like the law: both were invisible, but each had inflexible effects on those bound by them.

Wanting

Since Thio was ignoring Tiller, he talked to her.

"What is it about you, Thio? I saw something in your eyes when we left land, something I did not want to see. It made me want to know you in a way I've never felt before. I ignored it because you were the fish girl. But you tell lies so often, how could I ever know who you really are? My father could not tell the truth, Thio. Lies repulse me."

She scrubbed her fish board, rinsed it with sea water, and pulled tight the leather straps on a cask of dried oatcakes, ignoring Tiller.

He pressed on. "I cannot deny wanting you! But I can't afford for desire to cloud my mind, and at this point, I don't trust you at all."

Thio took her net from the peg on the side of the hull. She threw it onto the water and did not look at Tiller. He wished that they were alone so he could actually say his thoughts aloud.

A forbidden, taunting Fishgirl. Famines driving desperation at home. Sacrifice, with high stakes of danger. Too many lies. They were heading into another kind of storm, with no known route to safety.

Watching

Watch the sky for the clouds that mean land. Watch the water for signs. Watch for birds. Watch and observe. Watch the sky for the

122

clouds that mean land. Watch the water for signs. Watch for birds. Watch and observe. Watch and observe. Watch and observe.

Tiller watched everything, constantly. Just as constantly, Thio filled his thoughts, sometimes angrily, sometimes calmly, sometimes with worry, sometimes with hope.

Focus on what you know, he reminded himself. *Watch the sky for the clouds that mean land. Watch the water for signs. Watch for birds. Watch and observe. Watch the sky for the clouds that mean land. Watch the water for signs. Watch for birds. Watch and observe...*

...and try not to think about Thio.

———·———·———

Floating beside the boat today, so small he almost missed it, was a twig with a green leaf.

———·———·———

Another willow twig, and this one too had leaves. It floated along, a thoughtless messenger, in complete ignorance of the excitement it caused in Tiller. As it floated past the ship and out of sight, he knew the truth that it silently heralded. Somewhere directly north of them was ground where green things grew.

The whole ambition of his life lay ahead, the childhood dream that held every hope of a lonely, impoverished, mistreated boy. Men did not weep. What was this filling his breast so much that it hurt, and spilled out onto his cheeks? Tiller wiped the tears away impatiently. *Stay calm. This is just the beginning. You need to learn more.*

He would say nothing to anyone else. It was too soon. For now, though, he treasured the small twig in his heart, a priceless promise of more to come.

———·———·———

Tiller watched the water as intently as he could without drawing attention. Inwardly he felt wild anticipation, but the very intensity cautioned him to keep silent. Better to wait and be absolutely certain. Land did not mean 'safe landing'. There might be only cliffs that could crush the knörr between stone and sea.

———·———·———

The rowing shift was changing. Voices erupted in shouting. "Watch your damned oar!"

"Forget my oar, keep your cussed feet out of my way!" Soon there were fists, and men scuffled together once again on the floor of the foredeck.

"Thio!" he said quietly. She was watching the fighting men as she gutted the day's catch. Tiller dropped the rope he was repairing and stooped beside her.

Thio inclined her head, her eyes intent on the men.

"We are close to some kind of land. It will not be long now."

Thio's eyes widened in shock, but she gave no other sign of the momentous news Tiller had just spoken. The sounds of the scuffle got louder. Thio said, "Be ready as soon as I finish with this fish." Her expression softened, a flicker of joy mixed with fear and hope. Tiller's heart opened, and his lips parted, but he knew nothing to say.

Just as quickly, Thio's eyes frosted to coldness again. Her lips thinned in anger and she hacked savagely with her knife. Tiller, rebuffed, walked into the fight and for no particular reason cuffed the nearest two men, to soothe the pain of being a witless fool.

Approaching

A quarter-mark later, Tiller pulled the steering-board up and leaned over the side to inspect it closely. He did so daily, but now more than ever he needed to make sure it was in perfect condition.

The argument of a few moments ago had resolved without serious injury. A game of knucklebones had ensued on the front half-deck, and anyone not rowing was betting on the outcome. Thio complained loudly that she had not caught enough fish and threw her net overboard.

"How long?" she murmured.

"One day. Maybe two. Not long. We have to hope we don't miss it, sailing by too far east or west if it's small, or if bad weather comes. But something's definitely ahead of us. Only a matter of time until everyone knows."

For an instant, Thio put her hand on his arm and a thrill shot through him. Almost inaudibly, she said, "My gods. You are as good as they all say. You are wonderful!" She risked a sideways glance and Tiller could see the quickest flash of those blue eyes, suddenly sparkling with admiration.

His chest filled, and he looked at her with a quiet pride.

"I'm still going to do it, with or without your help," she said flatly.

"I still think there's no way they'll go through with it." *If it's true,* he did not add.

Thio looked at Tiller in complete exasperation.

"You *do* know it *is* going to be one of us?"

"Things almost always turn out differently than people expect."

"It *won't!* And I need you! That stupid covenant to 'protect' me? It was only to keep me 'pure' for the sacrifice! If they use you instead of me, what will my fate be then?"

It was an idea he had not considered, and Tiller had no answer. The nearer they came to land, the greater his concern for Thio grew, though he tried not to show it to her, and here was another unpleasant scenario. Apprehension and worry for Thio took turns with joy and excitement about actually finding a shoreline, and across the hours, Tiller knew no peace.

Land-Love

As the clouds started to speak to him of what they had seen, floating beneath them, Tiller felt it: the strange sensation, the coming-close, an insatiable longing, as exciting as sex and as irresistible as infatuation. He often sensed it long before the dark blur on the horizon appeared. Perhaps it was just instinct from observing small details, or maybe was something more mysterious in the souls of men, something that knew they belonged to the land, and felt her pull on them the way lodestones pull iron shavings in an irresistible need to come together.

Tiller had loved the land long before he ever loved a woman, and felt, deep inside, that perhaps he would always love the land more, the way she cradled little streams, and raised herself proud and strong,

126

arching along sweeping fjords. He loved the curves of her fields, and the fertile smell of earth opened by the coulter, and the sensuous waves of growing grain.

Did the land only lay claim to humans, or did she love them in return? Was it foolish to think that the heart of the land might lighten at seeing their sail, knowing how they wanted her? *Because we do want you,* he whispered forward across the waves. *We yearn for you.*

It was not long before Tiller sensed deep in his body the feel of her rising from deep, deep below, her loins lifting up from under the water, straining towards the ship. Soon they would see one another. Soon they would touch. Tiller's excitement grew at the prospect of this long-desired and yet-unknown beauty, a stranger to any man. But as he felt the land rising up under the sea towards the ship, as he tried to imagine what she might look like, it was Thio's eyes he saw lighting with delight, and Thio's body arching fiercely towards his.

——·——·——

Tiller's thoughts raced, but he could share his questions with no one. What if it was different land than they were used to, if strange creatures dwelt there, or it was full of monsters? What if it was nothing but rock and plants clinging to cliffs, or all swampland, with no place to beach and nowhere to grow food or to pasture the few animals that, remarkably, were still alive in their little pens? His beliefs in the gods were loose, at best, but Tiller allowed himself a moment to wonder what if this *was* Hel, or *Jötunheim,* the primordial place of ice-rock giants?

Too many wonderings. He could do nothing about them, so Tiller considered Thio. What would keep her safest? Following her plan, or disrupting it? It was critical to decide quickly. The signs in the water and sky could not be hidden any longer. It was time to tell the crew.

———·———·———

They erupted in cheers, surging to their feet. The strong men wept unabashedly, exchanging rough hugs and pounding one another with glee.

"What sort of land? Can you tell yet? Good farmland? Birch groves like Íseland? Pine forests like Nórsvegr? Bogs like Éireland? Is there a mountain that smokes as at home?" Their faces were like children hoping for gifts.

"There are signs of growing things. Trees at least. We'll learn more when we're closer."

For the next several hours, the crew rowed as if their muscles were fueled by magic, chattering together. Although the conversation was jovial, Tiller still sensed a taking-of sides, of two groups forming in opposition to one another, as they discussed the best way to build a longhouse or how to select a cove for landing. Finally, darkness came and night covered the ship. From the snores, some had managed to fall asleep, but most still talked, drowsily making plans.

———·———·———

Tiller could not sleep. How to spend what might be his last night on the ship...perhaps even his last night of life? He looked with gratitude at the stars that had guided him across so many waters. He imagined Thio lying under them on lush summer grass, her hair

128

spilling across the sweet green, her breasts like cream and berries in the moonlight. *One night to plan what I will and will not do. One night to seek reason and reject reckless fear, however it comes.*

__.__.__

LAND

Finding

Tiller told Thio what to look for. "It starts as the faintest *maybe* on the horizon. Just a blur, really, one that could also be a storm. Eventually a dark line will appear, and get distinct."

They watched in every direction. It could be so easy to miss.

———·———·———

It was exactly as he described.

———·———·———

At first, there was a haze. Slowly, it thickened. The crew strained towards it, speaking in anxious whispers, hoping it was not clouds and not an illusion, true land, and not Hel's nothing-land. They sailed closer and closer, hope building, until a coastline lay undeniably before them.

The stories were true. What Gunnbjörn Ulfsson had seen existed, and they had found it.

———·———·———

Their voices erupted with sound, cheering, the same words shouted over and over. "We found it! We *found* it! *We found Ulfsson's skerries!"* Ahead, sprawling across the horizon, lay the beautiful prospect of heroism, with outlawry and shame receding rapidly into the past.

All tensions and all enmity swept away in wild exuberance. The crew embraced each other and Thio was hugged over and over, so tightly she thought her ribs would break. They congratulated one another for every skill, every effort that brought them here. In the melee of hugs and laughter, Thio let go of Kurt to be enfolded in the next embrace, and realized it was Tiller. Lightning flashed from her body to his, and she felt it strike back in a delicious flash.

Tiller pulled back, startled. For the first time, Thio saw a smile, his real smile.

So that is what he looks like, his guard let down and his true self showing, she thought. Her face upturned to his, she smiled back, and they pressed into one another.

Tiller bent without thinking towards her open lips, but Thio twisted out of his embrace. *I will not give my heart to a man who will see me die within days. I will not do that to him.* She turned to the rail, biting her lips, and weeping not for joy but for what would come, her newfound happiness already destroyed by what the land meant for her.

A New Beauty

As the knörr approached it, the line in the sea grew thicker and wider. The crew searched every detail of it hungrily and sniffed the wind like dogs.

"How will we go ashore?" Thio asked. "You don't know where the coves are here."

"There will be a beach, sooner or later," answered Tiller. "We'll sail until we find one."

He noted that the current flowed north along the land. Ever since they left Íseland, the current had been pushing them hard to the southwest. Tiller squinted, thinking. Had they actually overshot the land, and were now approaching the western side of it? The more he looked, the more certain he became. That meant it must turn soon, somewhere close by in the south, and head sharply northward.

In his mind, Tiller saw shapes of land and currents move about fluidly, sorting them with a sailor's understanding as he absorbed critical navigational details of this new place. How lucky they had found it at all!

———·———·———

As the ship came closer to the shoreline, the crew could see stone walls rising steep and forbidding from an astonishing number of small islands. The sight was strange to eyes so used to wide bays that cut cleanly between far hills, forming huge swaths of sea on which to safely sail. Here, the sea tore into the land over and over, invading it every sea-mile, and the edge of the land had been broken and broken again and again into an endless tangle of islands that were empty of life. They were no more than gigantic stones, dangerous chunks of bread crowded in a *sup* of sea.

The land did not welcome them, but they welcomed it, their mouths open in awed wonder.

———·———·———

"Where is the volcano?" asked Kurt in astonishment. "Where is the smoke from Völundr's flames? Does he not work beneath a mountain here too?" It was the question of a boy who had not grasped the remarkableness of the island on which he had been born, where the Blacksmith's great forge spit smoke and fire to the skies.

"Not every place is home to immortals. Never forget you are an Íselander," said Tor. The crew looked at him in astonishment. He said nothing more, but looked over the stones standing in the sea. To him, also, it seemed startlingly still, the immense stones rising silent from the waves. Tor could not say what he was feeling. He had been taken from his homeland as a child. It had taken a long time for Tor to learn to love the rugged landscape of Íseland, but now he longed for the sight of those familiar places. Here, there were no longhouses or farms to greet them, no other ships plying the coast. Tor buried the lonely feeling deep in his immense heart, where the yearnings of a lifetime were stored.

"Are there forests?" Dagsson asked. "Timber would bring as much wealth as farmland."

They looked for anything approximating the forests of birch and rowan, juniper and aspen at home, but saw only stone, smelled only the odors of wet rocks and lichens.

The crew sailed on, their hearts in their throats, begging the gods to see something of hope and value. Olaf proposed that they should not beach at once, but sail until they came upon a good site for the settlement they had been tasked to start. It was an unpopular idea.

"No! We'll just find a place to stop for the night," Sig said, settling it. "We'll eat food that Fishgirl makes on land, and call it a feast. Now that we're here, there's no rush finding a decent place. I want to feel earth under my feet as much as the next man."

134

They passed sea-mile after sea-mile, looking for a flat-enough scrap of sand to serve as a landing site but seeing only the dozens and hundreds of harsh little stone islands and short inlets, their hope sharpened into a kind of frantic desire. The eighth-marks dragged on, interminably slow.

"What if there is nothing here but stone and sea?" Karl asked. "What do we do then?"

No one answered him. The question hung in the air.

In the end, most of them knew it mattered little what sort of land it was. It existed. Even if there were no good fields for flocks, sooner or later something would be found of value, something that could be traded: copper, tin, iron, silver or gold ores, or minerals to mine, or skins of animals, or rich fishing, something that men and women could use. It was land.

———·———·———

"Look there! Will that work?" Fishgirl pointed to where her sharp eyes had picked out what looked like a small cove, the stones colored a soft green with plant life. "It looks as though there might be some grassland. Our animals could actually forage!"

"She's right. Between those two hills," Lars confirmed. "Looks as if bit of stream is coming out."

"I cannot wait to feel earth in my hands!" shouted Ekka. "A stone, sand, anything!"

Soon Tor and Gierr had set the sail to run them up onto a narrow strip of beach. They manned all oars, four men to each to push hard onto shore, and plunged forward.

———·———·———

Thio wavered between excitement at being so close to making land and fear of what was coming. *Breathe,* she told herself again, for the hundredth time since morning. *Breathe. Don't panic. Tiller and I should be safe until we find a permanent camp.*

With all that pressed upon her, Thio realized she desperately wanted and needed to give way to the relief and happiness flooding her. *Maybe Tiller is right,* she told herself. *Maybe he is. Whatever may come, for this little bit of time I want to feel joy.*

———·———·———

The Breathtaking Sound of Beach

Tiller held his breath to better hear the sound of the ship meeting solid land, the instant when, after surging so long through the sea, a vessel built from trees once rooted deep in stone and soil came home to land: the sweet scrape of oak returning to earth.

The keel crushed against small stones which had lain on this unknown beach for untold centuries, and they accepted the strange vessel and held it fast. The grinding-grain-and-millstone sound, the beginning-and-ending sound, the coming-together instant of ship, sea, and land pinned everything to this pivotal moment, a long month from their departure day. The ship had arrived, and the search ended.

For the whole crew, the sound held a headiness never felt before. To the surprise of everyone, it was young Karl who found the words to express the moment.

"The words of the old sagas are no more! The old sagas are the past, and the past matters no more! *We* are the sagas! Our story is the one that matters! We are the land-finders! We are the hope-givers! We are *vikingers*, but not just any vikingers...we, this crew, will shape the future of our people!"

At Karl's words, the crew of the knörr felt awe. They were no longer just any men. To be immortalized in sagas for courage was an honor few could boast, but even those great accolades, so admired by the commonest of humans, were nothing compared to the prospect of being heralded as the heroes who would save their people from starvation. They had crossed the line of legend, and held the golden grains of hope in their hands, to sow in rich fields where a country's future could grow.

—·—·—

As quickly as the grinding sound began, it stopped, a rapid start-and-done, one thing finished and another began in that heartbeat of sound. The crew braced themselves for the sudden jerk of stopping, then leapt over the rails, ready to claim this place as their own. They shouted exultantly, rough and playful, less like grown men than puppies yelping with excitement. Whoops and shouts and laughter came from all sides. In twos and threes, they impulsively danced the steps of sailor-home-safe, and one by one, fell upon the earth and rolled on it, embraced it with their whole bodies, scooped handfuls of sand, and kissed it tenderly.

—·—·—

"I call for a fire!" shouted Nollar. "A gigantic one, a festival fire!"

At his words, all scurried in search of driftwood and dead branches. A great pile of sticks and logs grew, aided by one massive tree trunk that required four men to carry. Mitla fumbled for the flint stone in Fishgirl's tools. Not finding it, he threw Fishgirl over his shoulder and scuttled back to the ship, both of them laughing as Mitla fell into the sand and she tumbled off. Kurt and Karl mimicked them, dropping each another over and over, laughing.

Thio struggled to walk, startled at how odd her legs felt, now so used to the up-and-down of the swells of the ship. Her flint stone retrieved, sparks flew and the dried grasses gave off sweet smoke. Enraptured, the men and Thio listened eagerly for the sounds of crackling and popping as flames licked the logs, and soon the fire roared.

138

Tor's uncommonly rich voice sounded again. The man who had been a slave as long as he could remember was choked with emotion.

"We are free men now. We are outlaws no longer."

A deep breath filled each man's chest. They stretched their hands towards the fire, supplicating, grateful, and once again, tears ran down their cheeks. Thio looked at them and dared to hope, though she could not believe.

——·——·——

"We need moss! Seaweed! Wet wood!" Kurt looked around, scratching his chin. "It's like a crossing-over! Smoke should go to the sky!"

For a moment, the spell was broken. Randaal looked at Kurt, his quick anger flaring. "What do you mean, half-wit? No one has died here!"

For once, Kurt stood firm. "It is *we* who have crossed over. We were dead men, but now we're alive. We've crossed over into safety."

Randaal started to mock him, but Sigmund stepped in. "Kurt is right. I say we also make it a crossing-over fire for Hyulf and Bergr. What's done is done," he said, looking straight at Randaal, "but we had no way of honoring them, and we don't need them haunting us."

Randaal said nothing. Gierr stood stubbornly beside him, also refusing, but Olaf strode at once to a group of small trees and stripped off fragrant branches budding with leaves. Bolli found a wet log floating, and handfuls of green plants pulled from rocks above the shoreline were piled onto the fire, and bountiful dark froths of smoke tumbled upwards in the clear air.

Kurt's instinct served them all well. The fire roared and the smoke spumed, the sound and the sight claiming even the sky above the land, asserting *we are here! We are the triumphant!*

———·———·———

In the distance, a group of people bent over a bleeding body, the odor of entrails in their noses. They moved in rhythm, their knives stripping off sections of flesh. After a while they stood, arching their backs and talking of small things. One turned towards the sea, and gasped.

"What is that?"

The others' eyes followed where he pointed. A thing of darkness moved between the ground and sky, twisting angrily on itself. They stared as one, unable to take their eyes from it.

———·———·———

"We should go and see what that is. It is near where we hunted yesterday.

Seasoned eyes scanned the coastline in the distance. "He's right."

"Is it dangerous? What if that thing can hurt us?" Fear, so rarely felt, ran through them.

"Whatever it is, we have meat here that must not be wasted. We'll go after we finish. If it disappears before we reach it, all the better."

They turned to the carcass again, their cutting strokes more rapid. Soon long strips of red raw meat hung drying in the breeze, and they left, moving in the direction of the dark thing.

———·———·———

_____·_____·_____

The crew of the knörr fed the fire with driftwood throughout the afternoon. Knowing they must leave it soon, they watched the crossing-over fire until it fell to embers, delaying having to leave their moment of triumph and return to work. When the fire was little more than a soft glowing, the tide had risen almost full enough to lift the ship again. Sigmund and Tor pulled the wedging stones from under the knörr, and shortly the crew felt the deck move freely underfoot again as the ship headed back out to open water.

_____·_____·_____

The Others

The watchers lay on a low hill across the water, their bellies flat against the ground and their eyes fixed on the strange thing moving out to sea. Their stomachs were hollow, and their glances darted often to their wise-woman and her mate who had come on this one last trip, she said, before they were too old to do it again, silently asking, what is it?

But the elder-ones, too, felt only uncertainty coupled with fear.

They moved furtively, following the thing as it drifted steadily along their coastline, sometimes almost invisible in the fog that had blanketed the sea.

Each combed their memories of old stories. What could it be? Some kind of dead whale, huge with air? Or was it an enormous gull, sitting on the sea with that great thing above it that resembled a ...wing? It lurched along on the waves, horridly stiff.

All were hunters. They lay unmoving.

Shhhhhh.... shhhhhh.... watch....

———·———·———

"Look closely. It swarms with something."

"Are those some kind of beings? They have arms and legs - and faces!"

The beings on the thing had astonishing skin the pale color of bone, and their hair was mostly pale as well, the creamy yellow of birds' eggs. Some had hair covering their faces as well.

Were they animals? Or the Great Ones, the Land-and-Sea-Creators, come to shore in a great floating watercraft?

The watchers kept silent, straining to hear the strange sounds.

"Should we greet them, or stay in hiding?"

"They have not called out to us, have they? If they are seeking something, it is not us."

———·———·———

Searching for Safe Harbor

After the beaching, patchy fog came and went. For three days, the knörr moved slowly, the crew constantly on the lookout for rocks beneath the waters. Tiller dropped the lead-line often to check the water's depth. From gray morning to gray afternoon to gray night, they saw only rock cliffs and an impossible maze of countless smaller and even more broken islands.

"Does anyone see any animals?" asked scrawny Nollar. "I hope there will be plenty of game to hunt!" He actually slobbered in excitement.

The guffaws that followed offered a welcome break in the tension. The excitement of finding land had diminished across days of sailing with no more beachfront seen, and intense quarrelling had begun again.

"Just keep looking for green, Nollar, since grass is what they'd eat. Good green land is what they told us to find. That's what we want," replied Sigmund.

"Good green land, we're searching for you!" cried Nollar. "Green land means fresh meat for us!"

By afternoon, they came to an inlet that was wider than most and traveled up it, and by evening, Nollar saw something promising. As they dropped anchor to prepare for a morning landing, the late-day sun slowly brightened and the mist lifted. They took it as an omen.

———·———·———

"Steady, steady..."

They had waited until the tide was low. Sigmund called the strokes, watching Bolli's and Lars' signals as they approached. An archer could have shot an arrow onto the beach. It was tantalizingly close. They inched forward.

Lars waved frantically. "Pull to the right!" shouted Sigmund. Another underwater obstacle was avoided.

As they approached, Thio grew more and more desperate. She had no work to distract herself, and she picked her fingernails until blood ran. A long, unhappy glance passed between her and Tiller.

She lifted her eyebrows, asking silently, *have you changed your mind?*

No.

Any other ideas? Her eyes questioned.

To Thio's exasperation, Tiller's jaw tightened and he looked away.

The night before, as she banked her small cooking fire for the evening and climbed into her húthfat, she had wept, her tears blurring the stars that sparkled overhead. How beautifully they glittered, and how she longed to be safe at home. Every passing hour she felt more nauseated, remembering her first steps onto the cart path that ran past their farmholdings, and angry for every step afterwards that had led her here, and angriest of all for being forced into doing something inhuman, something that appalled her. At first she had only wanted to find out who had been in the boathouse, and stop them. She had asked herself a hundred times who all that might be, but there was no way to know for certain. Every time, she came to the same dismal answer. *I don't know who knows the plan. I have to assume they all do.* Slowly, she had come to believe there was only one way to be truly safe. *It means they all have to...*

The idea horrified Thio. Could she actually go through with it?

My mother and father and brothers have no idea where I am, and I am glad. The thought gave Thio some small comfort. *If they saw me here alone, and in danger, it would be so much worse for them. They know only that I disappeared one day in a tangle of lies I told. My stupid wildness has brought me to this jagged land that, one way or another, will cut me and Tiller and everyone else to pieces. The only thing I can do is try to save myself, and him. Just keep the two of us alive, and figure out the rest later.*

It was not the promise Thio had made to the woman from Jadar, but it was the best she could do now. Self-loathing filled her.

Jadar. She had never had a chance to tell Tiller. Had he forgotten?

She shook Tiller hard to wake him, but he was too deeply asleep, exhausted from the days of intense focus. The stars swept far across the night before Thio finally dropped into fitful dreams.

———·———·———

The grounding-grinding sound happened again, and the small jerk of stopping signaled another step towards the inevitable. This time, the cheers were subdued. Everyone was anxious to get ashore.

Nollar had seen well. A broad beachhead and low plain lay before them, rising to a hill to the east. They had run the knörr aground close to a stream for fresh water. Small groves of trees and low brush lined the edge of the attractive shoreline.

The crew immediately began to unload supplies. Soon sounds of *'hup, here, got it!"* and *"take this!"* filled the air as they worked to pull the crates from the ship, all except Nollar. Thio saw him just as he disappeared over a low hill.

She balanced on the rail and her boots landed soft on the small stones. Tiller came close, trying to look reassuring.

"Something will change, I'm certain."

Thio watched the men passing chests over the rail to waiting hands. "We may not have enough time for that."

What to do? Run to each of the men, confront him, and ask if he knew? Panic as sharp as the first few days aboard ship overwhelmed Thio. She looked about for a task.

"Tiller, will you help me carry the cooking tools to that flat spot? It's as good as any."

He walked beside her with an iron tripod in one arm and the chain for the big cast-iron cauldron slung over his other shoulder. Thio carried the small cauldron and a basket filled with spoons and tools. A light breeze could carry their words. He spoke quietly.

"We have to call for a Thing."

"Not now while they're working. Interrupt them and, they'll be irritated." Her mother had never learned that demanding her father's attention when Jorund was working always ended by one or the other of them stamping away angry. "Tonight would be better, after they've eaten." Thio felt miserable deceiving Tiller, but she could not trust a Thing. She had counted who might stand with her. It was not a certain majority.

The chain clanged onto the ground as Tiller dropped it. "I'm glad to hear you're not going to be rash. Do you want me to call for the Thing or will you?"

Thio did not answer. Finally, she muttered, "Let's decide when the time comes."

They returned in silence to the ship for another load. This time, Tiller took the small millstone Tor pushed over the edge to him. The quern rolled heavily along the beach stones, and sweat ran down Tiller's face. "Wait," he grunted, and had to pause every few steps.

Kurt and Karl called after them. "Fishgirl, are you baking fresh bannock? We saw the quern!"

The poor things. Thio hoped she would be able to protect them somehow, and Sigmund too, and Tor and Dagsson, when the time came. "Yes, you guessed right. It'll be ready soon."

Tiller gestured to the water as if he was showing Thio something. "You know that I do not believe this could actually happen, but if you're right, here are my thoughts about the Thing. For such a drastic action, they'll want consensus. That's their weakness, which we can use. I wanted to ask some privately about it on the ship, but there never was any opportunity. Then I thought, perhaps as soon as we made land, at the crossing-over fire, but it could have gone terribly awry. They might have rushed it right then and there." Tiller gestured back to the water again. Anyone watching would think he was explaining to Thio how to land the knörr.

"Keep talking, but let's get another load of supplies."

This time they left the ship with Tiller carrying her crate of cooking implements and Thio shouldering a precious sack of oats for the bannock.

Tiller continued. "If I go to one man and say, I want to talk about the sacrifice ceremony, it will put him on guard. If they do *not* know about it, they will not believe me, but they will still be afraid to stand against Olaf or Randaal or Gierr. And if they *do* know about it, they will likely lie. Even if they have the courage to say they don't support it, that is not the same as taking a vote in the presence of the others. So it gains us nothing to talk to them as individuals."

"I agree."

"But if we call all together now and say the same thing, whoever is in charge will resent having their plan interrupted, and first an argument will break out, then almost certainly a fight. Men we can ill

149

afford to lose may die, and of those that are left, the weaker will decide to go along with the more forceful. In the end, our chances are not much better.

"It is hopeless," Thio moaned. "I must do it. I must use the poison."

"No. Not at all. It is possible to change their minds, but we must strike at the one instant when it will be effective."

She looked doubtful, but hopeful. Tiller wished he could pull her close, but reassurance would be a lie. Instead, they dropped the heavy crate and the sack of oats onto the stones and stood resting for a moment.

"Let them be for now. Some don't know. The ones who *do* know but feel it to be wrong, let those men squirm. The closer it gets the more they will raise arguments in their minds against it. As for the ones behind this, let them suspect nothing. Behave as if all is well, as if you know nothing. When they tell the rest of the men, there will be a discussion, and disagreement, and at some point Randaal or Olaf or Gierr will put the matter to a vote. That is the moment they will be at greatest odds."

"Why do you believe that?"

"I have seen it in group after group. Opinions almost always divide evenly. Trust me, half will stand apart from the other half. What we say *in that moment* is critical. We need words to avoid a fight while keeping them from consensus, and other words ready to catch Randaal's anger --- and whoever else -- and draw it away, and weaken them. Once they are weakened and no longer have half the men, they cannot recover enough to carry any vote."

Perhaps Tiller would be able to sway them. Perhaps now that land was real, enough of them might be softened as well, and they would think the whole thing ridiculous. But Thio could not delude herself with hoping for a slim chance.

"How can you possibly believe that the best plan is one that might not even work? I want certainty, even if it costs terribly. The men inclined to be kinder, to forego the gothi's orders, are not the strongest and most stubborn of the crew. They will be swayed, or trampled, by the ones with harder spirits. Do you not see that?"

There was no place to where she could safely run away. No tent, and no food...Thio dug her fingernails into her scalp. *I would be like an outlaw at home,* she thought, the idea splintering her mind. *I would die in a matter of days.*

In that moment, Thio understood the desperation the men had faced, why they had accepted this voyage, and why they would do anything the council demanded, even kill her, to ensure their own safety. *We are the same, these men and I. They have planned to kill me to keep themselves safe. I have planned to kill them to keep myself safe.* The thought gave Thio an odd empathy for the crew. Tiller was wrong. It *was* hopeless. Even though it made her sick to think of it, she would have to be ready at a moment's notice to use the poison.

She needed to be cruel and cold, and steady her resolve to be as hard as the men.

Breathe breathe breathe breathe... she was back in the boathouse again, wiping vomit from her mouth *breathe breathe breathe what to do breathe breathe what to do* take the fire-starter and the water that Olaf is bringing say thank you for carrying that heavy cask *breathe breath what to do breathe breathe* find sticks for kindling find tinder *breathe breathe breathe...*

Once again Thio pushed back fear by focusing on small chores. There was much work to do to set up camp. The piles of boxes on shore grew steadily as the afterdeck was unloaded of crates: digging

151

tools, light coulters that could be pulled by a man to plow the soil, onion sets, shovels to dig turf for building longhouses against wet and cold weather, and the like. Axes, mallets, ingots of iron, an anvil, and Tor's blacksmithing tools. Chisels to work stone, charred coals to light damp wood easily, and oil and wicks to light the way in the night. The chickens and ducklings that Thio had tended each day were carefully passed down in their woven crates, their survival a miracle of good fortune. The chickens came tentatively from their cages and soon their gentle clucking softened the sounds of work as they pecked the soil. A trio of young goats that had been tethered in a dark corner of the under-deck were next. The animals were clearly happy to be off the ship, and despite her worries, Thio smiled as she led them to grass to graze. *My troubles are not the goat's troubles.* No, on second thought, they were. Goats were raised to be butchered. At least she had a chance. Three young lambs came next, and soon the small band of livestock was moving freely about the grass.

———·———·———

Thio walked the beach, picking stones of the right size to build a makeshift oven. She started a crackling fire, and the smell of wood smoke, at once exciting and soothing, spread on the air. While the oven-stones heated, Thio unpacked the bread trencher. She ground oats and filled the trencher with flour, added a little sea water, and honey from a stoneware jar.

Tiller saw her pull a string hanging around her neck, and scoop something from it into the bread bowl. She had mixed a little bubbling paste of flour and water the day Tiller told her they were nearing land, and tucked it between her breasts to stay warm.

"Ingenious," he muttered.

Thio ignored him and buried her hands in the comfort of dough.

———·———·———

As the hours passed and the men worked putting tent poles in the ground, the intoxicating smell of baking bread lifted on the chilly spring breeze. Thio saw them breathe deeply, and sigh.

Spare me and Tiller, she whispered. *He found this land. I will make it pleasant. Please.*

———·———·———

Did Tiller know which keg was prepared, how she had marked it? Their eyes met often, but neither said a word.

———·———·———

"Fishgirl! Mealtime?" Sigmund called a welcome rest. Muscles used to shipboard fatigued quickly as the men walked on sand and pebbles from the ship to the high-tide mark. Weary pleasure showed in their eyes as Thio brought the still-warm loaves.

When, Thio wondered. *When, when, when?* She moved quietly from one to the next, refilling cups and offering more food.

"I don't know what we'd do without you," Tiller said. "Already, you've helped us feel a bit of home here. This bread tastes wonderful." One or two grunted agreement.

"Tiller's right. We couldn't have done this voyage without you. Fishgirl, you're the finest asset we have here." Olaf's warm smile comforted Thio. She crossed him from the list in her mind. It was Randaal and Gierr, then, who had plotted. One more ally for her.

Thio made the same effort on Tiller's behalf. "None would be here without Tiller steering us on the sea. He's as gifted as they say. I trust he'll get us home safely."

"Maybe you're being kind to him because you think he fathered your kid, but you're right," agreed Dagsson. "He did get us here, didn't he?"

Thio waited, hoping for a response from anyone else, a hint even, but no one spoke as they ate and drank. In utter fatigue, one by one the crew stretched out on in the warm sun and fell asleep, relishing the feeling of motionless earth and safety.

"Wake us, Fishgirl, after an eighth. We still have much work before sunset," asked Olaf.

All too soon, she had to rouse them. The empty knörr moved on the still-rising tide. The men dug a trench in front of the ship. As it filled with water, they put shoulders to the lapped timbers and pushed the knörr away from the waves. When it reached the front of the trench, they filled the rocks and soil in behind it again, and with a long rope, tied the ship to an immense boulder, and pounded stakes to anchor the stones.

The ship secured, they raised their tents. Canvases were pulled over the tent-poles and fastened to withstand wind and storms. Others searched for firewood, storing it in one of the tents to dry.

"Tomorrow we'll start to explore, and see what lies around here," Olaf declared. "We need to see if this place is good to start the settlement, or if there is a place nearby with better fields. It's critical that we start planting some spring crops as soon as possible."

"Load all this back onto the ship again and move it somewhere else?" demanded Bolli.

Nollar laughed. "You'll load it. I'll watch."

154

Bolli started to protest before he remembered that Nollar had reappeared that afternoon with several hares swinging from a branch across his shoulders.

They worked hard to finish tasks for the day. As shadows stretched, weariness grew. The sun dropped below clouds in the west and its light reflected down from them.

"Look," Thio said, pointing, and they turned to see the sunset glowing across the entire cove, the ship, and their tents. Soup bubbled in a cauldron, and Nollar's rabbits were roasting over the fire. Whatever challenges tomorrow brought, today had been a good, good day.

———·———·———

The Others

"They've taken everything from their great vessel. Those things look like shelters. Does this mean they will stay?"

"Why are they burning those hares on the fire?" The watchers held their noses against the disgusting odor.

"Such strange animals they have!"

"Some of the beings laughed. We all heard that." Did Great Ones do such things?

"They also relieved themselves."

Apparently Great Ones had those needs as well? How strange!

———:———:———

156

Almost Time

"Is it time?" Randaal kept his voice low as he prodded his companion away from the others. The deepening sunset lit his rough features and shadowed the creases in his forehead.

"I'm uncertain when exactly we begin."

"The councilman wasn't clear, or the journey dimmed your memory?" Randaal scorned.

"Some actions he clearly described, but now that we're here, there is much he didn't explain. Do we use a post for the noose? We don't have one. Do we build a post, have everyone immediately start asking questions? Or tell them first, and then build it? Do it the first night here, or keep Fishgirl to help as part of our team and do the sacrifice right before we return to Íseland? The councilman was not clear on *any* of that!"

"Or on one other thing. Your gal's no virgin, either, it turns out." Randaal snorted.

"Did the councilman know that? Apparently not! And no one else on board knew she was supposed to be maiden-fair. Say nothing about it! We go as planned."

"The councilman said to instruct the others. Did you?"

The other man shook his head. "Not enough of them."

"Why not?" Disdain edged Randaal's words. *Councilman should've given the job to me.*

"I spoke to as many as possible before we left. On board, it was harder once she started feeding them. They like her. Hel's bells, *I* like her! But it's a job we must do, whether we want to or not. We have to do our best with this."

"Damned right we must. Let's sacrifice them both while we're at it, to be certain of meeting the council's expectations. We don't need a post. I can stand behind Tiller or Fishgirl, hold the noose tight. Getting it done matters more than *how* it's done." Randaal thought of holding the noose while Fishgirl squirmed against him and shivery excitement ran in his legs.

"Guard your impatience." Contempt edged Olaf's voice. "We get one chance at this. It must be done properly, or there is no point in doing it at all. Remember what he said? It's not a hog-butchering, it's a blood-ceremony for Odin. I, Olaf, had been sought out and directed by the councilman. I am the one they will question carefully on our return." Too much was at stake to let Randaal botch things. But this confusion... "Sigmund!" Olaf called.

The older man strode over, jovial. "What is it?"

"It's time...for..."

Sigmund's face fell. "You know I agreed to this long before we knew Fishgirl, or Tiller either, for that matter. They said she volunteered. I highly doubt that's true. She's not said a word about it, has she?"

"The councilman was clear! We must!"

"Come on, Olaf. We need them, both of them! She works three times as hard as Bolli! He spent half the day watching Tor dig holes for the tent-poles."

"That doesn't matter! What matters is following rules set by the council."

"The council! Fat lot of good they have done any of us. Besides, come home with news of land, they'll forgive us!"

Olaf's fists clenched. Sigmund did not know about Olaf's son. He flinched, remembering the councilman's voice. "*A fine son you have here, Olaf. Regrettable that you will be gone for such a long time, but*

158

fear not, he will live in my longhouse, and my daughters will treat him as a little brother. If you never return, I will raise him with honor and praise your name." The councilman's voice grew silky. *"He can have all your lands, except for those you stole from my brother, of course."*

Olaf had protested at the terms. *"Kill a woman, as a sacrifice? I could be put to death!"*

"Not likely. She's an orphan," the councilman said. *"But if you fail in this - if you find land, and do not bless it properly with her blood - this young son of yours will be taken to the cliffs, those, over your southern field. I will explain sadly that you did not love him enough to fulfill your duty. With those words in his ears, he will fall from the rocks. If he does not die immediately, he will do it slowly. Think of that when the moment comes, should your hand weaken, or if others argue. You must prevail, or this lad,"* the headman had caressed the boy's head gently, smiling warmly at the child, *"There's no need for me to say it again, is there?"*

———·———·———

Olaf and Sigmund and Randaal's voices grew angrier and louder as they argued. One by one, others looked up at the sounds of discord, and as words came across the beach, some of those who knew what was being discussed purposely avoided coming over.

Randaal's frustration deepened. He looked quickly up and down the beach. Thio was still at the cooking stones, a distance from where they stood.

"Enough," muttered Randaal, glaring venomously at Sigmund and Olaf as they argued. "They've not backbone to make this happen, but I do." He ran towards Thio, his feet churning.

Thio saw Randaal just as he approached her, and knew instantly what it was. She grabbed for a weapon, anything, but her hands found nothing. Randaal caught Thio's arm, twisted it back, and pulled until she was bent over.

"You've mocked me this whole trip, but not anymore," he bit at her. "No more!" As the crew ran towards them, Randaal shouted, "We are here because we broke rules! We have the chance to be men of honor now! Do not let her take that from us! Today, we will obey the council and not break their rules!"

Olaf ran full tilt into Randaal, knocking him off balance, and Tiller grabbed to pull Thio away. The four of them rolled on the ground, thrashing together.

"This is mad!" Tiller shouted. "Don't let a crazy old gothi dictate a terrible mistake!"

"Shut up!" cried Lars. "You have no say in this!"

"But *I* do," shouted Sigmund earnestly. "Tiller is right! The whole idea is madness!"

"What is going on?" Kurt shrieked. "Why are they fighting?"

"We've found land, and a good settlement spot! What's this ruckus about?"

Dagsson must know nothing, Tiller realized.

"It's you who's old and crazy, Sig! The Council must be obeyed!" Lars had caught Thio as she lurched to her feet and held her fast. Pulling his sax from its scabbard, he pulled Thio's head back. "Get back, or I will do the sacrifice right here!"

"Sacrifice? FISHGIRL?" Kurt and Karl cried as one. The words hung in the air as intense light under the clouds flashed along the blade of Lars' knife. He kept it steady and tight.

Olaf faced him, determined to gain control.

"Sigmund's words bear weight, Lars." He kept his eyes fixed on the knife. "We should have a Thing. Take careful steps. Nothing rash. Let everyone have their say."

Taking careful steps had kept Lars from getting caught for years. He got a fresh grip on Thio and snarled. "You want to discuss this? You're right. There's no hurry. No promises, and in the end, likely, no changes, but have it if you must."

Olaf sweated in the cool afternoon air. "I'll serve as headman. To keep Randaal and Lars satisfied, tie up Fishgirl so she cannot run."

Lars jerked his head towards Tiller. "Tie him up as well. He is thick as thieves with her. We need to keep them separated."

———·———·———

The watchers on the hill stared, aghast. Whatever they were, the god-beings on the beach were horrifying. Knives held against human throats? The female... one of the god-men had beaten her! The others had fought until they drew blood. What creatures treated each other so?

"I cannot believe the Great Ones behave like this," one cried.

"Then what are they? Humans? They are nothing like us."

"It is almost night. We are all hungry and tired, but we must keep watching. We'll take turns. Pair up. Who goes first?"

They divided, and two of them silently crawled forward again. The smell of spring grass and cool earth filled their nostrils as they pressed close to the ground.

———·———·———

The Logic of Fear

Tiller was tied up and gagged, but his ears and eyes were uncovered. Lars' face had a look Tiller had never seen before, a sinister smile of pleasure as he tied Thio's wrists. Randaal took Thio to a tent, pushed her in, and fastened the tent-flaps.

Tiller pictured Thio standing in the tent, alone and devastated. *Everything she said was true. I trusted in reason and doubted her.* Bitter shame flooded his whole being. Perhaps it was not too late; perhaps the men would disagree, but now, he felt doubtful.

"Now then, Lars. Why don't you speak first?" Olaf wanted to seem neutral to all.

Lars, unsure who knew and who did not, addressed his remarks to the twins and Dagsson. "Let's begin with who we are, as a people. Our island of Íseland was unknown for eons, discovered only a few generations ago. News of Íseland's existence resounded from land to land, because before that, *no one had found new land as long as anyone could remember.*

"Then came the Great Settlement: four hundred and thirty-five men and their families arrived, most fleeing from the Nórsvegr lands. Why? Because Harald, once only a chieftain of Vestfoldia, had declared himself king of all the North Way. Harald stole property from the rightful owners, and demanded outrageous taxes from them. The families left their homes of the Nor'way to seek safety on our newly-discovered Íseland. There, they began a new country. Because of Harald, we formed as free men with no ruler. We are *the only country in the world in which no king can tell the people what to do.*"

Lars paused for the weight of his words to be absorbed. Their voyage, the men began to see, was not just theirs. It belonged to a people of legacy, of whom they were a part. Their chests puffed with pride.

"People continued to swarm to Íseland. By the time of our grandparents, all the land had been claimed. I remind you of what you already know because it frames why this voyage is so important. It is more than a matter of one man or one woman's life."

Lars reminded them again of the powerful king in Nórsvegr whose power so many feared. "Harald Fair-hair took land that belonged to others – and his son is the same, even determined to tell people what gods they can and cannot worship! He forces the Frankish beliefs down the throats of his people, by the sword, if necessary. He wants to force his ways even to the shores of our country, by blocking trade with our allies! Fair-hair's son knows of our famines. He does not care if we starve unless we accept his belief and his rule.

Lars swung his hand wide, indicating those who lived at home. "Thorvald, Thorgest, Thorstein, Thordunn...Why do so many name their children 'Thor' now? It is to show our allegiance to our old ways, to show that we have the right to choose who we worship! Every son and daughter bearing the name of 'Thor' is a walking, breathing refute to Harald Fairhair's domination of us. But naming children in honor of the Thunder-Striker has not been enough to protect them from hunger or from Harald's schemes. The council believes that we must do more. We must find ways to show the gods that we are faithful to the ancient roots of our people, to have their blessings again. To do that, the council has given us a critical task, to honor Odin and Thor and all the other gods, and to gain their favor the way our people did long, long ago, by giving them a human life. This voyage was in search

163

of land, but now that we have it, we will bless it with *our* beliefs, not Harald's, and the gods will rain favors upon us!"

Seeing faces glowing with the imagined honor, Tiller despaired. At the same time, the men who had not known began to grasp the full import of Lars' words.

"A human life…you mean *Fishgirl's* life? Or *Tiller's?*" Dagsson cried. "Not a *goat?*"

"The council said the gods would expect a great gift in return for leading us to a new land. That's why Fishgirl came on the voyage. She was chosen. She knew it! She volunteered."

"Then why has she never said a word about it?" Sigmund demanded. "Ask her about it!"

"Maybe she had a change of heart! It doesn't matter. We have a duty," Lars retorted.

"What do I care if she volunteered or not, or how they enticed her? Her death would be on *our* hands, not the council's! How can killing a strong, hardworking, good woman, a woman who has helped keep us alive, possibly bless this place? These old ways… I don't remember hearing of a human sacrifice for Íseland!"

Lars voice hushed, and he looked over his shoulder with fear, as if something was listening. "You know the stories from the Land-naming. Ingólf and his brother Hjörlief were the first to leave the Nor'way shores for Íseland. Ingólf honored Íseland's land-spirits, the *landvoettir*, in many ways, and he prospered. Hjörlief did not, and his slaves killed him."

"Honoring the land-spirits doesn't mean Ingólf shed someone's blood."

"Agreed," said Olaf carefully to Dagsson. "It's an appalling idea. But can we just ignore the council's direction? We must at least discuss and vote on whether to heed the council's wishes, distasteful

164

as they may be. Otherwise, we are choosing to *ignore the entire council.*" He said the last few words slowly, with great emphasis, looking around the circle of men.

"Why *can't* we just offer a goat or a sheep?" Kurt asked.

"Because the *council* said to offer a *human!*" Randaal shouted, exasperated. Why in Hel had Olaf agreed to a Thing? "It's not a spring planting, it's a fukking *new land!* We'll live like chiefs because of this one woman...who...was...*willing!*"

At that, everyone began to shout different opinions. Their voices became louder and more vehement.

"You fool! Odin and Thor don't care what is sacrificed. Blood is blood."

"It is *you* who's a fool for thinking that these 'gods' exist, or that if they do, that they've told you what they want! When have you actually seen Odin, or asked his thoughts?"

"I don't care if Odin exists or not. I care about getting the gold and land the council promised when we return. If Fishgirl or Tiller are part of the deal, so be it. She won't be the first person I've cut, but she'll be the last. I've spent enough time outlawed. I'm going to be a rich and honorable man after this."

"Have you all lost your minds? We're talking about Fishgirl and Tiller! If a god wants them hurt, I want nothing to do with that god - or anybody who believes in it!"

"A sacrifice of a woman carrying a child? That's vile!"

"We need Tiller to get the knörr back home! He's the only one that knows the water roads. We can do without Fishgirl!"

"Hurt Fishgirl, and Tiller will retaliate. We'll never get home. "

"We don't need Tiller. We could get back on our own."

"What about that infant she carries? Like a spring lamb!"

"…a newborn's *blót*! Think about it! A newborn for a new land, and it would keep her here to work for us."

Sigmund snorted in disgust. "Do you even *hear* yourselves? It is one thing to expose an infant not likely to survive. But kill a healthy child? What kind of monsters are you? You think she'd work for someone who killed her child?"

"The gods just want a human. What do they care, adult or child? She might be glad to be free of a squalling infant. Which would you choose, a kid you never saw, or your own life?"

"Give both the mother and child as one! Do you not see the reason of that, stupid goats?"

"Yes! Give Odin the girl *and* the seed growing in her!"

At that, Sigmund finally had enough. "Fishgirl's not a thrall! She's the fish girl, and according to the rich and powerful men of the council, a protected sacrifice to the gods. You have no right to speak filth about such an important person in our lives! Let's end this nonsense and get a settlement started, and then head for home!" He cried out in heartfelt anguish. "I wish we had a *druwid* here, or a *völur*! A truth-seer could tell us what is right or wrong to do! We are simple men! How can we decide between obeying the council and killing two good people, or ignoring the council and bringing their wrath and the gods' displeasure on us? It is too much!"

A murmur of assent went around. They knew they must make a decision, and the burden of that truth weighed heavily on them. Two sides formed, and the argument resumed with even bitterness as each group dug in for battle, raging and reasoning with each other.

"And if her babe is still-born? We'll have wasted months. Let's not gamble with chance!"

"Him *and* her *and* the babe, all of them! One clean sweep, get them all gone…."

166

"Have some backbone, boys! When was the last time you heard of a human sacrifice, anyway? Some king's death in the sagas hundreds of years ago? Did the councilmen risk their own skin on this trip? Their sons or daughters? Ignore what they commanded! Ekka was right. If we come back with land they will forgive us anything!"

Olaf played on their fears. "None of us is a truth-seer, and no one knows the ritual for finding new land. What if we *do* cross some ancient spirit-law of which we know nothing? Or what if there are land-spirits here, and we anger them and they curse us? We might never make it home to tell what we found!"

In the end, the forces that united the men were fear and exhaustion. Some were too afraid of the wrath of the gods and the council of *gothar* to stand against the rest of the crew. The other dissenters became a dwindling minority who yielded as their numbers diminished, too exhausted to argue further. The decision brought terrible distress. It also brought the small comfort of consensus, and with the matter settled, they went wearily to bed.

———·———·———

Tiller knew true despair. Bitter self-doubt tormented him. Had he really stayed quiet because of his faith in human instincts, or from a fear of standing up for something, of confronting the men? Was it his father's fear of taking responsibility, of taking a stand, infecting Tiller? The answer mattered little. Tiller loathed everything he was, everything he ever had been.

———·———·———

The crew slept late, exhausted. Olaf was first up, and went to release Thio.

"Why am I a prisoner?" she spat.

Olaf made his face sad. "I did my best to help. I'm sorry. They were unanimous."

Thio crumpled to her knees in anguish. Olaf knelt and put his arms around her.

"Such hard news, I know," he said. "How can such a horrible idea exist? Or be tolerated? They said it came from the highest levels of the council." Safe in his victory, Olaf was eager to console. "But why do you cry, Fishgirl? Lars said you'd been foreseen by a truth-seeker: an orphan daughter of an orphan woman, alone since childhood and longing to meet your parents with Hel. Poor girl! A hard destiny, but one to be proud of, and that you volunteered."

Orphan? What was he talking about? "What else did they say about me?"

"I was not privy to any of the commands," Olaf lied, "but I understand that your name was made known to the council during the summer trials. A woman with a burning desire to please the gods." He stared into Thio's eyes, sizing her up for any sign of refusal. "Don't worry, being with child doesn't matter. It needn't keep you from your stated goal. You were chosen by the gods. Now I know why you showed such strength on the ship. You truly are remarkable."

"Did the council tell anyone my real name?"

"Of course not! We were told to call you Fishgirl, of course!"

"The highest levels, you said. The whole council, or just some? Who are they?"

"I don't know. Ask Randaal, maybe, or Lars."

"As if either of them would ever tell me anything," Thio said. Inwardly, she remembered words overheard in the boathouse so long ago. *'The gods chose this fish girl'*, the headman's visitor had said. So that was what they meant. Was there actually a woman who had intended to be on this voyage? Where was she, the one whose destiny Thio would fulfill?

Olaf patted her gently. "I must ask a tremendous favor, Chosen One. We had no dinner last night, as you know. You have an important duty today, but it is time for *dagvberthr*. I need to ask you to cook for us, one last time. Our daybreak meal, please."

"How preposterous for you to ask! Why should I?"

"Fishgirl, this was forced on us." His voice choked. "Sigmund's son...his wife..."

Thio guessed wildly. "Sigmund's family are hostages? Poor man! May I talk to him?"

Olaf looked at her closely, and his face grew cold and hard. "Thanks to you, they'll be fine. Someone else can cook the breakfast if you won't."

Thio shifted quickly. "Olaf, if Sig's been threatened, you don't have to tell me." She smiled bravely, making her eyes soft. "Of course I will serve you a last meal. The gothi at the village gave me many important responsibilities, and I will fulfill them all. He said that, should we find land, on our first real morning ashore I must prepare a make-land feast for the crew, to be eaten at midday. You knew about that, of course?" She held her breath.

Olaf looked surprised. "No, he said nothing."

Thio matched Olaf's surprise. "Oh, yes, he was very specific. His wife made me practice it twice, what to serve and what to say over the food."

"Then something small to hold us for now? I'll alert them about the make-land feast."

As he walked away, Thio gazed across the beach at the crew beginning to gather in the late-morning light. Her eyes lingered on Karl, and an ache grew in her heart. "Oh, Karl! And Kurt…and Sig. I thought you were my friends."

Even as she said it, her mouth grew flat and bitter. Olaf said that all had voted unanimously for the sacrifice. So be it.

Preparations

Thio took porridge to where Tiller was guarded by Randaal. "Untie him so he can eat."

"He's going to be a dead man soon. Dead men don't need food."

Thio braced her shoulders to broaden the untruth she had told Olaf. "The gothi told me very clearly what to cook when we made land. He said each man had to eat. *He demanded it.* Part of the ceremony, he said. Olaf commands that I must do exactly as the headman instructed."

Randaal was suspicious, but Olaf nowhere in sight. "Tiller doesn't get untied, though. You feed him. Like a helpless baby." He guffawed and sauntered away.

Thio lifted the spoon to Tiller's lips and spoke quickly. "I'm done for. You?"

"Both of us," he said, teeth clenched. "They're building a post for the noose."

Thio twisted her head to look at the men. So that's what that thing was. She began to shake, an uncontrollable shivering.

"I'm to feed them at midday," she stuttered. "They've agreed to that. I'm going to do it, Tiller. You and I lost. They all voted. This is our only chance to survive."

He could not answer, sick at heart. Thio bit her lip. "I loathe to hurt the twins and Dagsson and Sig."

"I was so stupid, Thio. I'm so sorry. I could have tried to help you, and I didn't."

"We all wish we'd done things differently. You're human." As she spoke, Thio considered the long trip that brought her to Ólafsvík, to the gothi's house. What would she have done differently?

Abruptly, the shivering left her. A song of survival whispered inside, a half-remembered fierce melody, entrancing, familiar from a long-ago memory at the Althing.

"It's not over yet. Be certain you don't drink any of the barley beer." Tiller dutifully swallowed the last of the porridge, and Thio left as Randaal returned.

Building

The hammers pounded without ceasing though the morning. Randaal, bored of guard duty, moved Tiller to where the crew was building the hanging-post. Tiller's wrists were tied behind his back and his ankles roped, with a rag wrapped across his mouth to silence him.

Thio kept glancing at the cask of beer where it lay nearby, the one she had mixed and marked early in the voyage. What seemed like a lifetime ago, the old wise woman had given her the ergot and deadly herbs that swirled in the amber liquid. Would the taste of beer cover them well enough? She willed the sun to slow as it continued its relentless climb.

Fury and frustration alternated with helplessness. One instant she would think *by the gods, I will watch them burn and bleed even if it means my death too.* The next moment she was second-guessing herself. *Tiller was right. We'll be alone. Eventually, we'll die too. Why don't I just give in and let it happen? I chose this path of my own free will. Maybe it is destiny. Maybe I should just accept my fate.*

She started the bread late on purpose, put the pounded fish in the cooking pot late so that it would not be done on time, so that nothing would be in their stomachs to dilute the poisons.

At last the hammers ceased their pounding. The men put down their tools, wiped their brows, and looked guiltily, anywhere but at Thio.

———·———·———

When the only options are death or death,
one must choose well and carefully.

- Thjodhild Jorundsdöttir

———·———·———

172

Thio stood at the cooking fire, defiant. She shouted over to the men. "You are finished building? Who will do this terrible thing to me? Sigmund? Kurt? Karl? Dagsson?"

They stood shifting uneasily around the hanging post, looking at the ground.

Seeing their shame, Thio's chin went up, and the fierce melody flashed inside her. Tiller had been wrong. Now was the time for battle. No poison! If the gods had brought her to this moment, she would not take a coward's way out. She felt her spirit soar. *I am strong. I will fight like the warrior I have always known myself to be.* The strength within her, the feeling she had first felt on the ship, surged through her, powerful and certain. *If I lose, I will become a legend in their minds, a woman of surpassing strength.* Her mother and father might hear of it weeping with sorrow, but they would be filled with pride. Suddenly, Thio feared nothing.

$$\underline{\quad}\cdot\underline{\quad}\cdot\underline{\quad}$$

She did not wait to be called. Thio held her head proud and her shoulders straight, and walked like a queen to where the men stood by the hanging-post. Powerful understanding filled her. *These men are just simple human beings, driven by greed and fear that the council put into their heads. I am their Fishgirl. I am their balance. Some have lost their way, terribly, but none of them were born wanting to be evil. They know goodness and strength when they see it. They will see it in me. Perhaps it will help them find their own way back.*

"Give me the knife," she said. Her voice sounded far away, not her own. "I will put it in my breast myself. That way none of you has to bear the guilt, or," looking fearlessly at Randaal, "take the credit."

173

"Fishgirl, you know this is a thing that we must do," said Olaf. *So close. No tricks now.*

"No, Olaf. It is a thing you are *choosing* to do.

"We voted last night, again and again. All finally agreed. We are in consensus."

"All may have voted and agreed, but your council was not valid!" Thio's voice rang clear, filled with honesty and courage. "You voted without getting all the required testimony!"

They looked startled.

Thio was equally startled. Questioning their intent on legal grounds had not occurred to her, but the words had come with certainty from her lips.

We need no king. The law serves us as it leads us! Thio had heard the words at every summer's Althing, but they suddenly spoke to her in a way she had never appreciated until now, when her life hung on them. Begging and pleading would have fallen on deaf ears, but a true legal challenge would bear weight. She knew most of the men had buried their guilty conscience in the belief that their decision had been sanctified by legal process. It was the simplest of ideas, and it bloomed in Thio at the very instant it had a chance of working.

The perfection of it burst sweet through her whole being. The law would carry her to safety the way the knörr had carried them across an unknown ocean. Thio felt the strength of the very stones of the land flowing up into her, steadying her. All the little strengths she had built across the voyage suddenly bound together, and the wild song inside her soared to a crescendo. She was free to speak or free to die. The result no longer mattered. Failure did not frighten her. Thio was dimly aware that she had become a *berserker*, absolutely fearless in battle and absolutely committed to it. She would challenge them, and free herself, and somehow free Tiller, as well.

174

Truth upon truth blossomed in Thio. *They* need *me to do this. I will free them from the odious task they feel called to do. Free their souls of sin.* Yes, even Randaal. If she succeeded, these men and she would stand on this beach victorious together. The darkness would be gone, and a new beginning started. That melody…

It's the song of the Valkyries, Thio realized with delight. *I can actually hear them.* Their wild battle music rang with freedom and courage. Thio drew her gleaming weapon of words, and went to war.

___.___.___

Olaf started to object, but Thio swung her voice-sword, silencing him.

"When did you ask for *my* testimony? I was not allowed to speak at your Thing. I claim my right!"

Olaf tried to refuse her, but Sigmund cut him off. "She is right, Olaf. The defendant must be allowed to speak. We all know it. We just forgot it with the insanity of yesterday."

Seeing heads nodding in agreement, Olaf realized he had no choice. Better to seem agreeable, and remind them later why they had voted together.

"I'm sure the Althing council weighed this carefully, so I fear, Fishgirl, that your testimony will have no merit. But speak, if you feel you must," he relented.

"You cannot say that my testimony has no worth, Olaf. You know that intimidating a witness causes blood-debt that must be paid by your family."

Olaf blanched. It confirmed what Thio had suspected that morning, that it was Olaf who had been threatened in some way, not Sigmund. Tiller saw it too, and came to the same conclusion. No wonder Olaf had fought so hard for the verdict, prolonging the discussion until the exhausted men just wanted it to be over.

Thio drew on the startling words she had heard that morning from Olaf. "You call me your Fishgirl. I may have served you as such, but I am not the chosen, truth-seen Fishgirl for this voyage, an orphan daughter of an orphan daughter. My name is Thjodhild Jorundsdottir. I am the daughter of Jorund Atlisson and Thorbjorg, his wife. *I am no orphan.* My family has a farm, a good one. My mother is not an orphan, either. Her parents live with us. The gothi forced me on the ship. I was never supposed to be on this voyage."

——.——.——

All eyes were riveted on Thio. Even Randaal had been surprised into silence, and he waited, angry and impatient, to hear what else Thio would say. She knew she must walk a narrow, treacherous track between telling the truth and the whole truth.

"We always travel to the merchant-fair at the midsummer All-Thing courts, to sell wools from our farm. I went to the trials whenever I could." She nodded at Tiller. "His was one of the most exciting. He was outlawed at the regional Thing, and the Althing council was to review his case. Tiller's father had been a violent man. The law-arguers were already convinced of his guilt.

"When I went home, I told an older woman who works on our farm about the trials. *'Thorvaldsson?'* she asked, going pale. *'You are certain?'* She had never spoken of having children. Who would have guessed that Tiller was her son?"

Thio knew this news would be both wonderful and devastating to Tiller. She had hoped to tell him in a better way, not in this cobbled-together half-truth. "I am sorry I did not say something before," Thio said directly to Tiller. "It was a personal matter, and with no privacy on board, I kept putting it off."

Tiller burned with questions, but Thio could not afford to be distracted. She stared from one man to another. "She became terribly sick when she heard of Tiller's conviction. I feared she would die. That woman raised me, more than my own mother did. I promised the gods that if they give her health back, I would find Tiller before he sailed

177

and tell him that his mother lived, and loved him, and wished him well."

Love for a mother can touch even the most hardened men. Thio saw many swallowing. She had not counted on her words moving them so much.

"I had heard the trial rumors: that a ship was supposed to sail from Olaf's Bay, come spring. I left our farm, saying I was going to visit relatives, but upon reaching them, I said I had to deliver wools to a merchant we met at the Althing. I kept heading towards Ólafsvík, telling whatever lies I could, until I reached the settlement there.

"When I arrived, the headman's wife received me impatiently, as if she'd been expecting me. I thought perhaps she'd been waiting on a new house thrall. I did not want her to turn me away, so I said nothing. She put me to work immediately. But she would not let me leave the house. Even a thrall has freedoms, so that was odd, but I had already asked many questions about the outlaw-ship, and did not want to draw more draw attention to myself."

Thio paused for her words to sink in, then continued. "I learned she thought I was the fish girl sent for this voyage. I said nothing. It seemed harmless to let her think what she wanted. I planned to leave once I had delivered the message to Tiller."

Thio's words sounded like a *winter-saga*, much dramatized for entertainment, but far more than applause hung on the tale. "But I never did have a chance to speak with Tiller. When it was almost time for the ship to leave, I told the headman I was not the fish girl, and demanded to be allowed to leave their longhouse. He was horrified at my words. I didn't understand why at the time, of course."

The story gripped Thio as she relived the terrible moment when her good intentions turned into an inescapable trap. "The gothi argued with his wife. He wanted to search for the woman really intended for the voyage. His wife declared there was no time, that he could not jeopardize everything over me. The fight between them…" Thio shuddered, remembering the escalating fury. "He was not as strong-willed as she. In the end, he gave in, and would not look at me or speak to me. The next day they locked me in chains and I was carried from the longhouse and pushed onto the ship with you."

Thio stopped speaking. Her eyes, vivid with challenge, caught and held the men.

"So you were not supposed to be our Fishgirl at all," Ekka said slowly.

"No."

"And you never went to the council and volunteered. They forced you."

"Correct."

Bolli's voice rang out. "Did you tell the gothi you were with child?"

An unexpected gift, those words. Thio shot him a glance of thanks.

"I told his wife. I know it is taboo for a fish girl to be pregnant. She slapped me and said that I was a liar. When I tried to tell the headman, she sent me from the room. I had no choice. I was trapped. I was afraid to tell any of you on board. I just did the best I could."

Many of the men started to remember the many small kindnesses Thio had shown them on the ship. Their brave, hardworking Fishgirl! She had been betrayed by the headman and his wife. Each of them knew too well what it felt like to be trapped. A fierce longing to fight for Thio began to bubble inside.

When Thio finished her testimony, her strength left her as quickly as it had come. She forced herself to keep standing but trembled like a birch leaf in the wind.

Sigmund said bluntly, "That's it, then. I rescind my vote."

Olaf shrieked. "You can't rescind it! The vote-total has been spoken!"

Sigmund laughed easily, his big easy frame a counterpoint to Olaf's wiry anxiety. "You don't make the rules here, and we don't *really* have a gothi to serve as leader, now do we? Besides, even if we did, the law is the law. Her testimony changes everything."

Karl and Kurt stood together, as always. "We want to change our vote too. This is all different than we heard last night. You said she volunteered."

Thio was astonished at their innocence. What woman would willingly have boarded their ship as an intended sacrifice? For *any* reason? Still, that made two more with her.

"Me too. I change my vote as well." This came from Dagsson.

Randaal whirled, red-faced and angry. "You are such fools. Everything that was discussed last night—about displeasing the council and angering the gods—none of what she just said changes any of that. *She is the one the gods sent to us, even if the path was different than we thought.* It is not our place to reject their gift!"

The long argument of last night was on the verge of beginning again, or worse, a battle. Desperately, Thio launched her last arrow.

"The only reason you each are still alive is because of Tiller and me."

The words served their purpose. Once again, all eyes focused on Thio.

"I learned about this matter of sacrifice shortly before we left. It is the other reason I said nothing about not being the real Fishgirl. I am ashamed to admit it, but it was my intention to poison all of you to prevent you from killing me. I would have lived here, terribly alone, but alive. But Tiller helped me to see that that was a wrong thing to do."

180

"What did he say? Why didn't you do it? Why are you telling us?" Lars frowned.

Thio faced Lars and told the simple truth. "Tiller sees the world the way he is: logical and straightforward. He believed you would never actually vote to take our lives. He refused to help me do wrong to you. In the end, I realized I, too, could not ...*would* not... choose to do wrong either."

Now would be the moment. Thio finished calmly. "Tiller's life and mine are in your hands now. You are outlaw, but you are good men." It was a kinder description than some warranted, but Thio felt filled with generosity. "I have been a friend to you during the trip. I have done my best to take good care of you. With all my heart, I believe that most of you were pressured into the decision, and that on your own, would never put a knife to my throat. But if I must die, I want to do it with the truth told, the full truth spoken."

There. She had said the whole of it. Never in her life had Thio felt so deeply or stood so strongly. The truth had set her free to cast fear aside and open fully to whatever life would bring. She already knew that her brave words had shone light on others. Gratitude and peace filled her, and she smiled.

"Damn you! *Damn* you!" Randaal charged across the circle of men. He snatched Thio and pounded his closed fist on the side of her head. She dropped to the ground like a stone.

Tor's great form moved with surprising speed to pull Thio away from Randaal, and Sig with him. "No more, Randaal," said Sig. "Never again. Put your fists away."

Randaal snarled with fury. "She's lying, you fools! She's trying to trick you! Ekka! Ulf!"

Even some who had at first favored the council's plan felt shame. *The council made the mistake. Fishgirl's right.* They regrouped, this time in her defense.

"It's over, boys," said Dagsson in relief. "The vote is void."

Tor carried Thio like a child in his great arms, and laid her carefully on the ground. Men who had come to genuinely like Thio crowded around her, grateful she was safe, that they had not been forced into an action that now seemed so revolting. They placed awkward pats on her shoulders, her cheeks, her hands, her legs. They had fulfilled the oath. They had sworn to protect their Fishgirl, and they had.

———·———·———

Dazed and disoriented, Thio sensed touch. As her eyes opened, she saw a familiar face, shaggy, with streaks of gray in the beard and kind green eyes. Thio searched for a name to say, but her mind would not work.

Need to tell … something. Her thoughts swirled in fog. Something terribly important.

"No drink…" she whispered.

"You need a drink? Somebody get Fishgirl a bowl of broth!"

The voice sounded so far away. Whose voice?

"No…no…! No …no… drink beer…" The once-beautiful song in her ears was gone. A low wail had begun, an eerie screech of fear. Her head pounded terribly.

"Beer? You want the barley beer? Yes, there is some! I saw a cask near your cooking fire!" The bearded face shouted commands, and soon Thio felt a cup at her lips. She could taste the ergot. Spitting it away, she looked him in the eyes intently and croaked out "No! Poison…"

No, No…

Lines around the green eyes crinkled together and Thio's brain said *smiling*. Something covered her brow, a rough hand across her hair.

"Shhhh, Fishgirl. You said your peace, and you didna do anything bad to us, so stop whispering and worrying. All is well. We're done with that sacrifice nonsense. It's time for us to celebrate!" He smiled broadly, lifted the cup to his lips and drank deeply.

No no no no no nnnoo nooo no nononono no nooo no, she called. *no no no…* The words stuck in her throat, and she gagging, tried again. *No no noo no nn no…*

Thio could see Sigmund's throat swallowing, his lower lip pressed against the rippled curve of the horn-cup. When he stopped, he spat upon the ground. "That beer tastes awful. It is so stale. I can't wait until we get home and taste fresh."

He patted Thio's shoulder and stood up, walking away. The wail in her head dropped to a funeral dirge. She moved her lips, but only blackness came.

—·—·—

Dagsson picked up the cask, but Randaal jerked it away. "Give me that! I worked hardest today!"

"You worked hardest because you wanted to see her hang." But Dagsson let Randaal prance off with his prize, his lips pressed to the bung hole and beer running down his chin, wetting the front of his kyrtill.

Was that the cask, Tiller wondered, the one whose bung Thio pulled after they left land, dumped in the poisons, and marked? He shouted, but the gag made his words unintelligible.

Randaal carried the keg to those who had sided with him. "Here! You were loyal to the council. They'll learn how the others let them down. You will have the best farms here! Drink to your success! Before the night is over, we might still see the blood of these two blessing this land!" Randaal guzzled greedily again, and passed the cask to Olaf, who stood with his hand pressed against his heart. It ached as he thought about his son. He shook his head.

The rest drank, happy to have plentiful gulps instead of the doled-out portions that Fishgirl had had to give. They took turns holding the small barrel over their heads, swallowing quickly before the next man claimed it.

Still Tiller shouted, struggling to his knees. Randaal kicked him to the ground. "None for you, Tiller. You could have been one of us, but you made your choice with her. Karl, leave off nurse-maiding Fishgirl. Come take a draught."

Karl came over, his eyes wary. "This doesn't change anything." Taking the cask, he drank, and wiped his lips. "I'm going to give Tiller some, no matter what you say."

Randaal held the cask to Tiller's nose so he could smell it, and laughed, mocking. Tiller butted it with his head, and Randaal almost dropped it. He kicked Tiller with annoyance. "No cause for that, ass. You don't have to spill what's left."

Tiller jerked towards the keg, shouting into the gag, but Randaal pushed him off. "No, you had your chance."

The men sat, sagging and weary from work and worry. One or another would cast a furtive glance to where Tor had placed Thio on the grass. She still lay motionless.

"You know she ain't going to be any sacrifice?" Dagsson said to Randaal. "You know the time for that has passed, don't you? Sig's right. It's over. No threats about what you might do later. It is over. For good."

Randaal grunted, sullen. His eyes felt odd, and he rubbed at them.

"Here, man," said Dagsson, knowing how unpredictable and dangerous Randaal could be. "No hard feelings. Look at it up there. See how rich the grass is up that hill? Your crops will do well, with or without a maiden blessing."

The cask passed for another round. Finally, Olaf took a turn. He jerked his chin to where Tiller knelt exhausted in the sand. At the gesture, Dagsson went over, carrying the cask.

"Turn around, Tiller," said Dagsson, reaching to untie Tiller's wrists, "You've some hard feelings, no doubt. Sit with us while it all gets sorted out and mended. A cask between friends or foes can be a mending thing." He turned Tiller around, sliding his sax under the gag. "Time to speak your piece. You've been trying to say some angry words. We deserve it, I guess."

———·———·———

Tiller spit the cloth from his mouth. "*Poison! Poison is what I want to say!* She didn't tell me where it was, but I'm thinking it was in that cask! You must make yourselves throw it up, immediately!" he shouted.

Tiller's words came too late. Already, their vision had started to blur, and the hallucinations traced lines of confusion in their thoughts, while their arms and legs twitched and burned. Tiller turned, and Gierr was on him, death in his eyes.

———·———·———

The watchers had changed teams through the night and across the morning. Now those in front crawled back to the rest and they huddled together as the group pieced together what each pair had seen.

Last night, the creatures had tied up one of their own and put the female in a huge thing that seemed to be a shelter. The rest argued for a long time. They seemed to agree in the end. This morning, the female was let out of the shelter. The male was still tied. The others worked on something. The woman made food.

The watchers had so many questions. Why were those two bound? Why only one female among so many? Why did the she feed them after they mistreated her?

The final confusion had been relayed by the two who had just taken their turn watching. *"The ones who were building something stopped. The woman spoke to them. When she was finished, one hit her. Others stretched her out and put her on the ground. She appears to be dead. She is just lying there, but they don't seem concerned."*

What kind of beasts would leave her body lying there, and not tend to her spirit if she was hurt, to encourage it?

"They all put something to their mouths, one by one. It looks like an enormous egg of some kind. It is brown, and round. Again and again they held it up, reverencing it, touching their mouths to it. Perhaps it is a ceremony to make her well again? Just now, they untied the other male. He yelled something, and then they hit him, and he fell down too."

Then something even worse happened next, something utterly strange and horrible. They began to dance, but a terrible dance, swinging their arms wildly, kicking and staggering.

"They all tore at their clothing until they were half-naked. They shouted, and screamed, and fought together. The big one who hit the woman carried her into the midst of the fight, and shook her until she woke and began screaming. Please come. We cannot bear watching alone. It is appalling."

———·———·———

Thio came back to consciousness to realize that Randaal was shaking her and screaming at her. "Look around, you disrespectful whore! Look at what you've done!"

In the fog of her brain, again, that warning. *Do not drink…do not drink it.* Drink what? Dazed, Thio saw the men tearing off their clothing, stamping their feet and fighting with one another. In a flash, she realized.

"No, no! No, this was not supposed to happen! No!"

"Well it did happen! I'm going to make you pay… Treachery…" Randaal struggled to speak, his focus vague. He held Thio tightly with one hard fist, feeling with his other hand in his kyrtill where the ceremonial knife hung hidden along his thigh. "Ah, here it is…" He lost his balance and fell, wrenching Thio down with him.

Thio screamed for Tiller in desperation. Her eyes searched wildly among the men thrashing on the beach, wrestling and hitting and stabbing themselves and one another.

"Help! Help me, someone!" But no one looked up, or saw the long dark blade that Randaal held to the sky, howling maniacally.

188

"Here we go. What were the words?" Randaal grunted. He frowned at Thio. "Help me, Fishgirl. There were words... I can't remember."

"Tiller! Tiller!" She kicked and screamed, but Randaal tightened his grip.

Olaf. The name swam unsteadily through Randaal's mind. Who was Olaf? An image of the boathouse and the councilman...

Randaal swung his head like a bear, clumsy, his motions large. "Olaf! My hands are burning! What are the words? Let's kill her and it will all be over! Can you help me?" His voice was plaintive, confused. "What are the words?"

Olaf lumbered towards the sound of his name, clawing at his clothes.

Randaal's head jerked from side to side. Something squirmed in his hand. He looked down, saw Thio in his grasp. *How did she get there?* A memory of anger kinked though the haze. *Oh, yes. The bitch. She dies, and we live. The councilman said so.*

"You're going to go to Hel!" Waving the knife, he shouted incoherently at the sky and sea, and then stabbed downward at Thio. Screaming, she twisted, and the blade missed.

"Karl, help me! Someone! Kurt! Tor! Dagsson? Someone, help! Tiller...Tiller!"

Karl did not hear Thio. He drooled as he watched Tor and Mitla fighting, his fingers entwined in his own pale hair, tearing it from his head.

Thio's voice...she's afraid...where is she?

Gierr had cut Tiller, but the gash was not deep. Tiller fought to get the knife from Gierr. Behind them, Ekka staggered up and tripped, and the three men tangled together, knives swinging. Tiller could taste blood in his mouth, gushing from someone's wound.

"Tiller! Tiller, help!"

Where was she? Looking frantically, he saw Thio struggling as Randaal groped for a firmer grip, holding the knife aloft again. Tiller ran, leaping as Randaal's powerful forearm drove the knife down again.

This time it sliced deep into Thio's arm. She saw the surprising gush of blood, then pain came and she cried out, twisting against Randaal's grasp, her feet kicking and fingers clawing.

———·———·———

Tiller slammed his body into Randaal and Thio. The three of them fell together at the water's edge, wrestling in the waves running onto the beach. Thio scrambled away and seized a rock as Randaal and Tiller churned over and around each other. She lifted it and swung down hard, and felt a sickening crack of stone breaking bone. Tiller still gripped Randaal's throat, but his body had gone limp. Red blood flowed into the tiny laplets of water at Randaal's shoulders.

Prostrate, wet, and stunned, Thio and Tiller gasped for breath.

Tiller pulled himself to his feet. "We need to get you off this beach." He put his arms under Thio's, helped her to stand. He bent to her belly and lifted Thio over his shoulder as he ran to a tent and closed the tent flap behind them. Casting about wildly, Tiller found a linen undershirt, ripped it, and wrapped a bandage around where the red ran from her arm. He laid Thio down and piled her with furs and wools, hiding her. He tied a rag around a cut on his own thigh as well. Minor, nothing to worry about.

Leaving the tent, Tiller ran to the men, but the blows were too many and their minds too sick. One by one they fell, their knives stabbing into the air, into each other, into themselves. The beach was strewn with the wreckage of bloody legs and slashed arms, gashed faces and broken jaws dripping saliva and blood, hair torn out, muscle hanging in hideous strips, the screaming of pain, of wrenching, writhing, gutted carnage.

He went to the nearest pile of twitching flesh. It was Tor. Tiller knelt and put his arm around the massive shoulders as Tor's life left. Bolli lay beside Tor, drenched with blood, his leg jerking, and his guts spilling in an oozing, reeking tangle.

Men groaned and died everywhere, and Tiller could do nothing to save them. Voices that had laughed and cursed and argued and sang aboard the knörr cried out in spasms of agony. As tears began to flow from his eyes, Tiller lifted his face to the sky and cursed the gods, anguish in his throat.

———·———·———

His father's voice sounded in Tiller's head. *You should have stood up to Randaal. You should have listened to Thio, confronted Olaf.* The voice grew harsh, the eyes reddened and bulged. Tiller passed a hand across his eyes, discouraged. His father's slurring censures mixed with the incoherent gasps of the dying men. *You should have taken responsibility for this before it became a disaster.* This from a man who refused to ever be accountable for his own actions. *You think it was I who was weak? That I taught it to you? You're weak, you've always been weak. Our line is cursed, boy. You came out here wanting to purge the parts of yourself that are like your father? You wanted to kill the weak Tiller? You gutless coward. You* are *me.*

———·———·———

191

Tiller went from man to man, checking each one. Most were already dead. The rest, their eyes glazed with battle frenzy, were unaware that death was taking them away from this lonely place. A few lay senseless and staring, but still breathing. There was hope, maybe, for them.

A movement caught his eye, and Tiller looked up to see Thio hip-deep in the surf, walking straight out to sea.

———·———·———

Thio's arms hung at her side as she moved into the water like one already dead. She grasped the ceremonial knife in her hand. In a step or two, she would fall. She would not fight the waves at all. A heartbeat in the cold water and she would be gone.

Tiller dashed towards Thio, but she fell as he ran. Splashing through the waves, he reached down, felt frantically, touched something and grasped it, but the wave caught him. They rolled in the deep surf, Tiller holding tightly to some part of Thio. As the chilly wave pulled back, he found his feet and dragged her back onto the beach.

"Thio! Thio, look at me!" Grabbing her head, Tiller turned Thio's face to him. She choked and water came from her mouth. He pressed on her chest desperately, turned her over and pressed again. More water came, and she gulped and breathed.

Her eyes opened. As they crossed Tiller's gaze, something was sickeningly wrong. Thio was alive, but she was gone. Only emptiness was left.

———·———·———

192

Unhinged

Thio could tell that her mind was not working properly, but she could not fix it. All that she was spun in a sickening whirlpool of blood and poison. She tried to tell Tiller, to ask for help, but the words came disjointed, and perhaps were never even said aloud.

"no *no no* FI sHg gir rl sn *poison* no non*ono no* **FisHGir** l No drink!! NO!!! *sick bleeding cutting* I killed them *spoi pois **killed*** pois*on* **Ikilled**lilled *pois posionne sick sick eye Sig*mmSig eye *green e*ye blood sand san d on ey eye*No NO NO* CUT no please nocheek cut *blood* sand in it eye on sand green eye S*mund dead? Sigmund dead? Sigmund dead! No No No* not fish girl sick sick*sic k* k s not Fishgirl sick*sic k* k sick no dri*n*K NO no eye *bleeding eye sand* no no no..."

———·———·———

"Thio, give me the knife." Tiller pulled it from her rigid fingers and jammed it into his saxe sheath. He carried Thio to where dried grass stood thick outside the tents. "I need to take off your wet clothing." Did she hear? She sat soaking wet, those broken eyes drifting.

Tiller stripped himself to the skin and took off Thio's ship-trousers. "Here, lift your arms." She followed directions. Dropping the sodden kyrtill on the ground, he lifted Thio into the tent and piled sleeping sacks like a nest.

She lay like a child, naked and shivering in the furs but absolutely still, staring without blinking at the tent roof. Outside, the embers glowed in the fire. Tiller put water in the small cauldron, and when it steamed, carried it to Thio. He blocked the thought of the men on the beach for the time. Taking care of Thio was his entire focus. When the blood was washed and he had cleaned the sickness from her, Tiller wrapped her again in the húthfat. He watched Thio's face for a moment. She had not spoken the entire time he bathed her. Sometimes those destroyed eyes slid over his, without recognition, interest or even modesty.

"It's time to sleep, Thio." She closed her eyes and lay rigid. Leaving the tent, Tiller braced himself for the horror ahead.

———·———·———

Humped forms twisted across the cove. Their nakedness shamefully underscored the devastation, with discarded clothing everywhere. Kyrtills, trousers, under-tunics, and even shoes had been torn off and thrown aside when the ergot burned within.

Olaf, Karl and Kurt still lived. Tiller could hear a heartbeat when he laid his head against each chest. Straightening their arms and legs, he rinsed their wounds with sea water and bandaged them as best he could using scraps cut from the clothing littering the beach. Tiller fetched their sleeping sacks and dragged them above the high tide line, and wrapped each man in tightly. If they survived the night, the furs would keep them warm.

The rest would have to burn.

There was no time for the mounting waves of anger Tiller felt for himself. Funeral rites needed to begin as quickly as possible. He needed a ship of stone.

———·———·———

The stone ship would carry each man's spirit to its afterlife home. If it was built with respect and honor and filled with things to help them there, the spirits of the dead would not linger. A dead person seen again – a *revenant* – Tiller winced at the idea. Honorable treatment gave revenants no reason to come back.

The gifts could be anything a person had used in life. For farmers, a plow, and seeds, and baskets to collect crops. To a skin-stitcher, fine skins and sharp new needles, and threads. Healers were offered a mortar, pestle, and spices. If lack of offerings kept the spirit from going to the afterlife, it might suffer, and could cause humans to suffer as well, with famine or sickness, or loss of those they loved. No matter what had happened between him and the other men, Tiller knew it was critical to help each one of them cross successfully over to Hel's care in Niflheim.

But their ship held survival supplies, and Thio and he would need them all. Tiller pictured an entire crew of returning revenants. As he combed the beach for stones, he thought frantically of how to outfit so many spirits, and still keep what they needed for themselves.

Reverence

Sigmund's ship had to be first. He had been the most-liked, most respected man aboard. In the discussion about the sacrifice, he had spoken of their country's traditions, the importance of ensuring their future safety, but always with respect for Thio. It took a quarter-mark to find enough stones to surround Sig, matched closely in size and shape.

195

A hoe to dig in the stones…one lay about somewhere. Ah, there, where Gierr had tested it against the grass turf. Soon the rocks had been stacked and dug in, forming a shape like the outline of a small ship. Another quarter-mark passed, and Tiller had enough driftwood and debris to make a fire.

Dragging Sigmund across the beach cost Tiller one grueling step after another. Exhausted, he sank down to rest and realized in dismay that he was leaning on Sigmund's body.

It was all Tiller could do to maneuver Sig's large frame onto the woodpile. At last, the body was ready. What should his funeral gifts be?

—·—·—

That knife, for certain. The beauty of its workmanship made it a knife for a leader. It had been destined for a strong woman, and in the end, she had triumphed over it. Tiller laid the knife ceremoniously across Sigmund's chest, wrapping the big man's fingers around the handle.

Sig's húthfat had good thick fur. Reluctantly, Tiller put it on the pile to burn, and Sigmund's shield as well. No one loved a game more than Sigmund, and his shield had often served as the table for knucklebone. A dried apple, his drinking cup, and a bit of smoked beef. With that, Sig was ready for his final *vik*.

Tiller carried a stick from the cooking-fire to light the dried sticks. He breathed deeply as the smoke began to rise on the near-dusk air. Sigmund was crossing over, and Tiller bid him a respectful goodbye. He spoke aloud to the form on the fire his remembrances of Sig's booming laughter, his fairness, his kindness to Thio. The words may

196

have helped Sig's spirit to cross, but watching Sigmund's body burn only deepened Tiller's desolation.

Seeing Things

What was that?

Tiller whirled. Did something just move on he opposite hill? It had felt odd, not like an animal's movement.

He looked intently but saw nothing else.

It must have been exhaustion and worry, he decided. The utter nightmare of the day had taken every scrap of energy. He shrugged. It was nothing.

Still…wait. Again, just a flick that caught at the edge of his vision. What *was* it?

———·———·———

The beings on the beach seemed less and less like gods, but less and less human as well. They had worked. They had talked. They had eaten. Humans did those things.

Beyond that, they seemed neither human nor animal. Creatures of fur and feather did not hurt their own, and these beings had done nothing but hurt each other. With the frightening dance over, only the once-tied man seemed alive. Why was he dragging stones and sticks? Why did he push the stones into the soil? Now he was moving one of the bodies. He said words, made signs.

Soon the pile of branches was burning. To their dismay, the once-tied man burned the body in the flames, but the movements had seemed kind and respectful. Was it a death-rite, an honoring? But why would one treated so badly give honor to those who did the hurting?

The smoke made the same dark-writhing shape they had seen in the sky days before. The People's eyes turned to one another in horror. Had they burned one of their kind then as well?

They debated what to do. The fact that the once-tied had shown respect complicated everything.

———·———·———

"Their faces when they touched foot to ground showed jubilation. Why?

"Where did they come from? Will it be just these few, or will others come as well?"

"What would such creatures do to us if they treat their own so badly?"

They mulled over this troubling thought. No one offered any other answer, so the snow-on-hair concluded the talk. "We are agreed about tomorrow, then?"

Heads nodded. It had been unanimous. Though fearful, they would take action.

———·———·———

Thio's thoughts still swirled in the sickening maelstrom. Somewhere deep inside, she fought to escape but could not.

no not Fishgirl **no** *no* no *cut c* Sigmunds*isigm*und's*eye*on my fault *MY* FAULT *my* fault the sand*sigmund* eye *drink*ing thep*pppoison***smiling at me hey** girl no poison *no drink!!!!* **will be well fish**girl no be knife cut cut *cu*t all dead *cu cut bl*eed *poisonedpoisoned t*hem sig sig sig no no drink no more no Sig no more no no no more Fishgirl no more Fishgirl no more Fishgirl no no nomorefishgir*lnonon*ono nonon *no more fish girl* nononono no more fish girl no never *never... ...*

———·———·———

Night came, and Tiller could no longer see well enough to do any more work. He wearily carried his sleeping sack into Thio's tent. She still lay as he had left her, but her eyes were open, staring steadily at the tent roof. She had not touched the broth in her *sup* bowl.

"Here, drink this." He held the bowl to her lips but she did not sip, her eyes still fixed on the ceiling. "Rest, then, Thio." He straightened her blankets again.

Picturing the dead on the beach, Tiller tied the tent flap more tightly. *Revenants.* He shuddered, and fell instantly asleep.

———·———·———

Tiller woke to Thio picking at her covers. It was almost dawn anyway. Time to get to work. He pulled Thio to her feet and took her outside where they had dug the pit for waste. Something automatic in her took over, and she bent down. In a moment, she stood again. As

Tiller pulled up her trousers, she gazed briefly as if to ask *who are you? What are you doing?* before her eyes drifted away again.

"It feels as if it might be warmer today, Thio. Will you eat something?"

After a long moment, her head moved. Was that a nod? He took it as improvement. More would follow, hopefully. "I'll make some food after I check…well, I need to check the beach." Right now, to see about Olaf and the twins was of utmost importance.

———·———·———

The once-tied man brought the pale woman out of the tent and took care of her. He went to where he burned the body the night before, and touched the bits of ash gently. Then he went to the three he had covered in furs on the beach, and bent his head close to the chest of each one. He put his hand on each of their foreheads, looked towards the sky, said some words, and covered them again.

The hill-watchers chewed strips of raw meat in silence.

That one did not seem to have the killing instincts of the rest, but he might still be dangerous. They would wait a little longer before moving in.

———·———·———

The breeze fanned the last embers inside Sigmund's stone ship. The fire had done its work. Everything had fallen to ash, and he was gone. Sigmund would rest in peace, Tiller knew, because he had been treated with honor.

On the beach under the covering of furs, Olaf breathed steadily, but did not respond. "I'm going to get you and the twins into a tent later today, Olaf," Tiller said to him. He spoke encouragement to the twins as well, but despair dragged heavily at him.

"Oh, Thio," he whispered, "I should have figured a way to prevent this. We are exactly where I feared. We are so alone. I promised to get you back home. How can I do that now?"

This expedition had been costly, with plenty of opposition about sending a group of outlaws to sea aboard a well-equipped knörr. The sun would likely cross the sky more than a thousand times before another ship set off. Even if another ship came, even if they found this land, what were the chances of Tiller and Thio being seen in the long tangle of stony coastline?

Or there might never be another ship. In a matter of days, the exultation of finding land had changed into a nightmare of hard, lonely years ahead.

So be it. Tiller straightened his shoulders. They were here, they were alive, and he needed to keep it that way. They had tools and supplies. Every day they would need to work to survive. What had he told Thio, early on the ship? *Focus on the task at hand.* Today, the task would be the grueling work of building the rest of the stone ships and setting funeral fires. Preparing food for Thio and himself came first, though. How long since her fragrant wheat loaves had filled their mouths? One day? Two?

Tiller poured boiling saltwater into the cooking pot in which oat kernels had been soaking and boiled them. He poured the porridge into a wooden bowl, added honey, and blew to cool it.

Thio did not move to take the bowl. He lifted the spoon to her lips, and Thio dutifully opened her mouth, took in the porridge, chewed mechanically, swallowed, and opened her mouth again. After a few bites, she turned her face away and would take no more.

Should he talk to her, tell her what was happening? Would that be better for her, or worse? Honesty was more difficult, but Tiller decided he would not hide the truth from her. Thio deserved to know the dead men were being treated properly. To see some good, any good, in the middle of all that had gone wrong might help. He led her to the stone ship, where a small group of rocks and trees offered a feeling of shelter. Chickens pecked the ground nearby.

"You'll be comfortable here, Thio. Watch the chickens." Tiller directed her gaze away from the grotesque bodies on the beach. She sat dutifully. "I am going to work today to build crossing-over fires, and give gifts to the men. Stay here where I can see you."

Nothing. With a gentle touch, he turned her face to the chickens. She considered the hens without interest, and stared impassively.

———·———·———

As piles of stones mounted, Tiller wondered when he had taken on his father's odious habit of always needing someone to blame. *Thorvald, you never took responsibility for anything. I, though, blame myself for everything. It is just as wrong to do that. All of us -- the crew, you, Thio, the council – we all had a hand in bringing us to this. Dwelling on who and how never fixes anything.* Shaming himself was

202

a luxury he could not afford, when every scrap of energy would be needed for the funerals and to care for Thio, Olaf, and the twins.

Despite his intentions, Tiller's thoughts kept turning to thoughts of blame. As he pried stone after heavy stone from the ground, truths unfolded slowly in his mind. Blaming others had kept Thorvald from ever seeing what was wrong in himself and from fixing it. Blame divided people: *you versus me, them against us,* drawing a line of conflict instead of resolution, whether it be between father and son, between Randaal and Thio, between one half of the crew and another. Blame was a divisive weapon of destruction. *What an ugly, useless thing blame is,* Tiller realized. *And yet, so hard to avoid when one has been trained to it.*

As Tiller sank the hoe against another stone to loosen it, his thoughts drifted to what people accomplished when they worked together instead of in conflict. *A crew pulling on oars...a shipbuilder teaching apprentices how the oak planks were to be steamed and shaped.* Common cause, common effort, made almost everything possible.

Ah, another stone came loose.

His father's voice sounded again through Tiller's effort. *Look how clever you are, with your big ideas.* His father's jaw jutting in anger, rising, looking for a fight. This time Tiller did not feel the shame and rejection, the usual seething resentment. There was only weariness, only the desire to let go of a competition he had never started, had never wanted.

I'm not so clever, Da. Look where I am, alone here on this beach. No need to mock me anymore. From now on, whatever happens will be the direct result of my actions. No one to blame then but myself, for certain, eh?

He saw blame for what it was, today, but still there would be no forgiving of himself or his father, not yet. Too much wrong had been done. But across hours of working, with only the sound of the waves to keep him company, Tiller felt something in himself shift from dwelling on what had gone so terribly wrong, and why, to considering what might be done, and how.

He noted the change in himself almost as if he sensed a critical change in the wind. Tiller had grown to manhood years ago, but stone by stone on the forsaken beach, he sensed with some astonishment the stepping-across of a threshold of importance, a path towards being a better person, a stronger man.

He lifted yet another stone, carried it, and heaved it onto the pile. His father's voice had finally ceased. With relief, Tiller heard other words sounding in his thoughts.

All that you regret is of yesterday. Forget it. All that you fear is of tomorrow. Let it go. Do as well as you can in this instant, and there will be less to fear tomorrow, less to regret when today becomes yesterday. Do what needs to be done now, as well as you are able. That is all that matters in life.

Another truth struck Tiller as soon as the words had sounded in him, the most significant truth of all. Blaming divided people – and blaming himself had divided Tiller from others, had given him the means and the misery of being always alone.

He spoke again to his dead father. "You blamed me for everything you could, Thorvald, so I blame myself…but it's just another bad teaching. Blame is wrong, no matter when or where or how or why it's done. It's just *wrong*. Now that I see so, I intend to change. And before your voice mocks me, saying that that will never work, hear this first: I understand that changing a lifelong habit will take years of practice. I'll just take it day by day."

Saying this, Tiller felt inexplicably comforted. Something deep in him felt as if it had shifted, ever so slightly, but significantly.

He considered the pile of stones. Carried one by one, they had grown into what looked like enough to build the necessary stone ships. It was time to start the task of gathering firewood. Tiller checked the height of the late-morning sun. The eighths were passing too quickly. Foxes in Íseland would be sniffing by now. Were there any here? The revenants would haunt him forever if he let foxes get to their bodies.

Tiller spoke aloud. This time he did not know to whom he was talking, so he spoke to the air around him. "So ironic and sad, isn't it? They wanted to sacrifice Thio to make this land prosperous and fertile. Instead, *their* souls will bless us, if they cross over successfully."

All of the funeral fires would have to take place today, even if that seemed an impossible goal. What was needed was less thinking, and more gathering of wood.

———·———·———

Thio stared at the chickens without seeing them. The nauseating images came without ceasing, one after the other, and she fought to breathe.

What had happened? Where was she? She knew she had been saying something, had felt brave. Randaal grabbed her again, and the sensation of falling, and waking to the horror of seeing Sigmund lying on the sand near her, his eye dangling from the socket, his face a mutilated mess. The horror on the beach. Randaal again. *Randaal cut me?* Her arm hurt. *No Randaal, NO! poisoned* her fault, all her fault *Sigmund eye on sand no no non o Ekka dead? No Tor, no no not Tor no no* all her fault *no no no no.*

The morning was mild but damp. The sound of chickens. What was the word? Cluck. Cluck Cluck. She could see the man *what is his name Jadar no not that* dragging first stones and then firewood. *he did not listen did not listen no no pppoison all de*ad fun*eral ston*es *sigmund eye on sand blood breathe breathe breathe breathe*

Tiller came over when the sun was half-high. *Eat now? oatcake no beer no drink no NO!!! No drink!* "It's broth, Thio, not beer." good *no poison no drink!*

"That's good. Just a little more, you must be thirsty." chew s*o tired* my fault oh *Sigmund so sorry so very tired*

Tiller put his arms around Thio. "It's good to cry. You need to cry. It will help you get better. Everything will be well." *No no Sigmund said everything all well drank poison killed him.*

Thio touched her arm gingerly, her eyes going to Tiller's like those of a child, confused, hurt, and wondering. *Randaal cut me?* The images from the beach swirled *going to be sick again*

The oatcake came back up, along with the broth Thio had swallowed. *So tired so tired poisoned them sorrso sorryso tired sorry tired sorr ry tire stired so rry so rry so sorry so sorry*

———·———·———

As the mound of firewood grew, Tiller looked again and again at the stone pile. How to arrange them? With Sig's spirit gone over, ten bodies still remained. What symmetry would please them? One big ship, with all the men lined up in rowing order? But what about the two men killed at sea, Hyulf and Bergr? Pattern after pattern came and went from Tiller's mind as he gathered all the firewood he could find, from the hills and the trees to the high-water mark and along the beach. He was at the farthest end of the cove when he saw the things in the water.

———·———·———

Ah, a good large branch, the largest of the day, long and thick and weathered to a dry silver color. Near it was another, one to pull in each hand. These two would be the last ones.

As Tiller stooped for the second branch, something in the sea caught his eye. He squinted, trying to make out what it might be. There it was again. Something was moving far out in the waves, well beyond the breakers at a distance to the west, glittering.

Whatever it was could not be clearly seen. Likely some kind of large fish were moving among the waves; whales, maybe, or dolphins, or sharks. Seeing a school of fish was always a good omen. Tiller kept walking and pulling the branches. A little later he glanced back. The sparkling motions were still visible.

Tiller stopped walking and frowned. Something was wrong. Sharks always cut cleanly through the water, their fins straight and steady. Dolphins leaped, with some arcs higher and some longer, a fluid dancing with the waves. Giant whale-fishes would surface and blow, then dive deep again in one smooth, slow motion.

These strange fish moved differently than all those kinds. They rocked slightly from side to side, staying at the surface of the water, level with the ocean swells. Was it a new kind of fish, native to this land? Tiller's interest grew as the bright motions drew slowly closer. The fish were swimming faster than he was walking. Soon they might be close enough for him to see them.

By the time he was almost to the woodpile, the distance between him and the fish had closed significantly. Tiller, studying them, saw something that could not be, something that was impossible. His heart began to thunder in his chest. What he had thought might be shark fins were men…and they were riding on the backs of giant fish.

Tiller could clearly see faces, and arms, and part of the beasts on which they rode. As they glided effortlessly, the men moved their arms, steering their fish. Tiller counted several of them, perhaps a dozen. It was so utterly astonishing that Tiller forgot where he was, forgot what he was doing, and gaped openmouthed.

A group of men, commanding fish and riding them on the ocean swells, and looking at Tiller, were coming straight towards where Tiller stood.

———·———·———

Like a fool, his mouth still hanging open, Tiller dropped the branch. He put his hand to his mouth in alarm, and then, not knowing why he did it, raised his hand.

The fish-riders stopped moving. They looked at one another.

Slowly, one of them lifted a hand as well. Tiller and the fish-rider stared at each other.

———·———·———

What he was seeing could not be real, but there they were. *What kind of man rides a fish?* And *how?* What were they? *Who* were they?

End-of-the-world guardians? People from Hel, coming to collect the souls of the dead? Their clothing was dark, almost all black. Their hair was black. *Blood of the gods, were these the spirits of the men on the beach?* Were these what revenants looked like?

Suddenly Tiller remembered Thio, alone and a good distance away. Should he run to Thio, or go the other way to keep them away from her? But that would leave her alone. Spirit of Thor, could things get any worse?

The revenants drew level with him across the water and stopped. Still, he stared at them, and they at him. Tiller did not know what to do. What if Thio came over, if they saw her? Would the revenants kill her? Randaal's spirit certainly would, he knew. Tiller looked at them closely. Which one was which?

Stay calm, he told himself.

Tiller squared his shoulders. "I am building your stone ship," he called, with no small amount of fear in his voice.

The revenants did not reply and did not move.

"I helped Sigmund cross over last night. Your fires will burn soon. Please, give me a little more time."

Still not a sound in reply. Could a revenant speak? Perhaps not. Tiller tried again.

"I give you my word I will honor you. Whether you liked me or not, you know I can be trusted. I've never broken my word."

Tiller picked up the branches, and began walking again, grim and determined, his eyes on the fish-riders. The revenants urged their fishes to stay near him. Together, they moved along the beach.

Revenants. Everyone had heard tales since childhood, but who had actually seen one? Did a revenant even have a face? Apparently so.

Gods, what a thing to see. What did revenants actually do when they caused bad luck of all kinds? Would they eat him and Thio? Perhaps the revenants would take his body and Thio's, and walk the earth wearing their skins. Tiller wished he had not thought of that dreadful idea.

Tiller's skin crawled. For all the stories of glimpsing revenants on dark roadways or around the corners of cattle barns, he could not remember one person describing exactly what happened. Did they normally wave in greeting? Had anyone ever described them riding on fishes? No, but the storytellers had never been this far at sea. If these beings *were* revenants of the men on the beach, would they see the work he was doing on the stone ship and appreciate it?

Would it be enough?

Thio had sacrificed her deepest self in doing battle with them. Tiller pictured the revenants getting off their fishes and surrounding Thio and him. As he did, the perfect design came to Tiller of the pattern the stone-ship must take. It was a beautiful, balanced design. In that, perhaps, lay their safety.

Dragging the branches along the beach towards the pile, with the dark creatures gliding beside him in the water, Tiller envisioned a second, larger stone ship with Sig's in the center: a ship within a ship, the crew around Sig in death as they so often were on the knörr. It was simple and strong, a gracious tribute. The design was so good that it gave Tiller hope. It would show respect, perhaps enough to let the revenants be at peace with their deaths.

Tiller remembered the words of a *druid-vitki,* one of those known for seeing mysterious truths: *"When reverent, and deeply connected to something good which can be felt but not explained, we are at peace,"* she said.

Yes, Tiller thought. The desire to do well for them surged within him and overshadowed his concern. He gestured respectfully at the revenants. "This ship will do you great honor!"

His words did not seem to have the desired effect. The revenants stopped their fishes again. Their heads turned quickly to one another and they appeared to be talking together.

That did not seem like something that ghosts would do.

——·——·——

"I think he said something to us."

"He sounds odd. Not right in his head."

"He is on a beach with a tribe of corpses. Who would *be right in their head?"*

"Was that some kind of challenge he just made?"

They considered the idea.

"We should not have let him see us. Bad will come of this." That was Iluq, always cautious. *"Change the plan. We should just stay here in the water and watch him."*

———.———.———

The revenants hovered just beyond the breakers. Tiller could hear their voices. *So revenants did talk, at least to each other. What did revenants discuss?*

Curiosity warred with a desperate need to work quickly. How much time did he have? Would they wait until he was finished and the fires were burning before they made judgment? Would they leave the fish? Float to land? Or could their fish crawl onto the beach?

Thio was asleep in her blankets, thank goodness. She was not moving and not easily seen among the grasses. He dragged stones to where they would be needed, sweating in the chilly air.

The fish-riders' hands rested quietly as they held their sea-horses still. From time to time Tiller called to them. "I'm working as fast as I can! Please let me finish!"

They stayed, unmoving, as the sun dropped from midday. Tiller worked feverishly. At some point he realized that no matter how good his intentions, he would have been too overwhelmed to actually do all the men's fires in a single day, too utterly exhausted, had it not been for the revenants. There truly was a silver lining, as legends said, to most clouds.

As Tiller dragged the last stone to the burn area, a shadow fell across him.

———·———·———

Tiller looked up, ready to jump from his skin, only to see Thio standing beside him.

"Are you all right, Thio?"

She said nothing. Had she noticed the fish-riders in the water? He glanced at them constantly as he worked. They never moved, hovering just outside the surf.

"It's time to start moving the bodies," Tiller murmured. "Stay very close to me."

Thio looked awkwardly away from the corpses, but Tiller had laid them out properly, not the contorted positions in which they died, and had covered each with cloth.

He pulled Gierr onto an improvised sledge, and dragged the body to its place. Thio stood silently alongside as he wrestled Gierr into place. Tiller could hear her too-quick breathing.

"Look away, Thio," he said. "Look at the hills over there. We'll explore them tomorrow." *Look away from the sea, Thio.*

———·———·———

"He's still at it."

"Yes. A hard worker. Determined. Like you, Iluq. Does that mean like you, he is good?"

"Hard work proves nothing. We do not know his reasons. He may simply be mad."

Snow-On-Hair frowned. The pale being had straightened the bodies and covered their nakedness. He was clearly building another of the strange funeral structures. She frowned more deeply. Funeral rites were something humans did. He seemed to be just a man, like them. It still confused her that even though the dead ones had hurt the pale man and the woman badly, he was serving their bodies. She turned it all over in her mind, considering carefully.

———·———·———

Thio ignored Tiller's instructions and stared fixedly as Tiller positioned Gierr onto the woodpile. He arranged Gierr's legs and folded his arms, then used the pickaxe to wedge stones into place, closing the symbolic ship-wall. Gierr's place on the funeral pyre was complete.

Thio went back and forth with Tiller to the woodpile as he readied the next position for Bolli. She moved beside him as he fought Bolli's dead weight onto the sledge, and then onto his section of the stone ship, and as Tiller tightly wedged Bolli's stones into the ship shape.

It was good to see her walking, to hear the sound of Thio's footsteps matching his. But it was not her feet he heard moving quietly on the pebbled beach behind them.

———·———·———

Tiller dropped his rock and caught Thio, pulling her into his arms, feeling like a fox with one leg in the trap. Defiant, he looked back, and nearly fell over in shock.

215

The revenants were standing close by. Holding stones, and offering them to Tiller.

———.———.———

They inspected each other.

———.———.———

Creatures so like himself, yet so different! The one closest to Erik was nearly as tall as he was, with skin was the color of rich dark leather, not pale, as Tiller's was. Their hair hung long on either side of the head in glossy black braids. It was perfectly, *perfectly* straight, and shone like the finest mink.

Tiller slowly studied the face of the one nearest him, proffering the rock. It was a serious face, stern even, but it was not unkind. The being had no beard. No stubble, nothing. No facial hair of any kind, with cheeks as bare as a babe.

Its eyes were the most startling of all. They were guarded and wary, but full of intelligence. They did not seem angry or ready for revenge. Around them, Tiller saw the kind of lines that came from smiling much and laughing often. What fascinated Tiller most was that, while his own eyes were round and blue, theirs were as dark as wet black stones, and...*not round.*

Tiller pushed Thio behind him. He bowed deeply to the being, bending forward from the chest, keeping his eyes on it and the other fish-rider one who stood a step back. With one hand, Tiller reached for the rock that the being offered, and it was released into his grip. The being mimicked Tiller's bow. His eyes remained locked with Tiller's.

Thio squeezed as tight as a duckling against his back, shaking, her head huddled against his shoulder blades. The being in front of him was breathing hard, too, and seemed almost to tremble. How could that be? A revenant, shaking with nervousness? One with laughter lines?

Lightning struck Tiller. This being was no revenant. It was a man like him. Different, perhaps, but still a man. *Dear gods and little gold fishes, there were people living on this land. Here, at the edge of the world, far from where anyone knew, were men.* No, wait; two of them were women. *How were they possible?*

It wasn't their gender that puzzled Tiller. It was the fact of their very existence.

People.

How had they gotten here? Where did they come from? How did they ride fish? Who were they? The questions spun too fast, and his head felt ready to explode.

Tiller stood utterly still, holding the stone, as he and the other man stared with equal intensity at one another. The man, his eyes still wary, reached for the rock he had just handed Tiller, who gave it back to him, reluctantly. It had been a weapon in Tiller's hand, and the man was taking it. The man gestured with the stone towards the funeral-ship, his eyes carefully questioning. *This way?*

Tiller nodded back. The man put his chin down and up. He was saying yes.

Tiller picked up his own stone, and took Thio's hand in his. They walked towards the funeral-ship. The fish-people followed. Two solitary *vikingers* who had crossed the sea in a knörr and twelve people who rode fish walked together, as unlikely a funeral procession as could be.

———·———·———

With the pickaxe, Tiller wedged the next stone in place, and then the next, forming the ship's wall. He and the strange people had labored together for two hours. The stone ship was nearly finished. As they worked, the people's serious expressions had gradually softened and they talked frequently in a strange language. Thio's blank stare had disappeared. She did not speak, but her eyes followed the visitors

218

constantly. At one point, Tiller was startled to see Thio sitting beside the oldest woman, still and quiet. The woman held her hand and gazed steadily into Thio's eyes, smiling gently from time to time and nodding. After a while, Thio began to cry. The woman took Thio in her arms and held her like a child.

———.———.———

not *fish girl* not Fish girl no no no nonono!!!   ...tTHi...thiO?

Snow-On-Hair sat next to the sick woman, marveling. The pale one's skin was creamy as a whale's tooth. It was almost as light as the fur of the Great White Bear.

The White Bear. A foreknowledge chilled Snow-On-Hair. The image of the white bear was a warning of some future pain, but one could not control these things. She let the thought go.

The sick woman's eyes were as blue as the sea. Snow-on-Hair was fascinated by the color. But the sea did not show such terrible sadness and loss as these eyes did. Snow-on-Hair offered gentleness, and waited.

"Do you know what I did?" Thio was surprised to hear the sentence come clearly from her lips. She had tried to speak earlier, but the words would not form, still too broken and swirling in a hideous mix since...the horror. "I...I..."

No, it still could not be spoken. Thio backed away from the abyss that threatened.

Snow-on-Hair took Thio's hand. She could not understand anything of what Thio was saying, but simply focused on holding her heart open. Words mattered little to the spirit.

Thio looked at small earrings against the other woman's mixed strands of silver and still-dark hair. Her mouth worked. "Your earrings are pretty," she said. "My sister has ones much like them. Carved from an antler, for good luck in love. I miss her so much. My family. I don't know what I was thinking. I just wanted to do a kindness for Tiller's mother, and to have a little adventure, I suppose. I just meant to go to the village, deliver her message and leave. Then all this happened."

220

Snow-on-Hair nodded as if she understood. In a moment Thio continued. "When I couldn't escape, and learned what they were planning, I made up my mind to stay alive. To do terrible things." She looked away, ashamed, then turned back to Snow-on-Hair, determined to be honest, her face pleading. "I did not want to, but I thought I had to. Do you understand?"

The older woman knew an important question had been asked. She nodded.

"Randaal... he cut me." Thio choked, touching the bandages.

Snow-on-hair touched them too. "That man hurt you," she whispered to Thio. "Deeper than the cuts." She put the palm of her hand flat against Thio's heart, her touch light. "Inside. Here."

"I didn't do it." Thio sobbed, the horrible guilt bursting into the open. "At the end, I didn't even *want* to do it, I decided I wouldn't, but it happened anyway! I mixed the poisons and the ergot! It's *my* fault they're dead! All of them! None of them, none of us will ever be able to go home, and it...is...all...my...fault!" Wrenching sobs shook Thio.

Snow-on-Hair pulled the pale woman close and held her. Good. This storm would wash things clean, for a while, at least. She held Thio until the sobs softened, and sleep came.

———·———·———

The last body was put into place. It was Tor. Tiller had chosen a place of honor for Tor at the rear of the stone ship, where a rudder would be. Tor would steer the other men.

It was time to give them tributes and gifts. Tiller had put Randaal's body at the pointed front of the stone ship. To Randaal, the cloak which had held the knife and the noose. It would double as a sail for the men's stone ship. *May you see things differently in the afterlife,* Tiller said prayerfully. To every man went a portion of food, his bowl, his cup, his shield.

It was not nearly enough. Would the spirits understand how limited their supplies were?

Tiller did not realize he had spoken his worries aloud. In response, Thio went to the tents and returned with a sealed crock of seeds. Tiller understood. He spoke to the bodies.

"A promise means an oath, but it also means hope. The promise of a better life was what made you say yes to this voyage. As you cross to Niflheim, take our oath-and-hope with you. We pledge not to give up on your dreams."

Thio nodded in agreement. The words were right. Tiller continued.

"To each of you, we give seeds symbolic of that for which we all hoped: farms, crops, and comfort. One day, when there *is* a farm here -- even if just with the few of us left -- we will bring you more gifts, of grain, and mead, eggs, and cheeses. We promise."

After that, Tiller said the words of passage. He brought a burning stick from the cooking fire. Because the fish-people had helped them, there would still be enough daylight for the smoke to reach the sky before twilight settled in.

Snow-on-Hair put her hand on Tiller's arm and stopped him. She spoke to one of the others, who brought a leather bag to her. Untying a cord from the neck of the sack, she poured a little oil from it onto the flame. It burned brightly. Tiller nodded.

They moved from man to man, pouring oil onto each. The entire group moved silently around the ship as the light softened. It felt decent, a respectful ceremony.

222

With that, Tiller touched the torch to the wood nearest him. It crackled as the branches started to burn, and the scent of fresh wood smoke brought comfort. The little group walked around the stone ship one last time, as Tiller touched the wood at the head of each man, and then at his feet. Flames climbed quickly, and smoke lifted skyward.

———·——·———

The woman with the silver in her hair sang. Her voice spoke of sadness, and of mystery, and the power of a drop of hope in an ocean of fear.

Tiller watched as dark tendrils of spirit-smoke curled towards the sky. He wished that he could abandon himself to the peaceful acceptance of the song, but grim reality spoke louder. With the grueling task of the funeral rites done, already the work of lonely survival loomed.

After Snow-on-Hair sang, there was a silence for a short while. One of the others said something to Tiller and gestured to the ocean, gestured to the others, and to the sea again.

"Of course you must go. You have a home, somewhere." So many questions he longed to ask. Where did they come from? What was it like there? How many of these people were there? Why had they come to help in such strange and terrible circumstances? Most importantly, would they ever come back?

There was no way to speak. His heart hardened at the thought of the bitter work ahead, but suddenly the words of the morning echoed again. *Do as well as you can in this instant, and there will be less to fear tomorrow, less to regret when today becomes yesterday. Do what needs to be done now, as well as you are able. That is all that matters.*

The people walked to where their tiny crafts lay on the sand. Far smaller than any boat Tiller had ever seen, each was barely enough for a single person, long, narrow and pointed.

Thio embraced the woman who had held her while she cried. Tiller grasped their hands one by one in warm thanks. The people said words in return, fascinating streams of sounds that Tiller wished he could understand, then climbed into their small vessels and pushed off.

"Look at them, Thio! They are barely a hands-breadth above the surface of the water. It does look as if they are riding large fish!"

The people paddled through the surf, lifted their hands in a last farewell, and began their odd, rhythmic rowing back in the direction from which they had come.

A tired and grateful sigh filled Tiller. Without these people there would still be bodies all over the beach. The beach – oh no, he had forgotten. "I need to move Olaf and the twins into a tent. I'll be back soon. Do you want to stay here?"

Thio nodded. The heat from the fire warmed her. She tried to name each man in goodbye, but the horrible images from the beach came, and the dangerous swirling. *Later,* she told them.

Thio reached for Tiller's hand and turned it palm up, tracing with her fingertips the rough callouses from working on the ship. The man standing beside her, like so many in Íseland now, was too lean. She did not know if he had had fields to grow his own food, or was landless and poor. That mattered very little to her here and now. She laid her hand flat over his, feeling how cut and swollen it was from the day's labor. It was the hand of a man who knew how to do the right thing; a good man.

Tiller would go to the beach, and then he would be right back, he had said. They would stand together and watch as the smoke covered the face of the full-again moon. She leaned against him ever so gently, holding onto that hand, and nodded.

———·———·———

In The Balance

Tiller bent over each man in turn and listened for his breathing. Olaf mumbled a word or two and lapsed back into unconsciousness. Karl did not respond, but he breathed steadily. Kurt moaned in pain and his breath came slight, with bubbles of blood. After Tiller had removed their wrappings of fur and washed the visible cuts, he returned to the tent where Thio was waking.

"How did you sleep?" He had been like a dead man himself.

"I can barely move my shoulder and hand." She said nothing to him of the shattering in her head, how words and images came and went but made no sense.

"It's normal for it to hurt worse the second day. I'll put some willow bark on it to help."

"Tiller…. the others?"

He gave her the truth, his words gentle. "Olaf seems steady. Kurt and Karl…it's bad."

"Have you put the honey on them?"

"Not yet. When we get you bandaged again, I need your help, if you are able."

———·———·———

Tiller lugged one of the small casks of honey into the tent. Thio flinched at the sight and smell of injury on entering the tent, then steadied herself. Tiller saw in her manner an echo of the Fishgirl who had done the stitching-up on board. She knelt over Olaf and checked him.

226

"He has three wounds, one along his forearm and one on his front thigh, and the third on his hip. The two deepest are on his right side. Here, put the blanket like this to support him. That will keep both wounds downwards, so they will drain."

She directed Tiller to pry the cuts open with his fingers while she poured honey into them. "These should heal cleanly. We'll need to wash out and replenish the honey once or twice a day. Thank goodness whoever supplied the knörr put so many casks on board."

Thio looked carefully over Karl next. Aside from superficial cuts, she could see nothing that was causing the stupor in which he lay. Her fingers found a large lump on his head, and another swelling over his kidneys.

"He's injured inside." She pulled Karl's eyelids open and scrutinized them. "You see it? The black part of his left eye is bigger than the right. Has he passed any water?"

Tiller nodded. "Yes. There's blood in it."

Thio's eyes filled with tears. With gentle fingers she spun a smooth coat of honey over the small cuts and kissed Karl gently on the forehead. "Rest deeply, young friend," she whispered.

Thio's eyes met Tiller's in devastation as she examined Kurt's still frame. "Oh, good gods, this gash goes all the way into his lungs. I don't know how to treat this."

"It's worse than that, Thio." Tiller lifted the bandage he had placed over Kurt's abdomen, and at the sight, Thio covered her eyes. The inner shattering began again, and the uncontrollable shivering. She panted, trying to hold on, and wrenched herself to focus.

"Get me seawater," she said. "Boil it. Make it even saltier. I don't know why; it just seems the right thing to do. Then bring it here to me -- and my sewing kit, bring that first."

Thio had never stitched a man's gut before. She forced herself to think of pigs butchered on their farm. It was not Kurt's stomach muscle under her fingers, not his skin she cut wider, doing things she did not know how to do. The terrible odor was not Kurt. *Pull the intestines out. Feel around, pull more, never mind the smell, never mind the blood. Nothing is cut inside, just the skin and muscle.* When Tiller came with the hot salty water, she tested it against her wrist until it was barely cool enough, then rinsed the gut matter until it was free of blood. Thio pushed the intestines back into his belly, poured the intensely salty water into the opening, then pushed on Kurt's abdomen so that the water gushed out again, full of blood and mess, flinching with horror. She filled the hole again, pressed it out again.

Thio repeated the salt-water pour on the cut between his ribs, talking to Kurt all the while as if he could hear her. "I don't know if this will help, Kurt," she said. "I know it must hurt terribly. I'm so sorry, but we'll try, won't we? Karl is still with us. Try for him."

Thio listened. Kurt's heart was still beating. "How long has it been, Tiller?"

"Since when?"

"Since they... Since the... Since..." her voice sounded dangerously unsteady.

"Two days, Thio."

"Two days, Kurt," she whispered, her head still on his chest. "You've made it two days. Tomorrow will be three. Stay with us." She choked as the swirling picked up in intensity.

"Let's let them rest now, Thio. Come outside. We'll make a bit of something to eat."

228

On board ship, focusing on one small task at a time had helped Thio stave off fear. Would it keep away the ghastly emptiness he could see returning in her eyes?

———.———.———

By the next afternoon, Tiller had stowed all the crates in the tents, to protect them from storms and scavenging animals. "They'll be safe there until I can get a small longhouse built." He dug hungrily into the food.

"My father does that, too. Do all men?"

"Do all men what?"

"Escape worry by throwing themselves into work. On the knörr, you were always fixing something. You ignored fatigue and stress, did what needed to be done. You don't seek appreciation. Work consumes you and protects you."

Tiller said nothing, simply shrugged and pulled another hunk of bread.

"Well, I am like my father, too," Thio said quietly. "I know how to work hard and I am not afraid of it, either." She had done everything she could so far with one arm hurt. "But the smallest effort is exhausting. I cannot imagine how you keep moving, with your thigh cut." He could not remember when it had happened, and had not shown it to Thio until she had finished caring for Kurt. "It must hurt with every step."

"We both know the sky of a storm. I cannot afford to rest."

"I wonder if it would have changed the men's vote, seeing us working for them."

"Doubtful. They were too afraid. Listen, I'll clean Olaf and the twins next time. Tiredness means you need rest to heal." Tiller paused, cleared his throat. "Something I do need to ask you, Thio. My mother…"

Tears sprang to Thio's eyes, and she cut off his question, shaking her head vigorously. "Not now," she gasped. "I can't, Tiller, I'm so sorry. Let me work on the chicken pen. Later."

But at bedtime, she said she was too tired, and turned away, falling asleep almost immediately. Tiller lay silent, yearning to know. Frustration battled with compassion.

Without discussing it, they had continued sharing a tent. Thio felt safer that way. Having Tiller nearby was like the close sleeping quarters of the knörr. A tent alone felt odd and wrong.

———.———.———

The sky was dark on the following morning, and rain fell heavily. After the furious pace of work since they had landed, to be forced by nature to rest helped. When she was not watching over Kurt and Karl, Thio spent part of the day sorting through clothing from the men's crates.

"Do you think Olaf and the twins will survive?" she whispered after they had eaten a small supper. The rain still drummed on the tent roof.

"Olaf's wounds are clean. I'm astonished that Kurt seems to be improving. Honestly, Thio, whatever you are doing is working. I don't have much hope for him. Karl, though…his gaze is worse, and he didn't pass any water last night at all."

Thio sighed with grief. "Remember when Karl asked me to describe rain at home? I wish I was there now. Rain always means inside work, the fire crackling and birch smoke lifting to the longhouse's smoke-opening. The quiet sounds of the animals nearby

230

in their stalls. The storm sweeping the fields with sheets of rain while we were snug inside." A wistful smile. "The smell of wool being carded or spun on the loom. Such little things, but so important."

"It sounds like good memories. Mine were not usually so warm, or happy."

"I promise I'll try to talk about her tomorrow. I feel stronger. I don't know why it's so hard. It's as if something sucks the heart out of me as I begin, but I know you want very much to hear." She was quiet again, hearing in her head the words she wanted to say. *On rainy days when we worked inside my brother would take his harp and sung wicked songs, until your mother would smack at him and laugh, and then he would play each person's favorite. Your beautiful mother would weave wools and dye them. She made the most beautiful colors of red, and purple, and blue. My cape, that astonishing bright red in it, that's her work.* " But Thio could say nothing. Those words would have felt like this good rain on parched dry earth to Tiller, but Thio kept silent, and he could know nothing of the person on earth he loved and missed most.

The peaceful feeling left them both. Lost in the enormity of their aloneness, individually and together, they laid down in their sleeping sacks. Not long after, Thio cried herself to sleep.

———·——·——

Olaf ate a spoonful of broth when Thio checked on him in the middle of the night. Kurt was awake. His eyes were locked on Karl, as if he was watching to see if his twin would grow stronger or weaker and was determined to follow, whatever the course. Thio held his hand and listened to the storm.

231

Karl's death-throes came while raindrops pattered on the tent roof. When his breathing and heartbeat were gone, Thio stumbled outside the tent and fell to the ground and was sick over and over. Another death on her hands, and Karl's hurt worst of all. She had cared very much for the twins during long, worry-filled days at sea.

"Oh, Karl! I cannot bear to lose you!" Thio sobbed, prostrate in the cold mud while rain soaked her to the skin. When shivering set in, she willed herself to die. *It is what I deserve.*

Thio had no idea how long she laid there. When she got up to check on Olaf, he glared weakly at her.

"Olaf, you are angry at me! What a relief! You are getting stronger!" She knelt beside him. "I won't forget that you tried to help me. I will do whatever I can to help you heal."

She glanced over at Kurt in fear. His eyes were closed. "Kurt, please stay with us if you can. Or go with your brother. You must do what is right for you." *Stay with us.*

Thio smoothed Kurt's tendrils of hair from his face. In the morning, they would take Karl's body to the stone ship to join the others. Filthy, wet, and exhausted, she longed to fall asleep for years. It felt as if they had been here an eternity already, with nothing but death. Who could she tell of the pain and loneliness that crushed in more every day? Tiller could not help. She would not increase his load any more. He needed rest. She would not wake him about Karl.

The dark swirling surged, and Thio hurried to get back to her sleeping sack. Her head split into thousands of sharp pieces that cut and cut and cut one another smaller and smaller, until all that was Thio was lost, and only the visible shell of her was left to walk and move and breathe, but could not feel, did not cry, did not know.

—·—·—

Tiller lunged awake from the terrible dream and then realized he was in the tent with Thio. He felt rested but was annoyed at sleeping through the whole morning. Thio, too, was sound asleep in her own húthfat. She usually stayed up half the night watching the twins, and rose again by dawn. Maybe the sound of the rain had helped her sleep. Good. She needed rest to heal.

The sky shone with the bright blue that celebrates a storm's passing, and the beach sparkled with the morning light. Tiller went straightaway to the men's tent, but there the brightness of the day faded. Olaf breathed easily and deeply, but Kurt and Karl's spirits had both left sometime during the night.

He decided to tell Thio that they had breathed their last together. It would soften the blow. "We'll take you to the stone ship, and you'll cross over together," he said to the twins.

At that, dread filled him. *Just Thio, Olaf and me now.* He had valued the twins so little when they boarded the ship, thinking them nearly useless. Now, their loss was crushing. Leaving the tent, Tiller poked up the fire and began to warm porridge for Olaf. *It couldn't be helped. We did all we could. We need to find ways to move forward. When the twin's fires are lit, I will go explore up the hills past the beach. We have seen nothing except this beach, and too much death. We need to figure out how to live. Maybe those strange people are close enough that they will come from time to time.*

Lonely despair crushed in on Tiller more every day. But who could he tell? Thio was barely holding on. No, he would not increase Thio's load one bit more. No one could help. He would go look at the hills, and hope for strength.

233

Going

"Thio?"

She was wrapped in blankets and furs in the little alcove near the stone ship, resting as they watched the fire. Kurt and Karl were crossing over, their bodies side by side, their hands clasped together, and smoke once again rose in the sky. On Karl's chest were the tafl board and its playing pieces, just beginning to burn. On Kurt's chest were the knucklebones. Along with those cherished items, Tiller and Thio had given more of their supplies than they could afford.

"What is it?" She did not take her eyes from the crackling pyre.

"I'm going to explore a bit this afternoon. Would you like to come with me, to see what lies beyond the hills? We'll be able to see the smoke from there." He knelt down and stroked her face. "They'll cross well, Thio. We offered them more than anyone else."

She kept her face turned away, and stroked the fur across her lap. A small sob escaped.

"Maybe it would make you feel better to walk with me a bit. I'll go slowly."

"No. I want to stay here. I want to fall asleep near their fire."

"What if those people come back, and you are here by yourself?"

"What people?" Her eyes drifted, resting momentarily on Tiller's face. She frowned. "What people?"

Yesterday Thio could not remember coming to this beach. She had pointed to the knörr, and asked when it had arrived. More confusion today did not bode well. "The people from the sea, who helped us build the stone ship. I don't want to leave you here by yourself."

"We are the people from the sea. There's no one else. Don't be silly. Go for your walk."

234

Despair filled Tiller. He could fix her wounds, but what about this sickness of the mind? *You cannot leave me too, Thio.* Yes, he could stay here and watch her, but there was too much crackling around the edges of his own mind. Sitting here would not make it any better. No matter what, he had to go, even if not for long.

"Stay here, then," he said, tucking the covers over her shoulders again. "Sleep as long as you want. Go back to the tent when you wake up. Rest and feel better."

Thio had already fallen back asleep. Tiller fought savagely with the laces of his boots, as if they would mend the chaos of his whole life, knowing full well that such a thing could never, ever be.

———·———·———

The hills rose from the beach to form a curving sweep of land around the water. Tiller struck out towards the rising hills. Nothing soothes the mind like putting one foot in front of another, and in just a handful of steps, even though nothing had changed, his heart lightened a little. Death, sickness, loneliness, fear and worry were still there, but as his feet moved forward, Tiller's thoughts turned to what he might discover. What would it be like beyond this hill?

———·———·———

The sun painted long blue shadows across the grasses as Tiller returned to the camp. He had a roaring appetite, and hurried across the last hill towards their tents with a hare in his hand. No smoke rose from the cooking fire, and the boiling-pot hung empty over cold ashes. Tiller took off his shoes and went into the tent, consumed with guilt. *I should not have left Thio.*

She sat half-naked in her blankets, her hair a tangled mess. She flicked a little string back and forth as Tiller entered, and looked at him with a childish, too-happy expression in her eyes.

"I've seen so much today, I can hardly wait to tell you about it," he said, as if nothing was amiss. "How's Olaf doing?"

She flicked the little string again. "Olaf?"

"Did you check on him today?" Tiller's heart pounded.

Thio glanced at Tiller, her eyes confused, then flicked her string and smiled at it.

"Never mind. I'll do it." His voice was harsher than he intended it, but her vagueness had immediately brought back all the strain the day's explorations had lifted. Thio said nothing. As Tiller left the tent, she flicked the little string again, back and forth, back and forth, smiling and humming to herself.

———·———·———

Olaf lifted his head and cursed as Tiller entered. The tent reeked of human waste, a less-than-pleasant reminder that Olaf was getting better. Tiller cursed, too, at the job of nursemaid, but buckled to the task. He rolled Olaf over and pulled the soiled bedding from under him. Olaf was able to sit up, groaning.

"Use the urn next time," Tiller growled. "We're running out of clean blankets."

"Where's our Fish-bitch?" Olaf growled back.

"Call her Thio," Tiller snapped.

"Where's Thio-fish-bitch?"

Tiller longed to hit him. "She's sick."

"That's one way of putting it. She's gone crazy is what you mean. How's she coming along with that babe of yours she's carrying?"

"There's no child, Olaf. She made it up, I'm certain, desperate to try anything that might stop the council's plans. Crazy or not, it's just the three of us now, and Thio's worked hard at caring for you, so try being decent to her. She doesn't know the things you say about her. I'm trying to protect her from any more strain, but I can't hide your meanness much more."

Olaf mumbled that if not for Thio he'd be fine and heading back to Íseland, but low enough under his breath that Tiller could pretend not to hear it. He checked Olaf's wounds and poured in more honey. There was a little porridge left in his bowl from this morning. He helped Olaf to eat and put him to bed for the night.

Tiller walked down to the shoreline and squatted on the dry stones. He had looked forward to spitting the hare and roasting it, but it felt too great an effort now. He would hang it for tomorrow. The small rounded stones of the beach ground under Tiller's feet as he walked wearily back to his own tent.

Thio was asleep. Tiller bid her good night anyway, and lay awake in the dark, worrying.

Yearning

Tiller worked for Thio every day. He woke her, made food for her, washed clothing, kept the fire tended. When she cried in the night, he held her, but no amount of caring was making her well. Thio was retreating somewhere deep inside where he could not reach.

Each dusk, Tiller walked along the shore and listened to sea birds calling to one another as they returned to roost. The water spoke to the stones of the beach. Tiller listened to their language as well. *We are not born of the sea or birds, but if we are attentive, they teach us their sounds. We must listen deeply to know them.* It was a distraction, a learning, but Tiller craved the human sounds of everyday community and work. With Thio, he listened and longed, but heard little. Would she one day be herself again, for good? *Maybe tomorrow.*

—·——·——

"Can you work at baskets today, Olaf? I cut some grasses and branch switches yesterday. I'll bring them on the sledge shortly." Olaf had already built small coop-nests for the chickens, but he was not strong enough yet for the heavy work of turf-cutting. Tiller had taken that task, cutting and pulling heavy earth blocks along a small longhouse foundation.

Thio was on the beach stones, washing their sealskins in vinegar and fresh water and rubbing them with mink's oil. They would be supple and soft to help keep the three survivors warm and dry in the winters to come. They had a small shed now, rough, but with a real roof. Tiller had moved all of their supplies into it.

The dry woodpiles for cooking and wash water grew tall. The traps for game were full. Each day was filled with hard work, but as the weeks and days passed, they adapted to a sort of rhythm. Returning with a brace of hares from the trap one afternoon, Tiller realized it had been several days since he had remembered to cut the counting-notch to keep track of their time. The days had grown steadily longer. To his shock, Tiller realized that a nearly whole moon had passed since they landed. Spring was in its last month.

"Do you notice something, Olaf? I realized today I never look behind me here, ever. It's lonely, yes. But we don't have to worry about being outlaws, either." Tiller stood straighter.

238

Olaf's bitterness poured out. "What I realize is that it seems forever since I have seen my wife or son. The gothi probably has my son calling him 'father' already. I am from a family of headmen! We lived like chieftains. Freedom? Thanks to you and Thio, I'm the king of nothing!" He stood unsteadily and limped a few faltering steps away, and Tiller watched him go.

———·———·———

That night, Olaf slipped from his tent under cover of darkness. He moved along the beach until he reached the stone-ship above the high tide mark, and felt his way carefully until he reached the center. Tiller said he had given the knife to Sigmund. Olaf ran his fingers carefully through the ashes. Rib bone, probably. Another rib. Breastbone. Spine. There it was. He fished the long ceremonial dagger from the pile of burnt bone, and felt along its length in the dark. Good; the heat of the fire had not warped it. Olaf slid the knife inside his tall sheepskin boot. No telling when he might need it later. Painfully, he made his way back to his tent, and hid the knife in his sea-chest.

———·———·———

Mild days of late spring afforded time for their first and biggest priority: starting crops to survive the upcoming winter. They ate well, with food plentiful everywhere they could see. Sugar kelp, dulse and other seaweeds grew plentifully on the shoreline stones, and blueberries and crowberries burst forth in early summer. A variety of game birds and animals came and went, peering curiously at the strangers who had taken up abode on the lonely green harbor.

Olaf had healed well. His arm moved almost normally, and he had a bit of a limp, but he managed to find a way to do most tasks. They all worked hard to gather vegetables and berries and to hunt for meat and dry or smoke above the longhouse fire, knowing that there would be no neighbors to ask for supplies should something run out over the winter.

Tiller watched Thio carefully. Many days she seemed completely normal. She had never regained the smile that had flashed from time to time on the ship, but she could work as hard as Tiller and Olaf, and she seemed to be healthy and strong. With no warning, however, something would change. The blank stare would abruptly return, and for a while, Thio would be like a stranger again, withdrawn and mute, not recognizing them, and trembling from remembered terror.

Maybe tomorrow was the only thought Tiller allowed himself on those days. *Maybe tomorrow.*

———.———.———

Each week brought new discoveries. A peace of sorts existed between the three stranded Íselanders, with each of them bound by need of the others. Spring opened to summer, and their small acreage of crops grew tall in the fields. They grew heads of barley and wheat and rye, and they watched the tops of the root crops grow leafy and tall. The moon waxed and waned, and summer yielded to autumn. Baskets full of grain and vegetable roots began to fill the small storage hut, and the rafters of the now-finished longhouse were full of smoked joints. Tiller, Olaf and Thio moved into the cramped but clean living space before the first snows came, with its small luxury of real sleeping benches. They had survived a first harvest.

A promise needed to be kept. On the first mild day after the harvest was finished and all the food stored away, Tiller took offerings to the stone ship, as promised. Olaf came with him, watching sullenly from a distance.

Thio did not come. Later, when Tiller and Olaf were busy with other work, she walked with great trepidation to the circle. She moved from one station to the next, and her hand reached tentatively to where the ash-piles had formed, now long scattered by the winds. Her lips moved in soundless words of apology, and then in anger, and then in heartbreak and loneliness. She imagined her companions from the ship standing there, looking at her.

"Sigmund!" Thio cried. "Kurt! Karl! Dagsson! Oh, Ekka, what I would not give to hear you prattle away about something! Nollar.... oh, dear Tor...."

There was no answer. When she looked up from crying, they were gone. Only the empty stone ship remained, the charred marks at each station a glaring accusation. Thio stumbled back to the longhouse, guilty and afraid.

———·———·———

The first gale of winter swept down the next day. The wind woke Tiller. Nearby on the longhouse bench, he heard Thio weeping in her sleep again.

Tiller pulled his sleeping sack next to hers as he did so often. "Shhh, Thio. Shhh... it will pass." Her nightmares usually would subside with comforting, and she would fall back asleep. This time, the sounds intensified.

"Thio, are you having a nightmare? Wake up!"

Thio rolled over and her arms went around Tiller's neck. Her body shook, and sounds of grief and terror poured from her throat. The intense sounds of anguish worried Tiller.

"Thio, please! Hold onto yourself! Don't go mad. I could not bear it. You *must* stay sane. I need you. I can't lose you. I can't. Please, Thio." Her mouth was open in agony, pressed against Tiller's neck, and still she wept. Incoherent words spilled out, tangled together. He nudged his sleeping sack closer to Thio and held her tightly. It was all he could do. Tiller wanted to make her better, and he could not. He could not.

——·——·——

Thio wept for as long as the wind blew. When the weather quieted, her body softened deeply against Tiller, as if the hurt and fear she had been holding in for so long had finally melted away, and she slept. With his arms still around Thio, Tiller slipped into sleep, loving her.

Joy

Tiller woke slowly to consciousness, full of a peace he could not remember feeling ever in his life. He dimly recalled hearing Olaf snort and stomp out of the small longhouse some time ago. In the dim quiet, Tiller could feel Thio's body stretched along the whole length of his. At some point she had removed her clothing and climbed into his húthfat. Her breasts were smooth and bare beneath Tiller's embrace. He knew desire as he never had before, but he kept his hands still. Thio had not been well for such a long time. It would not be right.

242

Tiller focused all of his attention on the sweet soft breaths that floated across his forearms. He stayed motionless, full of hope that the brokenness had finally left this woman he had come so deeply to love.

———·———·———

Thio woke, and stiffened. "Why are you lying with me?" Her voice was sharp.

"It is you lying with me! I woke to find you in my sleeping sack! I'm taking care of you."

"I don't need anyone to take care of me." She said it flatly, without emotion.

"But you were crying. I only held you, as I always have."

"I'm not crying now. I am awake. I am fine. Please leave me," she said coldly. "This is my sleeping area. You should be over there, nearer to Olaf. Not here. Not next to me."

———·———·———

Tiller joined Olaf at the outdoor work-fire pit. The other man stood peevishly poking the coals in the raw winter wind.

"Must have had some fun in there this morning. You're quite the lucky one, aren't you, laying abed with Thio? When's our Fishgirl going to make breakfast?"

Tiller glared at Olaf. "She stopped being Fishgirl a long time ago. Make your own damned breakfast," he said, and stomped away.

———·———·———

How was it possible for Thio to be so cruel when he had completely devoted himself to caring for her? Did she have no understanding of that?

Tiller had let himself dream of standing with Thio looking over their fields, talking of the crops they would plant and harvest, growing strong and happy by making the best of whatever life brought to them. He had dreamed of being with her through the dark cold of winter nights, snug in the longhouse as they waited for Olaf to fall asleep. They were the dreams of a man in love, her mouth against his, their legs twisted together as they shared themselves in hushed whispers to keep from waking Olaf.

Thio must have had only different dreams of the future, perhaps only nightmares, Tiller realized. Hope that had grown bit by pleasant bit in him spilled out in sudden gush, tearing great gashes in him. His desire for her body and his hope of Thio's love collapsed all at once into failure and feelings of betrayal, as bitter as bile. Tiller had never known such pain. He sank down near the stone ship and sat there for hours and did not move.

———·———·———

Another Spring

Thio sat throwing little pebbles in the field as Tiller plowed it with the small hand coulter, cursing. The task was easier this spring than it had been the first time, but he still longed for a decent ox to pull it. So much more land could be put under the plow that way! Tiller made up his mind to fashion a small yoke, to try on one of the goats.

Olaf, following behind Tiller with the seed-pot, cast the seed grains across the fresh earth. As he reached the end of each row, he raked the newly-spread kernels to protect them from birds.

From time to time, Thio would clap her hands, and smile a little.

"What's she doing over there?" Olaf demanded.

"Playing with her imaginary cat," Tiller answered.

He frowned. "Does she really see one?"

Tiller shrugged. "I guess so. It makes her happy."

"Crazy. Completely crazy." Olaf's bitterness had faded, from the sheer effort required to keep it up. Instead, he would wait for one of Thio's odd spells and mock her to Tiller, knowing how it annoyed him.

"Whose fault is that? Can't you just let it go? She wasn't crazy when she got onto the knörr, and she wasn't crazy when she got off of it."

Olaf eyed Tiller warily, then changed his tone. "Are you the cousin she trusts today, or the neighbor she doesn't like?"

Tiller sighed. "Neighbor."

"At least she sees you. When she's like this, I'm invisible to her."

It was true. As they worked the field, Thio threw her little stones, and ignored them both.

The Bad Voice

When did we move our farm to the sea? I didn't know we lived so close to the water. I cannot find my father or mother. But my cousin is somewhere. Oh, there he is. What is his name? What do I call him...? Jadar? No, that's a woman. No, it's a place. A woman from a place? I can't remember. So confusing.

"Thio, will you collect the eggs? I don't think any of us did it yesterday, and they are laying heavily now that it's spring again."

I don't want to go into the chicken coop. Something bad there.

"Fishgirl," Olaf taunted. He put the rake away and moved towards the coop where Thio stood, keeping his voice quiet so that Tiller would not hear. "Fishhhhhh.....girllll....."

Whose voice is that? Heard it before... She remembered falling to her knees somewhere, something in her hand, being sick. A scene came to mind, of sunlight filtering through the roof of a boathouse. *there had been another voice, and this one* Thio heard old words that felt old, from long ago *"No, you have to pull it like this...it's a sacrifice to Odin, not a pig slaughtering!"*

The memory of the boathouse and the frightening thing in her hand and the voice writhed with other images and sounds, horrific images of men on a beach, jerking in spasms of pain, terrible wounds *the poison...they drank the poison I put in the cask of beer Sig's eye eye eye on sand oh no the darkness no*

246

Thio rubbed her knuckles into her eyes, hunched her shoulders against the sound of the remembered voice from the boathouse. *They want to hurt me? Kill me! Stay still Cousin will come stay still Cousin will come stay still Cousin will come*

But the Dark thing ....still there? yes in front of me, threatening

—·—·—

Olaf blocked Thio, knowing she would not acknowledge him but would stand motionless and trembling, her eyes closed.

"Tiller's behind the longhouse repairing the fish nets. He can't hear me, but you can. I'll tell you, today and every day I get a chance, that one day, you'll pay for what you did to me. Not now. I need you to survive. But someday, Thio, I will have my revenge. Not because I am a cruel man, no. I will do it because if by some miracle, we ever get home, I have a son to save. I have a promise to keep. We were so close, Thio. So close. We could have started a settlement to welcome other ships, and sailed for home, victorious. I never wanted to hurt you. I would have done it cleanly, correctly. But you ruined it all, and I will never forget that."

Frightened tears fell from Thio's tightly-squeezed lashes. She did not see the angry ones on Olaf's cheeks as well.

Olaf cringed as he heard Tiller coming up behind him. Had Tiller heard? Unlikely, Olaf reassured himself. He always kept his voice down when he was taunting Thio.

"Get away from her, damn you!" cried Tiller. She's bad off enough as it is. Quit trying to make her worse." Tiller quelled the urge to crush Olaf's skull. It would be so much better if the twins had survived instead of Olaf.

———·———·———

Spring fish-runs came with the return of longer days. Thio stood knee-deep next to Tiller in the surf. She wore Ulf's oil-skin boots, too large for her, and curled her toes to keep them on as she strained against the weight of the fish in the net. The next few days would be spent scaling and gutting the haul. Their small smokehouse, such as it was, had charcoal stacked and ready.

"Hold tight, Thio! The net is pretty heavy. Can you manage it?"

From the corner of his eye, Tiller saw Thio startle. She dropped her end of the net and stared. Tiller looked across the water, following her gaze.

There was a familiar movement on the horizon. The sunlight glinted on something out in the water, just beyond the line of breakers.

The mysterious people were coming again. Tiller stood squinting, counting as they came closer. This time, there were far more than before.

———·———·———

"Tiller…" Thio whispered. "What are those things in the water?"

———·———·———

Whenever Tiller had tried to speak of the strange people from the crossing-fires, Thio became irritated, insisting that no such people existed. Although he had never stopped thinking of them, Tiller had long ago stopped mentioning them. So many months had passed since their visit that even for Tiller, it seemed more a dream than a memory.

248

Only the evidence of the stone ship was a solid reminder that they had existed.

Would they still be friendly? Would seeing their faces help Thio piece together her memory again, or would they take her mind to the breaking point?

"Those things are people, Thio. They travel in very small boats. Don't be afraid. Let's finish pulling in the net. We can offer them some of the fish. They are friends." *I think.*

"Keep me safe. Don't leave me. Tiller, keep me safe."

"I will, Thio." They heaved on the cords and hauled in the load of fish. "Olaf! Olaf! Come right away! The people of this land have come to visit again!"

———·———·———

So many of them! Tiller's chest felt tight as he bowed in greeting. Thio's face was pale and her lips pressed together, while Olaf stared openmouthed. The strange people climbed from their tiny craft, clustering tightly in a group and eyeing the seine net at Tiller and Thio's feet, bursting with fish. They exclaimed in their strange language as they pointed to it.

Once they were all standing on land, the people from the water lined up, facing Tiller, Olaf and Thio. Tiller bowed to them, and they did the same, as before. Each of the visitors raised a hand, and in turn, Tiller followed suit. It had been nearly a full year since he had seen them last, but some of their faces were burned into his memory.

"Thio, there is the woman who held you before."

Thio looked at Snow-on-Hair curiously. Some of the fear left her face, and she tentatively reached out her fingertips towards the other woman.

The two groups stared at one another with open fascination, and full of formality, a conversation began.

—·——·——

The woman who had held Thio stood in the center. She touched her chest with the flat palm of her hand. *"Tuniit."* She pointed to the others, repeating the same sound.

Ah. The people called themselves by that word.

"Tuniit." Tiller repeated, and she nodded.

Touching his own chest, Tiller said slowly "Íselander." He pointed to Thio, pointed at Olaf, said again, "Íselander." The woman mimicked him. *"Eyes-landur,"* and Tiller smiled. A soft murmur of *Íselander Íselander Íselander* rippled to the outer edge of their group.

The woman gestured around her. *"Nunaat."*

Wanting to make sure, Tiller pointed to the hills rising behind them, the beach, and the soil on which his feet rested. She nodded yes, and he knew the name for their land.

She spoke again, this time gesturing to the people and to the land. "Tuniit Nunaat!"

Tuniit Nunaat, the people of this land.

Their speaker pointed to herself and said a name, with many sounds. Tiller could not begin to follow it. She smiled at his confusion, and said again, *Aglaktiaputnujaq.* Then slowly, her eyes crinkling, "A-glak-ti". She repeated it slowly, until Tiller could say it correctly.

At his side, in a low murmur, he heard Thio. *"A*-glak-*ti. Aglakti."*

Tiller put out his hand. "Well come, Aglakti."

Aglakti's aging face was beautiful from a long life of kindness. A radiant smile beamed. She touched a young woman. *"Buniq."* Then she pointed to several men. *"Uukarnit. Kakrayok. Pukiq. Nagojut."*

250

Tiller and Thio repeated each until she nodded. Aglakti pointed to the second man again. Tiller looked at her stupidly.

"Kakrayok," said Thio. Aglakti beamed and pointed to another.

"Pukiq," said Thio. Tiller's face made them laugh.

How easy it seemed to trust these people, Tiller thought. Even without their help at the funeral fire, the people's quick humor today had the same effect. When Thio and Tiller had learned several names, Aglakti pointed to Thio, questioning.

Thio faltered. "Thjodhild Jorunds... Jorundsdottir..." She set her chin and said firmly "Thio."

Thio Thio Thio Thio passed among them like soft breath, and Tiller remembered the first time he had whispered the word, a lifetime ago on the ship.

Aglakti pointed at Olaf, who feigned disinterest. She made a questioning sound, gestured again. He continued to ignore her. Her face stayed carefully polite, but a small smile played at the edges of her mouth. The look in her eyes said she was undaunted.

"Olaf," said Thio. "Olaf Olsson."

They repeated *O-laaav Ol-ssen*.

"Olaf Olsson, King of nothing," Olaf commented sourly, but he clearly was affected by the small exchange.

Aglakti looked at Thio and pointed to Tiller.

"Tiller," she said.

———·———·———

No. I am not Tiller, he thought. *That is not my name.*

———·———·———

So common a thing, to call a person by the craft they mastered, acknowledging their skill as weaver, baker, miller, farmer, mason, silver-tapper, butcher, comb-maker, thatcher.

For most of his life, Tiller had been simply *Thorvaldsson*. Thorvald's son was a boy who had taken to *viking* at his first opportunity. It pleased him when people stopped calling him Thorvaldsson, and used his work-name instead.

Tiller, he thought as Aglakti repeated the word Thio had spoken. *No. That was my past. That was how I got here, how I climbed out of the chaos of my past. But my heart has always been with the land.* He heard his mother's voice from childhood, laughing and calling him by his given name. She had loved their home and their farm.

The man who worked on the sea is only a small part of who I am and want to be. It was time to crack the shell apart. *My father Thorvald taught me how to live badly, but it was his first lessons in the stars that set me on my course. Mixing poisonous arsenic into soft copper makes strong bronze. Perhaps that is the secret to life. One takes the poisons within -- our weaknesses and failures -- and faces them with honesty, and in the fire of that honesty, they mix with the good in us to strengthen it. We forge ourselves into stronger, better men.*

It was time to stop being ashamed of the past. It was time to smelt the bad of his past, to make it into something good.

An honest man would tell the whole truth to a woman whose love he wanted. With his hand over his heart, for the first time in his life Tiller spoke aloud his real name, the one his father had given him and the name his mother had called him. His voice was strong and proud.

"My name is Erik Thorvaldsson. I am the firstborn son of Thorvald Asvaldsson, son of Asvald, the son of Ulf, the son of Yxna-Thoris. I welcome you to our home."

252

———·———·———

The moisture in his eyes would have been an embarrassment had not Aglakti's face expressed the same confusion Tiller had shown earlier at an abundance of strange sounds. Tears changed into rich laughter rolling from his throat. He simplified it for her. "E-rik."

She repeated it, questioning, as if to say, *is that right?* Her pronunciation was a little off.

"*E-rik*", he repeated louder and slower.

Aglakti touched his wind-burned cheeks, pointed at the fire, said something, questioning. She made a slashing motion on her arm, indicated blood coming out, and said the word again.

Blood. Fire. What was it?

Aglakti spied the woolen cape Thio wore, and pointed at the red threads running through it, and said the word again each time.

Ruddy skin. Blood. Fire. Red threads. Ah... '*Erik*' sounded like their word for '*red*'.

"*Erik*," he confirmed. On an impulse, he added his own word for the color. "*Rautha.*"

Something broke from him and drifted away like ash. He was Tiller, but more than Tiller. He was Thorvald's son, but more than Thorvaldsson. He was Erik Rautha, the discoverer of a new land, survivor of blood and blade. He was Erik the Red.

———·———·———

253

Through signs and gestures, Tiller and Thio and Olaf learned that the land was an island. The visitors lived to the north, and moved from camp to camp across the year following game and fish. They had seen a pillar of smoke, and had come to see what it was. *No, not there,* gesturing to the stone ship where Sig's fire had burned first. *Over there*, pointing in the direction where the ship had first landed. They had found and followed the knörr, watching.

Tiller was appalled, realizing the ghastly sights they must have witnessed. The one signing saw the shame on Tiller's face. *Yes,* he nodded, and shook his head. *Terrible.*

They had watched Tiller working to build Sig's funeral fire, and had come to help when it was clear he was trying to do a kindness.

Thank you again, Sigmund. Your spirit helped us, Tiller thought. He had honored Sigmund because the man's actions deserved and demanded respect. In turn, it had brought this gift of people in this seemingly-empty land.

They had gone home to their camp, talked it over, and came back to learn more about the voyagers and their gigantic vessel.

In turn, Tiller signed that he, Olaf and Thio came from another island. *Where?* He pointed eastwards. *How far?* He could not say. *Many, many days,* he signed.

A long pause, and their faces grew tense. *Why did you come?* their eyes questioned.

How would they feel if they knew how those in Íseland craved the island these people already knew as their own? Tiller decided that the truth would have to wait. Instead, he showed that they wanted to build a farm, to raise crops.

Farm? Crops? They stared with uncomprehending eyes. All the signs in the world could not bridge that gap.

254

———·———·———

The Tuniit touched the knörr, marveling. Their fingertips traced the nails and the finely-trimmed timbers of the hull with wonder. With encouragement, they clambered into it and explored every inch. Even Olaf warmed, showing how the oar-holes swung open and closed, demonstrating by gestures how the ropes worked the sail.

Their small boats were equally fascinating. Made of leather carefully stitched over a frame of bone, *kayak* were ones in which a single person rode. An *umiak* carried a small group or supplies. The strange oars were *paddles*. They made a motion, and said the same word. Like *sail*, the same word was used for the thing and its action. One paddles with the paddle.

To Tiller's delight, they indicated that he should get in one of the tiny vessels. Two of them – Uukarnit? Nagojut? -- pushed him out into ankle-deep water and with astonishment, he felt the craft lift and float.

"This is so different than our rowing boats!" Tiller called to Olaf and Thio. "They are heavy and difficult to maneuver. This is so quick!" He demonstrated and nearly overturned it. The little vessel rocked wildly as the onlookers laughed.

Uukarnit and Nagojut each stepped into a kayak, showed Tiller again the movement of the paddle, and pointed to the sea.

———·———·———

Gone was the difficult voyage that had brought them here. He forgot Thio, forgot loneliness and isolation and guilt and frustration and pain, knew nothing but the bliss of *kayak* and water.

255

Tiller had loved the land all his life, and loved the sea nearly as much, but he knew that sea and man could never be one. She allowed humans to travel her waters, but trespassers in Rán's domain needed to remember that the sea was hers, not theirs, and she would fiercely remind those who forgot. Men were not of the water, like fish. They were not the sea's own.

Tiller knew that if he lived to be an old, old man, he would never forget this moment. This little leather watercraft floated so lightly that the delicate membrane between human and water became less of a separation and more a connection to the sea. It glided in complete fluidity with Rán-the-Always-Moving, she who lived dancing between the sky and the land, the great Depth who existed for herself with no need of humans. The kayak danced with her, lifting and floating, smooth and free. There was no word to explain the unbounded joy of the kayak, and Tiller surrendered utterly to it.

———·——·———

After what seemed a short time but turned out to have been almost a full eighth, the unfamiliar motion tired Tiller's muscles. The two men paddling alongside urged him back to shore.

Stepping off, he smelled bread baking on the cooking stones. Thio had set it to rise earlier that morning and must have started cooking it while he paddled. The Tuniit women and men looked with great interest at her work, and sniffed the air.

"Bread," Thio explained. "The fire cooks it. You knead it like so," she gestured, "and then you set it to rise." They watched her face and hands carefully. Thio explained in words they could not understand, but demonstrated the growing of wheat, the threshing. Tiller knew a second joy that morning, seeing Thio talking so normally to them.

256

"It is rude to laugh, but honestly, is there anything funnier than this?" Thio's mirth was music to Tiller's ears. "They look like children chewing honeycomb!"

It was true. The Tuniit chewed with their faces squeezed at the curious sensation.

They examined one another's clothing, and the longhouse Tiller was building, and marveled at the animals. Time passed quickly. Tiller began to dread the moment when they would climb back into their kayaks to leave. It had been so good to see human faces, to know that life was larger than their tiny camp of three. It was healing to hear voices in conversation, and to see smiles, and hear laughter.

Almost at the moment he thought of this, Tiller saw Aglakti speak quietly to the group. Heads nodded, and their faces were suddenly formal. Tiller could see something had been planned, and despite himself, tensed again.

The Request

Aglakti took Thio's hand and pulled the younger woman to her side. She made small gestures with her free hand and her expressive face. No, Thio was not well. Yes, something was still very wrong with her heart and her mind.

Aglakti pointed to Thio and then to the kayaks, and to the direction they lived. She pointed to the sky, made a small circle with her fingers and thumb. She opened her thumb slowly until her hand was flat, and then equally slowly formed the circle again. She held her hand flat against her heart, her forehead, and lifted her palm towards Thio, her expression full of care.

Tiller did not understand. Aglakti pointed at the horizon, made the circle motion again.

Moon?

She made the circle, and slowly opened it again. A moon's cycle? Thio watched silently. Aglakti pointed to Thio, to the boat, to the northwest. She waited.

"They want me to go with them for a month," Thio said suddenly. "To help me heal."

—·—·—

Ah, Thio.

Tiller now knew that it was truly possible to be of two minds about one subject.

—·—·—

No, Thio was not healthy. She acted as if she was two different people, and sometimes saw things that were not there. Tiller wanted nothing more than for Thio to be whole again. But to go with people she barely knew, even if they seemed kind? For an entire month?

"Do you want to go? Can we trust them?"

The woman with white streaks in her hair had helped Thio earlier, and today, she had seemed so relaxed during their visit. They clearly were good for her. But to leave with them? Maybe this had all been a trap, designed to trick them. It was a horrible choice to have to make. Would he ever see her again?

258

The questions hung suspended in the air. Her face ashen, Thio kept her eyes on Tiller.

"It is not what I want that matters, Thio, but what you need. Of course I am worried."

Confusion flickered in Thio as she looked back and forth between Tiller and Aglakti. She avoided looking at Olaf.

Abruptly, she turned to Aglakti, *Snow-on-Hair* who had helped her to talk, and cry, and rest.

"Yes." Thio indicated that she needed to get some things. Without another word, she walked away.

More

It will be good for her, Tiller said to himself. *These people are good. They are kind.* But bitterness pulled sour lines along his mouth. *All I did helped not at all. They arrived, and she is better.* Could he let her go? Stay here alone with Olaf? The idea wrenched him.

Thio came in and out of her tent, making a small stack of items to take with her.

They could start over. *Hello, Thio Jorundsdottir. I am Erik Rautha. You are so beautiful, Thio, and my gods, you are courageous. Tell me about yourself. What is important to you? What you will fight for? What delights you, and what discourages you? Tell me what your dreams are. Let me help you make them happen.*

A month without her face. It would be bitter and empty to hear only Olaf's voice. But if it would make her better, if it was what she needed? *I will not let my selfishness hold her back.*

"Let me help you gather your things, Thio."

259

As Tiller went after Thio, someone pulled at the sleeve of his tunic. Aglakti gestured to the men of the group. What else were they were signing? More about taking her?

————·————·————

They pointed at him this time, and to some of the men. Tiller could not make sense of the signs. They pointed to him and the men again, pointed to the boats. To the sea. *Another paddle before they left?* The indication of the moon again.

Aglakti pointed to the beach, pointed farther, and then even farther. Swung her hand to indicate the men, paddling, paddling, that sign of a month. Tiller signed, uncertain.

Me, paddling, with you, a month, that way?

Did they want him to go with the men as they traveled and hunted, while Aglakti took Thio to their camp for healing?

Heads nodded enthusiastically, and hopeful smiles spread across their faces.

Yes

How many days of backbreaking work and worry had it been at their camp, after weeks of tension aboard ship? How many months since he had gone with grim intent to get his high-seat pillars, and the killings, the betrayal of the trials? How many years of having to prove himself because of his father's reputation? A lifetime of feeling unwelcome crashed against those welcoming smiles. The hopeful invitation was almost too good to be true.

260

The people of this island knew nothing about his father's failings or his own. They did not know about the shame-mark, the outlaw tattoo that meant Tiller would never marry any daughter of good family. They were mindless of the blaming, ugly anger that flamed inside Tiller, with which he fought daily. All that they knew about him, they had seen here on this beach: hard work to honor the dead, caring for Thio, work to try and survive.

It mattered little to Tiller that he, too, knew almost nothing about them in return, save that they had once shown kindness to Thio and to him. It was enough.

"Yes," he said firmly. Then again, shouting, "Yes!"

———.———.———

Amid backslapping and general celebration, Tiller suddenly remembered Olaf. He stood aside and alone, not understanding what had just been decided. Tiller's heart sank. Olaf was not strong enough to paddle, and it would be presumptuous to ask. Even though Tiller had no liking for the man, to leave him alone for a month seemed a hard thing. Still...

"They've invited me to travel with them for a few weeks," Tiller said in explanation. "You won't be burdened with Thio. We'll both be back in a month." He cleared his throat, galled to have to ask the question. "Are you willing to stay here yourself that long?"

For the first time, Tiller saw through the bitter anger in which Olaf cloaked himself. "How can I?" he asked, his body tight with fear. "What will I do?"

"There is work you can manage. It will help you grow stronger. We need a larger yard fenced in for the animals. You're strong enough to cut willow canes and push them into the ground yourself now.

They'll grow fast enough to keep the sheep and goats out of the crop fields. If you feel strong enough, it would be good to start cutting turf for a second longhouse. Do what you can. Or just rest the whole time. Do what you want." Olaf would be all right, Tiller reasoned to himself, but selfishly, he did not really care.

Olaf was too ashamed to say what Tiller could see in his eyes. Tiller pretended not to notice, and turned back to the others, but Aglakti understood as well and came over. She pointed to Olaf, questioning. Tiller signed the moon, pointed to Olaf, to the camp.

No, emphatically. She bit her lip, thinking. Called to the others. Their voices did not raise to shouting, but it was clear there was significant disagreement.

———·———·———

"No, absolutely not!" Aglakti's mate Tupit was appalled. "That man was one who did the Hurting. What might he do to the children and old ones of our village, and to you?"

"You are worried that I will not be safe," she said in return.

"Of course I am! I listened to you about the woman. Anyone can see she needs help, and I understand your thoughts about taking the one called Red on our exploration. But this? No!"

"Look at him, my husband. We did not even know he existed until today. It is clear he was injured during the fighting. He must have been on the beach with the dead men when we came before. He is weak and afraid. Asa will be with us. There is nothing to fear."

"You are not afraid because you trust everyone!" Tupit could not bear to think of his beloved wife in harm's way.

Iluq, who also had silver in his hair, took Tupit's arm. "Brother, I am concerned as well, but not just about the fact that there was one more man here than we expected. You know my feelings. It is wrong for us to have anything to do with these beings at all. Look at us! We, who almost never disagree, are arguing. One day with them, and we are acting just as they do! What sickness do they have that so little a time and we are already ill with it?"

Aglakti spoke. "All the more reason for us to take him. If we are so easily infected by these people, we need to understand them. Our shamans need to see them, to feel their spirits."

"One sick woman, yes, we can help. One man who has been burdened and needs to regain himself, yes, we can help. But the third one, the hurter? No." Tupit was firm.

"What if more of them come?" asked Aglakti. "They say none will, but can one man control others, far away? If more arrive, better that we know everything we can of them."

Neither man could find an argument against these words.

"My brother, go back with Aglakti and my son instead of doing the circle-voyage with us," said Iluq. "Keep our people safe. I will watch this man Red to keep any evil from befalling our kin from him. When we meet again, we will each share what we have learned."

Tupit looked at Aglakti, pondering his choices.

"Our grandson has looked forward to his circle-voyage for a long time. He will be disappointed if you do not go because you think me a weak, defenseless woman," Aglakti said.

Tupit sighed. "What you are is a hard-headed and incessantly stubborn woman."

Aglakti's smile spoke years of understanding, love, and profound obstinacy.

———·———·———

263

Olaf and Tiller tried not to stare at the Tuniit group as they argued. Their gaze met a couple of times, and again Tiller saw the fear, but Olaf quickly covered it, spitting on the ground to show his unconcern.

Finally, Aglakti came to them followed by two of the men. She pointed to Olaf, pointed to herself and the group, pointed to their boats. *You come with us, too.*

Tiller felt relief mixed with regret, but Olaf blustered. "There is no chance in Hel of me getting into one of those toy-ships to sink and drown."

Aglakti stood in front of him, silent. Olaf blustered again. "Weird-eyed…dark people…weird boats…" Aglakti motioned, and a few others came to stand next to her. They, too, said nothing, but stood in silence looking at Olaf, their faces calm.

"Tiller, this is ridiculous! Call them away! I'll hit somebody, I swear I will!" Olaf balled his fists, bent his arms, ready to fight.

"Stop it, Olaf. They're just standing there. Going with them is better than being here alone." Did they know what they were doing? Olaf would be difficult.

Still the group made no sound, but simply gazed calmly at Olaf. He was encircled now. No one crowded or pushed. He shoved his way out of the circle of peaceful faces. They let him go, but reformed quietly when Olaf stopped moving. Again, he broke out, and again, they followed, encircling, each one gazing a gentle welcome directly at Olaf's face.

Olaf's blustering diminished little by little. At last he stopped, bent over and winded as if he had run a great distance. He straightened as if with great effort. "I'll go," was all he said.

———.———.———

Tiller thought later about the matter. The Tuniit had wielded calm as effectively as a weapon; more powerfully, in fact. No blood, no scarring, no death, no wounds. Just peace. Even more, he looked forward to the trip. He would learn more from them in that month than just how to paddle a kayak.

Freedom

With that, Thio and Olaf and Tiller turned loose the chickens and the ducks. They would roost wherever they liked for the time being. Tiller offered Aglakti's people the eggs laid that day, and was mildly disgusted when they sucked the contents out raw.

The goats and sheep would forage for themselves as well. Tiller stowed everything that could blow away or be damaged by weather. With many hands, they made fast work of it.

Last of all, he put out the fire that had burned since Thio started it the day they made land. Swallowing hard, he pulled out his oilskins.

At that, one of the men hit himself in the head gently. He ran to one of the *umiak* and pulled out a bulky package, offering it to Tiller.

The package opened to a set of clothing like the ones they wore. Leather on the outside and fur on the inside, beautifully made, simple and strong, and built to accommodate paddling. As good as his oilskins and wools were, these would keep him warm and dry even better. There were fur boots, too, to pull on and tighten with sinews, and a beautiful, dense outer coat made from an animal skin he did not recognize, with a great fur fringe around the rim. *Anorak,* they said. Even new gloves hung from a sinew threaded through the sleeves.

Someone had looked at Tiller carefully when the first group visited. They had noted his height and breadth, even his feet, because as he pulled them on, the garments fit perfectly.

Such magnificent gifts with many hours of work needed to create them. *Let the fruit of your gratitude be plentiful. Let it seed the future, when these people may need* your *generosity in return,* his inner voice told him.

Yes, he vowed inwardly, and took the clothing, humbled.

The deep moment was over, and the business of setting off began.

Into The Future

What did their tiny settlement look like to Tuniit eyes? The small sod house, a temporary one until a proper longhouse could be built, had cost grueling hours. The work had seemed huge and important, work Tiller could not have dreamed of leaving that morning. If Thio was healthy and laughing, they offered hope for some kind of future. Without her, they were just hardscrabble shelters, lonely and easy to leave behind.

Thio came over. "My cat --" she said. She held the small fur bundle she always carried.

"Are you taking it with you?" Tiller asked gently.

"It won't like their little boats. It could fall into the water." Her chin trembled.

"You can leave it," he said.

She shook her head.

"Thio, listen to me. This little thing you call your cat...your real one is safe with your family. This little bundle of fur, your Nunaat-

266

cat…let it stay here safely until you come back. It can't be lost on your voyage that way."

She nodded, her head against Tiller's chest. "Where shall we put it?"

They surveyed their camp carefully. Finally, she pointed to the stone alcove where she had rested the day the stone ships were built. "There."

Some green grasses made a little nest. Thio smiled a little at him, a first tiny glimpse of happiness in the quiet gloom that cloaked her. "I'm ready now. Let's go back to the others."

———·———·———

They took seats in the small craft, Tiller in a single kayak, and Thio and Olaf in one of the umiak with other passengers. The whole group pushed off through the breakers to the swells. Tiller realized the motion must have felt strange to Thio, bobbing on the waves, so close she could touch the surface of the water. Typical for Thio, she had held her fear in check and did not betray any expression of it. Olaf looked horrified.

The men in Tiller's group paddled east. After a few moments, they stopped and turned, lifting their hands in farewell to the others. Thio's group was approaching the curve of land at the end of the cove and would soon be out of sight.

Goodbye, Aglakti, Buniq. Thank you for caring for Thio.

Goodbye, Thio.

She did not wave at first. Finally, her chin lifted high, so like the old brave, defiant Thio, and she let go of her grip on the umiak. Her hand shot skyward, defiant and strong. She knew Tiller saw her. It was a parting gift. *I can do this.*

267

Thio would be with people who laughed and smiled easily, and would heal from whatever ministrations Aglakti thought might help. She was safe with them. Tiller had carried the weight of care for too long, and he needed release. Worry about Thio fell from Tiller like a heavy cloak at the end of winter. They were not alone in this place so far from home. They had friends. A new future had begun, and it held promise.

Tiller turned forward. How exhilarating to have a carefree month ahead! With a great wave of freedom, with hope floating powerfully across the water, with life calling and adventure ahead, the men paddled, surging forward under the spring sun.

———·———·———

Thio

That evening, Thio pointed to the fish. Where was a fire to cook it?

Buniq cut a bit of the fish's flesh and offered it to Thio. Why did Thio keep pointing?

How horrid! Had Buniq just put some into her mouth, raw? They ate fish without cooking it? Thio gagged. "Oh, gods above, that cannot be," she muttered.

Buniq held out anther strip of wet flesh.

"I don't mean to be rude, but that is nauseating!" said Thio. "Can't we cook it?"

"Thio must be hungry by now," Buniq told Aglakti. "But she refuses to eat any fish."

—·—·—

Buniq and Aglakti talked as they paddled. "She really did look disgusted, didn't she? So strange, with such a fine fish."

"Strange is the way they burn all of their food with fire!" Buniq mused. "But we ate that soft stuff. It tasted good. What was it again?"

"Ommel-bred. Something like that."

"Olaf won't take any fish either."

Aglakti smiled. "They will, sooner or later. Hunger changes minds."

"What makes a person like Olaf? What makes these people do hurting as you described?"

Aglakti struggled to find a way to make sense of the question. "To be truthful, Buniq, I do not want to understand. What settlement could

269

we go to, anywhere in Nunaat, where we would not be welcomed with open arms, home and hearth shared? Our people are different."

Buniq flicked her glance at Olaf. "That one is like ice that freezes, and then the tide goes out, and with nothing under it, it is a shell that crushes easily. What will be destroyed with him?"

———·———·———

Three days had passed. Buniq squatted beside Thio, pleading.

"Neither you nor Olaf has eaten since we left your home. You must be starving." She held the morsel of meat in her fingers. "You saw Kunwaktok kill it, it's fresh. The spirit of the seal was healthy. We offered to the sea and the land. Why won't you eat, Thio?"

Thio looked at the bloody seal meat, her lips trembling. Her eyes filled with tears, and she gagged. Shaking her head, she turned away.

With an angry cry, Olaf strode over and snatched the bit of meat from Buniq's fingers. He pushed it roughly into his mouth and shouted at Thio, his face in her face, and chewed and swallowed, then shouted at her again. He grabbed piece after piece, chewing, swallowing, spitting. Bits of bloody meat fell from his lips.

Thio kept her eyes fixed on the ground, trembling.

———·———·———

Blood bits bits eye blot eyes green eyes *SigmmSig eye green eye blood* poisoned them all *and san d blood blood* my fault my fault *sand eye on ey eye* voice know that voice *that* voice *cut sand in it* eye on sandpoisoned *blood agh chewed blood on sand* green eye all dead *should die*

too   eyeeyeeye   oh sig...   eye on sand

270

Buniq touched Olaf gently on the arm as he shouted at Thio. "Olaf, no! You must not!"

He glared at Buniq and stomped away. Kneeling beside Thio, Buniq put her arms around the shaking woman. "Shhhh..." she said. "Shhhh. Find your way back, Thio. Find your way."

___.___.___

Erik

"Here is how you paddle properly." Erik could not understand the words, but from his gestures, that must be what Tupit meant. "Hold your paddle so, and move it so. Your muscles" – he patted his chest, and then his upper arms – will last longer."

The lessons helped. Even so, Erik's muscles ached after his first hour. The Tuniit glided on effortlessly, their speed astonishing, rivaling a knörr's under a mild wind.

"Good work, Red," Tupit smiled. As Erik labored along the coastline, one of the Tuniit men always stayed with him. The others would speed off to one or another of the numerous nearby small islands, and quickly reappear with news of anything they had seen.

That first night, Erik was too tired to pay attention to how they set up camp or made fire, or ate, or not. He threw his sleeping sack above the high-tide line and fell asleep climbing into it.

———·———·———

Iluq and Tupit watched Erik Red sleeping. Tupit sighed. "Say your words, brother."

"It confuses me why no one else is concerned. The girl needs healing, but our help should be limited to that. These men should stay at their camp, no matter what Aglakti said."

"One learns about a man if he is pushed to exhaustion. We are learning about this one."

"They have done terrible things. They will hurt our people as well somehow, I *know* it."

272

"You're no coward, Iluq. They're here. We must learn what we can."

Iluq was used to being more cautious than the others, but to be openly ignored by his own brother? Already the strangers caused problems. Tupit and Aglakti's kindness had blinded them.

Time to Play

Erik groaned. *That cannot be the sound of people waking up.* He ached everywhere. Erik tested by stretching a little. Yes, everywhere.

Was that Pukiq poking at him? Or Nagojut? Erik found himself unceremoniously dumped out of his warm covering, and cold water tossed onto his face. Angry, he jumped to his feet, only to see both of them laughing and running away. They tumbled and wrestled like puppies.

"Men do not play like children where I live!" Erik shouted. He watched them as they laughed. What would it have been to have brothers like that? Erik smiled despite himself. "It is utterly childish to wake me that way," he said, but his tone of voice was mild.

Nagojut gave a hand to Erik, pulled him up, and knocked Erik's feet out from under him.

"Have it your way!" Erik gave chase, tackling Nagojut and then Pukiq. He received a pummeling as a reward, until they all lay on their backs along the shoreline, laughing.

"Where's our food?" Iluq called from the water's edge, and Pukiq mock-sighed.

Nagojut pulled on a string that trailed into the water behind his kayak. He lifted one of the fish secured to it, and quickly undid the thong threaded through its gills. He carried the wriggling fish to Iluq and expertly gutted it. In no time, slices were cut and laid on the fishskin.

Erik hesitated. How odd. Did they not cook it? He grimaced as Nagojut lifted his knife towards Erik with a raw piece, but he was their guest. Taking the slice of glossy flesh, Erik chewed quickly. To his surprise, it tasted delicious. As they ate piece after piece of the fresh, clean food, Nagojut pulled another fish from the line.

While he chewed, Erik noted that the wrestling had loosened his muscles. This second day of paddling had promised to be tortuous. Now it would only be completely uncomfortable.

————·———·————

"You're paddling faster, Red!" Nagojut said. Or was he saying *"Paddle faster?"* Erik had learned many words after five - or was it six? - days of paddling. Each day, his endurance had increased a little. He looked into the water as they glided along, trying to see fish. Nagojut pointed, saying words for *island, fjord, stone, surf, wave, fish, sky, sun, eat, laugh, cold, warm.*

"Others come," Erik said in Tuniit. *"Fast."*

They heard the rest of the paddlers returning, shouting with excitement. After a rapid exchange of words, the group started away again at a punishing speed. Shouts of *"Fast! Come!"* encouraged Erik to follow as quickly as he could.

As they approached a nearby island, the conversation picked up in intensity, with confusion and excitement in their voices. Eagerness filled Erik. What were they going to see?

————·———·————

The men leaped from their kayaks and ran. A short sprint, and the object of interest shone before them: a wide pool of water glimmered in the fresh air, steam hovering in delicate swirls.

"You've never seen a hot spring before?" Erik asked. It appeared that the Tuniit thought the water was on fire. "I've been in these since I was a little boy! There's nothing to fear!" He nearly laughed at their worried amazement until a better idea came: time to play a joke on *them*.

———·———·———

"Stand back!" Erik said loudly, his tone of voice indicating danger. He put his fingers in the water. Hot, but not scalding. He made a great show of gesturing to the sky and water, speaking in sonorous tones as if invoking spirit gods.

In fact, Erik's words were nothing of consequence. *Here we have a hot spring, how superb!* He bowed ceremoniously to it, and began removing his boots. *It will feel so good.*

———·———·———

They grasped one another's arms and shoulders, anxious. Erik pointed to Pukiq, indicated that he, too, must strip. Erik pulled off his shirt and trousers lined with fur until he stood fully naked, intoning, "I cannot wait to get into this wonderful spring!" He put his toes in the water, and shouted, jumping back quickly for effect. He walked away, rubbing his chin as if thinking.

The Tuniit were mesmerized. With symbolic gestures, Erik turned and slowly waded into the water, making his movements tentative, still

275

intoning as if to some spirit. When he was waist-deep, he shouted suddenly and submerged, thrashed about underwater, then erupted to the surface shouting, his hands clawing back towards the edge. Pukiq held out a piece of driftwood and Erik struggled towards it, wrenching as if something invisible in the water was pulling at him. Finally, Pukiq grasped Erik's hand, his eyes fearful and earnest...and Erik pulled him in.

———·———·———

Screams of terror erupted as Pukiq fell. He tripped again and again as he writhed towards the pool's edge. Finally, Pukiq crawled out and turned to help Erik.

Their new friend was bent double with laughter. Frightened faces turned confused, and slowly they realized they had been played in a joke. They bent and gingerly touched the water with their fingers, marveling at it. It was not long until all were naked and splashing in the hot spring, floating and looking at the sky.

———·———·———

"We should stop here for a meal, don't you think?" Tupit said to Iluq. "Set up camp for the night?" Even though the sun was quite high in the sky.

———·———·———

Iluq lay in the water, considering. The trick Red had played on Pukiq had been truly funny. Iluq had watched Red trying to paddle as hard as he could, struggling but not complaining. The man himself seemed likeable and decent, but a worry nagged at Iluq that he could not put into words. How to protect their kin and friends? It seemed that only he was concerned.

But it was hard to be vigilant in this strange warm water. Iluq moved a little away from noisy chatter of the others to think better. He stretched out his legs and fell pleasantly asleep.

———·———·———

Songs of hunting and travels and love lifted towards the high stars until late in the night. The next morning, the voyagers enjoyed one last soak. Erik's muscles still ached, and he could not remember anything feeling so good.

As they prepared to leave, Erik thought of Thio. She would enjoy this. Perhaps one day they could make their own kayaks and come here. The idea enlarged upon Erik's thoughts. Perhaps as he explored, he could scout the coastline for resources, for land that was even better for fields where he could move their camp. Also helpful would be a natural headland harbor, somewhere along what must be the nearby bottom of the island, where, if other ships ever came, one would almost certainly put in, and where he could at least create signs of their existence and where to find them. Perhaps it would be wise to even relocate there, little by little.

But how to explain farmland? The Tuniit did not use grains.

Erik was astonished how quickly he was learning their words. He could use *flat* from their signs describing the water and stones. *Land,* he now knew, and '*good*' from the meals they had eaten and a similar word they used when he paddled well. *Chickens*…Erik smiled. Nagojut would come up at random intervals, his arms bent and flapping like the birds he had seen at the camp. "Chickens, Red! Chickens!"

"Tupit?" Erik pointed to the nearest fjord. *Look flat land, please? Big flat land.* Looking, looking. *Good chickens.* He pointed again, in several directions, asking. *Big flat land...no stones, good chickens-and-ducks, near the ocean? Me paddle, look?* He may have been saying *flat land eats tasty chickens,* but it was the best he could manage.

Shoulders shrugged. They nodded yes. No one seemed in any hurry. As they got into their kayaks, a second idea came.

A mound built on this shoreline could mark the island, to make it more visible to a kayaker paddling among the innumerable small islands. Erik began putting stones one on top of another.

"It's not for a stone ship," he reassured them, but his fears were groundless. In a very little time he was pushed out of the way and they took over building it themselves. Shortly, a tight stone form stood on the shore, oddly resembling a human being, with shoulders and legs.

"*Inuksuk,*" Pukiq beamed. "In-uk-suk!" He gestured to the sea, the pool, and the men. The stones represented a beacon, a human calling to other humans.

"Inuksuk," Erik smiled broadly, and clapped Pukiq on the back.

They split into three groups. Erik's started up the nearest fjord, one went back to the inlet just passed, and the last group headed forward to the next one, looking for flat land.

———·———·———

"No good," Tupit said. *No flat chicken land.* The next fjords had some promising areas, but not the size that Erik knew he needed for a true settlement, and the spaces of green land were not close enough to the ocean to serve as a harbor for a ship coming in from Íseland. They continued on at a leisurely pace, with trial and error learning the sorts of place Erik was seeking.

At the next inlet Iluq signaled he remembered from an earlier trip that a day's paddle ahead, there was land flat and low to the water, with green growing plants, visible from the sea. They made camp for the night, ate, and crawled into night-sacks.

Quiet sleep-breathing soon filled the air. "What do you think of the stars in this place, Thio?" Erik asked the night sky. "They tell me that on the other side of this island, Íseland is due east. I was right! The storm must have blown us terribly far south." He lay silent for a bit, happy to know his navigating instincts were right. "I'm looking for a place now that will be a kind of port for incoming ships. We'll need that, if we ever can figure out how to get home." He considered a voyage home, and put the impossible thought from his mind. "But if we don't, Thio, it's good, being with these people. I hope you're finding it the same. We do only one thing: every day we paddle until nightfall. The days have no plan, no schedule to follow. No admonitions to *plant quickly* or *harvest right now*! No Kalendar's warnings about wasting Sól-eighths." There were no crops to get in, no shelters to dig, no animals to tend morning and evening, no sense of time, and no expectations; only the rising and setting of the sun to mark their days. The ocean was on their right, the land to the left, and freedom was ahead and behind.

It was not only Thio who needed help. Only a handful of days had passed, and in the endless paddling, Erik realized that he, too, was beginning to heal.

Discovery

Damp fog the next morning cloaked sight and sound. They had paddled along the edge of the coastline, staying outside the breakers but keeping land close by. They passed a long series of sharp rocky islands and then moved along a broad curve of shoreline, and the water moved like silk beneath the kayaks. The land continued along its wide curve until it seemed they would come full circle when Iluq finally directed them to a landing place. They beached their kayaks and ate quickly, with a little daylight still to explore on foot.

Iluq had been right. The land fit the description Erik had made – close to the sea, flat, and green growing things – but the soil was not rich enough to grow crops and keep livestock, and the shoreline curved out, not in as he would need for a harbor. But as they climbed the hill and looked across the inlet to the other side, Erik saw the thing for which he had been searching.

———·——·———

A wide plain spread out, nestled under a low hill. Yes, the land was stony, but there was enough grass to keep animals fed. The water reached in along a generous curve of beach, wide, flat, and good for ships to land. The shoreline curved so far inward that the land would be a perfect harbor, sheltered within a rounded cove.

Erik smiled broadly and bowed deeply to Iluq, his face beaming.

"He has found that for which he was looking," said Tupit.

"Good. It is far, so far, from our permanent homes," replied Iluq. "Maybe Red and the pale woman and the other man will live here. We will meet only if we choose to do so. We rarely come here. Even a circle-voyage does not happen every year."

"You are so worried, brother," Tupit replied. "But it comes from a good heart."

Understanding and Misunderstanding

The weather cleared the next day, and they paddled to the cove early and explored it. As they left and headed away from it, a thought troubled Erik.

There were so many inlets that all were beginning to look alike. How could he remember this one? Something like an *inuksuk*, but larger. Something that could withstand a winter gale and be seen at a distance from the water. Something like the night stars used for navigating. Something that could guide him to the fjord from *anywhere*.

A confusion from long ago clicked into clarity. Like many, Erik had heard about a man from a country far away, a man named Ahmad ibn Fadlan whose king had sent him on a long voyage to greet kings of other lands. The story of the adventurer had fascinated Erik not because of the man named Fadlan, but because of one detail that had confused him. The story described a flat piece of leather Fadlan carried, on which lines like rune-markings showed the flow of rivers, expanses of sea, the edges of land, and cities. The man would point to the leather thing to show people where he had come from, and where they were. He called it his *map*.

Erik had struggled for years to understand what a map might look like. He often took a stick and made lines on dirt or sand or snow, trying to make patterns, but would give up in frustration. Like the red berry in his neck-pouch, Erik had held it in his mind across the years, trying to understand.

Thinking of the red berry and the map, the dream of the petrel flashed into Erik's mind, and he saw the lines of the coast in the way the petrel saw them from the air, as patterns he could follow on land or sea. Perhaps it was not a true map like Fadlan's, but he could use it. Erik aimed his kayak to the shore, yanked off his anorak and his sealskin tunic and laid them on the sand of the beach, and quickly started a fire.

———.———.———

"What is he doing?" Iluq asked his nephew Pukiq.

"I don't know," Pukiq answered. He touched Red's arm, questioning.

Erik gesticulated, waving his arms around and pointing in excitement.

"He is so strange, Pukiq," Iluq said. The two men watched, one frowning and one intrigued, as Red poked the fire and held a small stick in it until it flamed.

He smoothed his sealskin tunic on the ground, and blew out the stick.

Iluq exploded. "He is going to ruin the sealskin! Your mother worked on that for so long! *No!*" He snatched the stick in Red's hand and yanked the tunic away.

Red spoke earnestly, reassuringly, pointing up the inlet, pointing to the sea, pointing to the tunic. He held out his hand, asking for it back.

"Whatever it is, let him do it," said Nagojut. "Maybe we'll learn something."

Iluq pressed his lips angrily. Again, his people chose the stranger's way. Again, they showed no respect for the gift of his advice. "Let's see what you learn when he ruins that tunic," Iluq said bitterly. He walked stiffly back to his kayak and paddled away.

———·———·———

The need to create the map overrode Erik's desire to be polite. He pulled another stick from the fire, blew out the flame, and smoothed the tunic again. This must be what metalworkers felt like, shaping silver or gold. He moved his hand in practice, looking at the cove, the wide inlet that led to it, the other fjords and islands they had passed. He pressed the glowing tip of the stick against the leather of the tunic, burning a mark into it. *This line would show where the sea forms the fjord, and here is the cove, so near the mouth of the fjord. These dots are the islands to the northwest of it. These lines, the fjords past them. Here the hot-spring lake. Here, the hot-spring lake, and here, the beach where our ship and camp are.* Erik indicated the direction where the sun came up and sank, and the northern star, the currents they had followed so far, and the ones the ship had fought on their journey. He put in every detail he could think of, and then held the tunic away from him, studying it. The drawing *did* look as a bird might see from the air. The guiding-shapes felt powerful, like an act of immortality, of creating land. In that moment, Erik experienced for the first time what it meant to value his own life.

Erik's traveling companions still watched, puzzled. He tried to explain, not yet knowing enough of their words, but just saying his own aloud. "There are things of every people that others don't understand. We cook our food, while you eat raw fish. You do not know bread, but it is a great treat to us. We farm, while you hunt and fish. I learned *inuksuk* from you today. I teach you a *map*. We learn from each other. Exploration and learning are the heart-blood of the world." Erik bowed to them. "You are explorers. It is an honor to be with you."

He bowed to them again to show his gratitude and respect, then stamped out the fire and carefully pulled the tunic back on. The day was early. They had more to explore.

———·———·———

Thio

"It doesn't matter. I no longer feel any hunger, anyway." In Tuniit, Thio affirmed her words. *"No eat. No."* She shook her head wearily. She had blacked out the last time she tried to stand up quickly.

Buniq offered again, her kind eyes worried.

"No."

———·———·———

Aglakti cradled Thio's head in her lap. The nausea had passed, but Thio still shivered, murmuring to herself.

"I'm sorry. I can't do it. Raw meat, raw fat. Raw fish. Raw anything. Don't you ever cook anything? Don't you ever eat anything but raw, raw, and raw?"

Aglakti did not know the words, but she knew the sound of distress.

"I realize if I don't eat I'll starve to death. I don't mean to waste it." She had thrown up every time she attempted a piece. Thio sat up wearily. "Let me try again, please."

Aglakti put another piece of fish into Thio's outstretched fingers. The pale woman put it into her mouth and chewed, and retched again.

———·———·———

Olaf walked to Thio. He stood looking down at her thinning face.

"Thio."

She stared straight ahead. A visible trembling started through her body.

"Thio, just eat the damned fish. It seems awful, but it's really not that bad after the first bite or two. Mostly just the *idea* of eating raw is awful, but if you don't, you're going to die. And I'm not going to be stuck out here alone with these people."

Thio still looked at the horizon. Olaf squatted down next to her. None of this was his fault. Damn it, Thio needed to understand that.

"I don't know who was behind it. Some of the *gothar*, and some from the Althing council. Someone I don't know, someone high, is leading them. They took my son not long before we were put on the ship. It was you or him, Thio. You or him." Olaf studied the ground and cleared his throat. His breath came ragged and angry. "Seven girls, and finally a son. Since he was young, he's carved. You should see his wine-cups. He's already done a set of pillars, and has orders for more. They'll pay for wedding feasts for the girls."

Overwhelming pain swelled in Olaf. He rubbed his hands together and stood. Self-righteous pride returned to his voice, and his eyes narrowed. "For Thor's sake, eat the food, Thio. I mean it. I'm not going to be stuck out here alone with these people. You got me here. You need to live."

Aglakti watched Olaf walk stiffly away. Thio had stopped looking at the hill and was watching him, too. She was not trembling. The only thing about her that moved were two lines of tears falling down her cheeks.

———·———·———

Another daybreak had come, of Buniq and Aglakti and Chena and Olaf and the rest eating raw-something. Thio's stomach no longer hurt.

She had been through enough crop shortages in the last years to know how dangerous that was, but she had lost the energy to care. She sat staring at the umiak paddles dipping into the water, out, in, out.

———·———·———

Buniq and Aglakti helped Thio from the umiak. Her hands were barely strong enough to hold theirs in return. A small group of huts was ahead, and people standing a short distance from them. They could hear wailing, the cries of a child mixed with a woman keening.

Olaf stayed behind. He never liked coming to a settlement, and would wait to come forward until the people had finished staring at Thio and touching her.

Thio asked Buniq what was happening, but the gestures in return made no sense. As they reached the edge of the group, Thio saw people look in surprise at her pale skin and hair. Instead of staring as others had, they grabbed at Thio, pulling her to the center of the group and pointing down. With shock, she saw the bloody thing squirming on the stones.

She did not wait for them to ask. "Give it to me," Thio demanded, reaching for it.

———·———·———

Thio was almost too weak to hold the shivering newborn. Aglakti and Buniq helped her to sit. Thio opened her anorak and put the shivering newborn against her warm skin.

"Why was it being left to die?" Thio asked Buniq.

With difficulty, her friend indicated that the baby's father had been killed in a sea storm not long ago. His body had washed ashore

287

overnight, pale and bloated. The baby had been born almost at the same time. The baby, such a strange color... They had been certain that the child's unnatural paleness came from the dead father pulling at the baby, trying to take its spirit, or body, to bring himself back to life. They were frightened."

Thio had seen a being like this once before. A young man with too-pale skin and eyes that were pink had traveled to their farm as companion to an elderly truth-seer. Besides poor eyesight, he had been normal in all other respects, and had eagerly helped with farm chores during their stay. Thio had become good friends with him.

"I'll take it," she said. "It will be my child. It will cause no harm."

Under her supervision, the infant was cleaned and wrapped in soft skins. The child's mother, frightened but encouraged by a murmuring crowd, nursed the baby, eyeing Thio with gratitude. When she was finished, she handed the baby the Thio. Laughter broke out at the sound of a very normal burp, and immediately the seriousness of the moment turned into an impromptu celebration.

The baby's mother offered Thio a slice of raw fish, with tears in her eyes and her lips trembling with gratitude. Thio glanced at the overly-pale child in her arms, now sleeping. With trembling fingers, she reached for the piece of fish and put it in her mouth. She quickly swallowed, and the bit of food stayed down.

"Another piece," she stammered nervously. "I need to be strong to care for this child."

———·———·———

Aglakti and Chena scraped sealskins that Chena's mate had brought them. An uncomfortable silence drew out between the two women. Aglakti sighed.

288

"Nothing to say today, Chena? You, who loves to talk? That means you are thinking."

Chena wiped her bone scraper and searched for the right words. "The Olaf," she began. "He is a sickness to our people. Before he came, who argued? Who felt fear? Now, it seems that that poison grows in us daily. Do you see it?"

Aglakti nodded reluctantly. "I do. Buniq spoke in anger back to him yesterday. Buniq! The sun does not set a single day but that harsh words are spoken, and always because of Olaf."

"Asa tries to help him. It makes me sad to see my beautiful son opening his heart to such willful wrong. Is it even possible to help Olaf? He seems determined to destroy himself, and he cares for no one."

Aglakti agreed. "I believed we could help him, but the longer he is with us, the more Olaf hurts us instead. He is changing us for the worse." Aglakti's voice broke. "This is my fault, Chena. I am so sorry. I was blind to what he is. I have hurt all of our people by allowing his spirit to mingle with ours. Terrible damage has been done to us, and I cannot repair it."

"We all make mistakes. You did it from a desire to help. Be at peace."

"I hope it grows no worse." Aglakti felt the white bear whisper, and shivered.

The women returned to their rhythmic scraping. For now, the work calmed them, but they fretted. It was one thing to talk about Olaf, a known problem. To feel afraid of what the future might bring was such a strangeness that neither woman could bring herself to speak words about that to the other.

———·———·———

Something was moving about ahead of the kayaks. The sound came and went in the mist. For the first time, Uukarnit had assigned Erik to lead the group. Should he ask someone about it?

Erik paused paddling and listened intently. There it was again. Low cries of people, maybe in pain? It was muffled by fog. Was it a village? His ears strained.

Suddenly Erik's questions were answered as a cacophony of snarls and roars erupted from the beach ahead. Shouts broke out from the other kayaks. "Quick, get the spears!"

There was another word he did not know, but quickly learned. They had found walrus.

———·———·———

Iluq and Pukiq led the hunt. From the hundreds of animals on the beach, they killed only one. As Uukarnit slit the animal from throat to vent, Erik studied the enormous teeth-like horns projecting from its mouth. "What do you call this?" Erik asked. "And this?" pointing to the huge leathery fin-feet. He practiced, and more words became familiar.

Uukarnit took out the liver first. He carefully placed it on a stone, and set aside the other organs. Uukarnit went to the water and cleaned his knife with sand while Tupit lifted the liver to offer an invocation, then made a careful stroke and cut a generous piece.

In the weeks he had traveled with the Tuniit, Erik had come to enjoy the raw fish that was the daily diet. But raw meat? And liver at that? He found himself gagging, but the importance of Tupit's gesture was clear. The bloody bit in his mouth felt wrong, but Erik kept his face calm and chewed as if it was the most important thing he had ever eaten.

The hunters watched carefully, eager for him to enjoy it. Erik swallowed hard, and bowed slightly to Tupit. His reward was enormous smiles all around, and a second, far larger piece.

———·———·———

"You have avoided me all day!" Iluq had pulled his brother Tupit off to talk alone.

"Iluq, I see you losing yourself in this worry. This man represents no harm to us!"

"But he *has* harmed us, don't you see? When was the last time you and I argued? We have been best friends since we were children."

"Iluq, it is not the man who is making us argue, but you, and your fear."

"I don't fear him day to day. I fear what he means to us in a larger way. They are different, Tupit, in ways we do not yet understand. They did the killing horrors!"

"Why judge one wolf by what another does? This one did none of that, we know."

Iluq sank to a squatting position, his expression worried. "The more Red tries to be one of us, the more fearful I become. If we allow ourselves to become friends with him, it will make us more vulnerable when the danger finally comes."

"But what danger?"

Iluq shook his head, miserable. "I cannot say, brother. I cannot say."

291

Nothing or Everything?

"It is so good, this life you live!" Erik signed and talked at the same time. "We sleep on the hard ground. I have no comfortable bed." When it rained, they pulled their kayaks together, and with extra skins, made a shelter to wait out the storm, talking and telling stories or just lying and thinking. "We rise at dawn and paddle all day. The coastline hardly varies: stone, inlet, islands, stone, inlet, islands, stone, fjord, islands. Raw meat and fish are our only food. We are wet by the rain, and dried by the sun and wind. I no longer think about yesterday and nothing of tomorrow. No hope, no regret, no fear. I live in the present moment. I have become an animal, but I have never felt more human, or happier."

It had been nearly a full month since the group had left the knörr. Erik wanted to ask when they would be returning to his camp without wanting to seem rude.

"It will be good to see Thio," he remarked.

"Where will you see her?" asked Pukiq.

"At our camp, where our ship is. Aglakti said she was taking Thio with them for a month. I intended to be back there at the same time as she arrived."

"You thought Aglakti signed a moon? And that our circle-voyage was a month as well? No!" Nagojut laughed. "Where did you get that crazy idea? It will be far longer before we reunite with them! Aglakti signed the leaving-of-the-sun and the coming-back, to see if Thio was willing to go for a full year, if need be."

"A year? A *year*?"

"They will be at Aglakti and Tupit's home village." They pointed. "In the always-snow-lands, far to the north."

"I need to go to her."

"I think that Aglakti made it clear you should be separated, until Thio is better."

Erik was stunned. He felt a sudden sense of tremendous loss.

"This is our way, Red," said Tupit, not unkindly. "You took a long voyage across the sea. We take extended explorations as well, along our land. Your companion Thio is safe. Aglakti knows the time we have planned to meet again. I'm sorry you didn't understand. Please trust that Thio will be fully healthy when you see her again. Accept it and be at peace." Tupit chuckled. "Be like that animal about which you were just speaking, thoughtless of time and care."

Erik stared at their faces, aghast. "Is there nothing I can do?"

Even Iluq took pity on Erik's unhappy astonishment. "No. But Tupit is right. We could all see that the pale one was very sick. She needs a long time to get better. Our people will help her. It would be better not to interfere."

A year, instead of a month? Erik knew he would never have agreed to it had he known. It frustrated him immensely to learn that their separation would be so much longer than he had expected, but worse, it galled Erik for Iluq, of all people, to dictate to him about Thio. Iluq was the only thing that had marred the days as their group had explored. No matter how hard Erik tried to fit in or work with the others, Iluq always found some small thing to criticize. Each time, Erik reminded himself to remain polite, that he was their guest, but Iluq seemed to push even harder then. It had become more and more difficult for Erik to swallow his anger. This news about Thio made it doubly harder.

Still, what was most important was what was right for Thio. Whether he liked it or not, Erik knew Iluq was correct. As sick as Thio was, a long heal was better, and she herself had chosen to go with Aglakti, without any questions. Erik breathed deeply, calming himself the way he had seen Tupit do.

The *viking* part of his brain found something to occupy his thoughts. Tupit had said it would take months to reach their permanent village. The island these people lived on was far larger than any he had ever heard of. Where did it end? Where did *all* land end?

"Nagojut, have you ever seen berries growing on Nunaat, about so big, perfectly round, and red?

Nagojut pursed out his lips, considering. "No. Red berries, yes, but nothing nearly that big. Why do you ask?"

"I was just wondering." Erik touched the small leather pouch hanging from his neck-cord. He thought about the dream of the petrel. He thought of the day he had found the red berry, and the mystery that small berry had opened in his mind. As he thought of how far Thio was from him, Erik wondered, for the thousandth time, from where that red berry had come.

———.———.———

Thorvald had stormed away from where a knörr stood ready to leave on an extended vik. They were to go first to Scotiland to trade for bronze ingots and glass smoothing stones, and then on to Nórsvegr for furs. Such a rich voyage would yield good crew-shares. Despite Thorvald's skills, they had refused to take him aboard.

"What do they mean, I caused trouble last time with the trading?" he fumed. "That jarl was cheating us! This is the thanks I get for stopping him? He didn't die. It was only a scratch."

Young Erik stayed well behind. When his father was in a mood like this, better to be out of reach. As Thorvald stormed away, he ran along the shoreline, following his father.

Up there, what was that? Something caught his inquisitive eyes. Erik ran to it.

There it was, wedged almost underneath a stone about the size of a cabbage and flat on top, something small and bright red. Erik picked it up carefully and looked at it.

It was a berry, perfectly round, and deep rich red, with some small green leaves.

Curiosity overcame Erik's caution. He ran to catch up Thorvald. "Da, what's this?"

His father gave the berry a cursory glance. He puffed his chest, ready to show off his knowledge. "It's a lingonberry. You know them perfectly well. A cowberry."

"No, Da. It's different. Look! It's bigger than any cowberry I ever saw. The shape and the end aren't the same either." Erik turned the small red sphere in his fingers.

"Let me see it." Thorvald took the berry. "It's a lingonberry, I tell you!"

"No, Da, it's not! I wonder where it came from." Erik held out his hand for the berry.

"You're as stupid as the jacks on that knörr. Here. Let your precious berry go vik with them." Thorvald threw it as hard as he could, and his rant shifted to the stupidity of his son.

Erik ran in the direction his father had thrown the berry. It bobbed in the very edge of the waves. Three attempts and wet boots for the effort, and it was his once more. He tucked it into a small leather pouch where Thorvald would not see it.

Erik's feet soon kept step with his father again, but his eyes and thoughts went westward across the sea, thinking of the waves that must have carried the berry to this shoreline.

There was nothing but sea out there. Where had it come from?

Gunnbjörn's skerries, something whispered, and the boy Erik had shivered in excitement.

———·———·———

Once again, spring drifted towards summer. The circle-voyage paddlers explored virtually every deep fjord, each one yielding its own secrets of mountain, stream, iceberg, land, growing things and living things. They paddled to the very south tip of Nunaat, and beyond, where the coastline turned suddenly almost due north on the east side of the island. Erik watched the currents and the winds intently, marking them in his mind for future reference.

As the long days of summer approached autumn, they headed back to their starting point. Uukarnit was eager to head north before winter, and Erik wanted to stop wandering for a bit, to find the familiar longhouse walls around him again, even without Thio.

As they left from a short visit to the hot-spring island and drew near to the knörr camp, Uukarnit saw another group of kayaks there. Erik's heart beat fast.

Uukarnit hailed them the traditional greeting. "Well met, family and friends!"

This group was a group of mostly men and some families who had come to what they called the magic-stone-shore, and were anxious to see for themselves the strange ship from afar.

Erik was greatly disappointed Thio was not with them, but he kept his thoughts private.

A happy exchange of news took place. Tupit's sister-in-law's brother had led a whale hunt and it had been successfully taken. Pukiq's sister had delivered twins, one a boy and one a girl. Her sister's best friend had adopted one to help raise it. At the word *Thio*, Erik listened intently, happy just to hear her name. Yes, the white woman, Erik's friend Thio, was still with Aglakti's group.

Was she healthy? Yes, she seemed to be so. Happy? Everyone liked her. Especially... there were snickers and pokes.

"Especially what?"

The speaker looked quickly and uncomfortably at Iluq. "Well...Asa."

"Asa?" asked Iluq, horrified. "Our Asa is with the white woman? Truly?"

Yes, they affirmed, she and Asa were partners now. They quickly changed the subject.

Iluq felt bitterness he would not have believed possible before the white ones' arrival. In a flash, his concerns for his people became personal, and his instincts began to harden into something darker.

Erik tasted the same gall. He made an excuse and left, his face burning with shame.

———·——·——

A few days later, Tupit and those who had come on the circle-voyage with his youngest son headed out with the stone-seekers on the long paddle north to home. Tupit was all smiles, full of pride in his son and looking forward to seeing Aglakti and telling her of their adventures.

Erik waved farewells and watched them leave, knowing it was perverse and possibly even stupid not to go with them, but the thought of seeing Thio was an obstacle he could not bring himself to face.

He had lost everything. All of his boyhood dreams of starting a settlement in a new land were gone, as well as the more recent ones, in which he had seen himself in front of the council, the pride and prestige his family had once known restored through his efforts.

But to lose this woman to another was a last and terrible loss. Erik did not try to deny to himself that he loved Thio. Instead, he had firmly instructed himself that if she loved another, he would try to accept it, because he wanted Thio to be happy. No matter how much he might want, he would not try to change Thio's mind, or force her to accept him.

He had struggled with the idea every moment since he had heard the news. In the end, once the decision was made, Erik forced himself to be at peace with it, but the cost was the stripping-out of his own feelings. All that remained in his heart was loneliness, and the desire to be alone. To actually *see* Thio with this Asa, whose very name Erik had come to dislike, was more than he could bear.

But he would not be completely lonely. Gone was the Erik who used to walk the beach and long for human voices, human community. He had learned to be at peace with himself, to live as a part of life and not demand so much from it. He had friends now, good ones. If he wanted, he knew where to paddle to be with them. He had fallen in love with this new land, so stunningly beautiful, with her bright blue waters and sparkling glaciers, the purples and aquamarines and blues of icebergs that floated in her bays and fjords, the wildflowers that colored the hills in spring and summer.

Erik addressed a family of seals on the beach. "I'm just like you now," he told them. "I know how to survive with what the land and the sea offers. I don't have to live on the sea, and I'm not tied to being a farmer. Pukiq and Uukarnit and Tupit and even Iluq taught me how to live as they do. As you do."

No, he would not stay at the camp, mooning over Thio and bewailing his fate. "It's decided, then," he announced to the seals as if they had waited on his decision. "I'll go to the hot-spring island again, and the natural-harbor cove. I'll build a small shelter at each, to use on future visits."

It was something to do. Another adventure. A long cold winter spent building a lonely shelter on the tip of the island was better than a long cold trip north to see Thio smiling warmly at another man.

———·———·———

Land herself must have known what was in Erik's heart. She took pity on him, and an idea began to play in his mind.

When he had left on the circle-voyage with Tupit and the others, they had straightaway headed to the ocean and the many islands that populated the coastline. The knörr camp lay on a small peninsula between two fjords. What was above it? Before he left for the hot-spring island, Erik made up his mind to first go up the waterway on either side of the knörr camp and see what lay further inland.

———·———·———

As the days passed, Erik often caught himself talking absentmindedly to Thio. It felt better to have a companion sometimes, even if she was far away, even if he could not see her. He missed her warm smile. In fact he missed everything about her, and more and more, Erik told Thio what was in his mind, sometimes speaking aloud, and sometimes just sharing his thoughts with her.

At some point, though, an imagined shadow would fall between them. *Asa.* At that point, Erik would wake from the half-dream of talking to Thio and turn his full attention bitterly to whatever task was at hand. Asa. He loathed the name.

———·———·———

Three leisurely days of paddling brought Erik to the head of the waters on the north side of the peninsula. Multiple glacier-feeds and small streams fed the clear, fish-filled waters.

He had been excited to see green ahead on the coastline as he paddled. Erik knew his dreams of a settlement were utterly pointless, but something in him still envisioned the green hills of his boyhood dreams. Part of him was always looking, still hoping to find it.

The green spaces had been promising, but far too small for more than one or two farmsteads at most. Worse, they were cut off from other parts of the peninsula. Ah, well. One river explored. Erik headed downriver again towards the knörr camp.

———·———·———

The other side of the peninsula at first seemed as if it, too, offered no land suitable for farming. Despite that, Erik paddled peacefully along to see what else was up there, watching birds building nests on the rocky hills. He was pleased to see the hills slowly becoming lower and gentler, and the land smoother, a promising indication.

By the end of the first day, Erik spied a long green curve along the shoreline. He beached the kayak and walked it, considering. A short

300

walk across the hills to the next fjord, it was not as expansive a piece of land as he might have liked, but still, it was the best he had seen so far. It would support a good number of fields, and all would have access to the coastline for fishing.

He spent the night there, exploring until it became too dark to see any longer. When morning came, he paddled even deeper up the fjord. A headland split the waters. Erik took the right fork first, but it led only to steep stone hills, soon ending in a glacier.

The other fork almost immediately showed another small green cove. Erik did not stop, but paddled faster as he continued north along the banks, encouraged. Ahead...was it really as green and flat as it looked? Would it be earth, not just moss-covered stones?

It was earth he had seen, green and rich and soft and deep.

Beckoning, calling to all of Erik's being, rolling rich and green with the verdure of late summer was a broad valley. It reached deep into the hills that would shelter it from the west winds. It stretched as far as he could see along the coastline.

Excited, Erik paddled as quickly as he could to where a stream had created a wide, stony beach. Gentle breezes flowed down from the rolling rim-hills. Already, he knew the soil would be fertile field-land.

"Yes!" Erik shouted as he leaped from the kayak.

The dreams of his childhood shimmered, real and green before him. There was bountiful room for flocks of sheep to graze, for fields to be planted, for farms to be built and for children to run between them. This was truly a place fit for a settlement. It practically sang with readiness, as if it had been waiting for Erik, calling to him through all the years he had dreamed of it.

Erik dropped to his knees, put his forehead to the ground, and thanked all that was Good.

"Home," Erik said. Again, louder, shouting joyous, exulting. "Home! Home! Home!"

HomeHome Home home home, his Tuniit friends would have murmured, hearing him.

Yes. One day, this would be his home, and he would welcome them to it.

———·———·———

It seemed natural to talk to the land as if it could hear him. They had been friends for years, and now they would become intimates.

"When the spring comes, I will walk these fields and choose a site for my longhouse. I'll start building it then, and little by little, move things from the camp here." He looked around, full of happy anticipation. "For now, though, I'm going to stick to my intention of exploring the southern end of the island again across the autumn and winter. I know my way around it now, thanks to my friends."

He waited for a response, but the fields were silent, peacefully basking in the warm sun.

"One more trip back and forth will get all these rivers and inlets fixed firmly in my thoughts. If I wait, it's so much ground to cover, they'll all be new again."

The fields did not offer any resistance. Erik nodded to them and got back into his kayak. As he paddled away, he smiled unconsciously. Behind was his home-place. He would think of a name for it across the days to come. Ahead, nothing particular beckoned, except the perennial desire to learn; to travel the next river, the next fjord, and to discover what might lie ahead.

———·———·———

302

Winter came. With the long dark nights came even more isolation, but Erik had learned by then to accept aloneness, something as natural and constant to him as breathing.

He became skilled at hunting by moonlight during midwinter when the days were cut in half. During storms when going about was impossible, he trained his mind to drift into a kind of hibernation, like small and large animals did, nestled tight in a shelter. He experimented with the seal-breath, and learned how to use it to connect to everything around him, from the animals he hunted to the howling winds to the changes of the moon across the weeks.

He studied the tides and currents around the tip of the island, where they turned from south on the sunrise side to north on the sunset side, and the coastline winds, and the changes of weather. He learned, with ever deeper understanding, about the nature of this land.

With no one else to talk to, Erik learned about himself.

———·———·———

Thio

Thio heard a sound she had come to dread. Olaf had huddled sullenly in his shelter across the winter, but with the spring, he was out and about, always looking for some sort of trouble. Thio could hear him roaring curses at someone. She put down the skin she was stitching and went to where he raged.

"Olaf! You must stop being angry with everyone!"

His face, once so implacable and superior, had grown lined and haunted. "It is they who pick fights with me!"

"Olaf, no one in this settlement fights except you, and you do it with everyone."

"I fight because I hate it here! How can you not? What about your family in Íseland? Have you forgotten them? What about your precious Erik?"

Gods, he could be stupid. "I would give almost anything to go home, but what am I supposed to do? Give up and die? I almost did that, earlier! What good would that do?"

"Well, at least you've got Asa now. Why don't you just get it over with and sleep with him?"

Thio looked at a miserable man, far from the world he knew, and frightened. "Olaf, do you have any idea how many weeks I spent watching the water, hoping we would see Erik coming? He could have come for me, but he never did. I'm here. He's where he wants to be."

They walked away from the settlement along a narrow path. "Olaf, we are not so different. I loathe that we have to soften leather by *chewing* it, for god's sake! Every single day, I gag, seeing a raw hunk of seal lying in a corner to be eaten. What I wouldn't give for a smoked leg of lamb, or stewed turnips, or apples, or soup! I miss the hot spring on our farm and the sweat-room in our longhouse. I cannot remember what it feels like to be really warm. What will winter be like, so far north? I miss the crackling sound of the fire catching. I long to hear my family, their voices speaking in our own language, not these peoples' words. I miss…Olaf, I miss everything so much that when I start thinking about it, I get so sad that for hours I just lie in my shelter and stare at the wall. So I don't think about it. But that doesn't mean I don't care. Does that show you we are the same, even if I appear happy? It's how I make myself survive."

Why was she telling Olaf this? It wouldn't change him.

"We should go back to our camp." His eyes fixed on hers, then wandered down her body.

Thio looked at him, confused. "You mean, to where the knörr is?"

Olaf's voice raised in excitement at the idea. "Yes! It's spring. We can travel to it now. Why not? Get the farm going, grow crops. Eat decent food, eggs, and goat's milk, and roasted birds. Every night, a fire crackling. If we are stuck in this country, why not live decently?"

Thio was astonished. "Olaf. I cannot. The baby…I can't! I need to be with the other women, don't you understand? I cannot take care of a child without them!"

"Yes, you could," he insisted. "If you wanted to. It's not that hard! My wife had eight. Stop being such a whining…" He stopped. "I can't stay here. You must help me start a farm."

"No, Olaf!" Compared to the distasteful idea of being alone with Olaf at the knörr camp, chewing sealskin and eating raw fish seemed infinitely more pleasant.

———·——·———

305

Damn that stupid woman, Olaf thought as Thio strode quickly away from him. He walked further from the camp to the tundra and watched the first stars coming out, picturing his farm at home. Equal-days had come, and with it, the *norther-ljós,* the dancing lights in the northern sky, were diminishing. It was time to shear the sheep. Maybe his son was doing that, and helping someone else with lambing.

Damn Thio, damn her, damn her! Olaf fumed. They had been so close to everything going right. The hanging post ready, a few days of starting a camp and sowing fields, and they'd have sailed for home. The idea of going back to the knörr camp, of living like people should, in a proper longhouse with proper food, began to fill him. Even just the two of them was better than this. Anything familiar. Anything. He had failed the council because Thio would not help him before. By Odin, he needed Thio to help him now. Surely she could see that.

Olaf watched the faint northern lights until his neck hurt, and then headed sullenly back along the track to the circle of huts. It was spring. He'd waited through the winter, but now, with the weather warmer, Thio was going back with him to the knörr whether she liked it or not. She'd gotten him into this mess, and she was going to get him out. She owed him that, at least.

———.———.———

"Let me help you with that."

Thio smiled over her shoulder at the sound of Asa's voice. "No, I'm fine. I have it." She knew he would ignore her and take the rope of the sledge and drag it for her. She knew also that Asa would find a way to brush her hand or briefly take her arm.

They fell into step together, not talking. Thio could see Asa smiling ahead at nothing. Asa's face was always lit by a smile. A pleasant feeling went through her. Olaf was right. She *had* come to look forward to spending time with Asa, far more than she admitted to anyone.

"Olaf is trouble again today?" Asa asked.

"What day *isn't* he trouble? Every day, he is worse. He tries *not* to learn your words. Thank goodness! If people knew what he was saying they would be even more offended!"

Unaccustomed to anger and shouting, at first the People had stared at Olaf, alarmed. Now, "*the mad wolf howls,*" they said, and went back to work, which infuriated Olaf more.

"What is it today?"

"Doesn't matter. I don't want to spend our time talking about Olaf, or you'll be over there trying to help him."

"Ah, so you want me here with you." His teasing voice held an invitation.

Thio had never met anyone like Asa. All the People were kind, but Asa was generous and friendly to the extreme. It was impossible to know Asa without loving him, and everyone did. He was the favorite of every settlement. A day rarely passed without one group or another arriving for trade or visiting. "Is Asa here?" was always the first question after greetings. Children asked, male friends asked, elders asked, and women, *all* the women from young to grandmother, asked. Asa deferred their compliments to others, and endeared himself even more.

"You only spend time with me because you're fascinated with new things. I won't always be the newest thing," Thio said briskly.

"I thought I might teach you throat singing today," he smiled.

"You know perfectly well I am already learning. Besides, throat singing is for women."

He laughed. "Let me teach you to hunt."

"I have no desire to lay motionless for hours waiting for a seal to come up and breathe. What else can you teach me?

"Soapstone carving?" Asa created beautiful miniatures of creatures as gifts.

"I'd rather you just make one for me."

He skipped in front of Thio and blocked her way. "You know what I want, and it is not to teach you anything. Or perhaps it is. Let me."

His black eyes locked on her blue ones and heat swept through Thio. Neither would betray a smile. The attraction between them had grown daily. It had become a playful contest of sorts, as if each was waiting to see who would yield first to the unspoken but almost-palpable desire first.

"Asa...I..."

"You know we can. Stop making excuses." His eyes were warm and now his smile was dazzling.

"But Erik..."

"Erik and I will be *aipak*."

Thio had learned *aipak*. She shook her head vigorously *no*.

"Erik is on the other side of the island. No doubt he has enjoyed the fine hospitality of some of our beautiful women. Our people are generous. Are yours?" Now Asa was laughing at Thio, mocking her gently, his hands on her hips, pulling them towards his.

She pushed him aside, half-laughing. Together, they dragged the sledge to where Thio was building a shelter for herself. With the stones unloaded, Asa took Thio's hand, turned it over, and held her open palm to his lips.

"Today, Thio? Tonight, perhaps?"

It was not the first time that Thio had wondered how those lips would feel against her own. The warm rush inside her deepened, and the word *yes* trembled on her tongue.

308

Suddenly she remembered. Others before had brought pleasure, but not this mysterious feeling. It was the same one that had swept through her at the Althing, when she had first seen Erik, the one from when they had almost kissed on the knörr.

The old darkness swirled at the edge of Thio's mind, and her voice hardened.

"No, Asa. No. Not tonight. Not ever. I hurt people, Asa. You should stay away from me."

Thio's words hurt more than Asa wanted to admit. He had often thought of the man Thio called Erik with kindness. He already thought of the other man as his *aipak,* but for the first time, he felt true brotherhood with this man he had never met, who his mother had said clearly loved Thio. He had cared for Thio in her sickness, yet she had left him to come to their village, and had never asked to return.

Rebuffed, Asa gently released Thio's hand and turned to go.

———·———·———

"Where's Asa's kayak?" Thio asked.

His mother Chena shook her head. "I hoped you knew. Perhaps hunting?"

Thio's heart stretched out over the water, seeking him. *I'm sorry, Asa,* she whispered. She moved to the fur-scraping area and picked up a stone, missing him terribly.

———·———·———

Snows began to fall almost daily as the days shortened rapidly. Olaf fought, and people whispered behind their hands about him.

Thio did what she could to pacify him and atone for his wrongs. She needed the People more than ever. If Olaf alienated them too much, would they blame her too?

"Erik, where are you? I thought you would come and find me," she said to the stars. "The People who have seen you say that you are almost one of them now. I am, too, but I have not forgotten you. Was I so easy to forget?"

———·———·———

"Asa!"

Thio saw him getting out of his kayak with Toonoq following close behind. The girls of the village were already crowding around. Thio pushed between them without caring how it looked to anyone. Her best friend was back.

———·———·———

Olaf wasted no time renewing his picking at Asa. "Maybe she'll give you the big welcome home!" he jeered. Not knowing the Tuniit words, he made vulgar gestures. Asa locked eyes with Olaf.

"No hurt Thio," he said.

Thio was astonished. Asa had practiced some words with her, but she could not believe he remembered.

"No hurt Thio," he repeated firmly and clearly. "Asa love."

For an instant, Olaf showed his inner brokenness. Thio reached towards him, but Olaf jerked away. "Your suitor better keep his eye on you," he said angrily, striding away. "No telling what might happen to a woman all alone."

310

Thio blushed. Asa loved her, and now had said so publicly...? The blush turned pale as Olaf's last words sank in, and Asa took her hand in his. Desire swept through her again, stronger than before, and this time, Thio did not push the feeling away. She squeezed Asa's hand tightly.

Asa felt the squeeze and saw the smile on Thio's lips. Not long now. His heart beat faster.

———·———·———

The wind screamed across the cove, and Thio was proud of her work. The strong whalebone bracings and stones did not move, and the covering skins and turf did not leak. She lay in the darkness, enjoying the feeling of shelter in a storm. It felt good to be in her own home, built by her own hands. The small oil lamp gave off a tiny glow and a comforting sound as it burned nearby. Aquuataq was nearby, with another family. Maybe it was overly cautious, but Thio had wanted to stay this first windy night in the shelter alone, to make certain it was safe for Aquuataq. A little thing, but something a good mother would do.

A good mother... So long ago, she had made a promise to Erik's mother, and had never kept it. Would she ever have a chance to right that? Sadness pulled at the corners of Thio's mouth. *But Erik never came for me. I would have told him. Why didn't he try to find me?*

Thio let herself think about Erik, something she rarely allowed. Her feelings for Erik were still strained and scattered. Perhaps she had imagined that instant of embrace on the knörr, when they had first seen land. Perhaps he had simply been kind to her, and she had misread it.

No matter what, in the end, he had tried his best to help her. She would always love him, no matter who he loved, or who she did. The

311

thought comforted Thio. She blew out the little flame and stretched out to sleep.

—·—·—

Thio smelled Olaf in her shelter before he found her in the darkness. He must have crept through the raging storm. She had only an instant to recognize the odor of him before Olaf was on her. She was dimly aware that she had been expecting this attack.

"Olaf! Get off me! Get away from me, you brute!"

Olaf yanked at her fur undershorts and forced Thio's legs open with his knee. Thio clawed at his face, her fingernails searching for eyes and ears. She screamed, again and again, fearing that no one would hear her over the howling wind.

"Olaf, get off me! I will kill you!" She would not beg him to stop. She would never beg a man for anything again.

His response was to slap her hard across the face. Dazed and furious, Thio shrieked and sank her teeth deep into his shoulder. It would not be long before he overpowered her.

To Thio's relief, she heard voices shouting, and felt hands grabbing Olaf in the darkness and pulling him off her. Someone carried in another oil lamp, and shaking, Thio lit hers again. Olaf strained against Asa and Toonoq. They had him tightly pinned, their chests heaving.

"Men do not attack women," Asa shouted at Olaf. "What kind of animal are you?"

"Do all your men treat women so badly?" Toonoq asked Thio.

"No," Thio said, her voice trembling. "No. My father is a good man, calm and gentle. This is a bad thing, something for which men who do it are punished." She paused, uncertain. They had no word for

312

Council, or gothar, or Althing. "A man who does things such as this would be taken to a meeting fire, to decide what to do with him."

"We need the ways of your people, then," Toonoq said. "This cannot be ignored."

"But tonight...?" Asa's eyes held a question.

Thio realized they had no idea of how to keep someone a prisoner. Ashamed to teach them, Thio tied Olaf's wrists with sinew. They dragged him from her shelter.

Asa turned back. "Do you want me to stay here with you? I promise nothing will happen."

Need for safety burned in Thio. She hesitated only a moment, then rushed to Asa.

He murmured words against her ear. *"Shhhh, little seal. Hush hush hush...."* Asa pulled Thio close as she buried her face in his chest and cried out months of strain.

Little by little the racking sobs subsided. For a long while, they stood in silence together.

———·——·———

Thio's heart had raced with fear when Olaf attacked her, and raced again as she wept. As her breathing slowed, her heart gradually slowed as well.

Thio's breath became steady and calm, but Asa still held her. She let herself lean against his quiet strength and soaked in the feeling of safety. Asa's cheek was against her hair, and the hard bone of his jaw filled the hollow of her temple. Thio's nose and lips nestled against his collarbone, and she could smell the leather and fur of his anorak.

They said nothing to one another. No questions needed to be asked or answered. They simply stood together, aware of what would be, letting it come.

Thio could feel her heartbeat rise again. This time there was no fear.

"Let me see you." Asa used his jaw to pull Thio's face upwards to his. In the soft lamplight, he looked carefully at her cheeks where the tears glimmered. His mouth parted slightly, tasting the salt on her skin and absorbing her tears with his lips. Thio did not move.

Asa gazed at her eyes, so close to his, and still, there were no questions, only understanding. His hands came up. Thio felt them brush against her face, smooth back her hair, and take gentle hold of each side of her head. She tilted her head back, waiting. The little flame guttered quietly. In the flickering amber light, his lips touched her lashes, taking the tears from them as well. Still, she did not move.

He gave her time. Again, he pulled her head close to his chest, his hands moving gently across her shoulders, down her back and up again, comforting her, letting the fear drain completely from her.

Readiness grew in Thio. For the first time, she pictured how Asa's bare skin would look, and imagined what it would feel like, naked against hers. She tipped her nose up, nudging his jaw. He pulled away and they considered each other seriously. After a moment, the barest hint of a playful smile flickered at the corners of Asa's mouth and in his eyes. His eyebrows lifted and dropped, the movement almost too quick to see, but Thio read its meaning clearly enough. *Well? What are you waiting for?*

Asa's hair was straight and smooth under her fingers. Thio grabbed fistfuls of it, pulled him to her, and knew the feel of his teeth on her neck, *yes.* She loosed the sturdy rawhide binding his braids and pulled the silky black mane free. *Yes.* Her fingers felt for the bone buttons of his anorak.

With a cry of desire, Asa arched his back, and Thio pressed towards him. Outside, the winds and the rains still pounded, but in her shelter, a different kind of storm rose. She opened to it, welcomed it, and yearned for it to soak her, to saturate her, to satisfy the sweet hunger inside.

————·——·———

Thio slept quietly, her breath soft and even. Asa slept too, but as he did, his spirit rose and left Thio's shelter. The storm had stopped, and he could see the light glowing from the shelter where Olaf was being held. As he watched, he saw a wolf coming, a strange wolf, large and white-furred. Its teeth shone in the lamplight as it lunged towards Thio's throat, unprotected where she lay sleeping.

Asa knelt, lining up his spear with the wolf, his arm pulled far back. His heart beat harder and harder until his chest felt as if it would burst. The throw was far, so far... Asa breathed and the spear flew, but to Asa's horror, the wolf was a man, and the man had Olaf's face, and the spear carried a death-throw towards him.

Asa's spirit, riding together with the spear, screamed *stop, stop,* but they flew fast and strong until he and the spearhead found the slender strip of muscle between the bones, and his spirit-spear pierced Olaf's heart. He fell soundlessly, and blood spread around his body onto the snow. Olaf turned towards Asa. *Why, Asa? Why do you kill?*

Asa felt revolting nausea rise in his stomach at the utter wrongness of killing a human, and he felt something inside him tear, something terrible and vital, as it ripped muscle and sinew along the length of his soul.

315

—·—·—

Asa sat up, his chest thundering in panic. Thio's whale-oil lamp burned softly in the peaceful dome of her shelter. Outside, the wind roared and the rain still poured down in torrents.

Sweat rolled down his back and chest. *It was a dream,* Asa told himself. *Just a dream.* He laid back down, listening to the hammering of his heart, and willed himself to try and sleep.

—·—·—

The storm lasted for two full days. A talking fire was impossible, but talking happened anyway as two and three and seven and ten people collected together. By the time the winds subsided, consensus had already been reached.

—·—·—

Olaf stood with a man restraining each arm, their faces unsmiling. A semi-circle of families stretched along the other side of the fire. Finally Asa coughed and began.

"Olaf, you have done a great wrong. It has been bad enough to seek and feed anger constantly. Now you have hurt Thio. We must not let you hurt anyone else."

Thio translated for Olaf, whose face remained stony.

Asa continued. "Our People do not kill other humans, and we do not hurt one another. We cannot abandon you, for you would die, which would be wrong. Because of that, we will keep you here until the summer fishing camp, and afterwards, we will take you back to your camp. While you are here, you will have food and shelter, but you will be invisible to us. No one will speak to you or look at you. Perhaps when being alone is unpleasant enough, you will try to live in peace among us."

Thio said the words. Olaf replied with contempt. "Tell them they can *fukke* themselves."

Thio said, "He does not respect the punishment."

"He has no choice," said Asa. "It is what we must do." He addressed the settlement. "Olaf must never be alone. Someone must watch him during the day. At night, he will be bound. He may not accept the punishment, but he will have it anyway, to keep us all safe."

Uncomfortable murmurs passed among the people. Asa's brows knitted. "I do not like learning this part of your people, Thio," he said sadly.

"Nor I." She had seen the dark circles under Asa's eyes. They did not come just from being awake with her at night. Something was eating at his soul.

It is happening again, Thio said to herself. She did not know exactly how, but it did not matter; what *did* matter was that once more, Thio knew she was nothing but trouble to those she loved.

——·——·——

Erik

Spring brought Nagojut.

Erik was returning from one of his first trips to his future home-site. At the knörr camp, he was surprised to see a kayak beached beside the ship and a familiar body sprawled on the grass, sound asleep. Erik beached his own kayak a distance off and crept up to play a trick on his friend, but Nagojut spoke without opening his eyes.

"Don't think you can pour water on me to wake me. I taught you that trick."

Erik laughed, and took Nagojut's hand, pulling him up. They embraced, clapping one another on the back. Nagojut pulled back and eyed Erik.

"Look at that fur growing on your face! You look more walrus than man!"

"Look at the wedding-mark tattooed on your cheekbones! Who's the foolish woman?"

They caught one another up with news. Nagojut had arrived a day earlier. Seeing signs that Erik was inhabiting the longhouse, he had decided to wait for a few days. Erik told him about the home-site upriver, and about his explorations across the autumn and winter, retracing the circle-voyage and expanding on it.

"Do you want to eat, Nagojut? Are you hungry?"

"I am hungry, but for something a bit north of here. I know you have been longing to see me and go paddling together. I have something to show you!"

Erik was delighted at the prospect of a companionable voyage. "Where are we heading?"

318

"Just a few days up the coastline. Maybe a little longer," Nagojut said vaguely.

Erik smiled. "Don't tell me, then. Yes, I'll go with you, and no, I don't care where."

———.———.———

"How much farther, Nagojut?" Erik asked, mentally trying to redraw his map again.

"Only a little farther. Isn't this day fine? We have had very good weather." He still playfully refused to tell Erik where they were going, and Erik still did not care.

Day after day they traveled the same direction: north, and more north, and ever more north. Erik looked at his paddle, unbelieving. He often adopted Thio's old habit of cutting a notch for each day that passed. After he and Nagojut had paddled a quarter-moon Erik had started counting the days of their trip. So many notches now, each one representing a day they had paddled north.

In the uncounted hours, Erik thought of the picture he had drawn on his tunic, the map showing the shape of land as a bird sees it. He counted, and recalculated. The farther north they paddled, the larger he redrew the map in his mind. The land-picture was becoming so big he could barely comprehend it. *Surely I've made a mistake,* Erik thought. *This would be bigger than any island I'd ever known. Bigger than any I've ever even* heard *of.* How big was it?

———.———.———

319

Kakrayok and Pukiq had joined them the evening before. As they rounded a curve in the shore, a ghastly sight oozed on the beach. The remains of a seal lay torn apart, bleeding profusely.

Erik pointed at it. "What did that?" he asked.

Kakrayok pulled a necklace from his anorak. He ran his fingers along the enormous teeth strung on it. "A bear, as white as the snow and the ice," he said. "A silent swimmer. A land walker. Killer of seals." His voice was excited and while not fearful, certainly respectful.

"Do we not want any of the meat, or the liver, or the skin?" It was clear that the seal had been freshly killed.

"No," Kakrayok said. "The seal belongs to the white bear and to her young. What we need to eat, we hunt ourselves. The white bear has left the seal for other beings of the ice. It nourishes those on which it will one day feed." With that, they paddled on, the seal ignored and forgotten by Kakrayok. But Erik thought long of the white bear, and hoped they would see one.

—·—·—

Iluq stood his ground, his face red and angry at Erik. "I am sick of you trying to tell us about your ways! We have our own traditions! We have no need of yours!"

"I am not trying to be better than you! I am trying to share what I have! Isn't that the way of your people, to share with one another?" Erik's face, too, was contorted in anger.

They had encountered Iluq's party a day ago, and the groups were travelling northward together. Immediately, the old tensions had flared again.

Uukarnit held up his palms to the furious men. "Brothers! Why these harsh words?"

"We were sharpening our knives," said Pukiq. "Erik showed me something called a whetstone. It made Iluq angry."

"Why anger over something that saves work and time, Iluq?"

"There is nothing wrong with how I do it!" Iluq searched the group for support. "New tools aren't always better than the way our fathers and grandfathers taught! I am tired of Red always trying to change our ways!"

"But Iluq, he has learned so many of our ways!" Pukiq protested. "Red is offering to share his. Change can be good!"

"What is so good about it, Pukiq? You are too young to know the value of the old ways. I am sick of all the thinking, changing, talking, talking, talking! Too much new!"

Uukarnit demurred. "Iluq, your concerns are deeper than how to sharpen a spear point. Your anger comes from Red being here in our land. Can you not be at peace with that?"

"No!" said Iluq passionately. "I want him and his kind to leave our land!"

"Iluq, their boat cannot travel without the dead ones. What you ask is impossible."

"What you ask of me is impossible, too," muttered Iluq. "I am so tired of no one listening to me, of always being criticized and mocked for trying to warn you. I will hold my silence!" Looking at Erik, Iluq spat bitterly. "As for you, one day your kind will be seen for the danger that you are. I only hope it will not be too late."

Uukarnit took Iluq by the arm. "Really, Iluq? It seems that great in your mind?"

"It is! You are blind!" He flung Uukarnit's hand away. "I will paddle on without you. Others will listen to me if you won't!" He strode across the beach, furious, got in his kayak, and paddled furiously away.

Uukarnit looked after Iluq and sighed deeply. It saddened Uukarnit that he was starting to wonder if Iluq was right. He had heard terrible stories from other paddlers about the man Olaf. Uukarnit knew that soon Iluq would hear them, and his concern would deepen to fury.

Uukarnit sighed again, more deeply. He was unused to this feeling in his chest, and had no name for it. It was too much for one man to understand. The Spirits had given no answers. Perhaps Iluq would calm down once they all reached the fishing camp.

"What now?" Erik asked. Uukarnit felt the breath of bitterness flow out from Erik, who stood behind Uukarnit as they watched Iluq's kayak grow distant. "Will I ever be more than a stranger to your shores? Will there ever be an end to this back and forth?"

———·———·———

Nagojut still would not say where they were going. The humor had left for Erik when Iluq's anger arrived, but he would not spoil whatever tremendous practical joke Nagojut was preparing. Apparently they were going to some kind of gathering, much like Íseland's Althing. More and more paddlers appeared daily. The groups traveled loosely together. Each evening, different combinations of people stopped together to eat, visit and sleep. Sometimes it was clear Iluq had been with the others, and greetings were not as warm as they might have been.

Today they traveled in mist so thick they could barely see one another, even staying close together. The usual banter between Pukiq and Nagojut was absent, each man lost in his thoughts.

They paddled beside a tall ice floe, towering over the kayaks as it drifted past. Erik continued smoothly along without looking up. He almost did not see the creature atop the ice floe, the same color as the ice, and as still.

"There she is." Pukiq pointed to a small dark spot. Erik realized it was the black nose of a gigantic white bear. They passed so close its enormous furred paw could nearly reach them.

"Do you see her young?" Two young pups nestled under the bear, their small faces peeping out. The paddlers stroked steadily and rapidly.

The she-bear moved, and Erik heard the smallest splash as it entered the sea water. There was no splash of cubs following her. She was hunting.

He kept looking back, dreading that the bear would emerge close to his kayak.

If the gods are going to grant my wishes so quickly, I will choose more pleasant things, Erik thought. Suddenly, he was back in Íseland, and Thorgest's dogs were after him. He could hear the howls and remembered being hunted.

Now he understood why the People gave a drink of fresh water as a kindness offering to the seal and walrus they killed. The animal needed to be treated with respect. Its fear needed to be soothed, so that the fear that filled its body did not transfer to those who ate of it.

Fear filled Erik as he paddled. His heart pounded, and he fervently wished for the white bear to be gone.

—— · —— · ——

Asa saw the bear as it watched Thio, unsuspecting, as she paddled past the ice floe. Its claws gripped the sheer side of the ice, and the

323

bear sniffed the air, seeking her. The massive mouth opened. Its huge teeth reflected the light.

Asa knelt, lining up his spear with the bear. His spear arm was pulled far back, and his heart beat harder and harder until his chest felt as if it would burst. The throw was far, so far... Asa breathed the seal-silence breath and the spear flew, but to Asa's horror, the bear became a man, and the spear carried a death-throw towards it.

Asa's spirit, riding together with the spear, screamed stop, stop, *but they flew fast and strong until he and the spearhead found the slender strip of muscle between the man's ribs. His spirit-spear pierced the man's heart, and the man fell, soundlessly onto soft snow. Blood stained the snow, and the man's face turned towards Asa.*

"Why, Asa? Why do you kill?"

Asa felt a revolting nausea rise in his stomach, the utter wrongness of killing a human, any human. Vileness spread through him, and something terrible and vital inside tore, ripping muscle and sinew along the length of his soul.

———·———·———

Asa woke to find himself slumped in his kayak and drenched with sweat, slowly drifting in the almost-still waters of the sound. He scanned the water around him in panic. The images of Olaf and the white bear were so frighteningly real, but he was alone. Thio was nowhere in sight. Nausea roiled through him still.

Why had he had that waking nightmare of killing Olaf again? Why a white bear? What was happening to him?

———·———·———

Another week passed. Erik had mostly given up asking where and why they were traveling, and Nagojut was skilled at deflecting any conversation among their traveling companions away from their destination. They paddled long hours every day, either silently or with good conversation, and the clear blue waters slid past under their kayaks.

Nagojut had been telling stories of the creation of his people. "At the end of the earth, Mother Sea and Father Moon glowed in one another's light," he began.

"Where is that place?" Erik quietly asked Uukarnit. "The end of the earth?"

"The end?" Uukarnit asked quizzically.

"Where there is no more land, no more anything," said Erik. "Before we found your Nunaat, we thought there was nothing but ocean west of our island. Some of our stories tell of the end of the world, of frozen giants and monsters, and waterfalls to nowhere. The sea brought us to your land, but surely, after this, it all must end somewhere! But where? And what is it like? Since spring, we have paddled further towards the northern star than I have dreamed. What is ahead of us to the north? What is west of these waters we are paddling? Is *that* the end of the earth? Are you taking me to see where the ocean finally ends?"

Uukarnit called to Pukiq. "If we paddle from our permanent settlements towards the setting sun, what is ahead, Pukiq? Where does the sea take us?"

Pukiq shrugged, and then answered carelessly, "To the lands across the water."

"And then?"

"You reach the wide marshes where the geese hatch their chicks in summer."

"And then?"

Pukiq laughed. "Land and more land. Rivers and islands, and more rivers, and more land. More and more and more."

"Where does it stop?" Uukarnit asked. "The land, I mean, or even the sea?"

Pukiq for once did not laugh. "I don't understand," he said. "It doesn't stop. The islands, the land, the sea…they go on forever." He shook his head, confused, and then repeated his words. "They never stop." Annoyed, he paddled off. Pukiq loved humor, not deep thinking.

Uukarnit glanced at Erik, waiting.

"Really? It just goes on and on?" Erik felt stunned.

"Really. I have traveled some of it myself, and I have talked and traded with others, who trade with others, who trade with our brothers on the far-western ocean."

"There's *another ocean?* And *people?*"

"Of course there are. Many, many peoples. Many tribes."

Erik's head felt like an overripe fruit, too soft. "Many tribes. It goes on forever."

"Yes," Uukarnit repeated. "It goes on forever. Our forefathers learned this from the tribes they met, and they learned it from the tribes they met. The land and the sea and people are everywhere. What is this you speak of, an end? The world knows of no such thing."

He paddled off as calmly as if they had been discussing how to make boots. Erik was left with his thoughts reeling. How could this be possible? He had struggled simply thinking of a larger island. His mind rebelled.

Where were they? How on earth would he ever get back to anything of his former life?

It was too much. Suddenly the earthy smell of growing crops came to memory, and a flood of other forgotten fragrances – flowers in spring, goat's milk cheese, oak planks, fresh and ready for shipbuilding. Without warning, with all his spirit and body, Erik desperately wanted to go home.

———·———·———

Iluq eyed men and women of the fishing camp who had met with him. "Friends and family," he said. "The stranger who traveled with us of whom you have heard, the man called Red, will be here at the summer fishing camp soon," he said. "I see in him and his kind a danger to our people. You say you share those concerns."

They shuffled, uneasy. "Why not discuss this at open circles in the camp?" one asked.

"Because some things must be done differently," said Iluq. "I have tried to make others see, and they do not. We must choose for them."

"We have seen the woman Thio and the other man Olaf. Thio is a good woman, but Olaf brought terrible evil to their settlement. Is the man Red a similar danger? We thought he was not like the Olaf."

Iluq felt a surge of power. "Yes! He may not be evil in his spirit as Olaf, but they are all a danger to our very lives! Red is the strongest of the three. He will arrive at the camp later today. We must find a way to show him that he must leave our people!"

"But how?"

"Tomorrow is the festival. It must be soon."

The group talked long. To cast someone from the circle of life was utterly foreign, but this man was foreign, Iluq said. They worked hard, grappling with this new thinking.

———·———·———

"Soon, now, my friend," said Nagojut. This time, he was as good as his word. As the early-morning paddlers rounded a long curve of land, Erik saw ahead the open water of a wide river. Ice floes glowed, rose and gold from Sól and blue and purple from the water, sparkling with reflections of the rising sun. Their paddles dripped silver with every stroke.

A whoop sounded from the riverbank on the right. Pukiq whooped back. Suddenly, kayaks sped from every direction, children in small craft with parents and grandparents alongside, young men and women, all moving quickly across the water, shouting ecstatic greetings. In moments, they reached the shore and were engulfed in people coming to make greetings. They pressed their nose and upper lip to each other's faces, breathing quickly in, circling around. Erik stood awkwardly aside. As each person came up, Nagojut spoke name after name. Each brushed their face to Erik's, nose-lip-tiny inhale.

"What is this place, Nagojut?" he asked.

"This river is home to our summer fishing camp," he replied. "Every other year, many of our people meet here. We catch delicious char fish, and celebrate being One People. They have been watching for us, knowing we would arrive soon. It's time for the Festival of the Night Sun."

The Festival of the Sun. Like Althing, during Sól's-stillness. He had guessed right.

"All the People come? Everyone?"

328

"Well, as many as can travel. Mostly everyone."

Erik swallowed, his throat tight. "Thio, the woman from my ship. Will she be here too?"

Nagojut called and received an answer. "Something delayed her group, but they are on the way."

"Did we pass her settlement?"

"Oh, no. That village is much farther north. You'll see her today, or perhaps tomorrow morning. Soon."

Erik did not want to meet the man named Asa. "Is anyone else with her?"

Again Nagojut called. "Naotak said that she brings the snow child with her."

Snow child? Erik's brain translated the unfamiliar phrase slowly. No, not snow. Not *whiteness-from-sky*. Nagojut had not said snow child. He had said *white baby*.

———·———·———

Erik's mind skittered away from the thought of Asa. What did it matter? She was alive.

There was no time to think about what might be or not be. People crowded in, wanting to see the strange pale man, and all talked excitedly about the festival to come.

———·———·———

———·———·———

Erik and Nagojut had barely arrived in time. The Festival began at middle-night, when the sun would kiss the land, and lasted straight through until midnight tomorrow. There would be games and contests, and plenty of delicious fresh char to eat.

Soon the water swarmed with kayaks and umiaks as they put to water again and started paddling. They needed to hurry.

———·———·———

The water became shallower until finally the group put their small boats ashore and walked along the river's bank. Erik heard shouting, and peered forward.

How many people were here? Dozens? No. There must be hundreds of them.

———·———·———

When was the last time he had seen so many people? Ah, it had been at the Althing, the summer he was outlawed. Had it only been two years since he had pleaded his case to the law council? Erik counted again, disbelieving. How had so little time gone by? It seemed a lifetime.

———·———·———

Throngs of people were catching char, gutting and filleting them, and tending racks of fish drying in the sun. They waved, greeting the newest arrivals. A fierce, proud feeling swept over Erik at the sight of

330

humanity alive and well and thriving. In what seemed a distant, lonely place, here was community. Here was everything people needed to live. This mass of human beings on the eve of Longest-Day was one of the most beautiful sights Erik had ever seen.

Such a bittersweet feeling. *Let the sweet rise,* Tupit always said, so he would.

Apart, Yet A Part

Once again there were the quick nose-lip-press-inhale greetings, many, many, many of them. Erik felt much like a collared bear at a fairing, with crowds of people eager to see him, to touch his skin and hair, so different from theirs. They asked him over and over to speak in his own language, marveling and laughing and asking again to hear the words so strange to them.

There were questions about everything. Tales of the knörr had grown until it was the size of a mountain. *No,* he smiled, and gestured. They asked about the sail, the woven fabrics, the strange foods, the animals brought. Thio said that Erik's people rode on something like caribou? How? The questions were endless, balanced against innate politeness and courtesy.

Erik told them about family life in his country, and children and holidays. The idea of crops and grains he had long since given up trying to explain. One day, when he was able to go back to that green valley, he could farm there, and show them.

Perhaps. He would leave that for the future to unfold. His life had taken such twists the last two years it was madness to think he could plan anything at all.

No Hurry

"It has been a long day, my friends," said Uukarnit gently. "Perhaps Red would like to rest and watch the char-catch."

It was Erik's turn, then, to be interested in how the char were caught and strung along sinews to dry in the breeze. Some would be taken home, and many would be buried in caches in the ground, as emergency food for future travelers.

The festival food would of course be fish, meat, blubber, fish, fish and more fish. What he would give for some roasted lamb, for cream and honey, or carrots sweet from the soil!

In the back of Erik's mind, he was keenly aware that Thio was approaching, somewhere along the same river he had travelled. The sun seemed to barely move. Erik forced smiles, and asked questions, answered them, and looked again at the sky.

———·———·———

Asa knelt, lining up his spear with the great white bear. His heart beat harder and harder, and he fought to calm his breath. He took careful aim and the spear flew, but to Asa's horror, the bear was holding a cub, a cub with the face of Thio's infant, the white child.

Asa's spirit, riding together with the spear, screamed stop, please, please, stop, *but they could not stop. They flew fast and strong, and found the slender strip of muscle between the bones, and his spear-spirit pierced the cub-child's heart.*

She fell soundlessly onto the soft snow, blood staining her white fur anorak, blood spreading out on the snow. Her face turned towards Asa. Why, Asa? Why do you kill?

Asa felt the white cub's mother at his back. With a terrible cry, her claws tore along the length of his soul, and she ripped his spirit from his body.

———·——·——

Asa staggered and fell to his hands and knees on the tundra. He panted for breath. Not far away, a caribou lay dead. Asa's spear protruded from its ribcage.

Toonoq called to him. "Asa, are you sick? What's the matter?"

Asa got up and lurched away from the caribou.

Toonoq ran after him. "Why aren't you gutting it? Are you just going to leave it there?"

"I can't... can't..." Asa wiped his hand across his forehead. Cold sweat glistened on his skin. "I am not well."

"It's only one more day to the fishing camp. Let's get you there so you can rest."

Toonoq did not say what he really meant. *So we can find a shaman to clear your spirit.*

———·——·——

What was that beating sound? War drums? No, that wouldn't make sense, not here. As Erik yawned and stretched from his nap, he woke to a sound no human ears could ignore.

Hands danced on stretched caribou skins, crafting an enticing rhythm that called across the air, insatiably luring people to scramble from their sleeping skins and pour forth from tents. Their voices raised, excited, as they ran to the sound. It was the festival of the midnight sun.

———·——·———

The drumming lifted in intensity and sound. It became louder and louder until it filled the entire camp. As people arrived where the drummers played, they began to move their feet and clap their hands, keeping pace with the drum rhythms. More and more of them gathered, crowded together where the drummers stood shoulder to shoulder on a huge flat stone.

Suddenly, on some unseen signal, the drums stopped and the entire group stilled all at once. The silence stretched, and the hairs on back of Erik's neck prickled. The drummers stayed silent, their hands suspended in the air over their instruments.

Erik saw it grow in the people's faces and felt it in himself: an intense longing for the drums to start again. It spread through him. He could feel his hands and his feet. His legs and loins yearned for it, a sound that would call them to move together in some kind of dance.

In the stillness, desire grew.

Fingers brushed against the drums ever so briefly, and then paused again.

A few dancers moved, anticipating, their smiling faces asking for more.

One of the drummers moved his fingers again, a few beats of sound, the barest breath of the rhythm to come. Slowly, seductively, the others built on it, the pattern, the sound, the tempo, and the building become a beckoning. The people reached forward, opening.

Erik could see them leaning in, craving it. Excitement grew in him as well, although he knew not for what.

More hands joined in the drumming and the sound grew even more demanding. The rhythm simplified, calling all into movement, a dance with the drums. One person after another began to clap, to step feet in patterns that matched the drumbeats, and they pulled one another in until all had leaped into the dance, clapping their hands, bending and twisting in one flawless flow. The drumming became yet louder, and more urgent, compelling, insistent, until finally all moved as one, and Erik with them.

———·———·———

Who not there could understand? The wild language of the drums brought the people into one Being, beyond place and time, in a way for which there was no human language. Connection bound them, and life-passion surged through them and from them, across the fiery water and sky, demanding all that they were, consuming them, and finally leaving them exhausted, refreshed, renewed, and laughing with silliness. Erik marveled that he, a person almost always apart and alone, had become part of a connectedness he could barely describe, and that at some point he had no longer known where he ended and another began, when *you and I* became *us-as-one, I.*

How could he explain that? He could not. He could only marvel at it, only a tiny part of himself still aware that he even existed. Once again, the drumming began, with a new pattern. The People joined with The One in the drumming and the dance, and he with them.

———·———·———

335

Asa knelt, lining up his spear with the white bear, his arm pulled back as far as he could. His heart beat harder and harder. The spear flew, but to Asa's horror, the bear's face became his own face, the bear's body his own body.

Asa's spirit screamed stop, stop, *but the spear flew fast and strong, and it pierced his heart. Asa fell soundlessly onto the ground, blood spreading out across the white snow.*

A woman's face leaned towards him. "Asa, this is not the way of your People. Why do you kill?" she asked.

"I did it for you, Thio", Asa's spirit wept as it left his body. "I did it for you."

———·———·———

Thio paddled quickly to Asa's kayak. They had almost reached the fishing camp when he had had another spell. His body had moved in odd motions, as if he was throwing a spear, and then he had slumped over in his kayak.

His heart raced and he was sweating and pale.

"Asa, what's wrong? Toonoq said this happened yesterday. Can you hear me?"

His eyes moved wildly. "I did it for you, Thio. For you."

"Did what, Asa? I don't understand." She gestured to Toonoq and spoke under her breath. "As soon as we arrive, we must find Asa's father and mother. He is very ill."

"Just let me rest here," he gasped. "Go on ahead without me."

"I don't want to leave you!"

Toonoq demurred to Thio. "I think he's right. You should go ahead. You are bound to cause a sensation at the camp, and Asa needs quiet. We won't be far behind. Once the initial excitement settles down, we'll find you. I don't think he's in any immediate danger."

Thio considered Toonoq's words. "Spoken wisely, my friend," she said. Thio touched her fingers to her lips and paddled away.

At Play

Through the remainder of not-night, the drumming and movement continued, among large and small circles that shifted and reformed, stopped and started again. When the dancers were too tired to move any longer, something else would fill the break until they rested enough to begin again.

"Red! It is time for the throat-singing competition!"

Erik watched as pairs of women took part in remarkable partner-duels of low, throaty music he had never witnessed before.

"They bounce the sound into each other's open mouth," Pukiq explained. The women simultaneously competed and supported each other in the singing until one of them fell out, giggling with good humor.

As the day brightened, other contests began. No, Erik could not gut a fish as quickly and as well as a girl-child of ten. He endured much good-natured ribbing for that loss. "You did not tell me it was a competition for children!" he exclaimed, and Pukiq shrugged, his eyes twinkling.

Yes, Erik was slower than others at passing a bladder-skin bag under a kayak, or making a spear-point of stone. Yes, even though he had become skilled, most of them were better than he at kayak racing. Erik knew he was urged to compete in every contest simply for his friends to tease him, but he did not mind. Erik made fun of himself as well, joining in the laughter and pantomime, in a marvelous, freeing experience.

With longer legs, however, he easily won the foot races. Admiration abounded at how very fast he could run. At last came the most important contest of all: the spear throw.

―――.―――.―――

"You know you have no chance of winning," Pukiq said, his face mock-serious.

"You may be surprised."

Pukiq gave Erik a look. "Did you practice all winter on your own?"

"I hunted to live. Didn't you?"

Pukiq chortled. "Bring your best, friend! Since Asa isn't here, I have no doubt that I'll win, but at least we can see how much you've improved!"

―――.―――.―――

Erik walked across the soft tundra to reclaim his spear from where it laid alongside others that had not flown far enough. Pukiq interspersed his impromptu victory dance with bragging.

"I am champion! My friend Red cannot throw anywhere near as well!" Pukiq laughed and danced again, following the steps from the night before. "Much practice but so little result!"

"Stop talking," Erik laughed. "You are far too pleased with yourself. Nobody cares."

"Of course, it's a good thing that Asa wasn't here. No one can match his spear-throwing."

Asa again. Erik was heartily weary of that name, but he said nothing to Pukiq.

"Truly, Red, your throw wasn't bad."

Pukiq was right. Erik had been pleased to finish among the top throwers. As he bent to retrieve his spear, a foot squarely stepped on his hand.

He had skirted clear of Iluq so far, but no longer, it appeared. Still bent over, his hand under Iluq's foot, Erik squatted down. He covered his eyes, looking up in the sunlight towards Iluq. "What are you doing? Your nephew made that spear for me. You're likely to break it!"

Iluq's expression was strange. "The festival is almost over. It is time certain things changed." As he spoke, other men and women whose faces Erik did not know drifted to Iluq.

"What do you mean? Why are you looking like that?"

"We must do what needs doing."

The people with Iluq surrounded Erik. Each gripped a spear.

Erik had not felt it for so long, but he recognized immediately: the feeling of being outcast, his anger building and his confidence crumbling simultaneously, knowing that no matter what he said, no matter what logic dictated, he was up against an angry, dark, uncaring force.

Would Iluq never let him stand a man, accepted by the others? Erik knew within himself a matching fury, a poisonous desire to lash out in frustrated anger. *Steady,* he told himself. *That's what led to you being outlawed. You are no longer that man.* He let go of his spear and stood.

As Pukiq protested, someone pushed him. "Don't interfere, Pukiq."

"You show your spear to me?" Pukiq retorted, undeterred. "What is happening?"

"This man Erik is an intruder to our land! He is not one of us, and he has no right to be here! We want you to leave! Go away! Go now!" Iluq shouted.

"You will not tell me what to do, Iluq." Erik stood his ground.

Iluq put his spear against Erik's throat, pressing the sharp against the skin. "We will not be refused. You must go to your camp. Stay there, far away from us."

"My understanding is that all the People of this land belong together! I have worked hard to learn your way, even though not born to it. Are you telling me that I am the only person on this island not welcome at this festival?"

"We are telling you that. You will never be one of us, Red Erik. Go away."

Pukiq protested again, to no avail. More spear tips were placed firmly against Erik's body. They pushed against him, their sharp tips threatening to pierce his clothing and his flesh.

"This is ridiculous. I will not stay here trying to reason with you while you cut me bit by bit. The camp is large enough for all. Stay away from me." Erik turned and walked away.

———·———·———

Iluq gave him a start of twenty paces and then followed with his group. Long legs helped, but spear-sticks still hammered about Erik's shoulders and head, and sharpened points bit into his skin from throws intended to hurt, not kill. Erik sprinted to the riverbank, directly towards the char-drying racks where dozens of people were preparing for the evening feast. People looked up, surprised, as he tumbled through the strings of drying fish, his pursuers on his heels.

"Damn it, Iluq," Erik shouted. "Stop a moment!" He wheeled, putting his hands up.

"Why are you chasing Red?" asked those working on the char-drying. "Is this a game?"

"No, it is not a game! This man and his kind are a scourge to the People! Too many of you do not see! We have gathered to help you to understand the dangers they bring! He needs to leave us, and we are explaining it to him in the only way *his* people understand – with weapons!" Iluq's voice rang with authority.

Another voice from Iluq's group. "His kind does these things! You all heard the stories!"

The attackers and Erik stood glaring at each other. Erik stripped off his destroyed anorak. Trickles of blood ran from his skin where the spear tips had pricked.

"But *your* kind does *not* do that, Iluq! For shame!" cried Erik.

"Yes, my kind does! The ones that came here on the ship, and some at home, yes, but not all of them! Far from it! Not even *many* of them! For the sake of the gods, *we are the people of the Law!* I have heard too many times that you think we will bring wrong to your people. But I have never hurt you, or any one of your people. Instead, I have worked to honor your ways. But it is never enough for you, is it? It is you who have harmed, Iluq! It is you who acts like the others on my ship...not me! It is you, with your misguided desire to 'protect' others, who has done the damage!"

Iluq's face grew even more flushed with anger. "Whether today's harm was started by you or by me, it is *because you are here!* You do not belong here. It will end when you leave!

"I *want* to leave! Do you not realize that? Who would not want to go back to their own home? But there is no way for it to happen! Even you could not kayak so far across the open sea! So I am stuck here with you, whether I want to be or not, and whether..."

Sudden shame filled Erik's chest. *Whether you want me here or not.* Drumbeats and dances meant nothing. He would never really be part of the life here, no matter how much he had fooled himself into thinking it was possible. A few accepted him as a friend, but to the rest, he was a curiosity at best, an outsider and a failure at their way of life. The contests had proven it.

I don't matter, Erik realized. He would never return on the knörr with news of land. Never be the hero of his own youthful imaginings. Those hopes, so long buried, once more burst forth bitterly. Yes, he had found a new land. Yes, he would have a farm on a rich hillside where crops would grow. But he would do it alone, living alone, and he would die alone. No celebration at an Althing, no cheers of the crowd, no sagas; that was a given. No one would ever know anything about him, beyond that he was once outlawed and then disappeared into the sea. And there was no community that welcomed him here, either. He was nobody's hero, and never would be.

Erik grabbed Iluq and viciously butted his forehead against the older man's face. As Iluq buckled at the knees, Erik bent over too, his hands on his knees, gasping for air. Around him, the men and women who had jabbed with their spears roared, the anger and fear inside them savoring the strange new taste of hate. They closed in on Erik.

———·———·———

Uukarnit waded into the brawl without hesitation. He helped Iluq to his feet, grabbed Erik, and pulled the both of them from the fight.

342

"Iluq, what were you thinking?" Uukarnit cried.

"We were teaching him a lesson in the only way he will understand!"

"A lesson about what?"

"That we don't want his kind. He and his must return to their camp and stay there."

"You have taught him a lesson, Iluq! That no one is immune to foolish action when one succumbs to fear! Do you not think this man has heard your dislike of him, over and over? Do you not realize he knows that lesson too well already?"

Iluq's shoulders hunched in self-righteous anger. His jaw jutted. "Clearly it hasn't been enough! Because here he is, among us!"

"He is here because Nagojut brought him as a guest! Our people welcome guests! It would be better to teach him a lesson truly from our own people, one you have forgotten: *that forgiveness is stronger than anger.* Like it or not, he cannot go home. He has no choice but to be one of us now. You are right that we must not learn anger from his kind, but you have forgotten to teach him the deep kindness of *our* People. The anger is here in us already. Of course it is; we are human! If we are to keep Erik's kind from poisoning us, we must do it not by taking on the ways of his people, but by standing fast in our own ways and sharing them with him."

Iluq stared away, angry and proud, refusing to hear the truth in Uukarnit's words.

"When the fishing camp is ended, let me travel with you, just us, alone together," Uukarnit urged. "We have grown too distant from one another. Paddle with me, cousin. We will talk. Whether we agree or not, I know you are a good man at heart, and a man of your word."

"We will paddle together, but you will not change my mind." Iluq walked stiffly away.

343

Uukarnit heaved a familiar sigh. He turned to Erik, his eyes deliberately resuming their familiar twinkle. "Well, now, Red. You are decorated with your name, yes? You have red all over you." He laughed, pleased at his joke. "Let's find you another anorak. You'll be cold with all the breeze-openings that Iluq and his friends have cut into yours."

Uukarnit's words had taken effect on those around Iluq. They had been uncomfortable with attacking the white man, but Iluq had said it was necessary. Uukarnit had brought them back to familiar ground. Shamefacedly, they turned away, murmuring shamed apologies to Erik.

Uukarnit's respect for Iluq and his calm approach had not been lost on the Íselander. These people really were part of one enormous family, deeply connected in ways he had sensed in the dance last night but would never achieve. At least he had good friends. It was enough.

"Another anorak would be good. I'll save that one to use in the summer when it's warm."

Uukarnit laughed with pleasure at Erik's wry response and slapped him on the back. They walked through the staring crowd, and Pukiq followed, for once subdued and quiet.

———·———·———

After the spear contest came the great char feast at midday, and storytelling sessions followed. Circles of people spread out like ripples centered on the enormous flat stone which the drummers had earlier occupied, the people full of good food, tired from the night of dancing and the day's contests, and ready for entertainment.

Women and men took turns speaking. They paused every few phrases so their words could be repeated outward from one circle to

344

another, so that everyone could hear the tales. Stories of the beginning of the world, of how the People and other humans came to be, of ice fathers and sun children, of whales and seals, and great birds that flew to the moon. Long fantastic tales spun through the afternoon.

They reminded Erik of the Althing law-readings, how the words and ideas were treated as a precious thing, something to be shared with everyone present. *We humans are alike in all parts of the world,* he thought. *We need the same things; shelter, sustenance, and the continuation of our kind. We are driven by the same desires, too; entertainment, answers, community, love.*

He listened to the stories with half an ear. Despite Uukarnit's steady presence, for Erik, the warmth of the festival was over. He would have left already if not for Thio. She should have been there by now. *Patience,* he reminded himself, but could not honor the meaning of the word.

———·———·———

There, in the distance? Several adults and children were walking along the river, their kayaks behind on the beaching-sand. Soon other people spotted them too, and called greetings.

Erik watched them approach. Two wore *amauti,* carrying infants. Might one be Thio?

Soon he was being pulled by young women, who had taken Erik by the hand and were calling ahead, "Thio! Thio! Your friend Red is here!" He felt thrilled and altogether terrified.

The approaching group stopped and listened, then started running towards them as well, dropping their bundles on the path. The gap between them closed quickly, less, less, and as they came together, he saw her, he knew it was her, and suddenly, there she was.

Thio and Erik took one another's hands and stared at each other.

For Erik, time stopped, sounds disappeared, and the world closed down to just her face, Thio's precious face, her eyes so close, her lips so beautiful, a face that had once looked up at him with love and joy, a face that he had lost for so long, and never, ever wanted to leave again.

———·———·———

Reunion

With the passage of enough time, even things once familiar had become strange.

How pale Thio's hair and skin were! Her eyes were amazingly round and wide, and blue. He had not seen such hair and skin and eyes in his life. *I'm seeing Thio as the People first saw us,* Erik realized in surprise.

Thio, unsmiling, searched his face as well. Where to start? So much had happened. So much time had passed, and so much was changed.

In Thio's eyes Erik saw the first thing for which he had long yearned. She was no longer the shattered creature of the knörr camp, wavering between reality and fantasy, unhappy and unhealthy. Now, she was strong, better than ever, sound of mind and healthy. Erik wanted to stand tall and straight and show her that he, too, had grown stronger and better. Instead, his eyes filled and Erik reached blindly for her, and she for him. They clung to one another as old pain poured out and joy surged into its place, wave after wave letting go of hurts held so long, and brining in tides of new hope.

After long moments, Thio pulled back. She wiped her eyes and smiled gently. "Well come, Erik. Welcome."

She said it in the language of the People. He liked it that way.

_____·___·___

They walked towards the great festival stone, with children following along, inquisitive, peeking and peering. Nagojut and Pukiq, too, had run with Erik to Thio. They had only seen her briefly, long ago, and their renewed curiosity helped an awkward, too-polite conversation.

Erik wanted to hear everything Thio said, to memorize it forever. Words trickled out at first, but soon became a torrent in which each could hardly talk fast enough.

Thio told Erik about the village to which Aglakti had taken her, and what things she did every day. She had learned to enjoy the food after a long struggle. She slept comfortably in an *iglu* in the winter, and could build one herself. She had built her own summer shelter, too. She loved throat-singing. That did not surprise Erik, as she often had sung aboard the knörr. What had she missed from the festival, Thio wanted to know. Really, Erik had danced *all night?* How many people were here?

They had almost reached the storyteller circles when the bundle in Thio's *amauti* made a small noise. Erik had been trying not to stare at the tuft of pale hair poking up from the furs. The white baby. Her child. Was it Asa's as well? He dreaded seeing it.

"Shhh, shhh," Thio comforted the bundle. "Just a moment, and we will stop to feed you." There was a sound of thumb-sucking, and the child quieted.

"What is her name?"

"We call her Aquuataq," Thio said.

Aquuataq, meaning *snow-white.*

Thio came to a boulder large enough to sit on. She twisted to release the amauti from her shoulders. A wail broke out. "Oh, you are really hungry!" she laughed. "Let's get you fed!"

A woman with their group took the fur-wrapped bundle from Thio and nestled it in the curve of her arm. She lifted her anorak and began to nurse the baby.

348

"You look so surprised, Erik! She's Aquuataq's milk-mother. Like a wet-nurse at home."

Erik said nothing, and turned the talk to other things.

———·——·——

Others joined them until the area was crowded with people. Some knew Thio and talked with her, while others just watched in fascination. Soon the milk-mother held the baby up to her shoulder, patting its back. When it had produced a burp, she offered Aquuataq back to Thio.

"May I have her, please?" Erik felt in himself a resolve to not be like Iluq. Belonging mattered, and hostility hurt everyone. No matter who fathered her, this child was part of Thio.

The bundle felt small and vulnerable in Erik's hands. That very vulnerability touched him to his core. She could not help being, could not change who she was, any more than he could.

Another piece of old bitterness broke away from Erik's heart, and he felt lighter.

Aquuataq burped again. The small sound made them all laugh. He pushed the little hood from her tiny face.

Truly, she *was* very pale, but plump and healthy. Her eyes opened.

They were not Thio's eyes. In fact, there was nothing of Thio in the child's face. Her eyes were pink, and most definitely the eyes of the People.

"She is not like you," Erik blurted. "She is not yours!"

"She absolutely *is* mine!" Thio replied.

"But she is like them…but white…"

"It's a long story," Thio said. "I'll help you understand."

Thio gathered her words. "You've heard the many stories about white bears and wolves and newborn seals. White creatures have a special place here, both revered and feared. The People believe that they are a link to the spirit world. This baby... Let me start a little farther back. When I left with Aglakti, each time we met anyone new, it caused a sensation. I was so different, and I'm sure I looked horrifyingly ill, but Buniq and Aglakti encouraged people to welcome me.

"When we reached the village where Aquuataq was born, there was no time for introductions. We saw all of them standing on the shore, and knew right away that something was wrong. When they saw me, instead of standing in surprised silence as others had, they literally dragged me into the circle, where I saw Aquuataq."

The newborn had writhed naked on the stones, struggling and crying.

"It is the same at home," Thio said gently. "There is no shame in it, if the child is sickly."

"They exposed her because she is an albino."

"Yes. They thought she wanted to be with her father's spirit. But then I arrived, and everything changed. Can you imagine? A strange white child born the same day a strange white woman arrived from the sea? I could not have refused her, even if I wanted to." Thio laughed. "It was the one village in which I felt immediately, truly, welcome."

Thio smiled, remembering. "Erik, it was so hard, losing Karl and Kurt. I was trying to hold onto myself, but I had lost that battle. My mind let loose. A ship with no Tiller."

350

Thio looked to see if Erik had caught her small joke. "I can talk about it now, Erik. I can face the sadness and honor their memory. I couldn't...back then. Leaving the camp, leaving my very last connections to anything of home, was terrifying, but some shred of sense told me to go with Aglakti, that I *needed* to leave it all behind to get better.

"But I wasn't getting better, not at all. I was barely alive. I was almost unable to walk, from not eating. But when I saw that baby on the cold stones, how she was so pale and helpless, I *had* to have her. She was alone in the world, and no one to love her...like Kurt and Karl must have been, once...I had to make sure she would be healthy and loved, had a chance..."

Thio's voice broke in a little sob. As he had so long ago, Erik put his arm around her, and Thio collected herself.

"Once 'the white woman' arrived to take 'the white baby', there was actually quite a bit of interest in her survival, and offers to help. We became a novelty, something almost magical. A young woman with her own child volunteered to come with us to feed Aquuataq. She has been mine, ever since." Thio's voice was still husky. She was quiet for a while.

"It helped so much to be needed by her. I poured myself into her. She helped me start forgiving myself. For Karl, for Kurt, especially at first. For all the crew." She smiled a little. "She helped me forgive you, too."

"Forgive *me*? I tried every way I knew to take care of you!" The bitter rejection of the morning threatened to flood Erik again. "Forgive me for what?"

Thio laughed gently. "Oh, Erik. For the fact that I loved your mother so much, a woman who loved *you* so much, that I ended up on that damned ship because of you and her. Now I understand what a mother's love means. For being such a decent man and not listening to my mad plans on the knörr that I grew to respect you deeply even while I was exasperated at you. For letting me go with Aglakti, and not even trying to stop me, which I *hated,* even though I knew I needed to go, which made me have to eat raw fish and meat, which I detested!"

The half-laughter left her voice and Thio's expression grew sad. "But most of all, for not coming to find me, ever." Her lips brushed Aquuataq's shock of pure-white hair.

"But you and Asa...I heard...I thought..." He stopped, miserable and feeling stupid.

"It's been forever. I thought you had forgotten me and didn't care about me. It hurt terribly. When I would hold Aquuataq, it helped. Asa helped."

Erik wondered if Thio could possibly believe that the very opposite was true. He had stayed away out of respect, but giving Thio freedom to love another man had instead destroyed her trust in Erik.

Thio said gaily, "Enough seriousness! It's so good to see you. I want us to enjoy the festival! Pukiq says you won the running contest? Well, I used to beat my brothers! I'll wager I can beat you, too!" She handed Aquuataq to the milk-mother and sprinted away from Erik down the beach.

He laughed and roared at her in mock threat. "There's no way you'll outrun me! I'll catch you and wring your mischievous neck, and you... will...be...*sorry!*"

———·———·———

As they ran down the beach, shrieking with laughter, Erik saw something move in the corner of his eye. A man at some distance stopped walking, stared intently towards Erik, and then knelt on this ground. He lifted a spear and pulled back his arm, clearly intending Erik as his target.

The spear flew. Erik twisted, but not fast enough, and the sharp stone point bit into his rib. Blood gushed immediately, staining the white snow at his feet bright red.

Erik stared towards the man, stunned. Was this one of Iluq's group again? Iluq had wanted to teach him a lesson, in hatred, yes, but without serious injury. This man had just thrown with deadly intention.

Why did that man just try to kill me? Why?

In the timeless eternity that it took for him to fall to the ground, Erik considered many things. Whoever had launched the spear was a master. It had been an extremely accurate and powerful throw from a long distance. Despite himself, Erik admired the thrower's skill. He had felt the blade hit a bone and stop, and knew, relieved, that there would be no real damage. He saw Thio turn back, saw her look of horror. Erik's knees hit the snow and then his chest, and as he fell, he heard her screaming *Erik! Erik!*

It was Thio's scream that snapped Erik into focus again. *Attacked again? Twice in one day? Damn these people! Would this never end?* He no sooner sprawled onto the snow than he rolled, as quickly as a cat and deadly furious, his seal-knife already in hand. Erik ran towards the still-kneeling man who had thrown the spear, preparing to kill him.

The man crouched with a look of shocked devastation on his face. Erik hit him full on with a body blow, and the man offered no resistance. His eyes were wide with terror as he fell. He saw Erik's blade, and instead of fighting it, turned his head to expose his throat.

"Whoever you are, you die today! I have had enough of this!" Erik shouted.

The man lay absolutely motionless, his eyes peering up.

"Erik?" he said, confused. "Thio is calling *Erik*. You are Erik?"

"Yes, I am Erik! The stranger, the intruder that one no one wants. Who are you? Why did you throw the spear? Tell me before I kill you, because I *am* going to kill you!"

"All that I have is yours," the man whispered. "Greetings and welcome, *aipak*."

———·———·———

Aipak?

Surely, it could not be, Erik thought, but Thio's voice as she ran to him, *stop Erik, no, no,* and the ghastly expression on her face said it was true, and his fury grew.

A crowd had come running at Thio's screams.

"Aipak?" Erik said to them in angry disbelief. He gestured towards the man whose neck was bared under his knife. "This man who just tried to kill me...*this* is *Asa*?"

———·———·———

Aipak, the word that meant 'other-me'. It was a term of trust and respect between two men, but not just any men, only certain ones: those who were pledged to protect each other's loved ones and children, united in a bond of life by a woman they loved.

Erik had seen men greet one another with warmth and happiness, using that word and saying that greeting. *"All that I have is yours! Greetings, aipak!"* They would embrace, more than friends, different than brothers. A man would give his very life for his aipak, if necessary.

Everyone, it seemed, had tried to convince Erik of the logic of an *aipak*, but he had never been able to stomach the idea. If you were to be away for many months, hunting or on a circle-journey, and your wife had a child too small to travel, your aipak's wife might accompany you as companion and helper, while your own wife stayed at home, living with your aipak and caring for him and his children. If you simply disappeared on the tundra or at sea, he would welcome your wife into his home to become sister to his wife, and your children to join his own. You thought of an aipak's children as your own, because they might well be yours, and yours his. The relationships created a deep bond of trust and loyalty between two families. It created security for children, and kinship among unrelated people.

To Erik's friends, the word 'aipak' was filled with respect and love, happy affection and implicit trust. To Erik, it meant beyond doubt that Thio had shared her body with the man Erik held in his grip. This man Asa had been given that which Erik had long desired and had been denied, Thio's heart. She *loved* Asa.

Why had this man tried to kill him? It was against everything their people believed in! But now that he had identified himself as Erik's aipak, instead of knifing Asa in self-righteous anger, Erik would be expected to honor that bond with a man whose very name he despised. Instead of stabbing Asa with all the fierce jealousy consuming him, Erik knew that it was his duty to welcome Asa...and thank him.

———·———·———

Loathing, well-whetted by Iluq's earlier actions, boiled over in murderous fury. Blood still ran from Erik's ribs as he held the knife above Asa, shaking with jealousy and wanting to strike. Instead, ridiculous logic came from his mouth.

355

"You are not my aipak! Thio is not mine!"

"Yes, she is. She may love me, but Thio's heart belongs to you."

Lies! Strike him dead! Kill him, kill your betrayer! Cut his throat with blood-justice. Kill Iluq, kill Randaal, kill the council, kill them all! Show them all that you are right! The words filled Erik.

But other words came as well. *Anger is a choice,* Uukarnit had said. *Forgiveness is harder than anger, which is why forgiveness is stronger.*

He would not be like his father. He would not let rash anger make his choices. It had been a long time since Erik had committed to such a path. The decision now was almost as difficult as the first time. Still, he could make it again, and he would.

"I will not act in reckless anger!" Erik shouted, still boiling with rage. His hand shook as he laid the knife on the snow beside Asa. Fury at Asa turned to fury at himself. How could he have been so stupid to let Thio go? To let this ass take advantage of her loneliness?

"I am sorry for threatening you," Erik said, forcing himself to courtesy. Everything inside hungered for vicious reprisal.

Asa still did not move. "It is I who must apologize for throwing the spear."

Spear? Erik looked at his bleeding side. He had forgotten it in the face of the deeper cut, the crueler hurt. "It will heal," he said scornfully. The other hurt inside would not.

"Let me see," Asa said. He squatted next to Erik, his fingers probing the painful gash in the recently-donned anorak. "It will heal, and quickly. Thank goodness you turned."

Erik did not answer.

"I have long wanted to meet you," Asa said. "It is so good to finally see your face."

356

Erik could tell that Asa meant what he was saying, which made Erik want to loathe him the more. So this was the oh-so-wonderful-Asa, beloved by all, working his magic. *Bah.*

Thio stood to the side. She looked uncertainly from one man to the other, caring desperately for both of them and uncertain what to say or do. "Asa...Erik...help each other," she finally said.

Warmth shone from Asa's eyes as he looked at Thio. "Of course we will. We are bound."

Asa's voice held none of the jealousy Erik felt. *He called me aipak. Aipak! How could this man care for Thio so much, and yet accept – no, welcome! – Thio's feelings for me?* Erik had spent a long time trying to deny Asa's existence. It was no longer possible to do that.

"What happened, Asa?" Thio asked.

Asa's eyes were serious now. "It was like the dream again, but this time, I knew it was real. I heard you screaming. You were running down the beach. Erik was chasing you. I thought he was Olaf, trying to hurt you again."

Thio shook her head. "Olaf is back where the kayaks are, with men of our village."

"He says Olaf hurt you?" Erik could not bring himself to say Asa's name.

Thio's cheeks flamed as she turned her face away. "Olaf tried to ...force me. I think he would have killed me after. Asa stopped him in time. They watch Olaf now. They keep me safe."

Erik pictured the last time he had seen Olaf, raging at the center of the quieting-circle at the knörr camp long ago. While Erik had been nursing his wounded pride, Asa had rescued Thio from that anger.

Today, to throw a lethal spear at the running figure he thought was Olaf would have been the most wrong thing any of the People could imagine doing -- to kill a human being! --yet Asa had unflinchingly chosen that action to protect Thio.

And Erik had wanted to destroy Asa for it.

And Asa had not uttered criticism or challenge to Erik, only welcome.

Erik sank down on his knees, weak and bewildered as revelation came on him. Blood soaked down his arm and stained both men with red. Asa's spear had cut into his rib, but something in Asa's spirit, flying with the spear, had pierced Erik's heart.

"I think of myself as one of the People now, but am I really?" A question to himself.

Yes, he could eat raw meat and sleep in the cold and paddle a kayak for weeks on end. Yes, he had grown calmer, less angry, more willing to listen and compromise. But he was not connected to his core the way the People were with one another. It was not a matter of giving up fences and property, or sharing caribou meat and wives and children.

The truth was that these People believed that they actually *belonged* to each other. The Oneness of last night's dance...Erik had tasted enough to know it was real. They thought they actually *were one.* An aipak was a closer bond, even more personal, than the Oneness. Because of it, Asa would have done the greatest imaginable wrong to protect Thio. Asa would protect his aipak the same way. It was why he had not even tried to fight Erik.

Friendship with Uukarnit and Pukiq was not the same thing. Friendship was good, but it still had barriers. The People had almost no barriers between one another. But Erik did. It was he who had kept those barriers in place between himself and the People, not they against him, not even Iluq.

Erik frowned, looking into himself. "I've never allowed myself to be close to anyone. Not really, not the way you people do, as naturally as you breathe. I had friends, but I kept barriers. I don't trust. How do you do it?"

Asa saw something unfolding in Erik. He had the wisdom to not answer, to let it come.

"I learned not to trust when I was young. I learned I couldn't depend on anyone. I didn't want to be hurt…so…the barriers. But they don't protect you. They isolate you." Another long pause.

"You would have honored me as aipak, refusing to hurt me, even as I killed you."

Asa had welcomed Erik into that sacred bond. Everything he owned, everything he loved, he must share freely. *Everything?* Selfishness rose in Erik, along with the old familiar dream of being a hero, but as it did, for the first time, Erik saw the lie it was.

"I wanted it so much; to be the hero. But why? It was nothing more than longing to be seen as someone of value. It was a weapon to wield against a father who made me feel unworthy and unwanted. It was a boy's fantasy, forged from loneliness. I wanted others to see me, not as worth less than them, worthless, but as an equal, and welcome."

No, that was still not the truth. He had wanted to be *better* than any other man.

His dream had been the false pride of superiority, and his aloofness a shield that pride had built it for him. *To keep you safe,* it had whispered across the lonely years. *Do not trust others. They will hurt you. They will take advantage of you. Build a strong wall. Build it high, and thick, and keep others out. Trust in me only. I, your pride,*

359

will protect you. He had believed it, had yielded completely to it. But pride had not helped his father. It had not helped Erik.

"You don't need dreams of glory, do you, Asa? And you don't need pride, either. Raised in the Oneness of the People, your happiness comes from sharing, not taking." Erik knew he was coming to the heart of the matter, a mystery that had kept him a prisoner within himself.

"Pride lies to us," he said to Asa. "It says it will protect us, but instead, it imprisons us. Pride separates us from those who care for us. The real truth? Pride lives only to serve itself. It cares nothing for us!" He cried out in anguish, seeing the terrible cost of pride over the years.

"Iluq was right. I have been a danger, unwittingly, perhaps, but no less so! No more! I will wrestle this stupid pride out by the roots! I will strip selfishness from my flesh and pull it from my bones. I will seek out and reject every lie pride tells me! I want to be a better person. I want to be like you are, like your people are!"

Erik's whole being exploded with new understanding. Struggling to his feet, he turned to the crowd that had gathered and shouted, throwing his arms out, wanting to open wider, to share more and more, to burst apart so that he could give everything he had, everything he was, everything he would ever be, give it all, share it all.

"I understand! I understand! I understand! Thank you for teaching me!" He turned to Asa, and clasped him in a great hug. "My friend, I am so glad that you tried to kill me, because in doing it, you have set me free! Your spear did not hurt me. It pinned us together! What a marvelous throw!" He held his chest, laughing, and slowly the world stopped spinning. "Friends, you know Asa, and now I do as well! We are aipak, Asa and I!"

He had never had a brother. But now, he had an aipak.

——·——·——

The drumming would start soon. Erik longed wholeheartedly for it. Last night he had danced in curiosity, trying to understand. Tonight he would dance with certainty, beside Thio and Asa, one in the midst of all of the People, one of *The-People-As-One*.

—·—·—

Olaf

Olaf felt a great weariness at the idea of celebration. Here they called it the festival of the midnight sun. Back at home they would be celebrating Longest-Day. What did it matter? Of all the Longest-Days he had celebrated, Olaf could not remember a single one making a difference in his life. *Except for the one in which they outlawed me.*

So there would be a lot of drumming and dancing tonight. Big *fukking* deal. At least after it was over he would be on his way back to the knörr camp. At least he could get back to a decent longhouse and decent food. All of these idiots would just go back to that godforsaken village in the frozen middle of nowhere and eat more raw seal. It was all just tiresome. He clenched his feelings down tight. If they saw his anger, someone would come and be nice to him. There was no escape from it. Nothing mattered any more. Nothing. Nothing.

———·———·———

Erik walked towards where the kayaks were beached. He saw the man between two others and immediately knew who it was. Even from a distance, he could see bitter frustration in every line of Olaf's body.

The man had done terrible wrong. But, he had also been a desperate man, and with newfound clarity, Erik knew his own part in causing that situation. He thought back to how afraid Olaf had been, thinking he would be left alone the knörr camp, and how much he had not cared. Back then, Olaf had thought he would be returned to the knörr camp within the month. It had been more than a year. No, it did not excuse Olaf, but he would not increase Olaf's pain.

Erik drew a deep breath. "Olaf." A simple acknowledgement.

362

Olaf squinted at Erik. "Look at how your braids are done. You're one of them now?"

"It's easier. I do what works."

"You wear all the same clothes too. Nobody would recognize you. I reckon you're quite the kayaker now, too."

"A good *viking* follows where the winds and the waves lead instead of fighting them."

Olaf looked away. "That's all you have? The great Tiller, mouthing poetry?"

Erik let the insult slide. "We don't need to fight, Olaf." Besides the fact that Olaf seemed old and tired, Erik's mind had suddenly quickened on something else.

"Did you hear what I said? They're taking me back to the knörr camp, to leave me there? Why are you staring through me like that? Your mouth is open."

"What I just said about following the winds and the waves. I just thought of something."

"What was it?" Olaf's voice sharpened with interest at Erik's tone.

"It's nothing. Nothing."

"Damnit, Tiller, look at me. You and Thio, you love it here. I'm a miserable, broken man, so don't lie to me. I heard it in your voice. You thought of something that affects me."

Erik spoke without thinking as an image turned in his thoughts. "I might be wrong. It came to me in a sudden flash, an image of how it might be possible to get the knörr back to Íseland. A way I never thought of before. I need to think it through."

Ironic that he always had to go so far to learn anything. They were the farthest Erik had ever been from the knörr, and *now* he was seeing a possible course for a return voyage. It was the slenderest chance, but still…it might work.

"It needs thinking," Erik said, but inside, he had already weighed the odds.

"What do you mean, it needs thinking? Tell me! There's a piss-pot chance we could make it back?" In Olaf's voice, Erik heard the same desperate eagerness as the shark-gutters on the shore so long ago. Unexpectedly, he felt compassion.

"All right then. I'll tell you. I just saw it in my head, like a…" No, not the explanation about the map. Olaf would not understand. "I spent the past winter studying the winds and the currents around this island. Added to what I learned coming up here, I think it might work. It was those words that made me see it: *follow the winds and the waves instead of fighting them.*"

"But without a crew?"

"We'd have to tie the sail. Go when the weather is best, the fewest storms. In all likelihood, everything would go wrong. Maybe even worse odds than when we came out here."

A shadow of Olaf's old commanding ways replaced the bitter, beaten look. His jaw bunched. "Let's do it, then. We should leave right away. We could sail before autumn!"

"By the time we kayak all the way down there, it would be too late in the year. I wouldn't trust the weather. We'd have to wait until next spring."

"Three more seasons? Almost a year? That's an eternity!"

"It'll go quickly. Look how fast the last two years passed."

"Nay, we shouldn't wait. Anything could happen in a year. Let's find Thio and tell her. We should leave at sunrise!"

Oh, gods, Thio. "Would Thio even want to come, with you aboard, after what you did to her?" And Aquuataq? Would Thio bring her, leave her, or stay here with her?

Olaf snorted his opinion. "And leave her baby? Not likely as long as that thing breathes. But she owes it to me, Tiller. I asked her to help me, but she chose these folks and that baby instead. You don't need to ask her. Just make her do it!"

"Olaf, slow down. I don't even know if Thio is planning on going back to the knörr camp with me. We've only just seen one another for the first time in years, and I just barely thought of this sailing route. It needs consideration. Besides, you're not going to make decisions for anybody, least of all Thio. We're right in the middle of this festival. There's plenty of time to talk when the festival is over on the trip back to the knörr camp."

"But you'll do it? If Thio will? You're game to try?"

Erik pictured the old dreams of riches and fame. He had just let go of them, but so quickly, he could feel their shimmering allure slinking back into him. He pushed the false promise aside. Riches and fame had their place, but he had a new life here.

But there were other things than riches, he mused. His mother, for one. He had long ago buried any hope of seeing her again. Thio had said she was alive when they left. Plus, there were people at home who might be starving, if the famines had worsened. What did he owe to them? To his mother, if she was hungry?

"Spring is a long time, Olaf. But if we get back to the ship and it is sound, and if the sail is in decent shape, and if Thio wants to go, I'll consider it. But those are three big questions, Olaf!"

Something buzzed *wrong, wrong* in his head, but the drumming would start shortly, and Erik pushed the nagging voice from his mind. "We'll talk later about this."

Olaf nodded. "As soon as possible. And…Tiller?"

Erik wanted to be away from the agitated look in Olaf's eyes. "What?"

"That big rock over there, where the people are gathering. That thing is the center of all this goings-on, isn't it?"

"Yes. It's the midnight-sun stone. Holy to these folks. You'll be able to see it all from here." With that, Erik nodded to the men who stood silently guarding Olaf, listening to the strange talk, and he headed off to the char-drying racks.

———.———.———

"Thio!" Olaf had convinced his guards to find her. "I have something important to ask!"

"You only just got speaking-rights back, Olaf. One wrong word, and you'll lose them."

"I have good news. For all of us—you, Tiller and me." Olaf put on a look intended to convey warm camaraderie. "Did Erik tell you that he has figured a way to get us home? You said not long ago you wanted nothing more. Well, we can go now, you, him and me as crew!" His hands were spread towards her, supplicating.

"What? *What?!*"

"Erik wants to wait, but I believe we have no time to lose. Tell him you'll do it!"

"Olaf, what are you talking about?" Thio backed away.

Olaf grabbed at Aquuataq. "You don't want to leave this little girl. I understand! I left my son! But she can stay with the milk-nurse! She'll be fine!"

"Well, I won't be fine! I'm not ready to try dying on the ocean a second time, and the *last* place I want to be is on a ship with you!"

Thio pulled away, but Olaf lunged forward, seizing her again. "I won't hurt you! I promise!"

366

"Let go of me! Get your hands off Aquuataq!" The guards restrained Olaf, and she wrenched away from him.

"You can *fukke* yourself!" Olaf shouted. "You, and your slant-eyed mate, and that damned ghost-child you drag around!"

He glared, seeing Thio nuzzling Aquuataq's face as she walked away. "Look at her, doting on that brat of hers, while my son pays for her treachery! That pink-eyed whelp...why would the gods make anything as pale as that? It looks like a sacrifice-lamb for Odin for Longest-Day."

A lamb...

Today was Longest Day...

Tiller had spoken of a way home...

It was a sign.

"Odin!" Olaf whispered to himself. "You sent the white child for me, not Fishgirl! She ruined herself as sacrifice, so you sent this one, and she stole it as well! I must take it back. That babe belongs to you!"

His son lived still, Olaf was certain. There was a way to get home. Only one thing still needed to be done. Aquuataq would serve in Thio's place; an eye for an eye. Today was Longest-Day. There was no time to waste.

Olaf broke free of the men guarding him and ran towards Thio.

———·———·———

In a flash, Olaf had wrenched Aquuataq from Thio's arms and sprinted away. He reached inside his boot and pulled out the knife he had kept hidden there for so long.

Thio ran after him, crying for help. "Stop him, stop him! Help! Olaf has Aquuataq!"

367

Olaf quickly gained the slight rise where the festival-stone stood and ran to the center of it. He ripped away Aquuataq's fur blanket and held the child over his head with the knife against her chest. Her pale skin shone in the afternoon light.

"Stop right now!" He shouted at people who had run at him from all sides. "You have your ceremonies? I have mine! This was predetermined a long time ago, and the gods have spoken through this child! We are going to leave your land and I am going home! But before we leave, I have the duty of blessing our finding. It will not be my son who dies. It will be this child, the legacy of the woman who ruined everything! Look at this child! *Look at it!* It was blood-born to bless this land! The *blót*-ceremony that was ordained will finally come to pass!"

Olaf started to chant the strange, unhappy words. He waved the knife in the air above Aquuataq. Olaf screamed as he reached the sacrifice-sayings, the final words. His voice shrieked hellish and determined as his knife pricked into the soft skin over the infant's beating heart, and Thio broke free of the people holding her.

———·———·———

Asa had whirled at the sound of Thio's scream. He saw Olaf on the festival-stone, saw Aquuataq, saw the knife in Olaf's hand, and knew instinctively what was about to happen.

Without thinking, Asa knelt, lining up Olaf in his sights, his spear arm pulled back as far as he could. His heart pounded and he fought to calm his breath. He had thrown his spear a thousand times, but never with such need. *Little Aquuataq!* The target was far, and the angle poor, and Thio was almost in the way. Asa knew he had only one chance. Taking careful aim, he breathed the seal-silence breath. The

368

whiteness of which he never spoke flashed inside, and Asa knew his aim would be true.

His arm moved and the spear left his hand. His spirit flew forward with it, speeding through the air towards Olaf, guiding the spear as it sought the opening between Olaf's ribs. The whiteness guided the stone tip so that it would not bounce off bone, but instead find the slender strip of muscle, and slide through, and keep sliding, seeking. Finally, it reached the thing Asa had sensed as he knelt in the snow, the malevolent anguish at Olaf's very core. Asa's spear-spirit drove deep and pierced the place of torment. Olaf gave a great cry and fell backward, still clutching Aquuataq, and Asa knew it was done.

As Thio reached him, Olaf wheezed in pain. "Thought these folks didn't kill, Thio...your precious Asa's no different than Randaal, is he? But he can't stop what must happen. The gods...the gothi..." Olaf pawed at Aquuataq. He felt weakly for the knife lying on the stone next to him and cried out in desperation. "My son...my son!"

Thio picked up the saxe that had terrified her so long ago. "Asa is in every way different from you and Randaal. Your death will devastate him. But I'm not that different from you, Olaf, and I will not allow Asa to bear alone the responsibility for your death. Now, by the law of our land, I forgive what you've done, and by that same law, you must forgive me!"

Thio gripped the pommel of the knife in her fist, plunging it straight into Olaf's chest. It stood side by side where Asa's spear protruded. "The evil that came here with you, dies here with you, Olaf. Go in peace." She picked up Aquuataq, clutching the little girl.

A circle of blood flowed across the great round stone, and Olaf gave a great cry and died.

—·—·—

The People stood horrified, their legs and arms locked in odd angles of running, their hands clasped over their mouths. Only heads and eyes moved. They swiveled from the ghastly corpse to Asa where he knelt in the snow, unmoving, his face ashen.

Asa had killed a man.

Laughing, happy, helpful, beloved Asa *had killed a man.* Asa, who would hurt no one, had slaughtered Olaf...on the festival stone, the very heart-center of the Dance of One People.

———·———·———

Thio might have finished it, but they had all seen Asa's spear, saw the death-throw.

Asa had done to Olaf what the strangers on the beach had done to each other. Their poison had reached to the very core of The People, and Asa was infected with it. Worse yet, they had *wanted* him to do it. They were all contaminated with the poison of Olaf of Íseland.

They knew the truth in themselves, and backed away from it, fearful.

———·———·———

Asa staggered to his feet and stumbled towards Olaf's body. People moved away as he approached, afraid to touch him. He stood over the corpse, studying Olaf in death. He pushed the body back and forth a little with his foot. It was flaccid and heavy.

Asa bent and pulled the ceremonial knife from Olaf's chest. He looked at it with bland eyes, then tossed it aside carelessly. He jerked his spear from Olaf's chest. He had made that spear over the winter, a special one for the competition. He looked at the spear point he had so carefully chipped, and then his hand dropped and the weapon rolled from his fingers unnoticed.

Asa sank down onto his haunches, staring at the body. No one moved.

First my spear flew to my aipak, and now it is Olaf's heart. Asa looked at the thought as if it was a bird looking for a place to land. The bird flew in erratic senseless circles.

On the same day, I tried to kill one human, and now I have killed another.

Suddenly Asa fell upon Olaf's body with a loud cry. He knifed it open from gullet to groin. A horrified gasp ran through the onlookers. Asa reached his hand into the bloody abdomen and savagely hacked out the liver. Holding it to the sky, in a broken voice he sang the thank-words for a hunted animal. Asa did not cut an offering-slice of the liver, did not offer spirit-food to the horrified faces staring at him. Asa did not see even them. His spirit was tangled with Olaf's, trapped in the detritus of Olaf's heart.

Holding the gory liver in both hands, Asa bit into it. He ripped the flesh with his teeth and chewed while blood spurted down his chin. He bit into Olaf's liver again, chewed in anguish, swallowed, and threw the rest on the ground. Choking and gagging, Asa flung himself full-length onto the corpse, his forehead pressed against Olaf's lips and the fingers of his spear-hand gripping Olaf's chest, holding the heart, rocking and sobbing with grief.

———·———·———

No one moved. Only the sounds of Asa's wretchedness broke the silence.

371

———·———·———

Thio handed Aquuataq to waiting hands. She crept towards where Asa sprawled on Olaf.

"Asa…" she whispered. "Dear one. Come away from that thing."

Asa did not move. She touched him gently.

"Asa, Aquuataq is safe. He was going to kill her. You did no wrong."

Asa rolled off Olaf and lay looking at the sky, and did not move.

———·———·———

Erik heard screams over the conversation at the char-racks. Was that Thio? He spat the fish from his mouth and took off at a dead sprint. *Wrong, wrong.* The festival stone? *Run faster.*

———·———·———

Erik pushed through the crowds pressed against the rock. "Thio! Where is she?!"

"I'm here," she called back, her voice shaky.

As he reached Thio, Erik saw Asa lying beside Olaf, the carnage, blood everywhere. "My gods, what happened?"

"Olaf was babbling like a madman about us going back to Íseland on the knörr. He snatched Aquuataq, and ran with her. He had the knife, the old saxe…was going to…Asa threw his spear."

"Is Asa alive?" There was so much blood, and Asa lay unmoving.

"He is. But…"

372

Thio did not have to put it into words. Erik had known his aipak for such a short time, and already he had seen the person that Asa was. This could destroy him.

Asa, of whom Erik had felt jealous when Pukiq described the amazing spear-throwing skills. Asa, who had saved Thio once, and had thrown the same spear only moments ago to protect Thio, had thrown it again. He had saved Aquuataq, but at what cost?

Erik knelt beside the man whose face was smeared with Olaf's blood. He took Asa's head in his hands. Erik had seen eyes like that before, when Thio had broken.

"Asa," Erik said quietly. "Aipak, look at me."

For the briefest instant, Asa's eyes, lost in pain, connected with Erik's.

"You must hold on to yourself, Asa," said Erik. "We will take care of you."

"I am no longer human," Asa whispered.

"No, Asa," said Thio. "You are the deepest kind of human, the rarest kind. You acted, without thought for yourself, so that a helpless child could live." She touched Erik's arm. "We need to get Asa away from Olaf and clean him."

Erik lifted Asa. He carried the man carefully and placed him gently on a fur spread. People crowded around Asa, kneeling, and reached forward to touch him. The same hands that had flinched from him earlier gently washed every trace of blood from Asa's face and hands. They took off his clothing, saturated with Olaf's blood and bowels, and cleaned Asa, and wrapped him.

Other hands carefully straightened and cleaned Olaf's destroyed body. The spirit of the hunted caught and held a piece of the hunter. They must protect Olaf until Asa was free of him.

They dared not speak their concern that the damage to Asa might be unrecoverable.

———·———·———

"What do we do now?" Erik asked Aglakti, who had been called from her resting-tent. The massive crowd parted at her coming—*it's Aglakti, let her pass*—and silently closed again.

Before she could answer, the crowd parted again for two more. Tupit stood shoulder to shoulder with Iluq, facing those who knelt beside Asa.

"What caused such a monstrous thing to happen?" demanded Iluq.

———·———·———

Iluq fumed. "But you said that Olaf has been in the same village as Thio and Aquuataq for so long! Why did he suddenly do this now?"

Erik answered. "I may have some inkling. You know, Iluq, how much you have wanted us to return to where we came from. Olaf felt the same. I always thought that such a voyage was impossible, but something today made me see a chance. I think that somehow, the idea provoked Olaf to madness."

Tupit and Iluq spoke in hushed tones together.

"Why was he not simply joyful to go home? Why hurt Aquuataq?" asked Tupit.

Erik struggled. Not knowing about Olaf's son or the threats against him, he did the best he could to explain.

"Pride. Fear. To gain the favor of other men. To be a hero."

"Hero?"

374

Erik had used his own word. There was none for it in the People's language. "Someone better than all others. One who is revered, and given the finest furs and the best meats."

They still did not understand. "We always offer one another the best meats," said Pukiq.

Erik tried again. "Someone whose accomplishments are so great that stories are told about him from one sun-year to the next and the next."

"Ah," said Pukiq. "You mean someone like Asa."

The last bit of dry shell that once held pride crumbled to dust. "Yes. Someone like Asa."

———·———·———

"I still do not understand!" shouted Iluq. "What about going to your home would make Olaf such a great man? We come and go back and forth from our settlements all the time."

The truth could not be put off any longer. Erik spoke them with pain and shame. "He would have been a hero because our land is not like your land. Nunaat is huge. Many people can live here and have plenty to eat, plenty of space to roam and build villages. Our land, Íseland, is much smaller. It is crowded with people. There is not enough food for everyone to eat. They go hungry. Sometimes they die of hunger. We need more land for our people. We came here looking for it. One who found that for which we searched would be greatly honored."

"They *die* of *hunger?* How is that possible?" The question came from many voices.

"Our people do not eat from the sea as yours do, and our land does not have plentiful herds of caribou. The only animals we have to eat, we must raise. Those animals require green grasslands. Besides their meat and milk, we need ground in which we grow plants that we eat. We simply have more people than our fields and animals can feed."

"Why *don't* they eat as we do? Seal and char need no grass lands!"

Tupit put a hand on Pukiq's arm. "People live as they do," he said quietly. "It is not for Erik to defend their ways. He is helping us to understand."

Turning again to Erik, he said, "So your water-vessel came here looking for grasslands. If you had returned, saying you found it, not only Olaf, but you, too, would have been *hero.*"

"Yes," said Erik. Shame filled him.

Iluq knew why. Scornfully, he said, "And more of your people would have come here."

"Yes."

"Why did you not tell us this ever before?"

"I never thought it was possible...and fear made me too selfish to be honest."

"How many more people like you?"

It was better that they knew the full truth. "You see all the People here for the Festival? As many as this, and even more."

Iluq put a hand over his eyes. The lines along Tupit's mouth deepened.

Pukiq murmured a guttural curse. "We need to take care of Asa and stop talking of this."

———·———·———

The truth-seeker known as Kunwaktok walked stiffly. "The dancing aches my old bones." She hobbled as quickly as she could, moving through the crowd to Asa. She touched his face with her weathered hands and his eyes opened. He looked at her silently.

Kunwaktok returned Asa's gaze steadily for a few moments, then nodded to herself and tucked the fur closer around his shoulders.

"So, wanderer," she said, without preamble. "What shall we do?"

Erik was confused. "I thought you were going to tell us."

"No. This evil came from your people. You must remove that which sickens Asa. What are you willing to do to heal your aipak?"

———.———.———

The answer was right there, of course. The only necessary decision was which choice. Erik would have to leave the People, just when he had learned to finally be one of them. The thought was terrible, but the prospect of losing Asa was worse.

"I can't speak for Thio. For myself, I can see two things to offer. I can go to my home-place near the hot-spring island, and live there alone, and never again be with your People. If they are not exposed to the evil in my culture, it may at least not hurt them anymore. Or, if Thio is willing, we can still try to take our ship back home, the way I told Olaf might be possible. If we never reach home, so be it. If we do, we can tell others that there is no land to be found, to stay there. Either way, you will be free of us. The choice is yours. Whatever you want, I will do."

Thio held Asa's hand in one of hers, and Erik's in the other. *Leave everyone? Even Aquuataq?* The idea crushed her, but she inclined her head towards Erik and nodded.

———.———.———

377

"So you would leave everything here? Give up the Oneness, to help Asa? Even choose your own death, if necessary?" asked Iluq harshly. "Knowing all the while it might not help?"

"Yes," Thio said. Her throat was husky. "Whatever we can do, we will."

Kunwaktok pulled open Asa's eyelids. They shared another long and silent gaze.

"This is the way of our people," she said. "To offer only generosity, to think more of others than oneself. Asa heard you. His spirit is terribly sick, but with such nourishment, it will one day heal." She turned to Iluq. "Now it is we who must make a choice."

"It is a big decision and it affects more than Asa. Should we have a Talking?"

A murmur spread through the crowd. Heads began to shake *no, no.* Tupit spoke for them. "Our lives depend on the Sun. We know it will begin to leave us after today, and we must honor it soon with the final dance. The choice must be made right away, so that we can offer it and honor it in the Dance of One tonight, to bless Asa."

He spoke to Erik. "You have spoken as one who truly honors his aipak. I can tell you that every man and woman here, most of all Iluq, appreciates your words. But what you say about people starving for food in your country still concerns me. We must choose to be kind to them, even if they do not know us. We must also recognize that they are desperate, as Olaf was. Regardless of whether you leave or if you stay, what of them? Might they not try again to find our land?"

"I cannot say," Erik spoke for both him and Thio. "It might never happen, or there might be another ship heading for your shores as we speak. There is really no way to know. There have been three years of famine in my country. Hopelessness might cause them to give up, but despair might make them try harder. The passage is difficult and long,

378

but not as long as one might think. If that is discovered, many will come, there is no doubt."

"If they came, where would they want to live?"

"I have looked at many inlets and fjords. Only those far south, and only a few of them, where there are large green meadows along the southernmost parts of Nunaat, would serve for farmlands. They would not want to be here where you live, or where Thio lives now. Not even here at the fishing camp. Your people thrive here, but it is too far north for our way of life."

"Would they not eventually come up here, as their children's children grew plentiful?"

"No," Erik said with certainty. "My people travel for trade, but we are farmers at heart. We want fertile fields for crops and herds, and harbors with open seas to take goods to other countries to trade. I cannot imagine them ever wanting to live in the parts of Nunaat where your permanent settlements are."

Tupit's fingertips brushed up and down, up and down the front of his anorak. He spoke almost to himself. "The lands where they would live are far from the lands where we spend most of our life. We go there sometimes for explorations, and for circle-voyages when a young man or woman comes of age, but many years none of us travel there."

He continued. "I can picture you, living in your green home valley, far from the coast of the sea. If others did come, they would likely never find you there. They would explore up and down the coast, looking as you did. They might find us instead. What would happen then?"

Again, the answer was painful, but Erik was honest. "Every man is different. Some would want to trade fairly with you for furs and the tusks of your narwhal and walrus, and come every year. Others would see you, your very bodies, as nothing more than trade goods. They would take your women for themselves, and make your men spend the rest of their lives doing hard work, without any freedoms." The People would not understand the word for *slave* or *thrall.* "It would depend on the men aboard the ship."

Tupit's wise eyes considered the sky, thinking. "And what if you were able to return to your land? You would tell everyone about this new place you have found, our Nunaat. You would show them exactly where they can find the good green meadows. You would tell them that further north is always cold and always covered with deep snow, to not bother exploring there because you have been there already and that they would find nothing for their trouble, only ice and stone. No green meadows. You would tell them that, yes?"

"Yes, and they would believe me."

Tupit's fingers stopped their slow brushing and rested on his breastbone. He tapped it slowly, still thinking deeply.

"Iluq, my brother, the way I see it, it may be safer for us in the long run if Erik and Thio *are* able to go home. Go and be the thing called a *hero.* Be the stuff of stories. More importantly, help your people to survive. Bring some of them here--but only where you carefully choose, where we will not overlap. Give them places to live, and keep them away from where we live."

"What if one of them sees one of you one day, by accident? It could happen."

"Then you must be a truth-seeker for them. You must so earn their respect that if you tell them we are a peaceful people with whom to trade, to leave us to our places and our people in peace, they will honor your guidance. But that would be a matter for a much farther future."

Tupit turned to the crowd. "Is there anyone here who has other thoughts?" He waited a long time, perhaps hoping for another opinion, but none were offered.

"They support your words. I do as well," said Iluq.

"Is it truly possible to get back, just Thio and you in that great kayak?"

"Possible, yes. But no one has ever done it. There is no guarantee it will work."

Tupit was silent in thought for a long time.

"If you stay with us, as one of us, together we will always be watching over our shoulder for others. There is no true peace in that. If you go to live alone, others might come, and separately, you and we will still always be watching and worrying. The only way that offers even a hope of real freedom is what some might have first thought was the worst idea: for you to try and go back and deliberately bring others; but in that you may almost certainly perish and fail. It is a hard choice. We must give the decision back, for you and Thio to choose."

Erik bowed his head and nodded silently. Thio said nothing, but tears ran down her cheeks, and she held Aquuataq even more tightly.

———·———·———

"But what about Asa, right now?" asked Erik.

"We will take him and care for him," Iluq said.

"I have a duty to him. I *must* help."

"No!" said Iluq. "There has been enough harm! I appreciate that you have spoken honestly and bravely, but Asa should be with me...with us, with his own people!"

Thio walked towards Iluq, until their faces were barely a handsbreadth apart. She looked earnestly in his eyes. "Asa and I talked often of Erik. Asa wanted to know Erik, to be friends with him. Asa killed Olaf to protect Aquuataq. He almost killed Erik while trying to protect me. You, more than anyone else here, must realize it is we who must help Asa heal."

Iluq's eyes no longer showed scornful pride, but only anguish. "I would not have had Asa love you of all people, Thio, but he did. He and Red are aipak, by Asa's own choice." He wiped his eyes. "But I beg you, please do everything you can to take care of Asa...my beloved son...my only child." Burying his face in his hands, Iluq wept.

———.———.———

Iluq...was Asa's father? Before Erik could feel surprise, Iluq's next action completely astonished him.

Iluq bent and kissed Asa's forehead and murmured to him. Erik stood awkwardly and put his hand out to Iluq in friendship, but Iluq brushed it aside. Instead, he drew Erik into an embrace and held him close. "All that is wrong between us is over. You are aipak to my son. That makes you my son, and Thio my daughter. What is mine is yours, and I wish only goodness for you."

Words and explanations had never been able to communicate what Iluq's simple words did. Finally, Erik understood what an aipak brought to a community. Iluq, who had persecuted him, was now not only a sort of father-in-law to Thio, but father-by-association to Erik himself.

"You honor us beyond anything we could hope for." Erik bowed, and this time it was he who wiped his eyes.

———.———.———

382

There was one last matter to decide.

"We need to free Asa's spirit from Olaf," the truth-sayer Kunwaktok said.

"We also need to free Olaf's spirit to leave the earth, so that it does not return to us," Thio added. "It is the custom of our people to burn the dead. We need to do that. To protect Asa. To protect all of us."

When had he stopped believing in revenants? Erik wondered. But the tradition was deep in his bones as well. It would feel wrong not to observe it.

"Not here," said Iluq. "Not at our festival-place." All nodded.

"Tomorrow, after the festival is over," said Iluq. "Can it wait until then?"

"We will cover Olaf's body. That will trap his spirit in it."

Iluq pointed to Toonoq. "Asa is your best friend. You will stay with him, too?"

"No, I will take him with them. Wherever the burning is, we must take Asa to it," said Toonoq. "He must be where his spirit can find him when it disentangles from Olaf's." The quiet acquiescence that had hummed through the surrounding people while Tupit was speaking sounded again. *Um-hmm, um-hmmm.*

"Thio?"

She nodded. "Yes, Iluq, of course. Erik, Toonoq and I, with Asa, will take Olaf's body to where we will burn it for him. After that, we'll travel south, towards our knörr camp, with whoever else wants to come. When Asa is well enough, and ready, they will bring him back home to you." She smiled at Iluq, and gratefully accepted his warm, hopeful embrace.

———·———·———

Thio bent to Asa and spoke softly in his ear. "Beloved, Olaf's body must meet with fire so that it will release you. We will start at first light tomorrow. We will keep you safe." His eyes were closed, but Asa nodded. The effort of breathing seemed almost too much for him.

"It is time!" Tupit cried. "Sound the drums! Our people have endured a great wrong. We must pull all of this into the drumming, to honor those who have tried to do what is good, to bless those who have struggled and failed, and to bring us together, in acceptance and gratitude, in forgiveness and survival. We must dance as we never have done before!"

——·——·——

They positioned Asa where he could sense the dancing. Thio curled against him, Aquuataq in her arms.

"I'll stay here with Asa. Erik, dance for us. Go on, Toonoq, you too." She gave a tender smile to Asa. "I'll help him be part of it, right next to him, where he can see me."

When Erik and Toonoq had left, Asa's eyes flickered open and closed again.

"Was there another way, Thio?" The whisper was so soft she barely heard it.

"I don't know. I cannot see a way to change the path that brought us here…step by step."

"How does one weigh the life of a lonely fearful man against a helpless child? What took us to the place where such a terrible choice had to be made?"

"You did not take us to that place, Asa. You never stopped trying to help Olaf. But he needed to try to help himself, too, and he would

384

not. Or could not. You have his death on your spirit, but it was done in love. You stopped him from having a far worse death—Aquuataq's—on his spirit." She stroked Asa's hair tenderly. "Those nightmares plagued you so long. I used to hate it when it happened. Now I think there was a reason that you dreamed it over and over, always changing. If you had hesitated even the slightest bit, Aquuataq would have been gone. The dream was preparing you."

He did not answer, but only nodded. Any further effort was too great.

"Now it is you who must try, dear heart," said Thio. "I know this brokenness. I have lived it. It may seem you cannot come back from it, but you can. It will take some time. The most important thing is that you must believe it is possible. We will be here with you."

Asa's grief for Olaf, for the wrong he had done to protect Aquuataq, went beyond his bones. He could feel it reaching forward, intent on destroying every happiness in his future.

"You will try, won't you?"

He nodded, but only because Thio wanted him to.

———·——·———

Olaf's crossing-over fire burned hotly. The smoke was visible for a long distance.

They waited long enough to be sure the flames were doing their work, and then prepared to leave, anxious to be moving forward.

"Come, Asa," said Erik. "Let's get you back to the umiak. We have a long way to travel."

They lifted the litter carrying their precious friend and secured it on an umiak. Fifteen voyagers set off. Aglakti had insisted on coming with them. "I've been on this voyage since the beginning. I'll see it through to the end." Thio was grateful for the presence of her trusted older friend.

When they reached the mouth of the river and turned south, Erik pulled a long blade from inside his kayak. The metal was scorched from Sigmund's funeral fire, but it still showed the strange carvings. "Olaf must have taken this from your crossing-over ashes, Sig," he said. "It didn't seem right to give it to him as a crossing-over gift."

Erik started to drop it into the sea, but an odd feeling stopped him. He shivered a little, and put the skramasax back into its wrappings and slid it into his kayak again.

———·———·———

A Child's Touch

They had paddled for three days, and Asa had barely spoken or moved.

"Let's see if you can work your magic on Asa the same as you did on me," Thio kissed the baby as she walked to Asa. "Can you hold Aquuataq for a bit, Asa?"

Thio folded her child into the furs tucked around Asa. He looked somberly at the little girl. With her pink eyes, she was unable to see well, but knew it was Asa. He had held her often at the home village.

Aquuataq reached up to feel Asa's face. Her small fingers explored his eyes, nose and mouth. As she felt his teeth carefully, she played a game, one special to her and Asa. She put her fingers in his mouth, waited to feel him pretend to bite them.

Asa did not bite, but the harsh lines along his mouth softened ever so slightly.

"I'll be back in a little while." Thio sat not far away where she could watch. Not soon after, Aquuataq fell asleep, her head tucked under Asa's chin, her thumb firmly in her mouth.

Thio helped Toonoq prepare food. When she took some to Asa, he took a tiny bit of fish and offered it to Aquuataq. The little girl took it, chewing seriously, and Thio saw a shadow of a smile on Asa's face.

"Leave her with me while the others eat, Thio." Asa held the little girl closer and closed his eyes. This time when she put her tiny fingers on his lips, he bit gently. Once or twice more, and he fell asleep again, but his dreams were troubled.

———·———·———

"I need to talk with you," Thio said bluntly.

Erik had found a whale's skeleton on the beach and was choosing some of the bleached bones to tow back to the knörr camp. "Why do your eyes look ready to jump out of your face?"

She got right to the point. "I want to know why you were outlawed. The whole thing. Not the version they read at the Althing. I already heard that."

"It's so strange. Two years, and we've never talked about it. Not on the ship. Not when we landed, or at the camp. You were unwell, then there was so much time apart. I'll tell you everything you want to know. I don't want anything hidden between us."

"Good. You can start now."

———·———·———

"Well, the first thing is that I've been outlawed twice. The first time…"

Thio cut him off. "I heard about that when were are at the Althing. Besides, it wasn't so much an outlawing as a banishment. We'll talk about it another time. It's the fight over your high-seat pillars I want to hear about."

"The pillars had been handed down in my father's family. They had been carved with my mother's heritage as well, as a wedding-gift to her, but my uncle refused to offer them, because he feuded with my father. Many years afterwards, when my father was gone and my uncle as well, I was on a trading voyage to Nórsvegr. I finally found them and had them shipped to Íseland.

"My friend Thorgest needed a set, and I wasn't ready to use mine, so I lent them to Thorgest. It was an arrangement that helped both of us. I would have had to store them somewhere, and it gave Thorgest time to have his own set carved.

"I came home from months of travel and went to Thorgest. I took an expensive gold-leaf luck charm to bless his new pillars. Instead, I saw my own seat-pillars standing tall and beautiful in Thorgest's longhouse, and him sitting on the high-seat between them. I demanded them back, but he laughed at me."

Erik's eyes darkened at the memory. "He told me *'The law says that if you do not claim your property in a year, it becomes mine.'* I reminded him I had lent them to him as a favor, and that he had agreed to return them when I requested. Those pillars were all that mattered to me in the world. He knew it."

Thorgest's words had cut hard. *"Your loss, Tiller. There is nothing between us but words. You have no bond-mark. There was no witness to our agreement. The law will take my side."*

"I have heard of this man Thorgest," Thio said quietly. "One must tread carefully."

"I know that now. Thio, I went away enraged. My father came from a good family. That's why those pillars..." Erik stopped. "I went to take them back, in anger, and stupidly. If I had gone back with others and made Thorgest face them as a group, he would have been shamed into giving up the pillars. Instead, I let self-righteous anger drive me to rash action."

"What happened?"

"Thorgest and his wives were supposed to be away for days for his brother's wedding. No one was supposed to be at home, so we didn't expect any trouble. I promised some men I knew a share each of the silver I'd earned on my last trading voyage. My friend Styr Thorgrimsson, and Thorbjorn Vifilsson, and Lucky Wolf of Sviney, and two of Brand's sons, from Swanfjord came with me. We made jokes about stealing the pillars back, and besting Thorgest at his own game. As soon as the wedding travelers were out of sight, we broke open the door. I did not want to collapse his longhouse, so we had even hauled replacement pillars with us! We worked like cart horses switching the pillars. Finally, we dragged my *setsstokkrs* out of the longhouse and loaded them onto the wagon and headed home, jubilant at how well our plan had worked. Each man was planning how to spend his coin. Styr talked of buying a whole new herd of sheep, and Einarr wanted to buy an apprenticeship on a knörr." Tiller's mouth clenched. "We crossed the valley ridge, and then the howling began."

Thio remembered from the trial. "Thorgest came home early and found you."

"Yes. He should have stayed the full three days of wedding-feasting, plus a day to travel back, but his sister was there too, and bickering broke out immediately. It was ruining the party, so Thorgest said he was not feeling well, offered a large gift and left for home. When he saw what we had done, he set his dogs loose, and his sons followed. Thorgest followed Thorbjorn Vifilsson across the river. Styr and Wolf got away, running straight up rocks only they could climb. We always said Wolf should have been named 'Goat'. Einarr stayed with me and the wagon."

It took long moments to for him to continue. Thio waited.

"Thorgest's sons caught up with us, of course. I pleaded with them, but they would not listen, and we fought. Einarr was not a tall man, but he was so strong and quick. We battled them with our fists and with our saxes. I had Thorgest's oldest son pinned down when Einarr came over and taunted him that his brother was already dead. Thorgest's son rose up, insane, and threw me off. He and Einarr wrestled on the ground, stabbing at one another. There was no separating them. The end came quickly for both. Einarr laughed up at me. To this day, I wish I could erase the memory of the blood bubbling from his lips. *'Tell my wife I fought well for a farmer,'* he said. And then he was gone."

Another long silence. "Thio, Einarr was a good man. And I had trained both of Thorgest's sons to sail. My rash anger cost all three their lives."

"Erik, who does not wish he or she had paused to consider the better way?"

"Thorgest came back and found us. I was waiting for him by the wagon. I wanted to face him as a man, take responsibility for the fight, and offer what redress I could. But he accused me of his sons' deaths, even though he could see the marks of Einarr's long knives in them. When the local council gathered, Thorgest lied about his promise for the pillars and made me look like a common thief. From there, it was a trial at the springtime Thornes Thing, then again at Althing. I was outlawed for murder. I did wrong, there is no doubt, but I didn't kill anyone, not that day."

Acceptance

Thio got up and walked about a bit. "Thank you," she said, finally. "I needed to know. Some of the stories at the Althing made you out to be a vicious killer."

"People want entertainment, Thio. A true tale is not as much fun to hear as one embellished by a storyteller. What did you think of me when you saw me at the Althing?"

"You seemed bitter," she hesitated, choosing her word carefully. "Not belligerent like some of the prisoners, not cocky or blustering.

391

Broken inside, somehow. I knew there was more to the story. Now it is your turn. Come to my tent. We are losing the light."

"Where's Asa?" he asked.

"He's in Toonoq's shelter. He's been asleep since we pulled to shore this evening. He paddled for a bit, today, did you see? Every day now, he plays the little game Aquuataq loves, where she puts her fingers in his mouth and he pretends to bite her, and she laughs, and he chuckles...and Aglakti said that Asa even smiled at one of Nagojut's pranks today."

Erik had seen that as well. They all watched constantly for the smallest of signs.

"He'll be able to sleep without you?" Thio usually stayed with Asa.

"I'm sure the paddling exhausted him."

Erik cleared his throat. "Thio, I have a question for you, too. You don't have to answer."

She shook her head. "I already know the question. The answer is no. My future doesn't lie with Asa. I have a life before him, and a future that depends on going home to Íseland. Of course I love Asa, but because I do, I will encourage him to find his own mate. I sleep with him these days to comfort him, but that's all. Now, I have difficult things to say to you as well."

———·———·———

Thio lit a whale-oil lamp and shivered, but not from cold. Erik realized it was the first time they had been alone together since he had cared for her in the knörr camp.

"It would never look as if there was a problem," she began without preamble. "Our farm is in a good location. The soil is fertile, the

392

longhouse well built. My parents worked hard and were respected. I know this is going to sound terribly trivial, compared to the troubles of others. Maybe if I hadn't longed for their approval so much it wouldn't have hurt so much, but it did. No matter how hard I worked, my mother never praised what I had done. I always could have done better, somehow, in her eyes. My father loved me, I *know* he did, but he could not show his love and pride. He just mocked me; I wasn't a son." Thio's eyes were sad. "So much effort, hoping to prove that I mattered.

"Some women seek to prove their worth through a profitable marriage. I wanted to prove my own worth. Besides, I had no desire for a husband. I saw how my parents fought in secret and I wanted no part of it, so I avoided the bride-fair at the Althing, and watched the trials. That's where I first saw you. But of course, I was there looking for you."

At those last words, Erik realized why Thio had brought him into her shelter. It was to give privacy to him, not her. "It's about my mother? I'm finally going to hear?" He felt impossibly eager.

"She worked for my parents," Thio began. "She just arrived at our farm one day. Even after she lived with us for years, she would still never talk about where she came from. She was kind to me in ways my mother didn't know how to be, but underneath, she often was sad."

Seeing his expression, Thio added quickly, "Erik, this story does not have an unhappy ending. I don't know where your mother is now, but she was fine when we went to the Althing."

"My mother was at my trial?!"

"No, I am sorry. I did not mean to say it that way. She never would go to the Althing with my parents, even though her wools commanded the best prices there. Erik, her colors were so beautiful!

393

But she always said, "*If anyone asks you, tell them you did the dyes yourself. Please don't mention me. No one must know where I am.*"

"The summer you were to go to trial, we heard about it, of course. Word had spread across the valleys about Thorgest's sons being killed. Thorgest's brother had married my neighbor's cousin, and...oh, it doesn't matter."

Erik knew differently. It *had* mattered. "When my father was outlawed, he brought me from Nórsvegr to Íseland. I never saw my mother after that. If we had—Hel, if *I* had--gone to wedding celebrations and harvest feasts, I might have seen her. I only wanted the pillars because they were all I had of my family, and especially of my mother. I could have found *her* instead."

"No, Erik, she almost never left the farm. And it wasn't like I said at the knörr-camp. She didn't find out afterwards about your trial. She knew *before* we went. The neighboring farmer's wife had come over. We were standing in the yard, perhaps a week before the Althing, sorting goslings to for her to buy. People were talking about some of the trials to be heard. Our neighbor's wife said, *'There's a murder going to be tried again. The man is called Tiller Thorvaldsson, the son of Thorvald Asvaldsson.'*

"Your mother became hysterical. We didn't know why. She just kept saying that she couldn't breathe. She seemed terribly strained all week, but she wouldn't say what it was. The closer we got to the time for Althing, the worse it was. I realized later that she desperately wanted to go, but she was terrified to go out in public. Your father, maybe? She never said, and I still don't know. Finally, she whispered to me one day that she had decided to travel with us this year. She packed the dullest cloak. A drab apron and dress. Clothes that no one would notice her in, I'm sure.

"The day we were supposed to leave, she put her basket on our cart. My mother looked at her in surprise and said, "Elína, you never travel to the Althing! We cannot take you on such short notice! There is no time to get someone else to watch the homestead!"

Hearing his mother's name wrenched Erik deep inside. It had been so very, very long since he had heard that word spoken by anyone. "But she should have come! Why didn't she? Her only son!"

Thio touched Erik's wounded face. "She had been living in some kind of terrible fear for too many years. She conquered that fear enough to *try* to go, but standing up to my mother, and blurting out that her son was the accused murderer? No. It was too hard. She said nothing, and my mother handed her the house-belt with the keys, and clicked her tongue to the horses. 'Thio, we are staying at your uncle and aunt's home for the night,' my mother said. 'Be sure you round up your brothers and arrive by dinner,' and my parents drove off."

"Your mother was crushed. She began weeping harder than I had ever seen anyone cry. She could barely talk, but she whispered to me, *'Thorvaldsson, the one accused of murder. Please find him. I thought he was gone from this earth, and he must think I am as well. Please tell him for me...tell him his mother from Jadar is alive, and loves him.'*"

"I gave her my word, Erik. That is all I cared about at the Althing, finding you and giving you the message. Twice I almost got close enough to tell you what she said. Both times my mother interrupted after she discovered that yet again this year, I wasn't at the brides-fair." Thio's face filled with remorse.

"You tried. That's what matters."

"When we returned to our farm, I told Elína that I had seen you and that you were a strong man, healthy and good-looking, yes! She was distraught to hear you were outlawed, but she was so proud of you for electing to go on the voyage to find land. I never told her that I had failed to deliver her message. The truth ate incessantly at me. When we were close to spring, I did as I told the crew: I hitched rides with one trader after another until I found one heading to the road over Snæfellsjökull, to Ólafsvík. The Althing council had said the ship would sail from there, on the first full moon of the new spring year. You know the rest of the story, of course. I don't know who the real Fishgirl was and why she never arrived. But she didn't, and there I was, stuck on that knörr, scared to death, wishing I'd never seen you, and still no way of telling you who I was and what she'd said, because now I had to think of how to try and protect my life, and, it turned out, yours. You might not have trusted me. You might have worked against me without realizing it." Thio felt exhausted from the telling of it.

"My mother, Thio? What of her?"

"I honestly don't know. She was at our farm through the winter. I don't know if she left afterwards, but she was there when I headed to Ólafsvík."

———·———·———

Thio moved closer to Erik and put her head on his chest. Erik kissed her hair, holding her tightly. "Thank you," he whispered.

They sat silently for long moments, absorbing it all, until Thio lifted her mouth to his and gave him a gentle kiss.

Yearning rose in Erik as he kissed Thio in return, and felt her lips open to his. He pulled her closer, kissed her harder.

Suddenly Thio jerked back. "No! The camp…Sigmund…I fell in love with you on the knörr… Her words became jumbled, her voice too high. "Asa… No! My parents…the twins…your mother… I hurt everyone who ever cares about me, Erik! I cannot allow it to happen again!"

She pushed Erik out of the shelter and followed him awkwardly. "Don't hate me, Erik. I hate myself too much already."

———·———·———

Asa knelt, his spear arm pulled back as far as he could. His heart beat harder and harder, until his chest felt as if it would burst. The throw was far, so far...he breathed in and released, and the spear flew. Asa's spirit rode on the spear, and they flew fast and strong. The sun sparkled on the snow beneath them.

The spear flew on and on with the wind. They flew over a white bear named Olaf, a bear that roared in pain, with a knife protruding from its chest and a cloud of dark smoke billowing from it. The spear went straight through the knife and the smoke, scattering them to nothingness as it passed. The bear straightened, stood tall and sniffed the air, then bent to catch a fish.

The spear-spirit flew under a little moon rising, and the face of a white child smiled in it. The spear and Asa's spirit followed the sun across the water and mountains. Finally, they slipped soundlessly into soft snow and whispered to a stop, in the valley where the shaman-stones were found. Asa's spirit stretched along the length of his body. Asa, it whispered, you, who have never had a brother, you have an aipak.

Asa stirred in his sleep and murmured. A dream of something had woken him, something white and good. He rolled over and pulled the caribou blanket tighter. Maybe he would visit the place he always found good stones for spearheads. *Why do I need a spearhead?* Asa wondered sleepily. Oh, yes. The evil that had been trapped in Olaf's heart had called Asa's spear to set it free, and also Erik's spear that his father Iluq had broken; both had been given to Olaf's body as a burning-gift.

I will make a new spear for my aipak, thought Asa. *And one for Thio, and one for me, perfectly carved. I will call my spear Five Freedoms.* He smiled and drifted back to sleep.

———·———·———

No one wanted to show how nervous they were as Asa opened the seal. He took a long time about it, looking at the liver. They made small sounds of encouragement. Thio held her breath, remembering the horrifying last time he had held a liver in his hand.

Asa cut the organ carefully and placed it on a rock, considering it quietly. A small smile began to play around his lips. Asa's eyes found Erik among the circle around him.

"Uukarnit tells me that you are especially fond of seal liver, Aipak," he said. Asa cut an extremely large piece and held out his knife, offering the first slice to Erik.

———·———·———

With Asa able to paddle again, those in the umiak returned home, to take news of Asa's progress to Iluq and the others.

Asa signaled Thio to paddle with him. "What is making you sad?"

Thio smiled. The old Asa, always wanting to help, was coming back. "Aquuataq's village was afraid when she was born because she was different. She might have another chance with them now. Shouldn't her own mother have a chance to have Aquuataq again? If they don't want her, then Aglakti will take her back to your home village. She needs more people than just Erik and me. She'll have more love, other children her age. It's just hard for me. I want what's best for her, but I'm going to miss her so terribly." Her voice trailed off.

Asa's paddle moved in unison with Thio.

"What was the name of Aquuataq's mother?" Asa asked.

"Qali. She wasn't at the fishing camp. Her parents were too old to travel.

"I remember her. Aquuataq has her sweet nature." Asa was quiet as his paddle moved in and out of the water several times.

"Her husband died at sea, yes?"

"Yes. I've not heard if she took another mate."

"Hmmm," murmured Asa. After that, he was silent.

———·———·———

Madness

Each cove took them closer to the knörr camp. "I've waited long enough," said Thio abruptly as she and Erik paddled together. "I didn't want to even consider it before, but I've had time to brace myself for the idea. How is it *remotely* possible to sail the knörr without...?" *Without a crew.*

Erik, too, had not wanted to discuss the idea since the disaster with Olaf, but the idea had been like the drip of snowmelt, coming faster and stronger the more he thought about it.

"It's a madman's plan, Thio."

———·———·———

He had watched the currents as they travelled on the knörr, and afterwards, paddling back and forth across the coastline of Nunaat. He knew the winds and the shoreline currents well, and compared them in his mind with the ocean roads.

"Thio, I believe we must have been *very* close to Nunaat when the storm hit our ship. I think it blew us into a current that swept us far south. Then we aimed due north, and arrived here. This part you already know."

He pulled out the worn piece of sealskin that had once been his paddling tunic, the original map now drawn in far smaller detail on the reverse side. "Now, look here at this. On this side of Nunaat, the west side, the currents push along the coastline up, towards the char camp. We're paddling against them now. On the east side of Nunaat, the water and wind push southward, and west. Out to sea on both sides of

400

Íseland, the sea and wind push the opposite direction, northeast, towards Nórsvegr. Those currents are why it is *called* the North Way."

Thio nodded, concentrating. "So where does it change?"

"I have an idea." Erik had marked Íseland, Nunaat, Scotiland, the North Way, and other places. "In Íseland, when we approach southern shoreline, the ocean pushes right up against it, splitting. Part goes west towards Ólafsvík. The rest keeps going northeast, and rejoins the North Way on the other side of Íseland."

Erik struggled to make the images and his gestures match what his mind had intuitively grasped. "Picture, Thio, the eddy of a stream or a riverbed or even a puddle of mud. Water currents swirl where they meet one another, where the water is then pushed in a new direction. Maybe the sea works the same way."

Thio frowned. "A place where the currents of the sea swirl and push one another?"

"Yes! Uukarnit said the land and ocean had no end. If you followed the currents from Nunaat southwest, southwest, southwest, where would they take you? Far, far southwest. If one could follow the north-way current in reverse, you would go southwest, southwest, southwest. Where does it start? Is there a place in the ocean where those two currents cross one another? What if there is a place where those great motions of the ocean come together, a sort of crossroads in the sea? I keep asking myself if it might really exist, and how far away it might be."

Thio grasped his reasoning quickly. "But how to reach it? From the east side of Nunaat, it would be easier, from what you are saying. Just follow the currents as far as you can."

"Exactly! If we could somehow ride the wind and water currents of Nunaat southwest far enough, towards that sea-crossroads, we might be able to catch and follow the North Way as it flows towards Íseland. It would take us home."

The next part made it hard to meet Thio's eyes. "But how far out in the ocean? And would it take us other places first? I can't say. Besides, I might be completely wrong. They may not cross at all. Where would we be then? Far from everything, and completely alone. We cannot sail the knörr in any way that requires tacking and changing course. Too many hands are needed for that, and you are not a trained sailor. But with the wind and water pushing us steadily and always in the same direction, it might be possible to manage it."

The plan had tumbled in Erik's mind ever since the fishing camp. By now it was like a stone in a streambed, and the sharp, uncomfortable idea had grown smooth, rounded, and familiar. The explorer in him wanted desperately to try it. What a thing to explore! But to endanger Thio?

"It really is extremely risky, isn't it?" She spoke simply and quietly.

"More than risky. It is downright fool-hardy. We both need to accept that. So many things could go wrong. A storm. Losing our way. Worst of all, the currents never actually meeting one another. It could be a trip to nowhere."

"Just as when we left Íseland. Many thought that was a trip to nowhere, too." She smiled.

"True."

"We could die trying this, Erik."

"It's very likely that we will! But it also might work. Danger and hope are twin sisters. The question is whether we want to stay here in relative safety, or try it."

They went over the plan again and again, checking it, questioning the details. Yes, it might be possible. Yes, it probably wouldn't work.

402

Yes, they were willing to take the risk.

——·——·——

The more tightly you hold ice in your fingers,
the faster it melts between them.

- *Tuniit Understanding*

——·——·——

Thio was dry-eyed. She had vowed not to let her worry show in any way, concerned that it might keep Qali from welcoming Aquuataq back.

Again, Erik marveled inwardly at her strength. Finally, he blurted, "Thio, you have the strongest heart I know. Even on the edge of breaking, you find a way to be resilient and generous. You are remarkable."

——·——·——

Thio bent against the light rain as she carried Aquuataq into the village in which she had been born. It was silent and empty. Most people were still at the fishing camp, finishing the char catch. Thio pointed to the shelter she remembered as Qali's, and Asa called a greeting inside.

403

Qali marveled at Aquuataq's round face and the touch of her small fingers. She yearned to hold the child but held back, not wanting to offend Thio.

"She's yours, Qali," said Thio, choking. "We're going to leave Nunaat, and may never be back."

Qali took Aquuataq eagerly, and pulled Thio into her embrace as well. "You will always be her mother. You will always be my sister."

Qali and her parents wanted to know everything about Aquuataq. Thio told them, from the time she had left the village with Aquuataq and the milk-mother right up to the festival, even the awful parts about Olaf. They would hear it from someone else soon enough, and she wanted them to know the full truth of it from her.

The swirling threatened when Thio kissed Aquuataq goodbye, but she pushed it back. *Those days are over. I will not let the sickness in again.* She filled her eyes and heart with a last look at her little girl, a luckless newborn who had been transformed into a healthy and happy toddler. Thio's provident arrival and adoption had bestowed on Aquuataq a kind of reverence, the beloved of *Thio-from-far-away*, but even without that, Aquuataq had a genuine dearness about her. She laid her small head against Thio's shoulder and cuddled close.

Asa reached for Aquuataq. "It is time for her to nap, perhaps?" he offered gently. He held the child close and ever so subtly, stood nearer to Qali.

"Asa?" Thio guessed softly.

"I remember Qali from when we were both children. We have some stories to remember together." He kissed Aquuataq on the head. "You needed this child once, Thio. You are strong again, and it is I who need her now. Aquuataq will miss you, but she knows me and feels safe with me. I can help comfort her here. And there is something else she can give me." Asa's handsome smile flashed at Qali, who blushed. "Perhaps, Aquuataq, you will help me become friends with your mother again."

This is why everyone loves you, Asa, Thio thought.

"It will ease my mind greatly to know that Aquuataq will see your face every day." She smiled her gratitude at Asa and at the woman who one day would be *her* aipak. "Qali, it has been an honor sharing your child. Now you will have her, and dearest Asa as well. Thank you for taking good care of them both."

Thio handed over a little doll Kunwaktok had made of pale leather. Aquuataq took it and laughed, showing her mother. Thio turned towards the kayaks without speaking again.

———·———·———

The small group pushed their kayaks back into the sea. Thio held together until they were out of sight and sound from the shore, and then her body bent forward, and the racking sobs came. They paddled into the nearest cove, and Aglakti wrapped Thio in her arms.

"Good can be so difficult sometimes, dear girl, and generosity as well. You did the right thing. This gift will make your heart happy and stronger, and it will make Aquuataq, and Qali, and Aquuataq's grandparents, and aunts and uncles and cousins, and one day, brothers and sisters, happy and strong as well. Asa too. Especially Asa. You did great good, Thio. Let it comfort you," Aglakti crooned gently.

———·———·———

How remarkable, to come around a curve in the shoreline and to suddenly see the knörr again, solid and thick! Erik laughed. "Gods, Thio, it *is* huge, isn't it?"

Thio gazed with the same expression, seeing it from the People's perspective. She pushed back her hood impatiently, and her mouth curved into a smile of delight.

"So long since I have been here! And so much has changed!" Thio cried. "We are almost completely different people than when we left!" They smiled in understanding at one another. This place where one long-ago voyage ended had been the beginning of another they could never have dreamed. It was an impossible story. Thio's laughter fed Erik's, and his hers, and their friends laughed as well without knowing why until they were breathless and their stomachs ached.

Suddenly solemn, Erik paused. "Right now, we are paddling where I first saw you, and you saw me," he said to Aglakti. "You were floating on the swells, almost exactly here, in your kayaks. I thought you were spirits, riding on fishes. I am so grateful to you for coming that day."

They beached the kayaks and could not get out of them fast enough. Thio ran excitedly from one thing to another.

"Look, Erik! The chickens are still here!" The birds had fluttered up into branches, startled at the arrival of humans. "The flock is larger now." Their peaceful sound, so familiar from home, caught at her throat. "And up there – see?" One of the goats peered from the crest of the hill, and in a few moments, the rest of the herd stood on the stony rise. "Curiosity will bring them down in no time. Oh, glory, soon we will taste milk and cheese again!"

Most beautiful of all was the small longhouse on which Erik had worked so doggedly.

"Erik, I love my life with the People. I feel almost that I am one of them but oh, our own land and heritage, and the things of home again... To even think we might one day hear the sounds of Íselandic voices. Oh, what a fine and pretty thing that knörr is!"

———·———·———

To their relief, the knörr's sail was intact and strong. They pulled the tents from where they had been stored in waterproofed crates. These, too, showed no sign of mildew or rot.

Their friends wanted to sleep in the tents and try them out, like children with a new game. In fact, everything at the camp became a source of amusement. Toonoq and Pukiq delighted in picking up and putting down the poor chickens until the birds finally despaired and flew up onto the crossbeam of the mast. They chased the goats, picking them up and carrying them about making goat-sounds and falling down laughing at one another.

———·———·———

"So *that* is what you meant all those times you said *plow!*" Pukiq and Nagojut watched Erik turning a field with the small coulter. "You tear the grass skin off the earth and rip it apart. But why?"

Erik showed them a handful of rye grains. "In spring, they grow into tall grasses. Each plant will make many more seeds. We save a few to plant again. The rest become our food."

Nagojut made a face. "Who would want to eat that hard dry stuff?"

———·———·———

"Let's build something," said Pukiq. "I want to see how your shelters are made, and we may not get a chance to learn your techniques again."

"I have a project in mind. A small one. We can do it quickly, before you have to return."

They used the whalebones Erik had towed, and the stoutest willow trunks they could find, to frame out a small addition to the longhouse. They stacked stones between the roof supports, and sawed thick blocks of turf to stack in double layers to keep the wind from blowing through the walls. Erik showed his friends how to split birch trees to make rough-timbered interior walls.

"You put hot stones in here," Erik said. "It's like being in the hot-spring island, but you can make it warm anytime you want, in your own shelter."

Nagojut looked skeptical. "You strip naked? To sit around and sweat?"

Erik nodded, waiting for the inevitable jest. "It makes you warm."

"Seems to me that you missed the point, my friend. I can think of much better ways to get warm when the clothing comes off." He laughed. "And you don't have to carry stones around."

———·———·———

The last sections of turf went on the roof. The men hopped down and looked over their finished handiwork. Erik had refused to let Thio

408

see inside until it was finished. She shrieked with delight when she realized what the small room was for.

"A sauna, really? I will be warm all winter!" Thio cried.

"Red will see you naked, so perhaps he'll manage to stay warm as well," laughed Pukiq.

Erik laughed, and Thio blushed. "It's not like that. But this truly is a wonderful thing," she said. "We'll enjoy it so much more because of your help with it."

Goodbyes did not take long. The paddlers were as anxious to head north as Erik and Thio were sorry to see them go.

——·——·——

"Why can't we leave now? Why must we wait the last part of autumn? It is clear, and the weather is good! Wait all winter until spring again? That's ridiculous! If Íseland is so close to the east, we should set off as early as possible!" Thio's words were heated. "They said we could come back early if we found land. What are you waiting for?"

"Suppose we can't find the ocean-crossroads? Do you really want to spend winter on the open sea, drifting?" She gave no answer.

"You know it's a terrible idea. Besides, living here with the Tuniit, you have forgotten what it was like when we left. We don't know how conditions have worsened since we left. Hunger makes people desperate. We told Uukarnit we would leave at Equal-Days-Spring, and that's what I'm doing. Just like the voyage when we came here. It gives us the most time."

Thio stomped off, exasperated. "Equal-length kyrtills on board? Not on your ship!"

"Already, only six moons left until spring?" The beginning of autumn had caught them by surprise. "Let's have an Equal-Night-and-Day celebration tomorrow," Thio announced.

They were stalking a caribou herd, and Erik hushed her. Thio continued undeterred. "The wind is blowing our scent away from them. It'll take our words too. What do you think?"

"Isn't that silly? Just the two of us? It's a waste of good firewood!"

"What are festivals for, if not for each spirit? Even if I was here all by myself, I'd have an Equal-night fire, and I'd make a special meal. To celebrate being alive."

"If it matters to you, I'll do whatever you want."

The caribou moved closer, and Thio expertly shot an arrow from her bow. "Good. You can roast that caribou's loin for it. There's plenty of salt in the seawater-drying trays to use."

———·———·———

Every task of making the meal became part of the celebration. Soon the rich smell of roasting loin mixed with a sweet fragrance of pottage made from of dried apples and the *kvann* plants that grew taller than Erik in summer. Thio made soft cheese from the goats' milk and flavored it with cloudberries and cowberries, and she roasted eggs. Even though a festival held by two had seemed pointless, he found himself looking forward to the meal more than any he could remember.

They walked to the knörr as the sun set and Equal-night began. To Erik's pleasure, Thio moved in front of him and pulled his arms around her. *Six months,* they said to one another and to the ship. *Six months,* they called on the wind to friends far distant and family at home. Not long now.

—·—·—

Thio came inside and closed the longhouse door as the last glow of daylight faded from the horizon. A satisfied yawn filled Erik. "Are you tired?" she asked.

"More than I thought I would be. I want to be up early to scrape and stretch the caribou skin tomorrow. He looked at her eyes sparkling in the firelight. "What about you?"

"Yes, but today is a special day. I want to savor it." Thio reached for her sax and went to the longhouse's main pillar. "Which side?"

"Left side until Longest-Night, and then the right side until spring."

She made a smooth cut in the wood. "We'll do this every night. It'll be a ritual to help us get through the dark of winter." Thio laid her sax carefully on the cooking table. "Now, something else." She took the cup from Erik's hand and put it to her own mouth. Thio drank, her eyes locked on his, their expression unmistakable.

Curse my need to know. "You said no, before. What changed?"

"The very obvious fact finally dawned on me that we're going on a ridiculous voyage and we'll probably die. Maybe I'm not the worst thing that could happen to you." She put down the cup and curved her hand around Erik's cheek.

Years of locking away desire for her kept him still as stone. "You're sure?"

"I'm sure," she smiled. "If you still want me."

Oh, gods, yes. He had been waiting forever. He could hardly believe it was finally happening. The sweet feeling of Thio's lips were soft against his, tentative as she left behind the safe shelter of chaste friendship and ventured into more uncertain, exciting waters.

The fire murmured to itself, the softest gray ash whispering amid flickering orange embers. Their yearning mounted in intensity.

"So long..." she sighed. "So sweet..."

She wanted more, and faster, more *now*, but fought the urge. There would be only one first time with him, and she pulled herself back to the desire to go slowly, to savor the feeling of him pulling her hips against his, the long muscles of his arms under her palms, the feel of his mouth pressing against the soft hair on her temples.

"Here..." she pulled the furs off the sleeping bench and onto the stone floor nearer the fire. "I want to be warm."

Erik stood over Thio as she stretched on the furs, watching the soft glow of the flames on her skin. His eyes drifted across those beautiful shoulders, the flat of her belly, at every place where the golden light cast shadows deep between smooth curves. She sat up and pulled her braids loose, and waves of hair fell over her shoulders.

"I want to remember everything about this for the rest of my life," he said. "Every barrel of food stacked in the corner. The smell of the smoke lifting up to the roof vent. The fragrance of the dried apples cooking and the sharp tang of skyr. The little hisses and pops of the fire, and the way a piece of firewood will feel in my fingers when I put it on the fire to warm you, your skin so lovely and naked. The cold smooth stone floor under my bare feet. How my body will yearn even more in a moment, so close to yours."

True to his word, Erik added a log on the fire, and as the flames flared up hot around it, Thio reached up and pulled him to her. He dropped to his knees, and she wrapped her legs around him. Sounds

412

of pleasure filled their shelter as they gave themselves to one another. It was love, but also selfish desire for survival, deep and wild, yielding to the mindless forces that drive humans. Muscle pressed bone to bone, and breaths gasped and released as if they were running, until finally first one and then the other cried out, and the act was complete. As the fever left them, they lay together, tangled and sated. Their breathing slowed again, their bodies cooled and they pulled the furs around one another.

The closeness they needed most from each other was finally theirs. Erik heard an owl calling, far in the distance, and then the night was silent. Thio murmured against him.

"What did you say?" he asked.

"Six months, and then we go home," she said. He kissed her tenderly, and they slept.

———·———·———

"Whatever will we say to the people we see first when we land?"

They tossed the idea back and forth for a while until Thio put up her hand.

"It's too complicated and too far off. We can talk about all that once we make sail. For now, with spring coming fast, we need to focus instead on every detail of the trip: what we should take on board, and what should we leave behind."

"I say we take all of our supplies with us. We'll likely never get back here for them. If we lose our sail and drift, perhaps we'll find Uukarnit's 'endless land' and create another camp."

Topic after topic was debated. Every possibility had to be carefully considered. Thio and Erik developed a habit of long hours in silence punctuated by short discussions in which they often disagreed, sometimes bitterly, but rarely in anger. Olaf had made that emotion intolerable for both of them.

Whatever the dispute, by tacit agreement all discord ended at the evening meal, when one or another of them would cut the counting-mark into the left-side pillar.

Four months and a week. Thio stayed awake, listening to the sound of Erik's breath as he fell quickly asleep. She watched him closely in the last light of the fire, her face unsmiling.

Four months and a week.

———·———·———

They used sand and the ship's store of boiled linseed oil to clean rust from the blacksmith tools. They hunted and dried as much meat as they could, packaging it in the containers that had once held barley seeds, now small green sprouts that peeked about the snow on warmer days.

"Most of the sleeping sacks are still decent. I'll start mending them in the evenings. Have you figured out how we're going to get the ship into the water, just the two of us?" Thio asked.

"Sort of. That's really one of the hardest parts of this. But we'll get it done, somehow."

"Are we taking any goat kids or spring lambs?"

Another disagreement. Another notch on the left side pillar. Another night in which the argument was suspended, or disputes settled on the furs by the fireside.

———·———·———

414

"Átta tigir ok fjórtán!" Thio exclaimed. "Eight tens plus fourteen! Do you realize we're almost halfway there? Nearly time to switch the counting-mark to the opposite pillar!"

Tomorrow, they would pull ropes from storage and begin to ready those as well. The next task was to rub pitch onto the lapped boards of the knörr.

Three moons and two weeks left.

___.___.___

Shortest-Day came. This time, with the pleasant memory of the last season-feast, there was no expectation that any work would be done. Instead, Thio and Erik held contests similar to the Longest-Day ones of the fishing camp. With only two contestants, in fierce competition Thio and Erik raced one another at skinning winter hares and building iglus. Each had carefully prepared for the much-anticipated climax of the day: the races, a flat-ground one for speed and another that simulated tracking game over a field.

Thio had made snow shoes. Asa had taught her to bend willow strips in oblong shapes, drying them by the fire each night. Now they were lashed together with strips of caribou hide and tightly woven. Erik would race on long wood *skíths* as everyone used at home. He had split and straightened and dried and waxed the supple skis and fashioned straps to bind them to his winter shoes.

"I win!" Thio announced her victory after both races were over. "Your skis were definitely faster in a flat race, but mine were better for tracking game. The tie should be decided by whatever would help us eat in winter!"

They had another feast, this time a stew of caribou and dried beans. Thio crushed dried juniper berries into some of the still-

415

plentiful sauerkraut. As the short day ended, they built a small bonfire and struck it with sticks to make the sparks jump into the night sky.

In the firelight later, Erik pulled back the furs as Thio slept. She had been so thin when they reached the camp after the long paddle. Her body had begun to fill out. He kissed her shoulder, pleased to see her so healthy now.

She murmured drowsily, "Tomorrow we can pull out the rest of the sealskins and sleeping sacks from the men's sea chests and rub fresh oil into them."

"Go to sleep, Thio. No thinking about work. It's Longest-Night."

———·———·———

By half-winter, all the food supplies had been readied. They turned to the matter of what things to take to prove that they had been to a land where people could live.

"The whale-tusk is the most important." A treasured gift from Asa to Thio, the astonishing ivory horn of a small whale twisted in fantastic curves along its human-height length.

"And some walrus tusks. Egret and goose feathers. Teeth of the white bear?"

They agreed on these matters, as well as skins of caribou and seal furs.

"Shaman-stones?"

"The Tuniit visit the places they are found infrequently, but still... Perhaps not."

"But it's only a few days' paddle north of us. Someone is bound to find them." The crystalline rocks were added.

"What about our anoraks?" Thio looked down at her warm garment with longing.

416

"We can't. They're too unusual. It would be like taking a kayak. The design cries out they are from a different people than our own."

They were taking nothing that might indicate the People already living here: no spears, no whalebone beads, no fishing tools. The worst thing that could happen would be for a slave-trader to catch wind of the peaceful Tuniit. It was one of the few decisions about which Erik and Thio were in complete agreement.

"We'll have to watch ourselves, to avoid using the words of the People."

"I never even thought of that! We will have to be so very careful."

They had one singular goal: to form a peaceful settlement of farmers, trading in goods, not human lives. They would strive for only that when – *if* – they made it home.

———·———·———

"Thio, I need some of your wonderful health. How you are getting so plump? I'm dropping weight every day. I can barely eat from excitement and worry."

Thio startled, and then laughed. "I'm putting on fat so I won't starve at sea."

"No need to worry on that score. You've proven your skills as a fish girl. Stop working on that and come here to the beach with me. You're a better *kalendar* than I am."

"I don't need to come to the beach. You already know you're right."

As spring approached, Thio had put sticks on the sand to mark the shadows cast by sunrise and sunset, with one between to signify midday. Every day the shadow from the midday stick had shortened as the sun moved steadily northwards.

"Just another week or so."

"The counting-marks on the pillars agree."

Equal-Night-and-Day, the beginning of *Springa,* which marked the first day of a new year. The exact day they had left Íseland in heroism and disgrace two long years ago. When Thio cut the mark on the pillar that evening, Erik pulled the small leather pouch from his neck, took out the dried berry, and looked at it. *Please let me be right. Help us find the way,* he whispered into dwindling night.

———·———·———

The great balance of life tips from the weight of small works.

- Tuniit Understanding

———·———·———

For the second time in his life, Erik was astonished to see people riding waves along the edge of the coast. This time, the astonishment was all joy.

"Thio! Thio!" They had just begun the exhausting task of digging the knörr's path to the sea so that, come departure day, they could push the ship to the water. Both sprinted to the water's edge, waving madly.

"Why are you here?" they gasped in delight. "We've promised to have no contact!"

Asa laughed and threw an arm around each of Thio's and Erik's shoulders. "Honestly, *aipak,* you never cease to amaze me with the stupidity of your questions. Yet you think yourself an intelligent man."

418

"No one knows we're here," Asa began, but Nagojut interrupted him.

"Of course they know! You told them we were going hunting for little-wing eggs! Everyone knows the best cliffs are only two day's paddle from this camp, and that eggs won't be laid for at least another two moons. But who would deny us the chance of seeing your great kayak sail again? You said you would be leaving sometime around Equal-Days. We've been paddling like mad, hoping to get here in time."

Most of those who had helped to build the stone ship were there; Aglakti, Pukiq, Nagojut, Uukarnit, Tupit, and even Iluq. With them were others who had become friends, too.

———·———·———

Asa and Thio sat close together, playing with Aquuataq near the stone ship. Erik watched them, a curious feeling in his chest. Not jealousy, but something akin to it, for sure, something that whispered to Erik that he mattered less than Asa. It was an old, unwelcome feeling.

Asa is your aipak and your friend, Erik reminded himself. *He kept Thio alive in more ways than one. Of course she loves him, but she says it is different. Let it be.* He took a deep breath.

It had not helped that Thio had wanted to sleep by herself more and more of late. "I'm so tired," she would say, or "We need to be up so early tomorrow. Do you mind if we just sleep tonight?"

Pukiq was eyeing the knife Erik was using to cut rope to tie seal bladders to the chests. It gave Erik a distraction.

"You like this knife very much, don't you, Pukiq?"

"Such a thing is a marvel. What do you call it? Bronze?"

"Here, Pukiq. Remember me." Erik passed the knife and its small whetstone to his best friend and the man he would miss most. The small act of sharing grounded him in Oneness, and he thought no more of Thio avoiding him. When she was ready, she would share herself again.

———·———·———

A roaring campfire was the background to what they were certain would finally be the last night before pushing off the knörr. They had readied for the final push of loading the ship over and over, but each day had held rain, or bad winds, or no wind at all. Despite Thio's increasing demands that they leave as soon as possible, Erik was equally insistent that they wait for exactly the right conditions to set off. Their friends, considering the whole experience a circle-voyage of sorts, were perfectly content to spend the passing days exploring Erik's hoped-for homestead or going to the shaman-stone digging site. Thio's temper grew short as she despaired that they would ever actually leave.

"Tonight the sunset has flamed as red as the fire. We are certain to finally have good weather tomorrow. Is there any *possible* reason to delay yet again?"

Erik considered this woman who had become so important to him. "You realize that a large part of my delay is love? I don't want to do anything that will increase the danger to you."

"Trying to protect me is driving us both crazy. I trust you. We need to get going."

Maybe Thio was right, Erik thought. Maybe he was being too cautious. The day did promise to dawn fair. They would likely not get a better one, and at least they would have willing assistance to load and turn the knörr.

That night, Thio cut the last mark into the longhouse pillar, and below it, a mark for each of their names. Spring had been here a month already. It was time.

———·———·———

"Nagojut, is there *nothing* you can't make into a game?"

They had redug a trench between the knörr and the low tide line. The task had been hard and brutally heavy, but at last a wave pushed through the thin barrier of soil and flooded the small ditch. First the water just touched the stern, but eventually, the ship floated.

"That's enough for now," Erik said. "We'll push it out to between the low and high tide lines, and load everything on board. When the tide comes, it'll lift the ship the rest of the way."

Dried fish and seal and caribou, hunting weapons and fishing gear were stacked on board. All of the sleeping sacks, the oilskins, the tents, the remaining seeds and tools, along with barrels of root vegetables went into the underdeck, jammed side by side with crates holding furs of animals and feathers of birds.

Nagojut made a contest of getting the small but heavy millstone aboard, and then the cooking pots and the blacksmith anvil. Aquuataq, now two and toddling everywhere, learned how to climb so that she could get into the pens with the newborn lambs.

Thio drew Erik aside. "I am finding it hard to look our friends in the eye. I worry that there are so many ways we could fail them. Our own people might betray us."

Erik reached to hold Thio, but she pushed him off as she had so many times recently. Nerves, he supposed.

Push Off

A perfect breeze held as the tide rose, offshore and stiff enough to fill the sail and push them away from land quickly.

"One last time, Thio." Erik had gone over and over the launch. "This is our last chance to practice." The most dangerous time would be just as they set off. "When the tide reaches full high, our friends will push the knörr into the surf and turn the prow towards the ocean. The steering-board will be lifted. You and I will raise the sail." He had re-rigged the ropes to make it possible for the two of them to do the job. "When we get clear of the coastline, we need to swing north."

"Why north?" Pukiq asked. "You've said many times your land is straight east of us."

"If we had a full crew—all the men who came here with us—we could go straight down the coast. The ship is not like a kayak that can be easily turned by one person, so with just Thio and me, and the way our ship is built, we have to follow the currents and the wind, to let them push us where we want to go. They will first take us up along the coast of Nunaat, just about to where the fishing camp is, or maybe a little beyond. Then, from what you've said and what I observed, the current and the winds turn away from the land, and go quickly south again. We should be able to swing around and follow *that* current far down into the ocean."

"What will you do then?" Pukiq asked.

"We'll keep the wind straight behind us for days, or maybe weeks or even months—but I don't think that long. At some point, I think our sail will start to luff – to flap, sort of like a bird's wing. That will mean we have reached the place in the ocean where we can catch a different current, one that will push us northeast towards our land."

It was a crazy strategy, but all his years of tillering and watching and observing and thinking told Erik to trust this one thing, more truly than anything in his entire life.

———.———.———

As the tide began to rise, a silent line formed. Erik and Thio passed along it, emotion swelling as they hugged each friend. Finally, their first and deepest friends stood with them.

"Go in peace, friend," said Uukarnit.

Iluq was next. He smiled, and suddenly there was a trace of Asa's face in his appearance, but it changed quickly to a sad kindness. "It honestly grieves me to hope we will never meet you or see your kind again. Travel in safety, my son, my daughter; friends of my son."

Aglakti hugged Thio. "What can I say?" She used the formal words of departure. "It is time for you to wander, my child. Come back to us one day." She pulled Erik into their embrace.

Pukiq had waited until last. "Here, Red." He held out a tiny bone kayak, perfectly carved. "In case you need to come back to us, and your great ship cannot carry you."

Erik could not answer, his throat too choked with emotion.

Finally, they climbed aboard the knörr. A few high waves, a few strong pushes, and suddenly, the ship was afloat. Erik staggered a moment before his legs remembered what to do.

With hands on the smooth hull, their friends pushed the knörr around to face the sea and Erik pulled the ropes to lift the sail. A sound of awe went among the Tuniit, and a cheer broke out. The great ship was under sail.

___·___·___

SEA

In Search

They kept the wind to their backs and the rudder straight back from the prow. Erik set a course in sight of land but not too close, and they began what Thio called 'the long goodbye', passing site after site where they had paddled, or explored, or found crystals in stones, or hunted, moving along briskly, the sail filled with wind. As they approached the char-fishing river, Erik and Thio waved their goodbyes, although there was no one present to see them.

"It's hard, isn't it?"

Erik shook his head yes. Thio's simple words spoke a lifetime of feeling.

———·———·———

The first test had been to get afloat and away from shore. The second was to make a complete turn from north to south, off the coast of the fishing-camp river.

It went as well as could possibly be. Erik felt the change in wind and waves, and adjusted the rudder ever so slightly, ever so slightly. The sail drooped and flapped.

"Let's drop the sail," he decided. "We don't want to blow over if the wind suddenly shifts."

They waited, with the steering-board pushed all the way to the right. Perhaps they would not have needed to do even that, for when the current turned, it turned quickly. In little over a half day, they had reversed direction and were sailing due south.

Now, however, they were unable to see land. The wind stayed strong and steady, but by the end of the third day, doubt began to set in.

On land, Erik had diminished the possibility and probability of storms. Now, each day of clear weather only increased his worry about impending disasters. The fair skies could not hold forever. Fear gnawed deeply at him, and once again, he dreamed of the sea monsters said to swim in the deepest, furthest oceans.

Thio, on the other hand, was light and unconcerned. They spoke of things that mattered little. Erik forced his words to be carefree. In truth, all of him waited for the sound of the sails luffing, to tell that the winds had changed.

"Surely, we have passed the knörr-settlement by now."

The next day. "I wonder if we have gone beyond the southern tip of Nunaat, where I lived two winters ago?"

Day after day passed. His ears and eyes strained, hoping.

Fragrance

Thio woke to feel Erik curved against her back and wondered what had brought her out of sleep. Nothing was different. With the sail down for the night, the ship rose and fell with the swell of the waves. Yawning, she started to fall asleep again.

Wait. There is a different smell in the wind, Thio realized.

"Erik, wake up. Smell the air."

427

It was a fragrance Erik could never describe, but one he knew well. "Uukarnit is right. The *land-that-never-ends* lies west of us!"

Even if they could not find a way home to Íseland, they could try to turn there and look for another home. With a sigh of relief, they fell back asleep.

———·———·———

It rained, sometimes in driving sheets and sometimes in gentle pattering drops. The sun shone. There was fog. There were days when the sail hung loose and empty.

Every possible variation of weather graced the ship, except for the one that they could not afford; a true gale. For days, it was sunny, or rained lightly, or there was fog that would last all day, and fog that would burn off by mid-morning. Rain, and sun. Wind, and no wind…but thankfully, no storms.

Days passed. A week, then two, and then a third week dragged past. How long would it be until they felt a slow but inexorable pushing, turning them to the northeast, towards home?

———·———·———

It started as the gentlest looseness of the sail. Erik thought he was imagining it, but soon after, he noticed Thio staring intently at the sail herself. She saw Erik looking at her, and flicked her eyes away, and busied herself at rinsing off the board on which she cut fish.

By nightfall, he knew it to be true. The relieved look in Thio's eyes told Erik that her light words had been as much a sham as his, to help keep his spirits up. Her easy conversation had been to try and divert him as much as herself. *Beloved, how strong* are *you?*

428

"How long until it is time to make the turn?" Thio asked.

"I don't know. Perhaps a day or two will take us into the full current, but it may be longer. I don't know how wide it is, and I want us to be deep in the flow, not at the edge of it."

Erik changed the steering oar as little as he could to keep the sail full. If they were barely at the edge of the current and a storm pushed the ship out of it, where might they end up? They could take no chances. He used everything he knew of the sea to push them into an ocean stream that daily ran faster and stronger.

———·———·———

"Erik, quickly! Help me get it with the net!"

Thio had spotted a green branch, bobbing in the waves along the hull of the knörr. It was laden with green berries. They were perfectly round, and bigger than lingonberries.

"It must have come from *the-land-that-never-ends*! We are so close to it!" Erik touched the talisman hanging from his neck. They held the branch and its beautiful green-ball berries, gazing in rapt fascination. "One day they will ripen to red."

"It is traveling just as we are. Taking the ocean road to Íseland." Thio smiled.

There really was no end to the land. All this time, it still was keeping them company, off to the west, out of sight. The innocent fruits were an astonishing affirmation that Uukarnit's land was just one of many still to be explored.

A Name

"What will we call Nunaat to the people in Íseland?" Thio asked. "The name will be so important, and this beautiful place deserves a good one."

Erik thought of cliffs rising steeply from waters that had once looked so forbidding, and of fjords that led to breathtaking glaciers. He pictured herds of caribou and walrus and seals, the birds and the fish, the brilliant flowers in spring, and ice floes on seas every color of blue and purple and green and rose.

"You're right, Thio. People will desire much more to go there if the land has a good name. What could possibly describe it? Something fresh and new, full of promise?

Her lips curved in a smile. Thio enjoyed puzzling out a question.

After a long pause, she offered, "Well, home is Íseland. Ice, plus land. Before that, it was called Snowland, when Naddodd discovered it. What if we call Nunaat by something that sounds like Íseland, but has good appeal?"

"I like that. It will seem familiar but new and exciting at the same time."

Thio's lips moved silently through words as she considered and rejected them. Erik waited, knowing she would keep at it until she was satisfied.

"What about *ice,* for the glaciers and the icebergs, and because it sounds like home; and *groen*, for the color of the grasses and tundra? Ice-green? *Groenice?* Would that work?"

"Green ice? No."

"*Groen* water?"

"No."

"Green forest?"

"No. People want croplands. Besides, there really aren't forests, just low shoreline trees."

"Ice-water?"

He chuckled. "Did you think before you said it?"

Suddenly Thio beamed. "Remember what Sigmund said, and then Nollar? *'Good green land, you're what we want! Green land means fresh meat!'* What about *Green Land*? A sister island to Íseland!"

While much of Nunaat was rocky or tundra, there were plenty of green meadows and valleys for settlements along the western coast. Erik tested it aloud. "Green land...Greenland. Thio, it's perfect! It describes what it is now, and what it will be even more one day, a land green with fields of rye and barley and meadow grass. We will get home and go to the Althing, and soon the whole of Íseland will know that we discovered a new green land, where there is meat and room for farms. Using Sigmund's words will honor him. Greenland it is!"

———·———·———

"Erik, good gods...I just realized. What do we say happened to the rest of the crew?" Thio was taking apart an old kyrtill to make a new one for herself. She paused, needle in mid-air. "Should we tell them the truth?" Her voice was uneven. "That their deaths were at my hand?"

"That moment in your life is too terrible, Thio. Could you bear hearing it repeated everywhere, over and over? We must tell what happened, but in a way that does not hurt you."

Thio looked long and silent at the work in her lap without answering. Finally, she picked up the needle again and began to sew.

———·———·———

The current moved rapidly, traveling smoothly northwest. Again, the days passed, and then weeks, but this time with the sun on a different side of the ship. Again, it rained, or was foggy, or was clear. Again there were days with strong winds and mild ones. Again, their luck held, and while there was plenty of raw, wet weather, there were no terrible storms.

———·———·———

The land-sense had started in Erik, but it was terribly faint. He felt as if he was racing, running towards something so fast he could barely catch breath.

"This must be what the truth-seer Kunwaktok's knowing is like. She sees inside the human body and spirit, while I sense things about land and water."

Thio had been exhausted for days now. She rested a great deal. "Um-hm."

Erik carried some fish stew to her. Thio was tightly wrapped in a sleeping sack covered with oilskins. Even with the covering, she was shivering from the steady drizzle.

"Eat a little?" Erik asked.

Thio sipped from the bowl. "I hope we reach shore on a sunny day. I want to see the shoreline shining and bright to welcome us home."

"We need better visibility. I don't want to miss Íseland, going too far south of it."

"I trust you." She set the bowl aside, still full.

432

Erik kissed her damp hair. "Rest some more."

Thio fell back and closed her eyes with a strained look on her face. Something did not seem right. Erik touched her cheek. She was burning with fever.

———·———·———

The rain pushed forward and the setting sun came in low behind the ship. It lit the knörr with golden light, and the swells of water shimmered gilt along their crests.

"Thio, look, there's a rainbow ahead of us," he cried, but she did not respond.

Please, wind blow. Get us there faster.

———·———·———

Sleep was impossible. Erik kept the sail up, scanning left and right constantly, but could see nothing. Thio woke often. She said nothing about the pains in her back.

A blinding sunrise greeted them after the long and excruciating night. Erik could see to the horizon on all sides. Now, they just needed wind, and the right direction to travel.

As the sky brightened, Erik thought at first he must be mistaken, must be seeing what was left of the rain, but no, it was true.

He could just make out the tip of a mountain, wreathed in morning clouds. It was covered with ice, and smoke came from it. It looked for all the world like an island of ice in a sea of clouds. Nearby was another, larger mountain, its steep sides also covered with ice. The snowfields of Glacier-Island Mountain glittered brilliant white in the rising sun, and its companion, the massive kettle-volcano Katla, sent plumes of smoke into the sky.

Erik exulted. He knew these shores, and knew them well! But his gratitude was cut short, as he remembered that only he was there to steer the ship…and that straight ahead, a line of vicious blackness jutted up from the frothing sea. It was the cliffs of Reynishdrangar, teeth of the dragon.

———·———·———

LAND

Oh, gods. The beautiful, familiar, sprawling mountains came closer, and soon he could see the black stone beach approaching. A little faster progress, and they might have crashed into the cliffs during the night. A little further south, and the sea-road would have swung them far out into the North-Way current for another half-moon at least. Either would have meant Thio's death.

Erik knew exactly what to do now. Only concern for Thio kept him from shouting for joy. Her face was horribly pale in the bright sunlight, but it was not cold; it was not blue. She was alive, and land was close. They still had a chance.

———.———.———

The horizon rose quickly. With a good breeze, Erik wrestled everything he could from it. As the knörr approached shore, all his hopes and fears of the past three years dwindled to two critical needs: to beach the ship, and get help as soon as possible.

He knew there was a string of farms near Vik. Erik aimed towards the first longhouses he saw, hoping that someone would be home, that there would be a man or woman who knew about healing.

He saw fields, saw faces look up from their work as the ship neared the shoreline, and shouted to them, not knowing if his words would carry. He saw people standing, pointing and calling to each other. At last, at last, they reached the surf. Tiller shouted to the unconscious Thio that they were beaching, and rammed the boat at full speed as hard as he could onto the shore, not remembering until later that wonderful feeling of making land.

He picked up Thio and leaped over the side of the knörr, calling to the people in the field, who stared in astonishment at seeing a man carrying a woman, running from a knörr, running, running towards them, running with the woman in his arms, calling, crying desperately for help.

———.——.——

They were hurried into the nearby longhouse. In no time a sleeping bench was cleared, and Thio's clothing was being removed, and warmed stones wrapped in linen placed against her. Soon a healer arrived, a woman who looked too young to Erik. She felt all over Thio. She asked questions sharply, felt Thio's belly and then put her hand between Thio's thighs. Erik heard Thio gasp in pain and groan something in reply. The woman glanced sharply where he stood.

People were crowding into every corner of the room. "Everybody out but him," she nodded towards Erik. "Plus the freeholder, and two women to help."

When the room had cleared, she spoke again. "Did you know she is carrying a child?"

Erik's shocked expression answered for him.

The healer snorted, a little humorously. "When was the last time you saw her naked? You'll not be the first man to get such a surprise. She must not have wanted you to know; some women carry small. It's quite early."

Ah. So that was why Thio had avoided him with one excuse after another, for weeks.

"At any rate, she's either delivering or miscarrying. If she survives, she will need to stay here for a while to recover. Can you settle up with the people of this household for it?"

Erik nodded. "There are supplies on our ship I can trade."

The freeholder spoke. "Who are you? Where's the rest of your crew?"

Erik started to reply, but the midwife cut him off, speaking calmly but with considerable authority. Her eyes never left Thio. "Those questions are of no help right now. Do your duty and offer hospitality to peaceable strangers. After we get through this birth, ask what you want."

Too soon, there would be questions to answer. Today was only this small room, these women bending over Thio. *She can't lose it. Too much like giving up Aquuataq all over.*

"Brace yourself," the midwife said. Erik did not know if it was to him or Thio she spoke.

One of the other women pushed hard on Thio's belly while the midwife reached inside her, feeling. Thio cried out in pain and crushed Erik's hand, but he could do nothing.

"It's breech," she said to herself. "Footling breech, I think." She felt Thio's belly again. "Her muscles are strong. Good. We need to delay the delivery as long as possible, and then move it very quickly. Was she standing when her water broke?"

"I don't know when it happened. The fever started yesterday."

The midwife spoke to her assistant. "We need to turn the baby. Try to make sure the arms are not over its head. Be very gentle." She cursed under her breath. "Everything is complicated about this one. Let's hope the baby carries good luck with it. We're going to need it."

The women sweated, working hard. The sun pouring through the door moved across the floor. Thio screamed, whimpered and apologized and cursed. Little by little, the baby came.

"One foot out. Not blue! Good."

"I've got my fingers on the baby's shoulder. The arms are down, and no cord on the neck. Time to push hard now, Thio. We must be fast."

438

The other women pushed Thio's belly down, over and over and Thio screamed in agony. The baby's shoulder appeared, and the midwife got her finger into the baby's mouth. The other woman pressed again, hard.

Suddenly the baby was entirely outside. They pressed a final time for the afterbirth. Thio cried once more in relief as the room filled with the smell of blood and the sound of new life.

—.—.—

Erik kissed Thio's brow. Her hair was soaking wet, and she barely responded. The midwife cleaned the baby, looking closely at every part of it. She wrapped it in soft linen and passed it to Erik. "It is a boy," she said. "It looks well-formed, but it may have trouble with one hip as it grows. It came terribly early. It's too thin and too small. Can you see it struggling to breathe? The next few eighths are critical. If the child makes it through them, it may thrive; but it may be a sickly child. Times are hard. It's for you to decide. Will he be kept and named, or..?"

Exposed? No. Of course he would be kept and named. All the feelings Erik had for Thio, for Aquuataq, and for the mother he had not seen since boyhood, but who now had a grandson, centered fiercely on protecting this small being. He took the bundle and held it in his arms. The infant's eyes were closed, his face drawn in sleep. *You are the future. One day, you will be heir to a beautiful farm on a faraway island.*

Heir. Erik liked the old word for it, *Leif.*

"Yes, he'll be named. His name will be Leif, if his mother agrees."

"If he had come even a day or two earlier..." She left her sentence unfinished, but rolled her eyes, and shook her head. "You're lucky."

439

"You have no idea how lucky," Erik replied, numb. "No idea at all."

She looked sharply at him.

"It's just that we have been traveling for a long time. Luck has been with us the entire way. It got us here safely to you. Thank you."

The midwife nodded. "I'll be back later to check in on them both. No food tonight. Just broth if she wants some. Beef, with spinach." She looked a question at the freeholder's wife, who nodded.

"I'll make some. It'll be ready soon."

"Good. Keep the baby warm, either right against her skin, or against someone else."

The midwife left. People of the household began tiptoeing in to peer at the baby. For now, it nestled snug in the arms of the freeholder's daughter, both of them wrapped in a lambs-wool blanket. At the midwife's instructions, she lightly stroked its feet whenever the tiny breathing stopped. Erik heard, but his attention was on Thio, too, watching her chest rise and fall with her own breathing. Already the fever was cooling.

"You might have told me, Thio," he said gently.

Her lips moved, and he bent to hear. "Tell you I was pregnant on a knörr again? You'd have believed that?"

He shook his head, chuckled, and kissed her again. "Maybe before that, then."

"No. You'd have made us stay on the island, with no midwife, thinking you were keeping me safe, and I'd have died." A shadow of a smile. "Admit I was right."

Beyond right, and once again, beyond brave. No matter how strong he thought Thio was, she managed to surprise him again and again. Erik kissed her forehead and she slipped quickly into sleep.

440

"Go walk outside," the freeholder's wife said. "It's been all day. Get some fresh air."

Erik stripped off his boots, still soaking wet from carrying Thio through the surf. The summer earth felt good on his bare feet. He thought of Nagojut running through the far-off barley-field furrows. Still stunned, he pictured a child running through those same fields.

I have a son.

"You've good land here," Erik said to the freeholder.

"We do," he replied. "Soil's rich. Wish there were more of it. You have a farm?"

Erik nodded.

"If you know farming, I could use your help while your wife's recovering. Your muscle would mean more to me than anything you could pay."

"I'd be happy to work. It'll help keep me from worrying."

The freeholder gestured towards a stony hillside. "We'll start clearing stones out tomorrow." He headed towards his barn to get his cows in for the evening milking.

Erik realized that something was needed that he had not thought about until this very moment. He had a son. He was a father in his own right. It was time for a farewell.

———·——·———

Erik walked across the fields to the beach and stood near the sea.

"You were really good, you know, Thorvald," Erik said. "At knowing the stars. At finding your way through the sea. How could it be so hard to find your way in life?"

His voice grew husky trying to get the words out. He wanted to say them aloud. "You blamed everyone else for your troubles, but I think somewhere deep inside, you knew how weak you were, and hated it. But you couldn't escape the trap you built for yourself, could you? Couldn't take the first, hard step of admitting where you had gone wrong."

Erik pictured his father standing in front of him. Thorvald wasn't as tall as he once seemed. He looked old and feeble.

"I grew up wanting to be different from you. In some ways I am, and in some ways I'm not. I learned I don't have to pretend I know everything. That red berry? If you'd said you didn't know where it came from, I might have tossed the thing aside, and never given it a second thought. But your insistence about something I knew was wrong made me stubborn about finding the truth. Look what happened from that!" A wry half-smile.

"I learned how to admit I was wrong. Uukarnit and Iluq and Asa taught me that. They taught me other things you couldn't. That anger is a choice, and that letting go of it is harder than holding on to it. Letting go makes us stronger than anger ever could. I learned how to see things from another point of view. How to pull together, instead of pulling apart."

Thank the gods for that red berry. Erik's throat ached, but he wanted to be finished with it, to leave it all behind once and for all.

"I wish I could just say I forgive you everything. I've tried, but I can't bring myself to feel that way, not yet. Too much disgust, and too much anger, at you for what you let yourself be, and at myself for letting you hurt me. All I can say is that I hope to forgive you one day. That's as much as I have in me."

Erik thought of the tiny being fighting for breath up in the longhouse. "I have a chance to be a father myself now. It's humbling. Looking at that infant…none of us comes into this world wanting to

442

do wrong, do we? How does it happen? Someone hurts us, and we hurt others in turn? Generation after generation?"

How pointless was it to talk to someone long dead? What could it possibly change? Still, he had to say the words. Erik could not breathe deeply enough, could not get enough of the fresh air into his lungs, cleaning out all that was old and broken.

"Maybe somewhere deep inside you knew the wrong of what you did, and hated yourself for it.. Maybe in there was a part of you that wished you had done better. In that way, I *can* forgive you. Whatever mistakes you made, whatever you might have owed me as a father, you don't anymore."

Erik struggled with an idea. "I know our Kalendars count time, but do even they understand how it works? Maybe my saying this can change things. Maybe not, but I hope, wherever in Hel you are, you can finally forgive yourself too. Fare well, Da."

Maybe the words were useless, but he felt lighter, and free from something long past.

———·———·———

Erik turned to go, and realized a second goodbye was needed.

He pulled the pouch from around his neck and took out the small leathery scrap inside. The question of the round red berry that had burned in his mind for so many years had finally been answered.

"Quite the voyage you made so long ago, bobbing along in the ocean, wasn't it?" he asked. "Maybe it's time to give you a place to lie quiet at last."

Erik walked along the beach until he found a stone that was about the size of a cabbage and flat on top, and squatted down next to it. He turned the dried morsel in his fingertips as he had so many times across the years, looking at it for the last time.

"Look what you started!" he said, speaking to it fondly. "You helped me get started on my own journey. Time I went on my own now, and let you rest in peace."

He placed the precious tidbit carefully beside the stone, a little underneath, but not too much, where, if it was fresh and bright red and round, it might have caught the eye of an adventurous young boy on the beach.

"Thank you," he said to it, and walked away.

———·———·———

Epilogue

Across the sea to the west, in fields that sloped gently towards the water, fresh green stalks of barley stood tall and strong. Their slender tips sparkled with drops from an early-summer rain. The breeze blew and the grain rippled smoothly, glistening, lit by the sun coming in under clearing clouds.

Another small gust of air played across the field, a child's-breath, so delicate and light, and under it, the green grasses bent and flowed. The breeze strengthened, and sunlight lit the valley as if it would never leave.

The sights and sounds of these faraway fields were whispered into the ear of a child who slept peacefully and breathed steadily easier, held close by his father. "Do you see it, little one? It is all waiting for us, a place your grandmother and mother and you and I will call home. You will run free and grow strong there. One day you will have brothers and sisters. People will know you as Leif, son of Erik. You are small now, but you will grow. My tiny son! Who can imagine what life will hold for you?"

Erik nuzzled the baby and kissed its small warm head. "Oh, my little Leif!"

The End

AFTERWORD

This book was a complete surprise to me. I had never intended to write about Viking explorers. Like many people, I had at best a basic fourth-grade understanding of Erik the Red, and no knowledge to speak of regarding Iceland or Greenland.

You might wonder, then, how nearly a decade of work and over four hundred pages were inspired. The answer is that one winter evening, I experienced a very startling epiphany, along with a very clearly-worded (albeit somewhat confusing) communication.

I went forward on faith.

Like Erik's voyage to Greenland, the journey of this book was uncertain, difficult, and often fraught with failure. The fact that your eyes are landing on these sentences -- and that you even *care* to read them -- is not lost on me in any way. I am incredibly grateful to you for your time and interest.

The 'Norse', who lived in the first millennium in the area we now call Scandinavia, too often are portrayed in stereotypes that bristle with images of horned helmets and bloody battleaxes and include the words 'pillage' and 'rape'. If one thinks more deeply, one soon realizes that some of the sagas are filled with long and relatively boring discussions of land ownership and law. One looks at the craftsmanship of Viking-era ships, and sees immense creativity. One looks at their jewelry, so abstracted and skilled that hundreds of years later, it still looks fresh and modern.

All of this artisanship and legal hairsplitting confirms that these people were intelligent thinkers who celebrated and supported the arts.

These were not barbarians.

446

I'll leave it to scholars to establish, beyond all shadow of doubt, that the people of 'the North Way', called Vikings -- whether explorers, merchants, or yes, some of those who were in fact part of the great struggle for land and power waged not only by their kind by but *all* countries and *all* rulers of the region! – were instrumental in establishing trade routes throughout Europe, which influenced cultural exchanges for centuries.

At the time of the events of this story, the people of Iceland had formed the first true democratic society, where laws were made and approved by ordinary men and women, not by kings and queens. The people of this book – the man known to history as 'Erik the Red' and his future hard-headed wife Thjodhild Jorundsdottir -- created the first European settlement in the western hemisphere, fully five hundred years before Christopher Columbus' celebrated voyage. Their son Leif Eriksson extended his parents' legacy with additional settlements in North America: l'Anse Aux Meadows provided the first irrefutable evidence of the sagas.

New technology gives us even more tools which are even now probing some of the most intriguing historical mysteries that exist regarding the Norse colonies in North America: the ever-intriguing *'where is Vinland?' What relationships existed between the native tribes of the Americas and the Norse settlers there? Of most interest: what happened to the Vikings who lived as Greenlanders, who one day simply vanished from Greenland but never showed up as 'arriving' in any of the historical records in Europe of the time?*

For so long, we thought those old sagas were the end of the story. We now know they were only the beginning of a fascinating chapter in human exploration, ocean navigation, and cultural exchange. Thank you for reading and for caring.

AUTHOR'S NOTES

This book is a work of fiction. While based on historical events, the telling of a day-to-day story requires a tremendous collection of events and details that were never recorded and needed to be carefully conjectured. I tried in every case to strike a judicious line between sagas, source documents, reasonable assumptions, and good storytelling – as I'm sure three hundred years of oral-tradition saga-speakers did. Here are some notes that may be of interest to those who love to delve into details:

Sagas, misrepresentation of Vikings in general and of Erik the Red in particular:

In studying all I could find of Norse and Viking history, I read sagas: oral traditions passed from storyteller to storyteller across hundreds of years before they were finally written down. Some of the tales contain outright impossibilities. A few were clearly created to inflate the ego of a ruler, embellishing his prowess beyond all reason. Most of them, passed from storyteller to storyteller across hundreds of years of oral traditions, almost certainly suffered from inaccurate repetitions and had personal flourishes added. In some, the hero of the saga became like our movie superheroes of today: no real-life James Bond could possibly do the things we enjoy in the movies, but we suspend belief in favor of entertainment.

Despite that, I have tried always to be respectful to the sagas. They are the living documents that contain the roots of truth, and likely some very *certain* truths, regarding the lives of the Norse people of that time.

448

Like many of those called 'Vikings', Erik is often touted as a violent man...but was he, really? His leadership of the Greenlandic colony he established appears to have been excellent. His son Leif was reputed to be a strong, quiet, well-liked and well-respected man - not the sort of son one might expect from a violent father.

(...and why, why, why is Erik nearly always referred to as 'likely having red hair"? He was Nordic! Nordic people of that time were almost uniformly blonde. Please.)

Learning the few scraps that survive about the man known as Erik Thorvaldsson, I came to be fascinated that this man, accused twice of murder and outlawed from his country, was not only entrusted a few years later with thirty ships – a massive undertaking – but would eventually became the elder statesman of a whole community, whose son lived for a time in the household of the King of Norway.

That is quite a transition.

I became quite engaged with how a life might change so deeply. That wondering formed the central question to be explored in the story. Erik the Red may be a big deal in history now, but somewhere around 980 A. D, he was just a man who had almost nothing left to lose and was trying to figure a way forward as he slogged through the mess of his life...the same day-to-day way many of us do. I wanted to see Erik not as an iconic figure long brutalized by history, but as a real human being: a man in his early thirties, bitterly frustrated by his life and determined to change it, and banging about, seeking his way.

Those very familiar with the saga of Erik the Red may be wondering about one diversion from it. I, too, was uncomfortable with it, but the story came to me in a particular way, and I chose to honor it. Let me just promise you that events in the next book will resolve the liberty taken.

As for Vikings in general, this group has not been treated very well by history. Scandinavian people in history are usually lumped together in the Pillaging Horned Helmet Wearers, an inaccuracy that would be laughable were it not such a vile misrepresentation. A small percentage of Norse people did go on raids and do battle with other cultures – *but so did every culture of that age.* I'm no expert, but it rapidly appeared in research that the vast majority of the Vikings invading today's England, Scotland, Ireland, France and Germany were people from the Danish islands…who were under huge pressure from *other* invaders to their own territory. It quickly becomes a 'who invaded who first', chicken-or-egg muddle.

Even written records of Viking invasions are suspect. History is owned by the tellers, but in my very first reading, I immediately found myself doubting the truth of the Anglo-Saxon Chronicle, which in 793 A.D. reported that *"In this year fierce, foreboding omens came over the land of the Northumbrians, and the wretched people shook; there were excessive whirlwinds, lightning, and fiery dragons were seen flying in the sky. These signs were followed by great famine, and a little after those, that same year on 6th ides of January, the ravaging of wretched heathen people destroyed God's church at Lindisfarne."*

This was written by a priest, a theoretically-truthful man of God.

Dragons, actually seen flying in the sky? Really?

The noted English scholar and ecclesiastic Alcuin of York (who was actually in another country during the Lindisfarne attack) expanded the account, writing *"Behold the church of St. Cuthbert, splattered with the blood of God's priests, robbed of its ornaments…Never before has such terror appeared in Britain as we have now suffered from a pagan race... The heathens poured out the blood of saints around the altar, and trampled on the bodies of saints in the temple of God, like dung in the streets."*

450

As I read these accounts, I found myself questioning how accurate they actually were, but also considering similar battles between English and French and Germans -- all of whom would have been Christians battling other Christians. Medieval weaponry indicates bloodthirstiness on all fronts, and the horrors later inflicted on other holy places during the Crusades and the Rhineland massacres indicate that the so-called Christians of the day were not averse to violence.

My point is simple: nobody's hands were clean. Vikings, I came to believe, were certainly no worse than any other culture, and perhaps far more advanced than many. It was a radical idea, but one which has grown more strongly in me from the evidence. This way of thinking is gaining strength from fact-based researchers. It will be gratifying one day to erase the tinge of brutal barbarianism which undermines every aspect of Norse accomplishment.

Did they, or didn't they?

One conjecture I explored was interaction in the book between the Norse explorers and people already living in Greenland. They would have been people of the 'Dorset' culture - the name archeologists give to a middle wave of groups from Canada who may have explored and lived in Greenland over a couple of thousand years. There are legends about these people from the modern-day Inuit, in which the Dorset people described as tall and gentle, and not at all warlike. The art objects which remain from them are really quite beautiful. These people valued the animals with whom they shared their world and questioned ideas beyond simple existence. I hope I have brought some of them to life again with integrity to the people they once were.

(Please note: the Dorset people were not the 'skraelings' of later settlements. These one-legged characters do not feature in the sagas

until at least a generation later, and were no doubt either a misinterpretation between storytellers or an outright fabrication.)

We don't know if such a meeting between Norse people and the Dorset inhabitants ever took place. We also don't know that it didn't. What we *do* know is that the Icelandic vikingers and the Dorset people shared the same territories right around the same time, and both groups were prodigious explorers and travelers. I choose to interpret that to believe that they likely *did* interact at this particular point in time – and considered what effect two very different cultures might have on one another.

Farming and flora in the 980s

Much debate has taken place (and in fact, is still taking place) regarding the climate of Greenland from the latter part of the first millennium through the middle of the second, roughly 900 A.D. to 1500 A.D. Was the climate really going through the Medieval Warm Period, or not? When did it change? How did that affect the Greenlandic Norse as well as the native Dorset (and later, Thule) cultures?

We know from archeological evidence that on the earlier end of that time period, the Icelandic Norse who settled Greenland raised wheat, rye, and barley – crops that would perhaps not be sustainable today – as well as sheep and other livestock. We know that there were small trees of willow and birch growing, which have since almost entirely disappeared. It is my hope that I did not misrepresent the Greenlandic climate in any way in the telling of this story.

Iceland, too, was different. It was likely to have been pretty well forested when the first settlers arrived, but in a few generations, all the land had been cleared for use intensive farming and livestock use. With Iceland's steep slopes and thin topsoil, what followed was a perfect scenario for landslides and for diminishing yields from croplands. These issues created significant problems for the people of Iceland in that transitional time.

The role of women

It's no secret that Viking-era Norse women really did have considerable freedom and often held the same respect and leadership as men of the time. A woman named Aud was among the first to settle Iceland, and she owned the ship on which she and her group sailed.

Evidence shows that women were part of voyages of exploration as well as settlement groups. A possibly-prior voyage to Greenland by Snæbjörn Galti - whether in fact it actually occurred or not - listed at least one woman on board along with the men who were exploring.

Looking ahead

My next book will pick up where this one left off and carry us forward into the years 985 A.D and beyond. There is so much more story to explore. I can hardly wait to share it with you.

Sincerely,

Katie

ACKNOWLEDGEMENTS

I wanted desperately to write, but found it all but impossible to do, thanks to an inner voice that said things such as *you...write a book? Who do you think you are? Besides, surely something far better has already been written by someone more deserving and with more ability than you!* Low self-worth and fear of inability combined with unreasonably high expectations of myself to create a mental prison. I speak about this with extreme candor in the belief that honesty is the best way to encourage others who may face similar barricades.

The person who showed me how to escape the prison was Peter Smith: family therapist, clinical social worker, and professor at the University of Maryland School of Social Work. I will always be profoundly grateful to Peter for helping me to move forward as a writer, as well as for his significant role in helping me become a stronger human being. Peter is a rock star among therapists.

M. Louisa Locke, author of a cozy Victorian San Francisco mystery series and a founder of The Paradisi Chronicles, was a godsend, first for understanding the complexities of life...and when my hopes for traditional publishing did not materialize, Louisa gave unstinting help with self-publishing. I can never thank her enough.

My husband Mark, our oldest son Zach, and friend-and-wonderwoman Julie Hagen read and critiqued the first drafts. I'm so grateful to them for not insisting that I keep my day job. Louisa Locke and my brother-in-law Brad Ritter plowed through the 'final' manuscript (laughing...*not*...) in detail. Brad kept me honest about how certain scenes played out, and Louisa's sharp sense of timelines caught what would have been embarrassing mistakes.

Rebecca Lochlann, author of *The Child of the Erinyes* series, did a meticulous, superb job of critiquing and copyediting – and somehow, the hawkeyed Dick LeGates found even *more* corrections needed. Bibi Bendixen did the final edits (*how* could *there still be more? And yet, there were!*) and UK-based Aussie Cathy West offered some last-minute critiques along with encouragement to muscle up and get them done. Prior to releasing to me the rights to self-publish this book, agent Irene Goodman encouraged me to not be daunted by a 400+ page rewrite...or a second one...or a third...or more.

Richard Benning, an artist in The Netherlands whose artwork is on Behance.net, did the stunning cover image, with which I fell in love the instant I saw it. British cover designer JD Smith used Richard's artwork to design a truly beautiful cover.

To my husband Mark and our sons Zach, Gabe, and Ben: thank you for rarely minding that I was clearly deficient on homemaking skills but long on adventure. I owe you. Oh, my sons...what *does* a four-wheeler plus nine years of interest total? To dear Amelia, my constant love and gratitude; you are always right there with me.

I wanted my father Robert Aiken, who was an enthralling storyteller, to be proud of my work. He passed away before he saw this book become a reality, but I owe so much to him and my mother Barbara Aiken. Likewise to Dr. William Hogue, head of The Tome School, and to Swarthmore College, who changed my life.

My in-law parents Leora and Joe Ritter offered much-needed encouragement at every obstacle, and celebrated each success as if this project was their own. My sisters, brother, sisters-in-law and brothers-in-law and extended family members offered steady support – as did a select, extremely valuable group of wonderfully enthusiastic friends in my home community and on Facebook. Through one tough moment or another, each of you helped me keep going, one step at a time. In nine years of working on this book, there were plenty of tough moments. Thank you.

Endless websites provided critical bits of information. *What did the Icelandic Norse eat? How did they celebrate weddings? How did they count, and how did people mark time? What musical instruments were used? What trade items made their way from country to country, even to remote areas? Where might the Dorset people have traveled? How does one preserve meat in a culture where fire and smoke are very limited?* I am grateful to the many organizations and individuals who work to keep this information both available and accurate.

To Jennifer Sheets Harrison and Francis Bruno and April Forrer and Nathan Gunther, thank you for being there since the beginning, (and Michael Neff for being the reason I met them, and for his cold-water-in-the-face introduction to the realities of writing; but *not* for his daunting assertion that I would *'never, ever, ever sell a Viking book'*.) Rick Bader, thank you for forming with me our semi-annual writer-support group of two...and also to the Alabama Writer's Conclave for blessing me with a treasured award for the novel.

Posthumous thanks go to the man who first encouraged me to write: Wilson Ballard never rode a nag, but fortunately he *was* one, and he pushed me to try.

Lastly, to those who gave this story to me along with an admonition to *'set the record straight'*: I'll never know who you were, but rest assured, the connection with you was unforgettable. Thank you for your charge, your trust, and for the privilege of doing work that apparently meant so much to you. I hope this book accomplishes what you wanted.

Onward.

Dear Reader,

I appreciate more than I can say that you took the time to read this, my long-in-coming first novel. I truly hope that you enjoyed it and will recommend it to friends and other readers.

Will you consider taking a quick moment to post a review on Amazon? Your words are worth <u>far</u> more to me than any advertising I could ever dream of affording. Your experience in reading this book, in taking this journey, is important to other readers.

Thank you from the bottom of my heart
for taking the time to do a review.

Ps…it may be crazy hard to not mention the plot twists…
but let's keep everybody guessing!

With great appreciation,
Katie

Stay in touch!
Goodreads – Katie Aiken Ritter
Facebook.com/KatieAikenRitter.Author
Twitter@ThinkKatie
Amazon review VIKING: THE GREEN LAND

CPSIA information can be obtained
at www.ICGtesting.com
Printed in the USA
LVOW12s1619290916

506736LV00004B/763/P